WITNESS ON THE RUN

CASSIE MILES

EXPOSING COLTON SECRETS

MARIE FERRARELLA

MILLS & BOON

First Published in Great Britain 2020
by Mills & Boon, an imprint of HarperCollins*Publishers*
1 London Bridge Street, London, SE1 9GF

Witness on the Run © 2020 Kay Bergstrom
Exposing Colton Secrets © 2020 Harlequin Books S.A.

Special thanks and acknowledgement are given to Marie Ferrarella
for her contribution to *The Coltons of Kansas* series.

ISBN: 978-0-263-28040-1

0720

MIX
Paper from
responsible sources
FSC® C007454

This book is produced from independently certified FSC™
paper to ensure responsible forest management.

For more information visit: www.harpercollins.co.uk/green

Printed and bound in Spain
by CPI, Barcelona

Cassie Miles, a *USA TODAY* bestselling author, lives in Colorado. After raising two daughters and cooking tons of macaroni and cheese for her family, Cassie is trying to be more adventurous in her culinary efforts. She's discovered that almost anything tastes better with wine. When she's not plotting Mills & Boon Heroes books, Cassie likes to hang out at the Denver Botanic Gardens near her high-rise home.

USA TODAY bestselling and RITA© Award-winning author **Marie Ferrarella** has written more than two hundred and fifty books for Mills & Boon, some under the name Marie Nicole. Her romances are beloved by fans worldwide. Visit her website, marieferrarella.com

Also by Cassie Miles

Mountain Midwife
Sovereign Sheriff
Baby Battalion
Unforgettable
Midwife Cover
Mummy Midwife
Montana Midwife
Hostage Midwife
Mountain Heiress
Snowed In

Also by Marie Ferrarella

Colton Baby Conspiracy
Mission: Cavanaugh Baby
Cavanaugh on Duty
A Widow's Guilty Secret
Cavanaugh's Surrender
Cavanaugh Rules
Cavanaugh's Bodyguard
Cavanaugh Fortune
How to Seduce a Cavanaugh
Cavanaugh or Death

Discover more at millsandboon.co.uk

WITNESS ON THE RUN

CASSIE MILES

To Carla Gertner for her inspiration and knowledge of New Orleans and, as always, to Rick.

Chapter One

The Day of the Dead celebration unleashed a parade of floats, bands, ghosts, skeletons and zombies that wended through the night in the French Quarter of New Orleans. Some people carried tiki torches while others waved neon lights. Alyssa Bailey stood with a crowd on the curb and watched. The thought of dancing in the street made her self-conscious. She had turned in her ledgers and calculator three years ago when she first entered the witness protection program, but she still had the soul of a quiet accountant who liked to have every *i* dotted and every *t* crossed.

This year, she vowed, would be different. No more standing on the sidelines. She was twenty-seven and needed to join the parade before life passed her by. During *Día de los Muertos* on the weekend after Halloween, the veil between the real world and the afterlife thinned. The dead craved laughter, song and revelry. Alyssa was determined to get into the spirit of the thing.

Just before she got off work at half past nine, she'd gotten a phone call from someone anonymous saying they'd see her at the parade. The voice had been so garbled that she couldn't tell if the caller was male or female, but she intended to keep a lookout for a familiar face.

Gathering her courage, she took a giant step into the

street, where she shuffled along to the irresistible beat of drums and death rattles. Her eardrums popped when the trumpets and saxophones wailed. People in crazy costumes bumped and jostled. She told herself that this was fun, fun, fun but didn't believe it. The wild display of neon, color and confetti made her feel like she was inside a raucous, whirling kaleidoscope.

A masked ghost dressed like an 1800s pirate approached her, whipped off his tricorn hat and swept a bow before he grasped her hands and spun her in a circle. The music shifted gears from a dirge to a more upbeat tempo, and her pirate led her in an energetic dance that was half waltz, half polka and one hundred percent exciting—more thrilling than the handful of dates she'd had in the last three years.

He leaned close and said, "Tell me about your costume. Who are you?"

She'd put together a ragged outfit of pantaloons and an old-fashioned gown with a low bodice, lace trim and a tattered skirt. The clothes were meant to honor her mother. Mom had been born and raised in Savannah. Though they'd lived in Chicago for as long as Alyssa could remember, her mom would always be a southern belle. Five years ago, she'd been killed in a hit-and-run.

Tilting her head, she gazed up at her pirate's silver half mask. Though she couldn't see his eyes, his mouth was visible. He had a divot in his chin—very sexy. She swallowed hard and said, "I'm supposed to be a zombie Scarlett O'Hara."

"Good choice, *cher*. With your dark hair and green eyes, you make a real pretty Scarlett."

Her mom had always said the same. "Did you call me?" she asked. "Was I supposed to meet you here at the parade?"

"We didn't have an appointment."

"Well, we should have." Alyssa gestured to his white shirt with full sleeves and his burgundy velvet vest with gold buttons. "Are you a famous pirate? Jean Lafitte?"

Again, he doffed the hat and bowed. "I'm the ghost of Captain Jean-Pierre Fournier, an original pirate of the Caribbean and one of my ancestors. I am Rafael Fournier."

"I do declare," she said in a corny southern accent. Unaccustomed to teasing, she wasn't sure she was doing it right. "I'm ever so pleased to make your acquaintance, Rafael."

"*Enchanté, mademoiselle.* Please call me Rafe."

He twirled her again and then held her close. Their posture felt strangely intimate in the midst of a wild crowd. Her half-exposed breasts crushed against his firm chest. Their thighs touched. He guided her so skillfully that she felt graceful, beautiful and sultry. Before she knew what was happening, they were dancing a tango. *A tango? No way!* She didn't know these steps but must have been doing something right. People in the crowd made way for them and applauded as they passed by.

When their dance ended, he dropped a kiss on her forehead. *"Merci, ma belle."*

With a flourish, he disappeared into the crowd—an impressive feat for a guy who was over six feet tall with wide shoulders and puffy sleeves. He'd kissed her and called her *belle*, beautiful. *Moi?*

Their dance gave her courage. Life was meant to be celebrated. When a laughing zombie placed a beer in her hand, Alyssa took a huge gulp and wholeheartedly threw herself into the parade, bounding along the street, snapping her fingers and shaking her hips. Her mom would have loved this scene. If she were here, she'd have danced all night. It was Alyssa's duty to celebrate in Mom's place, dancing with pirates and looking for mysterious people who left anonymous messages.

On a street corner, she encountered a guy dressed like Baron Samedi, the voodoo master of the dead, with a skull face and top hat. He blew a puff of chalky powder at the crowd, making everybody more ghostlike. All around her, people were laughing and waving, drinking and dancing. New Orleans took every opportunity to party—from Mardi Gras to funeral processions to *Día de los Muertos*.

Dodging around a dour threesome in skull masks, she joined a group of zombie belly dancers with tambourines. A four-member band played "When the Saints Go Marching In," and she sang with loud enthusiasm that was hugely out of character. She danced along a street where the storefronts were mostly voodoo shops. The fortune tellers stood outside, enticing tourists with offers of special deals. For a small fee, the bereaved could have a conversation with loved ones who had crossed over. Instead of dismissing the voodoo promises as illogical and absurd, Alyssa imagined how wonderful it would be to talk to Mom one more time.

A loud, raucous laugh cut through the music. Alyssa knew that sound. A shiver prickled between her shoulder blades, as quick and creepy as a spider running across her back. She peered toward the fortune tellers on the sidewalk. Amid the crowd, she saw a woman who looked like her mother. She stood in a doorway, laughing with her head thrown back and her long silver hair rising in a cloud of curls around her head.

Could it be? Her mom couldn't be the voice on the phone. Alyssa would have recognized her. And she was dead, very dead—Alyssa had identified the remains. She caught another glimpse. The silver-haired woman looked so much like her mom. Could she be a ghost?

Alyssa broke away from the parade and ran toward the place where she'd seen the woman. A trombone player got in her way, and then a high-kicking can-can dancer. The music shifted to a minor key as a feeling of dread swelled in her chest and spread through her body. The shop where the woman had been standing was closed, and the door was locked.

Frantically, Alyssa asked if anyone had seen her. Nobody knew anything. Nor did they care. *Laissez les bon temps rouler*—let the good times roll.

But Alyssa couldn't let go. The woman's resemblance to her mom was too uncanny to ignore. Operating on instinct, she darted through an alley and came out on a street where there weren't as many people. She crossed at the stoplight and entered a park with a large brick patio and bronze statues of jazz legends. Pacing back and forth, she scanned in all directions.

At the edge of a grassy area lined with fat palm trees she saw the three men in matching skeleton masks who had been at the parade. She'd noticed their cold, serious attitude. Why were they here? Had they followed her?

The tallest asked, "Do you need help?"

"I'm looking for a woman. She has curly silver hair."

"Oh yeah, we saw her. Come with us."

The three of them surrounded her. She was trapped and beginning to be scared. "Forget about it. I'm sorry I bothered you."

He edged closer. "You're coming with us."

For the three years that she'd been in the witness protection program, she'd lived in fear of this moment. The dangerous criminals she'd testified against wanted to take revenge, and she figured that it was only a matter of time before they found her. She pivoted on her heel, tried to run.

The leader grabbed her arm and yanked. The other two closed in. One of them slapped a cloth over her mouth to keep her from calling for help. She couldn't breathe. A sickly-sweet antiseptic smell penetrated her nostrils. She heard the men in skeleton masks laughing, telling witnesses that she'd had too much to drink and they'd make sure she got home.

She struggled, kicked at their legs and lashed out with her arms. She clawed at one of the skeleton masks, and it came off in her hands. She found herself staring into flat, dark eyes above a sneering mouth and hatchet jaw. A cruel face—this man would show no mercy.

Her vision blurred. She was losing her grip on consciousness.

In half-awake glimpses, she saw another man come closer and shove one of the skeletons. It was her pirate. He demanded they release her. She tried to warn him that these were violent men, but her throat closed. She couldn't make a sound. The pirate attacked the others. She thought he had a stun gun but really couldn't tell.

When the skeleton let go of her arm, she fell onto the grass and desperately crawled. Her head was spinning. Her body was numb. She had to escape. One of the skeletons kicked her. She barely felt the pain.

Alyssa staggered to her feet, concentrated on putting one foot in front of the other. Her legs were rubber bands, incapable of supporting her. She fell again.

The next thing she knew, she'd been flung over someone's shoulder and was being carried. She attempted to wriggle free but couldn't move. Her last reserve of strength drained from her, and she went limp. She was caught. They had her. She hoped it wouldn't hurt too much when they killed her.

She was dumped into a car seat. Someone reached across to fasten her seat belt. Forcing her eyes open, she saw the dashing pirate. He had come to her rescue. *Merci, Captain Fournier.*

Chapter Two

Alyssa woke with a gasp. Her eyes snapped open. *Where am I?*

It appeared that she was in her bedroom, lying flat on her back with her arms tucked straight down at her sides under her vintage chenille bedspread. A small lamp with a glass base and fringed shade cast a soft circle of light on the bedside table. She saw her music box with the twirling ballerina inside—a gift from her father.

Still night—it was dark around the edges of the window blinds. What time was it? Gazing across the dimly lit bedroom, she tried to read the red digital numbers on the alarm clock that stood on her dresser, but she couldn't see it. How did she get home? She remembered the parade, *Día de los Muertos*. There had been dancing, and she'd seen the ghost of her mom before she was attacked by skeletons. *Was it a nightmare? A dream?* Her thoughts disintegrated into static.

Hoping to ground herself in reality, she turned her head and looked toward the music box. When the lid opened, the tinkling music would play "Lara's Theme" from *Dr. Zhivago*, which was perfect because Lara was her real name. She hadn't been allowed to bring photos when she entered WitSec, but she'd refused to leave the precious music box behind. Her father was long gone.

She couldn't remember what he looked like and had never known his name, but he'd loved her enough to give her this present on her fourth birthday. Small reassurance, but it was better than nothing.

She realized that her cell phone wasn't on the bedside table. Matter of fact, the charger wasn't there, either. *Strange.* She *always* charged her phone at night. The only thing on the table other than her music box was a cut-glass bowl of her homemade potpourri. She inhaled a whiff. The familiar scents of orange, cinnamon and vanilla should have comforted her, but she was growing more anxious by the minute. Her bedroom felt oddly foreign. She peered through the shadows at the Toulouse-Lautrec print on the wall opposite her bed—a can-can dancer at the Moulin Rouge. She'd picked it out herself. Of course, she was home.

Focus, I need to focus. The music box looked different, less battered. When she pulled her arm from under the covers and reached for the box, she saw a swelling on her upper arm, the beginning of a bruise, and a bandage wrapped around her wrist. When she touched the bandage, she felt a stinging sensation. That wasn't her only pain. As soon as she moved, she experienced a pulsing headache. Her ribs throbbed. Lowering the bedspread, she looked down at the bruises on her side and gauze bandages on her knees. She was wearing nothing but her black sports bra and silky blue panties.

Sitting upright on the bed, she held the music box. Seeking comfort from a familiar object, her fingers stroked the worn wooden edges of her talisman—a souvenir of another time, another home, another life. She lifted the lid. The delicate ballerina pirouetted on tiptoe, and the jingly music played "Twinkle, Twinkle Little Star." Not her tune! Not her music box!

The door swung open. A man strode into her bedroom.

More outraged than frightened, she demanded, "Who are you? What are you doing in my house?"

"Not to worry, *cher*. You'll understand as soon as I turn on the light."

The overhead light erased the shadows. Her gaze slid across the walls. The window was in the wrong place. Her shabby chic furniture had been replaced with stuff that was plain old shabby. *Not my house!* "Where am I?"

He took a step toward her. "You have no cause for alarm. I can explain."

"Stop where you are. Don't come any closer."

But the stranger took another step, murmuring about how she was safe. She didn't believe him, not for a minute. With as much force as she could muster, she threw the music box at him. It crashed against the wall.

Though logic told her that this wasn't really her bedroom, she struggled free from the blankets, climbed out of bed and ripped open the drawer to the bedside table where she kept her snub-nose Smith & Wesson .38. The drawer was empty. She snatched the bowl filled with dried, scented leaves and drew back her arm to throw it.

The stranger held up a hand to stop her. "Wait!"

She hesitated. "Why does this bedroom look like mine?"

"It's all right, *cher*." He offered a disarming smile. "Put down the bowl. You don't want to break it and get glass on the floor. No, no, *ma chérie*. Step away from the potpourri."

As soon as he spoke, she realized the absurdity. Dried leaves weren't a lethal weapon. And he wasn't wrong. Breaking the bowl would make a mess. "Where am I?"

"Nothing to worry about," he said. "Don't you recognize me?"

His face seemed familiar, and he was so appealing that she wanted to believe he meant no harm. But Alyssa wasn't a fool. She needed to figure out who this charming Frenchman was and what she needed to do next. "This is the last time I'm going to ask. Where the hell am I?"

He rattled off an address. "That's about six miles northeast of the French Quarter."

"How did I get here?" A sliver of memory pierced her mind. She recalled being carried and placed into an SUV. Her seat belt had been fastened by the man who rescued her—the man who now stood on the opposite side of the room. "You—you're my pirate."

"Rafe Fournier." His sweeping bow was far less effective when he wasn't wearing the swashbuckler's costume. Jeans and a black T-shirt weren't dramatic. "At your service, *ma belle.*"

She should have recognized him sooner with his subtly accented voice and sexy grin, but he'd been masked from the nose up. She warned him, "You shouldn't have gotten involved. This isn't your fight, and those men are dangerous."

"They're cowards. Any man who lays hands on a woman needs to be taught a lesson."

Very gallant but not real bright—he could have been killed. When she shook her head, the pain ratcheted up a few notches, and she regretted leaping from the bed. Her entire body was stiff and sore. The inside of her mouth tasted like cotton. Physically, she felt miserable, but her brain was beginning to sort out the details. Fact: Rafe had appeared in the nick of time. Fact: He knew a lot about her. Fact: He had created a duplicate of her bedroom. *Very suspicious!* "You were following me, weren't you?"

"This explanation is going to take a while. Why don't you settle down and rest?"

As her mind cleared, she came to the obvious realization that she was nearly naked. She dragged the chenille spread off the bed, wrapped it around her and draped the fabric over her shoulder like a toga. "Why did you take my clothes off?"

"Accept my apology, *s'il vous plaît*. I needed to treat your cuts and scrapes and make sure you didn't need medical attention."

A rational explanation, but she wasn't about to let him off the hook. "Where's my stuff?"

"In the closet." He pointed to a closed door. "Everything is there, except your cell phone, which I am charging in the kitchen."

Intending to grab her clothes and get out of this crazy, through-the-looking-glass bedroom, she stumbled toward the closet and made it all the way to the foot of the bed before a wave of vertigo overwhelmed her. She stood still until she'd regained her balance. When he moved toward her, she snapped, "Don't come any closer."

"You don't trust me," he said.

"Damn right, I don't!" His timely appearance when she was attacked might be part of a larger scheme. She'd never believed in coincidence.

"You're dehydrated." Several plastic bottles of water stood atop the dresser. He grabbed one and tossed it onto the bed. "Drink."

Cautiously, she picked up the bottle. The cap was still fastened, which meant he hadn't tampered with the contents. Taking a few sips shouldn't be dangerous. She raised the bottle to her lips. The cool liquid moistened the interior of her mouth and slid down her throat. After another sip, she felt marginally improved. "Tastes good."

"Have some more. The liquid will dilute whatever is

in your system. If you like I can give you something for the pain."

"Do you really think I'm dumb enough to accept mystery meds from somebody I just met? For all I know, you could be the one who drugged me in the first place."

"Do you remember being drugged?"

"Not very well." But she knew that Rafe wasn't responsible. She recalled a cloth being pressed over her mouth and the antiseptic smell of whatever chemical formula had knocked her out. "There were three skeletons. I can't remember how I got all these bruises."

"You were attacked, three against one."

"Who were they? What else did you see?"

"Not much. I got you away from them, put you in my car and brought you here." He folded his arms across his torso and leaned his shoulder against the door frame. "It's your turn to speak, *cher*. Tell me what you remember."

Though grateful to him for helping her out, she didn't owe Rafe an explanation. "Why do you want to know?"

He pursed his lips and gave a very Gallic shrug. "If we share information, we might understand who those men were and why they attacked."

His logic made sense. If she could figure out the names of her attackers, she'd know what to do to evade them. Leaving the investigation to WitSec was also logical, but the marshals weren't likely to share details with her. Rafe was offering her a chance to face the threat. There was no harm in talking to him. "What do you want to know? Where should I start?"

"The beginning."

"I got off work at the bistro at half past nine." *Don't say too much!* Before she even got started, she was throwing up mental roadblocks. She stumbled backward and braced herself against the bedroom wall. To her immediate left was a window. Peeking through the blinds, she saw that they were on the first floor. *I should get out of here. It's time to run.*

"Are you all right?"

She picked up her narrative. "In the employees' locker room, I changed into my costume. At first, I wasn't sure I'd go to the parade, but I got a phone call from somebody who said they'd meet me."

"Who called you?"

"Anonymous," she said. "Nothing showed up on caller ID, but I took it as a sign that I should go and try to have fun."

"Did you know the voice?"

"No." The phone message could have been a trap. The men in skeleton masks might have been luring her. But how did they know her phone number? Who were they? From the street outside, she heard the clang of a streetcar. "It could have been a man or a woman with a low voice. It could have been you."

"But it wasn't."

"Almost as soon as I joined the parade, you approached me. Why?"

"I promise, *cher*, to tell you as much of the story as I can. But first, I've got to hear your recollections. Details might help the cops find the bad guys."

"No police."

In situations like this where her cover might be blown, the protocol required her to report to WitSec. She should make that call right now, and yet something held her back. The attack had warped her perceptions. She wasn't sure who could be trusted. And how could she make that determination?

After another drink of water, she scrutinized Rafe. When she was first taken into protective custody and the marshals started asking questions, she'd gotten good at describing the criminals she'd encountered in Chicago. She formulated an analysis of Rafe. His height was about six feet two or three, and he probably weighed 185 or 190 pounds. The dimple in his square chin counted as a distinguishing feature. Other than that, he was a standard version of handsome with wavy brown hair, gray eyes and a smile that could melt your heart.

Those were the physical details, and they didn't help her decide if he was trustworthy. "I remember our tango," she said.

"We fit together well."

"After you vanished into the crowd, I joined a group of belly dancers with tambourines. We were clapping and dancing, and I sang along with them."

"You have a strong voice. Not a good voice, but strong."

"Did you hear me singing? Were you watching me?"

"Always, *cher.*"

He sounded like a stalker. "Do you make a habit of following me around?"

"I usually know where you are. You stick to a regular routine."

The marshals in WitSec had warned her not to be so predictable. She was supposed to take different routes to work and to shop at different supermarkets. At first, she'd followed their rules. But after a while, she established her own itinerary for handling danger. It might be time to put her plans into effect.

She finished the water and lobbed the empty plastic bottle onto the bed. "I'd like another, please. And I need my phone."

If she decided to notify WitSec, her life in New Orleans was over. She didn't relish the idea of starting over in another city, but that was the deal. She did what they told her, and they kept her protected…except for tonight. Somebody had fumbled the ball.

Without coming too close, Rafe dropped another bottle onto the bed. When she picked it up, he held out a small container of nonprescription painkillers. "The seal is intact," he said. "You can see that I didn't touch the pills."

Grateful, she took the container. After fumbling with the childproof lid, she shook out three capsules and gulped them down. Though still in pain, she felt better than when she'd bolted from the bed, more in control. "About that phone?"

"How long were you singing with the belly dancers?"

"A couple of blocks. Then we moved into that area with voodoo shops." And she'd heard her mom's laugh. "There was a silver-haired woman on the sidewalk. Did you see her?"

He nodded. "An attractive woman wearing dozens of shiny Mardi Gras necklaces."

"She looked so much like my mom that I had to find her, had to talk to her. Even though I knew it couldn't be Mom. She died five years ago. Her name was Claudia."

"I know," Rafe said.

"How do you know her name?"

"I know a great deal about you. Continue with your story. What happened next?"

"I ran in the direction I thought the woman might have gone, went into that park, then the guys in skeleton masks surrounded me. I never should have let them get so close. When they grabbed me, I clawed at one of the masks. It came off in my hand."

"Did you see his face?"

"Yes."

"Did you recognize him?"

"No." But she'd seen that heavy jaw before. His empty, soulless eyes would haunt her nightmares.

"Maybe," he said, "maybe you're remembering, maybe just a little piece. Was his hair blond or brown?"

It seemed wise to keep her secrets to herself. "I don't know."

"I want you to look at mug shots."

Though Rafe hadn't moved a whit, his attitude transformed from casual street pirate to alert professional. "You sound like a cop."

"Good guess, *cher*. A while back, I used to be in the FBI."

"And now?"

"Private detective," he said. "Two and a half weeks ago, I was hired to keep an eye on you."

She sat on the edge of the bed and drank more water. "Who hired you?"

"I can't give you a name, but I can assure you that my client means you no harm."

She wished she could believe this tall, handsome, gray-eyed man, but life had taught her not to give her trust so easily. The price for naivety was steep. She came at the question of his client's identity from a different angle. "Did this mystery person tell you to decorate this room like my house?"

"My client thought the similarity in the room might make you more comfortable."

"Why would anybody think that? I'm not a child who needs her favorite toys, especially not the music box. It played the wrong tune, you know."

"Duly noted," he said. "My client wanted you to feel at home."

"Why would that matter? I have no intention of staying here." Anger sparked inside her. "You didn't think you could keep me locked in this room, did you?"

"I did not."

A horrible thought occurred to her. "How do you know what my bedroom looks like? Did you sneak into my house?"

"I avoid breaking the law whenever possible."

"Did you take pictures?"

"Photos were taken."

And if he didn't enter her house, how did he take pictures? Did he use a drone? Or dangle from a tree outside the window? "You spied on me. Like a Peeping Tom."

"I was careful to respect your privacy."

How could she believe him? The first chance he got, he'd stripped off her clothes. His rationale of treating her injuries made sense, but it was still a violation. "You said you were hired two and a half weeks ago—"

"Sixteen days," he said.

"And you've been watching me ever since. You know what I call that? Stalking. You're a damn stalker."

"Not stalking," he said, "protecting."

"Why?"

He shrugged. "It's my job to keep you safe."

If that were true, he shouldn't have any objection to contacting the WitSec offices. *Make the call!* She was angry and, at the same time, exhausted. She scooted back against the pillows and pulled the bedspread over her body. "What if I said I wanted to leave? Would you let me walk out the door?"

"Of course, but you might want to take a moment— while the assault is still fresh in your mind—to figure out who is after you. Who was the man behind the skeleton mask?"

"Why should I tell you?"

"We're on the same team. I can help you. I learned techniques in the FBI to jump-start your memory." His voice was gentle and cajoling, so charming. "We can try a few simple concentration techniques. You're smart, *cher*. You'll remember."

"Leave me alone."

"Allow yourself to relax. Close your eyes."

Though she didn't agree to cooperate, her eyelids slammed shut. She believed in meditation and was good at controlling her breathing. While he continued to talk in soothing tones, she focused. In her mind, she saw the face of the man who attacked her. Ignoring the terror she'd felt, she waited until his features became clear. With sandy hair and cold dark eyes, he was average-looking, except for his hatchet-shaped jaw. His mouth was wide, and he had big teeth, horse teeth. *I know him.* She didn't have a name or a title, but she'd seen him at the WitSec offices. The man behind the skeleton mask was a US marshal.

Her body tensed under the covers. Her subconscious mind had been protecting her. That was why she didn't call WitSec. She couldn't trust the marshals—couldn't trust anyone.

Rafe encouraged her. "Tell me. You figured something out."

If she was straightforward with him, she doubted that he'd let her walk out the door. *Trust no one.* The only way she'd escape was to make a run for it. She gave a huge, deliberate yawn. "I need to sleep. You should leave."

"We have more to talk about, *cher*."

"Not now…too tired. Please turn off the light and close the door."

She heard the click of the switch for the overhead light. Darkness descended. Opening her eyes a slit, she saw the circle of light on the bedside table where the music box had been.

He lowered his voice to an intimate whisper. "Sleep well, *cher*."

The door closed, and he was gone.

Chapter Three

Outside the bedroom door, Rafe walked down the short hallway toward the bathroom with a purposely heavy tread. He figured Alyssa would be lying in the bed and listening—waiting until he was out of the way before she made her move, which, he suspected, would be to run away by sneaking down this hallway or climbing out the window. Though he wanted to believe that she'd rest for a while and then wake up and have a reasonable conversation, he doubted that would happen. She didn't trust him. Nothing he said or did would make her think differently.

For the past couple of weeks while he'd been observing Alyssa, he had developed a pretty good idea what to expect from her. Her sweet, bashful attitude was genuine, but this pretty lady could also be as stubborn and immovable as a block of granite. When she made up her mind to do something, she carried through. If she successfully managed to disappear, she'd be hard to catch, especially since she already distrusted him.

Someone else might have better luck convincing Alyssa to cooperate. Another woman could reassure her and let her know that Rafe was on her side. In the kitchen of the very small house, he made a call to a confidential informant he'd worked with for many years. Sheila Marie knew everybody in New Orleans and heard every rumor.

Her connections stretched from the parish courthouse to the voodoo dens in the bayous to the wild parties in the French Quarter.

His CI answered after two rings. "Rafe, you pretty man, why you calling me?"

The strains of a jazzy saxophone wailed in the background. "Sounds like you're celebrating the Day of the Dead."

"Where you at? I expected to see you parading like your pirate uncle. Did I ever tell you about the day I saw naughty Jean-Pierre himself peep over your shoulder? And I heard his rumbling voice. He be liking you better as a gumshoe than a fed."

Sometimes it was handy to have an informant who talked to ghosts. "I have an assignment for you."

"Sure 'nuff."

"I'm looking for someone who was at the parade, near Jolene's gris-gris shop. This woman is tall and skinny and has curly silver hair. She's in her sixties."

"Prime of life," Sheila Marie said. "I'll ask around."

"And if I need help from you later tonight?"

"I'm at Becca's Bar on Canal."

He truly appreciated her help. "You are *magnifique*."

"Betcha say that to all the ladies."

"Only you, Sheila Marie."

He put away his phone. Stepping lightly, he returned to the bedroom door and leaned against the wall beside it, lurking and listening. Alyssa was half right when she called him a stalker. Much of his work as a PI or an undercover FBI agent involved sneaking around in the shadows, hiding behind other identities and lying. The difference between him and a run-of-the-mill Peeping Tom was that Rafe didn't get a buzz from watching.

He wanted to tell Alyssa the truth, but the time wasn't

right, and he wasn't altogether sure this lady could be trusted. His investigation into her background had uncovered some potentially unusual maneuvering with finances. He knew she had at least one fake passport. And she kept two safe-deposit boxes in different banks.

Tonight, she hadn't told outright lies but had been misleading. Most suspicious was her reluctance to call Wit-Sec. That should have been the first thing she did when she regained consciousness. If she'd insisted upon making that contact, his mission would have become even more complicated, but Alyssa never even mentioned witness protection.

Maybe she didn't believe the marshals could keep her safe. Given the events of this evening, he couldn't fault that opinion. Those masked skeletons were clumsy in their approach, but they'd known where she'd be. One of them might have made the anonymous phone call encouraging her to come to the parade.

From behind the closed door, he heard the bedsprings creak. In bare feet, her movements were a nearly silent shuffle, but he could tell when she turned the knob and opened the closet door. He hadn't left her defenseless when it came to clothing. Not only had he draped her Scarlett O'Hara rags on a hanger, but he'd added a couple of his own shirts and a pair of gym shorts that would undoubtedly be too big for her. In a pocket of her Scarlett pantaloons, he'd found a slim wallet with a couple of bucks, identification and a credit card. There was also a key chain with a fob and four keys. Though he left those things in her possession, he'd scanned every bit of her stuff until he was dead certain that nothing was bugged. The only item he'd taken was her cell phone, which he'd disabled so her location couldn't be traced.

When he brought her here, he made sure they weren't

followed. The security he had arranged at this location was similar to an FBI safe house with alarms, surveillance cameras and sensors. If she opened a door or a window without his authorization, he'd be alerted by a silent alarm. None of his electronics rang through to the police. Rafe didn't want to share his secret safe house with the authorities or anybody else, not even the man who'd hired him.

There were a couple of thuds from inside the bedroom, and he heard her curse under her breath. Getting dressed in the dark shouldn't be that difficult unless she'd decided to put on that old-fashioned corset, which had been complicated and utterly unnecessary for a woman like her. Alyssa didn't need to cinch her waist. Her natural curves, firm muscles and long legs were spectacular, truly *magnifique*. Her job as a sous chef at the bistro had taken a toll on her hands and forearms, which were reddened and freckled with spots from grease burns. But her midriff felt as sleek as satin. The bruise on her rib cage where she'd been kicked had infuriated Rafe. There was something deeply wrong about harming such a delicate creature.

Even if he wasn't being paid as a bodyguard, he would have instinctively wanted to protect her. The first step would be to identify her attackers. While she'd been lying on the bed in a meditative state with her eyes closed, he'd seen her fists clench and her brow pull into a scowl. He suspected that she'd been touched by a memory. The skeleton she had unmasked might be somebody she knew from Chicago. Unfortunately, she hadn't chosen to share that information, didn't want to say the name. She didn't trust him.

When he mentioned mug shots, she'd reacted the same way. *No police*, she'd said. Why not? He didn't want to believe that Alyssa was on the wrong side of the many crimes her old boss had committed, but she was a skilled bookkeeper, capable of hiding her involvement in money laundering and fraud.

Her accounting talents had worried Davis James, the man who'd hired Rafe. The client had made a compelling argument about his personal interest in Alyssa and his fear that she might be in danger, but Rafe had smelled a rodent and had used Chance Gregory—a computer genius who occasionally worked for the FBI—to trace his client's background.

Chance uncovered a steaming pile of dirt, starting with his client's name. Davis James was really Viktor Davidoff. He owned six used car lots—Diamond Jim's—in the Chicago area, and he was the alleged boss of a multimillion-dollar international group that specialized in smuggling exotic vehicles. When Davidoff hired Rafe, he'd refused to reveal how he'd learned that Alyssa was in New Orleans. Who had leaked that vital information? Who else knew her location? How were they connected to the men in skeleton masks?

From inside the bedroom, he heard the scratchy noise of the window being gradually raised inch by inch. The alarm system connected to his cell phone messaged him with the same info. Alyssa intended to make her escape that way.

Knowing that she'd need a few minutes to remove the screen and slip outside, he crept down the hallway to the kitchen and out the back door. His lightweight Kawasaki motorcycle was locked in the garage behind the house. For a moment, he considered trailing after her on foot but decided against it. On the bike, he had greater maneuverability and could continue to follow if she hailed a cab.

Taking a position on the breezeway beside the house,

he watched her cross the lawn, stumble on a crack in the sidewalk and hide against the trunk of a live oak until there were no headlights on the street. He imagined her heart beating fast and her gaze darting through the night, looking for skeletons and for him. Her outfit was a little bit crazy. His extra-large black Saints T-shirt with a gold fleur-de-lis drooped over her lacy Scarlett pantaloons. On her feet she wore black dancing slippers with two-inch heels and straps.

Chasing her down and dragging her back to the safe house was one option, but he knew Alyssa wouldn't respond to bullying. If he could convince her to trust him, he could keep her safe. And he was curious. A logical, organized person like Alyssa wouldn't forget about WitSec, and she wouldn't rush off into the night without some kind of plan. If he followed, she might lead him somewhere that would explain what she was doing.

When she was almost a block away, he started up his bike and eased into the street. Two blocks away was the streetcar that ran all night on weekends. It was only a little after one o'clock, early for a Saturday. Even in her baggy T-shirt, she wouldn't stand out in a crowd of partying zombies and ghosts from *Día de los Muertos*.

Staying out of sight, he circled the block and found a parking spot where he could see her. He turned off the motor, kept his helmet on and watched as she waited at a stop for the trolley. If she intended to go to her house, she was on the wrong side of the street. Alyssa didn't make careless mistakes, which meant that her escape included a return toward the French Quarter. *An unexpected direction.* Maybe she was heading back to the bistro where she worked, or maybe there was a friend who would give her shelter. Countless possibilities presented themselves.

For sixteen days, he'd managed to watch her without

attracting her notice, but now she knew him and could pick him out of a crowd. Surveillance would be ten times harder. He took out his cell phone to arrange for a meet with Sheila Marie. He needed backup.

In the meantime, Rafe would continue to be a stalker.

Chapter Four

Waiting for the streetcar, Alyssa kept to the far side of the sidewalk where a break in the shrubs that lined a wrought iron fence gave her a place to hide. Her entire body hurt. From her head to her rib cage to the palms of her hands and the scratches on her knees, she bristled with pain and tension. Taking another pain pill and falling back to sleep would have been nice, but she didn't have that choice. She had to run. There was no time for slumber—she needed to get away from the danger that had found her in New Orleans.

Though the night was cool, sweat dampened her forehead. She welcomed the sultry breeze that coiled around her bare legs like a torn veil. The mist limited her field of vision and gave her the hopeful illusion that she was invisible. Except for the squeaky window, she'd been quiet when she slipped outside and fled from the house, but that didn't mean Rafe hadn't figured out what she was doing.

She wished she knew who hired him. His refusal to tell her the name of his client worried her. She hated to think he might be working for someone who hated her, someone she'd testified against. Rafe had fought the guys in skeleton masks, so he wasn't connected to them. But he admitted he'd been a fed. Agents from the FBI, like the US Marshals, could be after her. *Why? Has the whole world turned against me?*

Paranoid and in pain, her life was a wreck. Crouching back into the bushes, she scanned the area. Only a few cars rolled under the streetlamps. She didn't see Rafe. Not that she trusted her powers of observation. During the time he'd tracked her, she hadn't noticed a thing. Either he was really good at sneaking around or she was oblivious.

The clang of the trolley alerted her to its approach, and she limped forward so the driver would see her and stop. When she'd first moved here, she'd memorized the streetcar routes. From here, she'd go about a mile and transfer onto the Canal Street line, which would take her close to her destination. After growing up in a big city, she preferred public transportation to the hassle of searching for a parking space. And she enjoyed the New Orleans streetcars. This one was painted a cheerful red with yellow trim. She hopped inside and slid onto a mahogany bench seat. There were only five other people— a young couple, a nurse in scrubs and two waitresses in pink uniforms with aprons. The young ones were busy staring into each other's eyes, and the ladies didn't look like violent criminals. *Relax, but don't let down your guard.* She held up her window-side hand to cover her face in case Rafe happened to be outside peeking in. There was no sign of him.

She really didn't know what to think of the tall, handsome man who'd introduced himself as a pirate. On the plus side, he'd helped her escape from the bad guys. For that, she would be forever grateful. Then Rafe had taken off her clothes to treat her abrasions. *A plus or a minus?* Administering first aid counted as positive. Stripping an unconscious woman was…not good. She decided to leave the naked question aside. He'd taken her phone but left her wallet, which gave her enough cash to pay the buck-and-a-quarter fare for the streetcar. Rafe's really big negative, the one that counted, was obvious: he'd spent over two weeks spying on her. Still, if he climbed onto the streetcar right now and sat beside her, she wasn't sure whether she'd scream her head off or snuggle into his warm embrace.

If only life could be more black-and-white with the good people wearing halos and devil horns for the bad ones. Some of the criminals she'd testified against were the very definition of evil. Monsters capable of committing terrible violence, they showed no remorse, possibly weren't capable of empathy. Rafe wasn't one of them, thank God. But could he work for them? Money spoke a universal language.

Hiring a private detective seemed too subtle for those thugs. She figured that if her enemies from Chicago found her, they'd take lethal revenge with a bullet in the gut or a knife across her throat or something more torturous and terrible. A shudder twitched across her shoulders. She couldn't trust WitSec, not anymore. Her survival depended on her ability to defend herself. During the last three years in New Orleans, she'd prepared a number of escape routes using new identities and different forms of transportation.

At her house, she had four sets of different license plates for her car, two prepacked suitcases, cash and the paperwork required to start over in another place. Unfortunately, going home was out of the question. The WitSec guy she'd recognized would know her address and would also know where she worked, which meant the emergency evacuation bag she'd hidden in the employees' locker room would have to be abandoned. Too bad! She had three disposable phones and a new credit identity in that bag.

Exiting at Canal Street, she blended into the small-ish crowd on the street outside a restaurant. Closer to the French Quarter and the downtown area, there were more people—some in costume and some with masks. In her baggy T-shirt, she felt awkward, embarrassed and scared. The creeps in the skeleton masks had drugged her and nearly abducted her. What if they found her again? The fifteen minutes it took for the connecting streetcar seemed like hours. She climbed aboard, relieved when they finally jolted into motion.

Again, she shielded her face from those who could see her through the streetcar window. Peeking through her fingers, she stared out at the scraggly palm trees that lined Canal Street, barely looking up when a woman with long dreadlocks sat beside her.

"It's late," the woman said. "You hungry?"

"I am," Alyssa said, realizing as she spoke that the gnawing pain in her belly wasn't entirely due to injury. She needed to eat. "I'll stop at Café du Monde."

"The café got the finest beignets in the world." The woman chuckled, showing off three gold teeth. "You know what to do, how to take care of yourself. That's good. Rafe said you were a smart gal."

Rafe? Alyssa looked up sharply. Her gaze riveted on the woman sitting beside her who could have been any-where from forty to 140. Strands of gray twined through her dreads, and her eye shadow was purple. She looked like she came from the voodoo shops in her long, dra-matically patterned skirt, red and yellow tie-dyed tank top, and abundant jewelry.

"Excuse me," Alyssa said. "Did you say Rafe?"

"Such a pretty man, dontcha think? He tole me not to get you riled up, hon."

Alyssa was hit with a sense of déjà vu all over again. Meeting this woman felt a lot like when she danced with a pirate, caught a glimpse of her mom's ghost and woke up in a bedroom that looked like her own but wasn't. After the upside-down day she'd had, the approach of yet another odd person should have made her paranoid and scared, but her anger overwhelmed all other thoughts. No way would Alyssa play a cat-and-mouse game with this woman.

She wanted answers, and she wanted them now. "What's your name?"

"Everybody calls me Sheila Marie."

"Why did Rafe send you?"

"Wassamatter. You don't trust him?"

"Not a bit."

"Smart." Sheila Marie's eyebrows knitted, and her full lips pursed. "It's dangerous to put your trust in a man, any man. Rafe Fournier, the great-great-great-great-grandson of Pirate Jean-Pierre, is better than most. He's a good person but still a man. You know what I mean, hon? Can't help himself—his brain don't work right. And that's why he sent me."

"Let me get this straight," Alyssa said. "He thinks I'll trust you, a person I've never met, who has no credentials."

"Credentials," she said with another flash of gold teeth. "You think I should have a business card? Maybe a diploma?"

"I want to know what you do." Was she a psychic, a medium or a voodoo witch doctor with a dozen spells in her pocket? "If you had a business card, what would it say?"

"Mostly, I'm a helper. I'm good at finding people who have gone missing. The pirate said you were looking for a tall woman with silver curls."

Alyssa gasped. Her lungs clenched, and she stopped breathing. When Mom died, she'd tried to contact the spirit world and had thrown away hundreds of dollars on a fortuneteller in Chicago who came up empty. Did Sheila Marie have the answers? Could she make that connection? "Did you find her?"

"Not yet, it's only been a couple of hours." When she stood, her many necklaces and bangles jingled musically. "Come on now, this is our stop."

Café du Monde was right around the corner on St. Peter. "How did you find me?"

"Hush, hush. You'll find out soon enough."

Alyssa got off the trolley and walked arm in arm with her strange new companion to Café du Monde, a twenty-four-hour-a-day bakery that was always busy despite the fact that they didn't serve alcohol. She spotted Rafe standing at the far edge of the patio awning with a white bakery bag in his hand. In his brown leather jacket and blue jeans, he looked almost as dashing as when he'd been costumed as a pirate. Somehow, he seemed taller.

After he greeted Sheila with a kiss on each cheek and gave her the bag of beignets, he turned to Alyssa. "We need to be moving along, *cher*."

She rooted her dancing shoes to the sidewalk, determined not to go any further without an explanation. "How did you know where to find me?"

"Secrets, secrets," Sheila Marie said with a snort. "You two deserve each other."

Rafe asked her, "Can you stick around for a while?"

"I'll do you one better, give you an escort. Follow me."

She entered the café, where she greeted several people

like they were long-lost friends. When Rafe took Alyssa's arm to escort her, she resisted. This wasn't the escape she'd planned. She'd figured out every detail of how she could disappear, and she wouldn't let a stubborn pirate hold her back. "How did you know I was coming here?"

"Come with me, and I'll tell you."

Reluctantly, she followed in Sheila Marie's footsteps. "Start talking."

"Last week, when I was doing surveillance on you, I saw you come here. You bought beignets and drank a cup of chicory coffee. And then you walked a couple of blocks until you got to that old brick building halfway down the block with the painted advertisement for Za-tarain's on the wall. You purposely walked past, then came back and went to the office where you paid cash for something to the guy at the front desk."

Why hadn't she noticed him? The whole reason she'd paused for coffee was to observe the area and make sure she wasn't being followed. "I must be blind."

"After you left, I checked with the office. You're rent-ing a storage space in that building. Don't worry, I didn't break into it." He tugged her forward. "Quit dragging your feet, *cher.* We need to hurry."

"Why?"

"As soon as you got in line for the Canal streetcar, I knew where you were headed. That's when I alerted Sheila Marie, who was close enough to intercept you. If I can figure out your escape plan, so can others."

Every word he said was logical. He was making sense, and she had to believe that her enemies could be here right now, watching and waiting. She might have ridden that cheerful red streetcar into a trap.

Chapter Five

Rafe's warning had the effect he wanted. He saw a glimmer of fear in her green eyes. Alyssa was still angry, no doubt about that, but she was also scared and she had good reason to be. If somebody was searching for her, they might have followed the same markers that led him to Canal Street.

Her gaze darted as she searched Café du Monde, trying to see the possible danger that might lurk among the mostly empty tables and twinkle lights. With the black Saints T-shirt hanging down to her knees and her hair a mass of tangles and the vestiges of ghost makeup on her face, she looked miserable and raggedy. Not like a person who belonged in this warm, fragrant bakery. Her voice creaked when she spoke. "Did you see anyone?"

"Not yet," he said.

"They could be anywhere," she whispered.

Sheila Marie handed Alyssa a cardboard cup of chicory coffee, looked up at him and said, "You'd best find a place where Missy Alyssa can catch a few winks. This little birdie is ready to drop."

"Don't leave me," Alyssa pleaded with her. "You have to tell me about the silver-haired woman. She looked like my mom. And when she laughed, I heard my mom. I can't come so close and have her slip away."

"Hush now, honey." In a swoop, Sheila Marie gathered her into a one-arm embrace while holding her own coffee in her other hand. She spoke in warm, musical tones. "Your mama passed a few years back."

Rafe couldn't remember if he'd mentioned that detail to Sheila Marie, but he must have said something. Either that or his CI had hooked into her psychic abilities. Her voice was gentle but firm. "You listen to me, missy. Right now, you got to do like I tell you."

"But I—"

"Straighten up." She kissed Alyssa's forehead. "Come along now."

Sheila Marie shepherded them through the kitchen, where a minimal staff worked at a leisurely pace. A beignet is always better when eaten fresh; the bakers couldn't stockpile dozens in advance and had to keep cooking. The staff watched through droopy eyelids as Sheila Marie escorted their little group through the kitchen and out a side door.

Rafe hadn't been able to make Alyssa budge, but Sheila Marie had everything under control. Contacting her was the smartest move he could have made. Instinctively, Alyssa seemed to trust the other woman. Never would she have allowed Rafe to take the lead. *Malchance*, it was bad luck for him. At times like this, he missed working for the FBI, where nobody questioned orders. They simply obeyed. Alyssa needed to accept his leadership. He couldn't be expected to choreograph a song-and-dance routine every time a decision had to be made.

Leaving the restaurant, they navigated through the streets until they came to a stop, huddled in a doorway. In a low murmur, he said, "Remember that you're in danger, *cher*."

"I know."

"The men in masks tried to drag you off into the night."

"Yes," she said.

"You can't go jumping out the window of my safe house and running away. It's not safe."

"I don't trust you." In the reflected glow from a streetlamp, he watched her brow furrow as she continued, "This isn't your problem, Rafe. It's mine, and I can take care of myself. I have plans. I've made arrangements."

"Bless your heart," Sheila Marie said. "You got a former FBI agent who's over six feet tall and as pretty as he can be. Let him shoo away the bad guys."

Under his breath, Rafe said, "I'm not the only one who wants to protect her."

"Are you saying there's somebody bigger and badder than you?" Sheila Marie took a bite from her beignet, sending up a cloud of powdered sugar. "Do tell."

"WitSec." He focused on Alyssa. "Why haven't you called them?"

"I don't want to say."

"I'm not inclined to play guessing games."

"And I'm not going to tell you."

Stubborn, difficult woman! How had she survived until now? It wasn't easy to qualify for witness protection. Her refusal to take advantage of the well-run, efficient program must to be due to something more than orneriness. He glanced across the street. Halfway up the block was the tired old building he'd seen her enter. "Give me your key and tell me what you want me to take from your storage locker."

"I'll get it myself."

This was exactly the sort of situation he wanted to avoid. Rafe didn't want to waste time by listing the many reasons why she shouldn't act alone, starting with the obvious fact that she wasn't armed. If ambushed inside the storage building, she would need backup. A lookout on the street would be useful.

"Sheila Marie, I'd appreciate if you'd wait at the café and watch for suspicious characters." As if on cue, two zombie princesses walking a spotted Great Dane sashayed down the street. Half the city was suspicious-looking, but he trusted his CI to recognize real danger when she saw it.

When he reached down and took the gun from his ankle holster, Alyssa asked, "What's that?"

"A Glock 43 nine millimeter."

"I know it's a gun," she said. "I thought you were the type who carried a stun gun."

"I'm former FBI," he reminded her.

"Didn't you use a stun gun on the three skeletons?"

"I suit the weapon to the occasion. You're in serious trouble, *cher*." When he met her gaze, he silently repeated a mantra: *Don't come with me into the warehouse, don't come with me, don't come...* Aloud, he warned, "You should stay with Sheila Marie. Do as she says."

She shook her head, and her tangled curls bounced. "Compromise? I won't go in there alone. You can come with me. We need to go around to the back."

He waited for the headlights of a delivery van to pass before he stepped off the curb into the street with Alyssa close at his side. In spite of a slight limp, she moved athletically. From the first time he'd seen her, he'd known that she was healthy and fit. Part of her daily regimen always involved exercise. He'd enjoyed watching her workouts—a detail he would never share with her. She had already called him a stalker. He didn't want to graduate to pervert. A flagstone courtyard between the four-story Zatarain's building and the two-story neighbor to the left made it easy to access the loading dock at the rear. Up a short flight of concrete steps was a door. Before he could reach for the handle, Alyssa elbowed him out of the way.

"I've got this," she said.

On the back side of a metal post beside the door was a small box with a combination lock. With a few flicks of the wrist, she had it open. The key inside opened the door. Before entering, she slipped the key back into the box and closed it.

"You made arrangements," he said. "Smart."

"I figured I might need to get to my storage unit at odd hours. I pay extra every month for the lock combination."

He followed her into the warehouse. The silence hung heavily. The stink of dirt and rat droppings oozed from the brick walls. A faint glow from high windows thinned the darkness, but it was still hard to see anything but edges and shadows. He took a slim Maglite from his jacket pocket. The beam spotlighted a beat-up wooden desk, a couple of file cabinets and concrete floors that created a maze through the rows of boxes, lockers and storage units.

He didn't hear any other sounds and figured they were alone. Still, he didn't want to take chances. "Don't turn on the lights."

"You didn't happen to bring another flashlight, did you?"

"*Pardonnez-moi*, but no."

"How much can I take from storage?"

"Only as much as you can carry." He had to wonder what she'd packed into her unit. What items did she consider necessary to survival?

"You know," she said, "it would be easier if I had the flashlight. I'm the one who knows where we're going."

No argument. He handed over the Maglite. "I'm right behind you."

She set a vigorous pace, charging along a straight four-foot-wide path between wall lockers and smaller center units. At the end of the building, she made a sharp right. They stood in front of a freight elevator with an ancient wood-slat door that rolled up like a garage. She lifted it and stepped inside.

"C'mon," she said. "My locker is on the second floor."

He hated the idea of being trapped inside the rickety old elevator but didn't want to waste time arguing. Though the elevator was a wide area, designed to move large objects from one floor to the next, he felt tense and crowded. Under his lightweight leather jacket, he was sweating. When she pulled down the door and hit the button for the second floor, the machinery rumbled like ten swamp gators with indigestion.

"Too loud," he said, wishing he'd figured that logic earlier. "If anyone is here and planning an ambush, they know exactly where we are."

"You're right," she said. "I should have considered that."

As soon as the elevator door opened, he scooted out. Carelessly, he bumped her leg. When she winced and gasped, he jumped back and cursed himself for being so clumsy. Just a few hours ago, she'd been knocked around by those men in skeleton masks. Her bruises had had enough time to ripen.

"The pain," he asked, "is it bad?"

"I wouldn't mind a long soak in a hot bath."

Though her quest to escape infuriated him, he had to admire her bravado. In spite of injuries and fear, her determination remained strong. She deserved every effort he could make to protect her.

The second floor of the warehouse was even more dreary and dark than the first. A few barred windows spilled light across rusted storage units. The big, square, filthy aluminum doors had numbers stenciled on the scarred, peeling paint. Her unit was 224.

She passed him the Maglite and reached under her giant T-shirt to retrieve her wallet and key chain. He focused the light so she could see where to unlock her unit.

"It's a five by five," she said. "I figured this was all the space I need."

The first thing he saw when she lifted the door was a sleek, shiny ten-speed bike that looked like it had never been ridden. She turned on the bare bulb light inside the unit, and he saw a tower of plain cardboard boxes pressed up against brand-new camping gear, still in the box. There was a tent, a sleeping bag, a camp stove, a lantern and miscellaneous tools, some with the price stickers still attached. Labels on other boxes showed premade food that was "better than the MRE."

He picked up a small hatchet. "Have you done much camping?"

"Not since I was a little girl and visited my grandparents in Georgia."

"How did you choose this equipment? Why?"

"I thought it might be a good idea to hide out in the backwoods. So I went to a sporting goods store and asked the salesman to give me all the gear I might need to survive for a month."

Rafe hoped the clerk had been working on commission. Providing the high-quality camping supplies this naive Yankee woman might need must have been an expensive proposition. "Did you happen to buy a gun?"

"Two of them," she said, "but I don't keep them here."

She climbed around the boxes and grabbed the heavy-duty straps on a gigantic backpack. As soon as she had access, she unzipped a small pocket on the side of the pack, dug inside and pulled out a bottle of extra-strength pain reliever. While she found a crate of bottled water in her space and helped herself, his cell phone buzzed, indicating he had a text message. Very few people had this number, which was specially encrypted so he couldn't be tracked or called unless he wanted to be.

He stepped away from her unit and checked his phone. The text came from Davidoff in Chicago. It was brief: Alyssa is missing. What do you know?

Rafe didn't reply. The message bothered him. Alyssa had been attacked by the three skeletons only a few hours ago. Already, Davidoff knew she'd gone off the grid. Where was he getting his information? Was somebody else keeping an eye on her? If others were involved, Davidoff should have informed him. Not that Rafe had expected ethical treatment from the infamous crime boss. Davidoff was no Boy Scout.

He glanced back toward the storage unit in time to see Alyssa strip off the oversize Saints T-shirt and change into a brown polo from her backpack. She'd already replaced her raggedy bloomers with a pair of jeans. Perched on the edge of a cardboard box, she changed into sneakers. With the addition of a denim jacket, her outfit was complete. Nondescript and practical, she'd blend in with any crowd. He couldn't explain why he preferred the zombie Scarlett clothes, but he did.

"Who was on the phone?" she asked.

"It was just a text." If she had been more forthcoming with him, he wouldn't have hesitated to share information.

"We should go," she said. "I have a hotel where you can drop me off."

Not a chance. She might think a local hotel was safe, but he doubted it. Rafe wouldn't abandon her to whatever thugs or skeletons might be on her trail. When they left this storage unit, he'd take her back to his safe house with the fully functional alarm system. On this issue, he refused to listen to any objection. Her safety was top priority. Either she came with him or she went to WitSec.

She hefted the backpack, which was almost as big as she was, onto her shoulders, grabbed the Maglite and staggered to the end of the row, where a casement window allowed a square of moonlight to spill across the concrete floor. This window started at her waist and went vertical for four feet. In summer, it could be cranked open and used for ventilation.

Alyssa peered through the grungy panes of glass. "Oh, no."

"Qu'est-ce que c'est?" He moved down the aisle toward her. "What's wrong?"

She pointed to the window. "There's a man across the street. I recognize him."

He peered through the window. The silhouette of a man—average height and weight—was readily visible. Though dressed in black, this guy wasn't good at fading into the shadows. He stood just outside the alley with the streetlamp illuminating his features. "How do you know him?"

"He's the man behind the skeleton mask that I pulled off. I realized that I'd seen him before, but it wasn't until just now that I recalled his name."

"Who is he?"

"Hugh Woodbridge," she said.

His phone buzzed again. He glanced down at a text from Sheila Marie that said, Three bad guys incoming. Get out!

Across the street, he saw two others join Woodbridge. "Why do you know this man?"

Chapter Six

Alyssa watched Woodbridge and his two colleagues saunter across the street toward the warehouse. They were coming after her again. She'd been running on adrenaline ever since she regained consciousness, and her energy was almost depleted. Her backpack felt like it weighed a thousand pounds. Her vision was foggy. Her bruises ached. Escape from this warehouse without Rafe's help would be nearly impossible. At this point, she had to trust him, even though he was an admitted pirate/ex–federal agent/private eye who'd been hired by an unnamed shady character to spy on her.

She tilted her head to look up at him. "Do you have a plan?"

He took the Maglite from her hand and replaced it with his Glock 43. "Don't shoot unless I tell you."

No need to worry about that. She'd never fired a gun at a living being and doubted she'd be able to start now. "Is the safety on?"

"Don't touch the trigger, and you'll be fine."

She followed him back to her storage space, where he used the flashlight to dig through her belongings until he found what he was looking for—a generous length of woven blue rope and a couple of those metal clippy things. He pulled down the door to her unit, closed it and locked it. "You ought to send a thank-you note to the sales clerk who ordered your gear. I doubt you asked for rock-climbing equipment."

"Rock climbing?"

"The rope and carabiners," he said. "These supplies might save us."

Before she could open her mouth to ask questions, she heard loud noises from downstairs. *A door being flung open? The heavy tread of men in boots?* They'd broken into the building.

Now was the time for action. And Rafe didn't hesitate. He seemed comfortable giving orders, which, she supposed, was SOP for FBI agents or captains of pirate ships. Whichever identity suited him was fine with her. Too nervous to think or plan, she fell into line, ready to do whatever he said.

He stopped in front of a casement window, which he managed to crank open. A breeze swept into the warehouse. Only a few blocks from the river, the air felt damp.

"Take off your backpack," he said.

"Will I have to leave it behind? There are things in there that I need."

"We'll take it, but you can't carry that much weight."

As soon as she slipped the straps off her shoulders, she felt better—not much stronger but lighter. She watched him use the carabiners to secure the woven blue rope around a pillar beside the window. After it was fastened, he tied a knot near the end.

"What are you doing?" she asked.

"Making a loop. Stick your toe into the loop, and I'll lower you down."

"That's a long drop. I could break my leg."

"Which is why I will lower you," he said. "Let me help you climb onto the sill."

The window opening was wide enough for her to pass through. From downstairs, she heard the rumbling squawk of the freight elevator as it descended to the first floor. Woodbridge was coming closer. She stuck her foot into the loop. "Now what?"

"Put your weight on your foot in the loop and slip through the window. Hold tight to the rope, and I'll let you down gradually. Brace yourself against the side of the warehouse."

Peering down, she stared at the narrow sidewalk between buildings. The drop was only about thirty feet but seemed as deep as an abyss. This window was strategically placed on the only side of the building that wasn't exposed to public view. The loading dock was in the rear. The front opened onto the street. And the opposite side looked down on the flagstone courtyard.

Though she tried to prepare herself for the descent, her hands trembled. Her bruises throbbed. She was so weak! How the hell was she going to jump out a window and climb down the side of a building like a spider?

"I can't do it," she said. "Do you have a plan B?"

"We're out of time."

Woodbridge and his men were calling to each other as they made their way through the storage units. Rafe was right, again. There wasn't a spare moment for hesitation or logic or fear. She climbed through the window, used the loop to support her weight and held the blue woven rope with all the strength she could muster. Slowly, he lowered her. Her leg began to buckle, and she kicked against the wall.

Above her, Rafe offered encouragement. "You're almost there."

She looked down. Not that far from the ground, she hesitated while he lowered her another few feet, and then she swung her free leg until her foot touched the side-walk. She'd made it.

Gasping, she collapsed on the ground, unfastened the toe loop and watched as the blue rope snaked up the side of the building toward Rafe. He leaned out the window and dropped her backpack. Quickly, he climbed into the window frame.

She noticed that he was wearing black gloves as he held the woven rope. He braced his feet against the wall and climbed down. His descent looked easy, almost graceful.

"We made it," he said.

"We did."

For the first time, she thought of them as a unit. They were no longer him and her—their escape had turned *them* into *we*. He had saved her and protected her. Was he, finally, the one person in the whole world she could trust?

He hoisted her backpack to his shoulders. "Come."

From the window above, she heard voices. Looking up, she didn't see anyone peeking out, but Woodbridge and his men were on the move, coming closer. She had no time for questions or planning. No time to handle the situation in the organized manner she preferred. All she could do was run down the alley behind Rafe. Usually, she was fast and agile. She prided herself on staying in shape with workouts, sprints and three-mile runs twice a week. But now, she stumbled on every other step. *Exhausted. Clumsy.*

When they got to the street, two blocks down from Café du Monde, Rafe grasped her arm and rushed her along the sidewalk. He stopped beside a motorcycle, took a helmet from the luggage carrier and handed it to her. "Put it on."

Not her favorite form of transportation, but she

wouldn't argue. They had to get away fast; these streets were too vulnerable. He fastened her backpack onto a rear luggage rack and helped her climb onto his bike. Before he got on, he flipped up the visor on her helmet, stared into her eyes and asked, "Are you strong enough to hold on?"

"I can make it." Though she'd agreed to let him take the lead, she didn't want him to think she was a wimp. "There's no other choice. Turning myself over to the cops is no guarantee of safety, not with a US marshal on my tail."

"About Woodbridge," he said. "No more secrets."

"The same goes for you."

"A question, *cher*." He stroked his jawline and massaged the dimple in his chin. "May I ask why these guys are really after you?"

"It's got to be revenge," she said. "My testimony got one guy a life sentence and prison terms for three others."

He leaned closer. His gray eyes were mesmerizing. "Tell me why a US marshal in New Orleans would care about the prison term for thugs from Chicago."

Breaking eye contact with him, she glanced over her shoulder. "We should get moving."

"If they want you dead, why not hire a sniper to shoot you on the street?"

"They don't want my death to be easy. They want to hurt me. That's the only thing that makes sense."

She refused to think about the other possibilities and unknown dangers that had haunted her ever since the FBI came knocking on her door asking for her testimony. Her old boss, Max Horowitz, had been a fence who owned a pawnshop. While working for him, she'd entered millions of dollars—receipts and billing, payments and expenses—into her neat ledgers. She was aware that a certain level of danger was attached to handling that much money. The FBI asked a million questions about the balances.

"It's possible," Rafe said, "that you have something they want."

"Not your problem." The moment of trust had passed. She returned to her normal, suspicious attitude. "If you don't mind, I'd like to be dropped off at a hotel. The address is—"

"I'm still in charge, *cher*. You go where I tell you." He put on his helmet and mounted the bike. "Hang on."

Alyssa wrapped her arms around his torso. His body was lean and muscular, radiating with heat. That warmth comforted her, even though he was being deliberately contentious. He cranked the bike, and the engine roared to life, sending shivers through her body. She tightened her hold and leaned against his broad back, rubbing her cheek against the supple leather of his jacket.

Though perfectly capable of taking care of herself, she had to admit that she liked being with Rafe. What had Sheila Marie called him? A former fed who was tall and dark and pretty. He was protecting her, and that level of concern felt unfamiliar to her. Mom had done her best to take care of Alyssa, but Mom was flighty—more attuned to playing games and having fun than providing a safe environment for her daughter. Alyssa's aunt Charlotte had never been someone she could turn to for wisdom or help. Mr. Horowitz was kind, but he was only her employer. There had never really been anyone who was dedicated to defending Alyssa. Not when she was growing up and certainly not now.

As the motorcycle swerved around a street corner, she leaned into the turn. The breeze wove around them, and she was glad to be wearing her denim jacket and jeans.

Before she could get her bearings and figure out which street they were on, Rafe yanked the handlebars to the right and drove the bike into an alley. Where was he taking her? When they emerged from the alley, she heard jazzy music and laughter from a bar on the corner. The sign above the bar identified it as Hurricane Harry's, named after a signature rum drink with a cherry and orange slice garnish. A woman dancing on the sidewalk looked like Sheila Marie…or maybe not.

Her memories blurred with glimpses of street scenes. When Rafe drove on the long, open stretch at the river's edge, she gave up trying to determine their destination and closed her eyes. Images from the parade flashed through her mind. She remembered the skeletons. Why did they come after her? Rafe's question had been perceptive. If they wanted her dead, why not just shoot her?

After dozens more twists and turns, he exited the street and drove up a driveway. She opened her eyes as he parked on the breezeway beside the house—the same house she'd escaped from only a few hours ago. "We're back here?"

He climbed off the bike and removed his helmet. "I told you I used to work for the FBI. You remember?"

She nodded.

"I know how to set up a safe house. You need surveillance, weapons and secrecy. Done, done and done. I have cameras, sound and motion detectors, infrared vision— all the bells and whistles. There's plenty of weapons, the more high-tech the better. And nobody knows this hideout exists. You're more protected here than in a hotel."

"What about your client? He must know the address."

"Let me worry about him."

When she dismounted from the motorcycle, her legs

were rubbery. Too exhausted to think, she'd ask other questions in the morning. Right now, all she wanted was sleep.

AFTER RAFE GOT her settled in bed and activated the security systems that turned this plain little house into a digital fortress, he sat at the kitchen table and took out his cell phone. He'd told Alyssa that he could take care of his client, and it was time to make good on that promise. The conversation would be difficult. Rafe had been hired by Davidoff to protect Alyssa, which didn't mean that the Chicago gangster had good intentions. By reputation, he was smooth but ruthless—much more dangerous than a rogue federal marshal like Woodbridge. Why was Davidoff so interested in this young woman?

Davidoff had fired off four more text messages, each more demanding that the one that came before. He went from the first polite inquiry about Alyssa's whereabouts to a demand. The last one, received at 3:17 in the morning, said, Where R U? Call me. Now.

Another benefit of Rafe's safe house security was a cybershield that made it impossible to trace his computers and cell phones. It was now 3:34. Rafe put through his call on the phone number Davidoff had given him. Audio only—he didn't want to show a glimpse of the house.

"Why, why, why…" Davidoff spat the words, rapid-fire like a semiautomatic. "Why did you take so long to call back?"

"Prior engagement."

"A woman? Is that it? Did you ignore my text because you're getting laid?"

"I have been with a woman this evening," Rafe said truthfully. "But tonight was about the celebration of *Día de los Muertos*, Day of the Dead. I had hoped to contact my pirate ancestors."

"Your voodoo games and your sex life don't interest me. Tell me about Alyssa."

Though Rafe had never actually met Viktor Davidoff, aka Davis James, aka Diamond Jim the owner of six used-car lots in Chicago, he'd done plenty of research before accepting this job. Photos showed Davidoff to be heavy-set with shoulders like a bull and a thick neck. His head was shaved, and his black beard was neatly trimmed into a goatee. Though he had a reputation for being well dressed, Davidoff had the strong hands of a peasant, with thick, blunt fingers.

If Rafe expected to learn anything from this client, he needed to ask the right questions and avoid giving away too much. "When do you think Alyssa went missing?"

"After her shift at the restaurant, she didn't return to her house."

"She might have a date."

Davidoff scoffed. "You've been watching her. Does she have a boyfriend?"

"Tonight, there are parties in the street. She could have arranged a casual meeting." Rafe shifted the direction of the conversation back toward the other man. "Do you have someone watching her house? Who told you she wasn't at home?"

"Should have been you!" Davidoff fired his accusation like a bullet. "I'm paying you good money to watch over the girl. And don't get me started on your so-called expenses."

Setting up the bedroom to his client's specifications had been costly, but Rafe turned the focus back on Davidoff. "Have you hired someone else to handle your business in New Orleans?"

"Why the hell would I do that? I'm not made of money."

"Who told you Alyssa was missing?"

"Not that it's any of your business, but it was the FBI agent who recommended that I hire you as a bodyguard."

"That was Jessop, yes?"

"I never said his name."

"But I'm correct." As soon as Davidoff had contacted him, Rafe had his FBI computer whiz do a search, and he'd found a link. "Your contact in the FBI is Darren Jessop, *n'est-ce pas*?"

"I don't have to tell you a damn thing, Frenchie. You work for me, got it?"

"But of course."

"I want to know where the hell she is."

Rafe decided to let this fish off the hook. "She's spending the night in a safe location. I can guarantee that she won't be harmed. Tomorrow at noon, I'll send you a photo of her."

"Thank God."

His relief sounded genuine. "She's important to you. Why?"

"Let's just say that I knew her mom well."

Davidoff didn't seem like the kind of man who took a sentimental journey. There had to be another reason for him to be invested in Alyssa's safety, and it probably involved money. Rafe probed, "In her job for the pawnbroker, she handled money. Is there some sort of payoff?"

"I'm done talking, Frenchie. Send me her picture tomorrow." He paused. "Maybe it's time for me to come to New Orleans myself. Alyssa will be happy to see me."

Rafe had his doubts. "Does she even know you?"

"We've met." He gave a sinister chuckle. "You might say I'm the most important man in her life."

"Why is that?"

"Let's just say that without me, she would never have been born."

Davidoff was her father?

Chapter Seven

The next morning, Rafe woke up thinking about the Chicago gangster with the thick neck and stubby fingers. If Davidoff truly was Alyssa's papa, he had a good, even noble, reason to hire a bodyguard to watch over her. But his claim was hard to believe. According to Rafe's internet search, no father was listed on her birth certificate. No man had claimed to be her parent, not in Chicago or in Savannah, where she'd lived with her mama for a few years.

Last night before she fell asleep, Alyssa had spoken about her family. She'd told him that her papa stepped out of her life when she was five years old. She never knew his name. Her mama said he was dead, and she had no reason to think otherwise.

Sitting on the edge of his bed, Rafe stretched and yawned. The early light of dawn crept through the window blinds. It was only a few minutes past seven, which was early for him and most of the NOLA night owls, but three and a half hours of sleep would have to be enough. He knew Alyssa was an early riser.

If Davidoff was her papa, why hadn't he come forward before now? After her mama died, Alyssa had no other family. When she'd witnessed a murder, she'd almost been killed before she was taken into protective custody. What kind of father would abandon his daughter when she so desperately needed him? Diamond Jim was a powerful, dangerous man who wielded great influence. Maybe he thought he was doing Alyssa a favor by distancing himself. If his enemies didn't know of her existence, they wouldn't go after her.

If those were the true circumstances, Davidoff could be considered gallant. But Rafe didn't think that was so. More likely, Davidoff was after the so-called payoff—a mysterious stash gleaned from the accounts of Alyssa's boss. When Special Agent Jessop referred Davidoff to Rafe, he'd mentioned that Alyssa was not only pretty but might have access to serious money. Rafe should question Jessop and dig out more information, but he had reservations about contacting the feds. Yesterday, Jessop had reported to Davidoff that Alyssa was missing. Had he also betrayed her WitSec location? *Très* suspicious, *n'est-ce pas*? Agent Jessop could be hooked up with the US Marshals. It might be wiser to keep the FBI in the dark.

Without turning on the light, he got out of bed. If he'd been alone, he wouldn't have bothered with clothes. But Alyssa was here. He pulled on a pair of sweatpants and shuffled barefoot into the kitchen. First order of business: brewing a pot of chicory-flavored coffee.

After he set the coffee to perk, he checked his surveillance cameras and alarm systems. All clear. He hustled down the hallway to the single bathroom in the house. The door was locked. From inside, he heard water running. Alyssa had gotten there first, which shouldn't be a problem. He knew from observing her that she typically hopped into and out of the shower in less than fifteen minutes, even when she washed her hair.

Back in the kitchen, he poured himself a mug of coffee. His brain would work better after a hit of caffeine—

maybe then he could figure out who was after her and why. This morning, Alyssa ought to be more willing to share information. Hadn't he saved her cute little buns last night? Surely her opinion of him had changed.

Last night at the storage facility, there had been a moment when she let down her guard and trusted him. He needed that attitude to continue. Acting as her body-guard was hard enough without having to worry about her sneaking out windows and taking off on some improbable scheme. He considered his plans for the day. If she agreed to cooperate, he could leave her safely tucked away in this house, where the security was top-notch. But he couldn't be one hundred percent sure that no one could track her to this location. If the bad guys found her, she didn't have the skills to defend herself. Therefore, he had to bring her with him when he left the house.

He sipped his coffee. Today he should consult with Chance—the computer genius—in order to uncover information on Davidoff and on Alyssa's former boss, the Chicago pawnbroker. And, of course, he'd talk to Sheila Marie to find out the gossip on the street. First, he needed to get into the bathroom.

Peeking down the hallway of this narrow, shotgun-style house, he saw her walking toward him, wrapped in a blue, yellow and orange beach towel. Her hair was still damp from the shower. The overhead light in the hallway spread a golden mantle across her bare shoulders. Her cheeks flushed pink. Her eyes were bright. "Good morning, Rafe."

"Allo, cher."

Her gaze dropped to his naked chest. "I didn't expect to see quite so much of you."

His nascent plan to assert his authority disappeared.

With nothing more than a smile, she had disarmed him. "I made coffee," he said.

"I'll throw on clothes and join you in the kitchen." She tossed her head. "We need to make plans. Because it's Sunday, I can't get into the safe-deposit box at my bank. But I have other things to do before I leave town."

"It is not safe for you to leave New Orleans before you have a safe destination and a plan."

"It's worse if I stay," she said. "And I'm good at figuring out what to do. I'll need to use your computer to look for locations."

Instead of objecting, he dived into the bathroom. The mirror was still steamed over from her shower, and he could only see a hazy outline of himself, which was fine with him. Rafe didn't want to confront himself directly after allowing Alyssa to roll over him. The way she talked about her plans sounded like she was calling the shots.

He rushed through a shower, brushed his teeth and dressed in cargo pants and a T-shirt. Though he was moving fast, she beat him back to the kitchen. When he entered, she was on tiptoe, reaching for a high shelf in the cabinet. Her mint-green blouse rode up, giving him a glimpse of her silky midriff.

"I thought I'd make oatmeal," she said. "Why do you keep it way up here?"

"I prefer grits," he said. "Step aside, I'll cook breakfast."

He took the container of stone-ground grits from the lower shelf and got started while she settled herself at the square-topped wooden table.

She tasted her coffee. "If there's anything I can do to help, just tell me."

Without measuring, he poured milk and water into a saucepan to heat. Grits for breakfast had been a standard since childhood, when Grandmama Lucille prepared most of the meals for his active family. Both his parents were professors at Tulane, and his three sisters were older and busy with their own lives. Nana Lucille had taught him how to cook, and he'd enjoyed his time in the kitchen where the air was redolent with Cajun spices and his mouth watered in anticipation of the treats to come. The kitchen was a soothing place, good for talking.

"I know the basics of how you came to be in Wit-Sec," he said, "but it would be useful to hear the details from you."

She groaned. "I've told this story a gazillion times. Are you sure you need to hear it?"

"We need to determine who is after you and why. So, yes, *s'il vous plaît*, tell me how you got yourself into so much trouble. Start with your old boss."

"Max Horowitz?"

"How did a nice girl like you get a job working for someone like him?"

"Through my mom," she said. "Mr. Horowitz used to come into the jewelry store where Mom worked as an appraiser. Long story short, she arranged for me to take a part-time job at his pawnshop after school, which was a huge step up from the pizza joint where I'd been working."

He set the cast-iron skillet on the range to heat before he cooked the bacon. The part of her account that she'd omitted with a casual "long story short" intrigued him. "What else was going on in your life at that time?"

"It was about ten years ago, just after Aunt Charlotte ran off and was killed in a fire. Mom missed her and spent a lot of time crying. She wasn't purposely ignoring me, but I felt isolated. I liked the distraction of working."

He glanced at her over his shoulder, noticing that she'd

used the coffee mug with daisies that he seldom touched. "Did your mama know that Horowitz was a fence?"

"Are you insinuating that my mom didn't take good care of me?"

"You tell me, *cher*."

"When she was in a good mood, she was the best— beautiful, funny and talented. On weekends, she used to sing with a band at weddings and, of course, with the choir at church." Alyssa fluffed her still-damp curls. "Mom raised me by herself. Money was tight. Not that we were broke or anything. But there were times when she might have dabbled in petty crime—things we didn't talk about. She never hurt anybody, always had my best interests at heart."

Her tone had become defensive and sharp. She loved her mama and wouldn't tolerate any negative allegations against her, even if they were true. He had to wonder about her mom's untimely death, killed in a hit-and-run.

"And so," he said, "you took a nice, quiet office job as an accountant in a pawnshop."

"I jumped on it. Mr. Horowitz was a sweet older gentleman."

According to internet gossip, that kindly old man with his walrus mustache and rumpled suit had stabbed a robber with a sword disguised as an umbrella. "Tell me about your job."

"The office was on the second floor of the pawnshop on the Near West Side, which was a fairly decent neighborhood. Mr. Horowitz assured my mom that it wasn't dangerous, and he did everything he could to make sure that was true. When I got to work, he buzzed me in. The door between the staircase leading up to my office and the shop was always locked. There were only four attempted burglaries during the five years I worked there."

"Only?" He stirred the grits and turned the bacon in the skillet.

"Pawnshops are tempting targets for thieves. It's a cash business. Mr. Horowitz had a built-in safe in addition to the cash register." She left the table and joined him at the stovetop. "I'll do the grits. You take the bacon."

He'd considered frying up andouille sausage to mix with the grits but decided to keep it simple. Making an incredible breakfast wasn't his primary goal. He wanted her to relax and give him the real story. But he didn't want her to make a mess with his food. "Have you made grits before?"

"I'm a cook at a bistro."

He'd wondered why she'd taken that job. When her mom died, Alyssa had been left with substantial assets and a big insurance payoff. She didn't need the money. "Do you enjoy being a chef?"

"Not as much as I thought I would. All the food in New Orleans sounds so exotic—gumbo, jambalaya, crawfish étouffée. Learning how to make those dishes isn't easy, and I've had several disasters."

He liked her curiosity and her interest in his hometown. So much about her was appealing. "You mentioned burglaries," he said. "Did you get involved in one of them? Is that how you ended up in witness protection?"

"You are so wrong. The incident didn't come until later, and it didn't happen at the pawnshop." Using a wooden spoon, she swirled the grits. "Should I add butter?"

"If you like."

"Everything is sweeter with butter."

"Spoken like a true daughter of the South."

"Don't forget," she said, "when you first met me, I was dressed as Scarlett O'Hara. I'm not a belle, but my mom was born and bred in Savannah. I've spent enough time there to understand their customs and habits. Not to mention the past few years I've lived in New Orleans. I like this town, and I'll be sad to leave."

"Perhaps, *cher*, we can find a way for you to stay."

She shook her head. "The best thing is to pack up my tent and move far away. In a new city, I can start over."

"And if they find you again?"

"I'll stay on the move."

While leaning over her shoulder to check the grits, he caught a whiff of her hair, a peach fragrance that didn't smell like any shampoo he'd ever bought. She must have brought her own hair products in that giant backpack. When he inhaled again, she turned her head. Their faces were inches apart. The tip of her nose almost touched his chin.

Kissing her lips would have been natural, sexy, pleasant and…*très, très, très stupide*. Such intimacy was destined to end in a slap. He pulled back and said, "Cayenne. I like to add pepper to the grits."

"So do I." She stirred in salt, a pinch of cayenne and a glob of butter. "I like my food sweet and spicy."

Precisely the way he liked his women. Not a topic he intended to mention to her, not even as a joke. "Tell me more about your work at the pawnshop."

"Mr. Horowitz made it easy for me. At various times during the day, he handed over paperwork that showed what merchandise had been taken in and how much he paid for it. I recorded the transaction in a digital file that could be checked against the counter receipts. After I'd been there for a couple of months, I started doing larger shipments that were delivered to the warehouse. After that, I recorded estate sales where Mr. Horowitz picked up antiques and artwork. Sometimes, Mom went along on those trips."

Her work sounded straightforward. Products came in and cash went out. "I suppose the business expenses had their own records."

"There were several different files. Mr. Horowitz liked to see monthly figures, detailed quarterly tax data, profit and loss statements to verify how much he was spending on different parts of the business. Everything was computerized, but my boss was old-fashioned. He liked the ledger system that he'd used when he first went into business."

"How did you do that?"

"I translated the figures by hand from the computer to neat, tidy books. Some were bound in leather. Others were less fancy. He kept them on floor-to-ceiling shelves behind his antique desk in the upstairs office. My workstation was across the room by the window."

Rafe took the skillet filled with thick strips of bacon off the flame. "Are you saying that there were two sets of books?"

"Actually, there were three. I used to take a photo with my phone of the computer sheets to copy into the other ledger. Before you get all excited, I should tell you that FBI forensic accountants went over the ledgers and other data. They were satisfied that Mr. Horowitz wasn't committing fraud."

Still, the complicated system was suspicious and offered many opportunities for disguising amounts and burying payments. Using a high school part-timer to keep track of business accounting seemed risky. While she finished with the grits and sprinkled cheddar on top, he whipped up scrambled eggs. With breakfast assembled, he sat across the table from her and raised his coffee mug in a toast.

"Here's to us," she said.

"And here's to finding the men who are after you…"

"…and locking them up in handcuffs, and then we'll throw them into a swamp, where the gators eat them piece by bloody piece."

Her grin belied the danger in her words. Not unlike the zombie Scarlett she impersonated, Alyssa had many secrets she hadn't revealed. For one thing, she made the pawnshop sound like a cute little neighborhood business. He knew better. Horowitz Pawn & Exchange had been a multimillion-dollar business. Not only did the old man with the white mustache deal in over-the-counter trades, but he handled raw diamonds and antique jewelry with untraceable provenance. And he was a fence who regularly dealt with criminals and probably laundered their cash.

Though the FBI accountants hadn't found evidence of fraud, that didn't mean her boss had been cleared. When Alyssa came forward to testify, Max Horowitz had disappeared. He hadn't been heard from since.

"We should make plans," she said. "I'd love to get into my house."

"A joke?" Because he wasn't laughing.

"I realize that it would be difficult, but I hate to lose everything I own."

She might be hiding something of significance at the house. "Any particular item? Perhaps jewelry?"

"As if I'd be foolish enough to leave anything valuable lying around."

"*Mais non*, you are too clever." He watched her expression as he continued. "You might have hidden something under a loose floorboard or in a secret compartment of a desk or in the freezer section of your refrigerator."

"I might have tried a stunt like that...when I was twelve." While holding eye contact and looking innocent, she dug into her breakfast and moaned with pleasure at the first taste of grits. "If Mr. Horowitz taught me anything, it was how to keep my treasures safe. My mom was the same way. When I was a kid, we used to play a game where she'd hide a diamond brooch and I had to find it."

"And now that you're grown up?"

"Well, you saw my storage unit. And I mentioned my safe deposit boxes. I have a locker in a gym and at my work."

Her green eyes sparkled so brightly that he was distracted. He looked forward to the time when she stopped playing this game of cat-and-mouse with him. They were on the same side. The more he knew, the better he could protect her. "In any case, you cannot return to your house. They could be watching or have rigged booby traps. Your car will most certainly have a tracking system so they can find you."

"You might be interested to know that I have another car. It's in a private garage, all gassed up and ready to roll."

"Is this vehicle in your name?"

She bit off a piece of bacon with her sharp, white teeth and chewed before washing it down with coffee. "Technically, Alyssa Bailey is an alias. That's the name I use for everyday business, but I have four other identities, two with passports and all with credit cards."

It sounded like she changed names the way other people changed clothes. "Did you have any of this paperwork while you lived in Chicago?"

"Only one," she said. "I added the others during my three years in New Orleans."

She made falsifying her identity sound like a hobby. Where had she gotten the paperwork? How had she obtained credit in different names? He suspected that Horowitz had taught her more than rudimentary accounting procedures. "I would like to see these documents."

"Not a good idea. After all, I might need to disappear from you." She dabbed at her full lips with a paper napkin. "Maybe we can pick up my second car or visit the locker at my health club."

"We'll see."

He had no intention of allowing her to call the shots and drag him along on her secret and possibly nefarious agenda. After another sip of coffee, he scooped up a forkful of fluffy scrambled eggs. The food was good, but he ate too fast and only savored every other bite. Alyssa had thrown him off his game.

After they cleaned up the breakfast dishes, he took her into the small pantry off the kitchen so he could show her his array of surveillance equipment. Four screens from cameras outside the house were divided into four smaller pictures. None showed suspicious activity.

He explained the sensors. "If you jiggle the doorknobs or rattle the windows, an alert rings through on my cell phone."

"Last night, you knew exactly when I made my escape." Her tone became accusatory. "Why didn't you stop me?"

"I wanted to see where you'd go."

"And why is that, Rafe? Did you think I'd be meeting a contact?" She whirled to confront him. The walls of this tiny room seemed to shrink as she demanded, "Do you suspect me?"

That was a big question with many shades of gray between gleaming innocence and pitch-black guilt. Hoping not to destroy the cooperative mood that had been building during breakfast, he distracted her by holding up her cell phone and replacing the battery. "If you want to check messages, you can turn it on for a few minutes. I have enough security in this house to shield phone transmission and tracking."

She snatched the phone. "Thank you."

He watched her scroll through texts and messages. Her manner was casual, and he didn't sense that she was looking for a contact from a partner in crime. "Are you expecting a call?"

She shrugged. "I have a message here from Anonymous. Should I play it?"

He perched on a stool in front of the screens. "If you please…"

The voice of Anonymous reminded him of her earlier account. Pitched low with husky overtones, Anonymous could have been male or female. The message was brief: "Sunday morning, nine o'clock services at the Hope and Peace Church in the Ninth Ward. Be there."

She played it again. "That's the same person who called me last night. I'm sure of it."

"But you don't recognize the voice."

"There's something familiar, but no."

He glared at the phone in her hand. Though he wasn't in the mood to dash across town without knowing what he was looking for, they couldn't ignore this message. "You need to get dressed in a hurry. We're going to church."

She bounced to her feet. "Give me eight minutes."

Most women would take longer than that to put on makeup and style their hair, but Alyssa was a clever little chameleon. In his bedroom, Rafe changed into a dark blue suit and a white shirt with no tie. Before he donned the jacket, he added a shoulder holster. Then he ran a finger over his jaw. No time to shave, but he wasn't too scruffy-looking. He combed through his thick, dark hair with his fingers and called out, "Ready?"

"Almost."

He stepped into the hallway and came face-to-face with a blonde whose long hair curled past her shoulders. Out of curiosity, he checked his watch. Exactly eight minutes had passed. "How did you know the timing?"

"I've practiced changing into my disguise." She wore extra-large black sunglasses with rhinestones in the corners. Her patterned pink sundress had a full skirt and low-cut neckline. With her fists on her hips, she stuck out her impressive cleavage. Then she pursed her lips, which were painted neon pink, and asked, "What do you think, sugar?"

"Subtle."

Alyssa Bailey, the former accountant from Chicago, had transformed into a femme fatale. Those huge sunglasses hid her green eyes. The bright color of her dress was a distraction. Any witness describing her would focus on the long shiny blond hair. She had a natural talent for disappearing in plain sight. Rafe had years of undercover experience, and he approved of her disguise.

Chapter Eight

In moments, they were out the door and on their way, riding in the black SUV that had been parked in the detached garage behind the house. Scrunched down in the passenger seat, Alyssa felt twitchy and nervous. Not scared—not yet, anyway. The misty morning sunlight spread a sultry glow over the city streets near the French Quarter. Last night's parade had left behind debris. Mingled with the trash and discarded flowers were glittery threads of fine memories. New Orleans was like a woman who'd spent the night in the throes of passion and was well pleased with herself on the morning after.

Alyssa envied the sensual indolence of NOLA. In comparison, she seldom allowed herself to relax, seldom let her guard down. When her life whirled off balance, she hated the disorientation from scary memories in the past and the threats of the future.

Behind her giant sunglasses, her brow furrowed. She had to remember and to plan and, above all, to trust no one—not even Rafe, even though he seemed to be helping her. In his blue suit and crisp white shirt, he looked as sharp and well groomed as any other gentleman on a Sunday morning. But not harmless. His eyes flicked from left to right and back again, scanning for danger as he drove. She hadn't missed the fact that he wore a shoulder holster under his jacket.

With the sun visor pulled down, she took off her glasses and studied her reflection in the mirror. *More blush, more lipstick.* When she first started playing with makeup, she'd been amazed by how simple it was to change her appearance with a wig, eyeliner and a push-up bra. The bra had proved especially effective. Most men—and some women—were so impressed with her bosom that they barely noticed her face.

When she unpacked last night, she'd had a feeling that a disguise might be necessary and had taken this pink outfit that she'd named Baby Doll from her backpack. She'd shaken out the long blond curls and hung up the dress. Though she would have preferred platform heels to complete Baby Doll, her backpack was only big enough for pink ballet flats, which was probably just as well. She wanted to be appropriate for church.

Glancing over at Rafe, she asked, "Am I dressed okay?"

"You look fine."

That rote response was the kind of thing men said to stay out of arguments. It didn't tell her much. "Where I grew up in Savannah, our church was nondenominational Christian with a super-dramatic pastor, a lot of clapping and singing. Mom was a soloist in the choir, and she was really good. When she sang 'Ave Maria,' the congregation wept."

"Are you sure you're her child?" He teased, "I ask because I heard your singing voice at the parade. You almost made me cry, but not in a good way."

"I didn't inherit her talent." And she didn't appreciate the reminder. "Is the Hope and Peace Church the kind of place I'll feel comfortable in a wig and sunglasses?"

"Don't know, *cher.* I've never been there."

The location and the anonymous phone call worried her. "Why do you suppose the mystery caller wants to meet at a church?"

He shrugged. "The message was left on your phone. And so, I suspect, the location is meant to have some kind of significance for you. When you think of church, what comes to mind?"

She closed her eyelids and concentrated. She hadn't been a regular churchgoer in years, and her memories were mostly of Bible stories and games they played in Sunday school. "It's not a bad place to meet. I don't expect any of the bad guys to attack me in a church."

"Are you afraid?" he asked.

Not something she wanted to admit. Alyssa opened her eyes and focused on him. "Did you go to church when you were growing up?"

"My family is Catholic. Nana Lucille took me to St. Louis Cathedral."

An incredible building with triple steeples, sky-high vaulted ceilings, ornate carvings and statuary, St. Louis was a symbol of culture in Louisiana, one of the oldest cathedrals in the country. She was reminded that, unlike her, he came from a traditional family with deep roots. Maybe he'd grown up in a mansion with pillars that looked like Tara. "Do you still have family in town?"

"Not anymore."

She sensed there might be an interesting story about the Fournier clan, but she didn't want to hear too much about Rafe or get too close. He had charm, an enticing grin and silver-gray eyes that sparkled and flashed. But she didn't dare trust him. Not until she understood what he was really after. Not until he shared the identity of his mysterious client.

Headed toward the Ninth Ward, he drove on mostly

deserted streets toward the bridge across the Mississippi and the canal. "I want to hear more about you, *cher.* You never finished your story about why you're in WitSec."

She'd been hoping to avoid reliving the actual murder. She could have gone on and on about Mr. Horowitz and how much she'd liked working for him. "Where did I stop talking?"

"You had explained your job."

"Right," she said. "By the time I graduated from high school, I decided that I wanted to be an accountant, a CPA, which meant I needed to get a degree. Mr. Horowitz agreed to pay for my college if I promised to continue working for him for four more years after college."

"A fair offer."

She agreed. "He's a really good person. I guess, maybe, I suspected that he was a fence. But is that so terrible? It's not that different from an auction?"

"But it is," he said. "A fence usually handles stolen goods."

"Don't patronize me." An irritated sigh puffed through her lips. "What I'm trying to say is that a lot of the jewelry that gets sold in a nasty divorce might as well be stolen. The same goes for expensive works of art used to pay gambling debts."

"Possession is assigned by law."

And she believed in the law. "You're right, but I hate to think of Mr. Horowitz doing anything illegal. It made me furious when the FBI agents questioned me and kept insisting that he committed fraud and laundered money. According to them, the fact that he'd disappeared after the murders was proof that he'd ripped off his clients."

"Did they have other evidence?" Rafe asked.

"Nothing but vague accusations." She hated their lies and how those suggestions implicated her. "Mr. Horowitz was kind and generous. I saw him give two thousand dollars to a widow who had to pawn her husband's Purple Heart. Later in the day, he arranged for the medal to be returned to her."

"It's possible to be a decent human being and a criminal at the same time."

"Is it?"

"I should know," he said. "My ancestors were pirates."

"Those guys in the FBI are so damned self-righteous. Again and again, they asked if I might have made an accounting mistake. Of course I might have. It's called human error. I didn't always balance to the penny. But they were talking about a ridiculous sum—seven million, six hundred thousand dollars."

He stomped the brake, whipped to the side of the road, tore off his Ray-Bans and glared at her. "Repeat."

She did so and added, "I never should have told you."

"Au contraire." His unshaven jaw clenched. "That money is a powerful motive. It gives over seven and a half million reasons why those guys are after you and why they need to take you alive. They think you know where the money is."

"They're wrong."

"They might also be after your boss. Do you know where to find him?"

She lifted her chin to confront him. "Even if I did, I'd never tell."

He rattled off a long string of French phrases, some of which she recognized as curse words. Then he put the SUV in gear and merged into traffic. "Do you remember the names of any of the agents who questioned you about the money?"

"There were a bunch of them in Chicago and in court. Be more specific."

"What about the locals?" he asked. "Have you spoken to Agent Darren Jessop?"

"Tall and muscle-bound, blond hair and baby blue eyes," she said with a nod. "I remember him. The guy looks like he works out three times a day. Do you think he's after me? Working with Woodbridge?"

Instead of answering, Rafe stared straight ahead through the windshield as he drove onto the bridge. "Finish your story. I might as well know it all."

The dark waters of the river stretched as far as she could see on either side. So many secrets roiled beneath the surface. She'd confided in Rafe. *A mistake?* It felt like he knew more than she did and therefore had an advantage. They needed to be on equal footing. "I told you about the money. Now it's your turn. Why are you interested in Darren Jessop?"

"He knows my client, the man who hired me to protect you." He looked toward her. "I had hoped to talk with Jessop today."

"In person?"

"Or on the phone." His shrug had a touch of French nonchalance. "Back to your story. You claim that your job was not dangerous. And yet, you witnessed a shooting."

"Not in the pawnshop. My upstairs office was totally protected and private. I didn't deal with the people who came to pawn their treasures, and I didn't mess around with the merchandise. Other people did the stocking and made sure everything went where it was supposed to go."

"What was the regular procedure?"

"Lots of stuff was kept at the store, especially if Mr. Horowitz thought the person who pawned it was coming back. There was a huge walk-in safe downstairs, but much of the valuable stuff was stored at a separate location, a warehouse in Bedford Park."

In her mind's eye, Alyssa saw the neighborhood, which wasn't gritty but wasn't gentrified like the Fulton River Warehouse District. The warehouse used by the pawnshop was a square two-story redbrick building with a two-bay loading dock. Unremarkable on the outside, but the inside had been broken down into smaller containers with clean, white walls. These enclosed spaces were humidity and temperature controlled to maintain the artworks in peak condition and to keep the wood on antique furniture from warping. Walking among these containers had reminded her of a labyrinth.

Memory crept over her, and she shuddered. The air-conditioning in the SUV felt icy cold. She didn't want to talk about this. They exited the bridge, and Rafe drove east.

"Are we almost there?" she asked.

"We have enough time for you to finish your story," he said. "Tell me what happened at the warehouse."

"I hardly ever went there. In the five years I worked for Mr. Horowitz, I'd gone to the warehouse only ten or fifteen times by myself. On that day, I was checking balances in the ledgers against inventory sheets for an audit, and I discovered a discrepancy."

"How large was this discrepancy?"

"At the time, I thought it was huge, close to twenty thousand dollars, and I figured it had to be a mistake— *my* mistake. I was juggling a heavy schedule in college while working full-time, and I was exhausted. I didn't want to think I'd written the numbers wrong, and I hoped this was a simple matter of merchandise being misplaced in the warehouse. Mr. Horowitz was out of town, and I figured I could clean up the error before he came back."

As the memory became clear, she went silent. If she'd stayed in her office behind her desk, none of this would have happened. But she'd been full of herself, thought she could fix the problem with a wave of her hand. *Wrong, wrong, wrong.*

"Tell me about the discrepancy," he said.

"When I got to the warehouse, I should have known right away that something wasn't right. Frankie Leone, the warehouse supervisor, wasn't behind his desk. At the time, I was glad to slip inside unnoticed."

"Did you say Leone—Frankie Leone?"

She nodded. "Do you know him?"

"Continue with your story," he said. "You were glad to be unnoticed because you hoped to correct the discrepancy without anyone finding out."

She wished he'd stop saying *discrepancy*. It was her choice of word, and she hated herself for trying to be aloof, trying to turn her twenty-thousand-dollar mistake into something less stupid. "I botched things up, okay? If I hadn't gone to the warehouse, Ray McGill and his brother would have cleaned up the body and gotten away with murder. But I was there. I was a witness."

"Not your fault, *cher.*"

"Then why do I feel guilty down to my bones?"

"This was a large warehouse, yes? What kind of outsize items were stored there?"

"Construction equipment, motorcycles and vintage cars," she said. "Once I saw a speedboat."

"Do you know Diamond Jim Davidoff?"

"Everybody knows Diamond Jim. I bought a used Honda from him."

"And so? You are personally acquainted?"

She shook her head. "He's much too important to work on the lot, but I shook his hand at a fund-raising event. When I called his office about buying a car, he passed the word to the car salesman that I was a special customer."

"Continue your story, *s'il vous plaît.*"

"I wandered through the containers until I found the wall safe where furs, designer gowns and jewelry were stored along with small antiques like clocks and lamps. I used the combination, opened the door and went inside the ventilated, temperature-controlled safe. That's when I heard gunshots."

And her heart had stopped. She hadn't wanted to believe that the popping noise was gunfire and went to the door of the safe to look out. "A man staggered toward me. His sweatshirt was covered with blood. When he got closer, I recognized him as Frankie Leone. Before he collapsed in my arms, I saw Ray McGill shoot him one more time. I grabbed Frankie and shut the door to the safe. It automatically locked."

"And you were trapped inside with Frankie Leone, a man who was dying."

She appreciated the way he mentioned the name of the dying man. The FBI agents and the marshals had always referred to him as the "victim." Not acknowledging his given identity seemed to diminish his passing. "There was so much blood. I could tell that he was in pain. His eyes squeezed shut. He passed out."

Every time she spoke of those helpless, painful, terrible moments, Alyssa felt one step closer to death. She'd called 911 on her cell phone and managed to get a tenuous connection before the phone went dead. Desperately, she'd needed to believe that help was on the way, but she didn't know for sure. Frankie Leone lay unconscious in her arms. How to save him? She tried to remember first aid. Was she supposed to wake him? Or put pressure on the wound? She didn't know CPR but had seen it done.

When she pushed up his sweatshirt, any thought of pushing on his chest was erased. Blood oozed from his wounds. He'd been shot several times. From outside the safe, she heard more gunshots, which had to be McGill and his pals trying to break inside. She wrapped Frankie in a full-length mink coat to make him comfortable.

"He never opened his eyes," she said. "His breathing stilled, and then it stopped. The police took over an hour to arrest McGill and get the safe opened. By then, Frankie had started to turn cold."

She'd held him tightly. Though Frankie was beyond help, she'd wanted to protect him. This might be the hundredth time she'd told this story, but it never got easier.

To her surprise, Rafe reached across the console, placed his hand on her forearm and gave a gentle squeeze. He didn't say anything, but the physical contact soothed her. The warmth of his hand melted the chill that had enveloped her body.

When she looked up at him, she could tell that he had experienced a similar trauma. They didn't need words to communicate. Coming close to violent death had changed her forever, and she was certain that he felt the same way. If she hadn't been strapped in by her seat belt, she would have climbed across the console and wrapped her arms around him, pressing herself against him so she could absorb his heat and his strength.

He pulled over to a curb and parked.

"Are we at the church?" she asked.

He nodded.

She'd been so distracted by the telling of her story that she hadn't noticed their surroundings. The Ninth Ward had been devastated by Katrina when the levees broke, and parts of the area still looked like a war zone. Other streets—like this one—had been rebuilt and replanted. The road itself was in need of repair, but the homes on either side were tidy frame houses, some painted with bright colors. She noticed a one-story house with purple and yellow stripes. The church took up several lots on the corner and had a parking lot, which Rafe had chosen to ignore.

The rebuilt church had a simple design with a white steeple. Along both sides were tall, narrow windows with gray hurricane shutters. Behind the main building, she saw a patio with a barbecue and a garden. A long, low one-story structure, probably a recreation hall, stood on the other side of the patio. The church entrance was up two wide stairs and had an arched double door made of heart pine. Two women stood outside talking. One was black, the other white, and both wore sundresses.

Alyssa pulled herself together. "I'm ready."

"If we encounter danger," he said, "we leave. *Immédiatement.* Do you understand?"

"I get it. The bad guys might recognize me. I know my disguise is distracting, but I'm not invisible."

He came around to the passenger side and opened the car door for her like a gentleman. She was equally ladylike in her Baby Doll pink with the rhinestone sunglasses. She took his arm as they strolled up the sidewalk. The clean concrete looked like it had been recently poured.

Though the Peace and Hope Church seemed to live up to the nonthreatening name, a shiver of fear twitched across her shoulder blades. "We could be walking into a trap."

He didn't deny her statement as they strolled toward the church doors, one of which was opened. From inside, they heard clapping and singing as "If I Can Dream" came to an end. With a polite nod to the ladies at the door who handed out programs, Rafe escorted her inside. They stood at the rear and watched as the congregation got comfortable in the pews.

In the raised sanctuary at the front, the pastor—a handsome, barrel-chested man in a double-breasted burgundy suit—strutted back and forth behind the railing. His energy couldn't be confined to the pulpit; this man had to move. His speaking cadence was rhythmic, almost musical, and he reminded her of speakers who had come to her family's church in Savannah.

The design of the sanctuary was simple with little more than a cross, a pulpit and benches for the choir. But the decorations were plentiful, including tall bouquets of dahlias and mums and fragrant roses. The floral scent mingled with the waxy smell from yellow, green and orange candles of every shape and size. Hanging from the overhead beams, embroidered banners displayed messages of love and friendship. The pastor wrapped up his message, and the choir, dressed in burnt-orange robes, rose to their feet.

Peace and Hope was actually very similar to her childhood church, with a diverse congregation and plain decorations instead of statuary. Still, Alyssa was surprised when the pastor spoke of her church and introduced the visiting soloist as a member from that congregation. Her name was unfamiliar.

The organ player hit the opening chords, and a woman stepped away from the others in the choir. She stood tall, her hands clasped at her breast. Her curly silver hair was tucked into a bun on the top of her head.

Frozen in place, Alyssa stared. This woman could have been her mom. She had the same high forehead, the same wide-set eyes. When she sang, her soprano resonated with the same compelling vibrato as Alyssa's mom, Claudia. That voice filled the sanctuary and the nave and flowed out the door all the way to the street. "Amazing Grace" would live forever in Alyssa's fondest memories.

She closed her eyes and imagined that her mom was still living, thriving and having a chance at happiness. But that was a lie. Mom was dead. Alyssa had seen her in the coffin, had wept at her grave.

The silver-haired woman currently raising her voice in song was, most likely, the anonymous caller who had summoned them to the church. But that wasn't all. This woman was presumed dead ten years ago, though her body was never found. For better or worse, this beloved and infuriating woman was Alyssa's aunt Charlotte.

Chapter Nine

The shock of seeing her aunt crashed into Alyssa with a paralyzing force that rattled her bones and twisted her muscles in knots. *This can't be! Aunt Charlotte is dead!* She was so tense that when Rafe touched her shoulder, Alyssa bolted away from him like a scared rabbit, darted across the back of the church and cowered in the corner. Her heart beat louder than the sonorous voice of the pastor as he directed his congregation to the next hymn.

Rafe eased up beside her and whispered, "Should we go?"

"Not until I talk to her." Somehow, she had to figure out what had happened ten years ago. And why, oh why, had Charlotte returned now? *I don't understand.* Alyssa wasn't rational, couldn't think.

"Who is she?"

She was surprised that he didn't know. "My aunt Charlotte."

"The one who is dead?"

She nodded. When Charlotte died…or disappeared… Mom had been devastated. Alyssa had been unable to assuage the grief they both felt. Even now, ten years later, she experienced the loss. A sob crawled up her throat, but now was not the time for an outburst. She pressed a hand over her mouth to stifle her sorrow.

Rafe took her other hand. "Come with me."

Her initial horror was beginning to ebb, leaving her numb. "I'm scared."

"You were right, *cher*, when you said we need to talk to her. Why is she here? What does she want?" He squeezed her hand and gave a tug. "It must be important. Why else would she return from the dead?"

Being with Rafe boosted her courage. With him at her side, she could move forward. She had to know why Charlotte was here and what kind of game she was playing.

The Hope and Peace congregation—filled with the spirit—sang "Wade in the Water" with gusto and hand clapping, barely noticing as Rafe guided her down the aisle under the windows. In spite of the emotional chaos that raged within her, she found herself humming along with the old-time spiritual, a familiar touchstone. When she was a kid, she'd stood in the front pew and belted out hymns in her imperfect alto while her mom and her aunt stood on either side of her and sang like angels.

When they approached the altar rail, Charlotte gestured to them and moved toward an exit at the back of the sanctuary. Rafe led Alyssa past the choir into a hallway. A door at the end stood open.

Before entering the room, he scanned the hallway. His jacket was pulled back, revealing his weapon, and she remembered that he was a bodyguard. They needed to be vigilant. The innocent-looking congregation might be harboring a snake—three snakes, to be more precise, Woodbridge and his two companions. Was Charlotte working with them? Would she hesitate for one minute before throwing her niece under the bus?

On one level, Alyssa was happy that her aunt was alive and well. No longer alone in the world, she had family again. But she was also furious. Charlotte had chosen to leave. Faking her death was bad enough, but she'd made it a hundred times worse by choosing to stay away from them. When her mom died, Alyssa could have used the loving support of her aunt, but Charlotte couldn't be bothered to come home.

Alyssa stalked toward the open door. "Let's get this over with."

"I'll go first," Rafe said as he drew his weapon.

She followed him into a plain, windowless room that seemed to be used for storage and changing clothes. Tidy but musty, there were cardboard boxes on the floor. Shelves and cabinets lined the walls. Choir robes in burnt orange, burgundy and green hung from metal racks.

Standing with her back to a full-length mirror, Charlotte waited for them. Over six feet tall in her high heels, she was long limbed and chic in a sleeveless black dress with a heavy gold necklace. Her generous mouth stretched in a grin, and she held her arms wide. "Come to me, my sweet niece."

Alyssa caught her breath. "No."

"Why not?"

"I can't forgive and forget. Not without an explanation." She was hurt and angry. Surely, that was understandable. There had been many gallons of water under this bridge. "The last time I saw you, I was sixteen. And you were a brunette."

The platinum and silver bun on top of Charlotte's head was coming undone. Wispy curls tumbled artlessly and encircled her face. She pointed a long, bony finger at Alyssa's blond wig. "At least I'm not trying to be a princess."

"Neither am I." Princess was a game they'd played when she was a little girl. Aunt Charlotte was the best when it came to imagination and dress-up. Real life wasn't her thing.

"Remember?" Her voice held a teasing note. "We had to slay the dragon."

"I'm not dressed up like this for fun and games. This wig is a disguise I'm wearing because somebody is trying to abduct me." Resentment bubbled up inside her. "I suppose you know all about that."

"Why would I?"

"You called and invited me to the *Día de los Muertos* parade. Am I right? Was that you?"

"So what if it was?"

"At the parade, you signaled me and I got attacked. Coincidence?" Alyssa didn't dare take off her sunglasses; she didn't want her tears to show. "Who are you working for, Charlotte? I hope they're paying you enough to make it worthwhile. What's the going rate for betraying your family?"

"I'm disappointed in you, Lara."

"I don't use that name anymore."

"After what you've been through with WitSec, I thought you'd understand the terrible problems that have plagued my life. For ten years, I've been in hiding—a woman without a home. Not that it's been all bad. I have enough cash and assets to get by, and my singing career is doing fairly well."

"You sing in public," Rafe said. "That doesn't seem like hiding."

"You're not a pro, so I wouldn't expect you to understand. In every big city, there are dozens of dreadfully anonymous piano bars. When I hook up with a band, I can sing at weddings and parties. If I didn't have to keep such a low profile, I could be a star."

Alyssa gave a snort. "Yeah, sure, just like I could be a princess."

"Don't sass me. I did what was necessary to survive. Sometimes, it's best to run away and live to fight another day."

"Where did you learn that? From a fortune cookie?"

Rafe inserted himself between them, spreading his natural charm like a healing balm on this most horrendous of family reunions. He introduced himself to her aunt and said, "I know your first name is Charlotte. What's your last name?"

"Take your pick," she said with a toss of her head. "Do you want my maiden name or my surname from one of my three marriages? Or maybe I should give you one of my aliases."

"I get it," he said. "Your life is complicated, and you have much to discuss with your niece, but now is not the time for a chat. The church might not be safe for her."

Her green eyes narrowed. "I'd never do anything that would put Alyssa in danger."

"Why are you here?" he asked.

"In the Ninth Ward at this church? I knew the pastor and contacted him when I got into town. He invited me to do a solo. I'm not getting paid, but I never turn down a gig."

"I meant," Rafe said, "why are you in New Orleans?"

"To contact Lara or Alyssa or whatever she's calling herself. I had hoped we'd meet at the parade." Her head swiveled toward Alyssa. "We missed connections."

Or maybe Charlotte's call was an excuse to draw her into danger. "Your phone call came from Anonymous. Why didn't you identify yourself?"

Charlotte rolled her eyes like a disgruntled teenager. "I figured it was better to meet for the first time in person. If I announced myself on the phone, it would have been a shock."

"Did you think it would be better to pop up like a re-turned-from-the-dead, zombie jack-in-the-box?"

"Sarcasm is such an unattractive quality."

"So is stupidity." Alyssa didn't want to be mean but couldn't help herself. "What did you think would happen when I saw you on the street?"

"A warm hug? A kiss on both cheeks?"

"I thought you were Mom's ghost. You scared me out of my skin." Alyssa shook her head. "Enough of these guessing games, just tell me the truth. Are you working with Woodbridge?"

"Who's that?" Her eyes widened in what might have been an innocent expression, if this woman had been capable of truth or sincerity. "I've never heard that name."

"Who wanted you to come to New Orleans and find me?"

"I can't tell you."

Alyssa turned on her heel and took two long strides toward the door. She felt her aunt's gaze boring a hole in her spine, but she didn't look back. "I admire your ability to survive, Charlotte. And when it comes to singing, you're incredible. But there's more to life than talent and money. You hurt me, and you hurt Mom."

"What about me? My pain? It wasn't easy to walk away. Yes, I lied, but I've paid the price. My life has been a living hell."

Alyssa paused with her hand on the doorknob. "Why did you do it?"

"If I had stayed in Chicago, they would have killed me and probably would have come after you and Claudia. It was my fault. I double-crossed Frankie Leone."

Alyssa whirled to face her. Frankie Leone was the

man who had died in her arms. She glanced at Rafe and saw a similar recognition on his face. Alyssa cleared her throat. "Keep talking."

"I was dating Frankie. I think he was involved with the McGill crime family, the same guys who are after you. In his apartment, I found a stash of money and merchandise that he was holding for them, and I gambled it away. Frankie tried to protect me, but I had to disappear—just like you had to change your identity in witness protection."

Alyssa asked, "How did you manage to escape?"

"I had a few powerful friends." She twined her hands at her breast—a dramatic gesture. "They helped me fake my death in that fire. One of them arranged transportation and set up an account to pay my living expenses."

Now we're getting somewhere! Alyssa demanded, "Who was this friend?"

"He made me promise never to tell anyone, especially not you."

Alyssa couldn't think of a single reason why her aunt's secret benefactor would single her out. Until the moment when she accidentally stumbled over a murder, she'd been a quiet accountant who juggled numbers and kept to herself.

"Your benefactor," Rafe said, "did he send you on this trip to New Orleans to find your niece?"

"Yes."

"What does he want from her?"

"Information." Charlotte exhaled a dramatic sigh. "A large sum of money has gone missing, and he thinks Alyssa might know something about it. Listen, I'm one hundred percent sure that he means no harm. He's basically a good, decent person."

As if Charlotte was a good judge of character? Alyssa

wasn't buying this story. If this decent person had nothing to hide, why didn't he just call her? Why set up this elaborate ruse? "You can tell your so-called friend that I don't know anything about the seven million, six hundred thousand dollars, which is exactly what I told the FBI and WitSec."

"Can I see you again?"

"There was a time when I would have done anything to be with you again." Alyssa steeled herself inside. "But I don't need you anymore. I'm totally independent. I've learned how to take care of myself."

"I used to think the same thing. And I used to be just as proud as you are. That was before I spent ten years moving from place to place, always looking over my shoulder. I couldn't put down roots or make friends. There were times when I would have traded all my talent and my money to be normal—just a normal woman who could fall in love. When you're on the run, you can't trust anyone. Without trust, you can't build a relationship." She glanced back and forth between them. "I envy you, sweetheart. I could never have what you and Rafe have."

"What? Me and Rafe? We're not a couple."

A knowing smile curled Charlotte's lips. "I see the way he looks at you. And I caught you looking back."

Before Alyssa could voice another objection, Rafe stepped into the conversation. "I have two questions, Charlotte. First, do you know Diamond Jim Davidoff?"

"Sure, everybody does."

"Was he one of your special friends?"

"The last I heard, Diamond Jim was too busy running his auto scams to mess around with anything else."

"Second question," Rafe said. "Is Darren Jessop one of your associates?"

"Special Agent Jessop? As a matter of fact, he's a

pal. When I first got to New Orleans, he set me up with a place to stay."

"Does he know you're here at this church?"

"I'm not sure."

"I'll take that as a yes," Rafe said. "Therefore, we must say adieu."

Alyssa allowed herself to be propelled from the room without saying a proper goodbye to her aunt. Charlotte was mistaken in thinking that she and Rafe had a relationship. He was her bodyguard, nothing more. Why would she even consider her aunt's opinion? The woman's life was one terrible decision after another, and she was wrong about almost everything. Alyssa couldn't pinpoint the lies in Charlotte's story, but she was certain that her aunt hadn't told the whole truth.

Rafe hustled her out a rear door that opened onto the garden between the church and the recreation hall. Members of the flock were drinking coffee and nibbling on homemade muffins and cookies. It was a charming, normal scene on a pleasant Sunday morning that contrasted the wild, jagged emotions tearing through her. She and Rafe moved away from the crowd, nearly running.

In seconds, they were in his SUV. As he pulled away from the curb, she pressed her back into her seat and inhaled a deep breath, struggling to release her tension. "Is somebody after us?"

"It's possible, *cher*."

"As soon as Charlotte mentioned Agent Jessop, you dashed out the door. Do you think he's here?"

"I do," he said. "Jessop has been in touch with Charlotte since she came to the city, and he's FBI. That means he has her under surveillance and is tracking her movements."

She realized that he was speaking from personal experience. "Is that what you would have done when you were a fed?"

"It's standard procedure."

"Similar to the way you followed me." For more than two weeks, he'd been on her tail, and she hadn't noticed him lurking in the shadows. Rafe was clever and skilled. There was no way she should trust this pirate. And yet... "Jessop is a federal agent, right?"

"Correct."

"Why do you think he's dangerous?"

"I don't know, but it could be for the same reason that Marshal Woodbridge dressed like a skeleton and tried to kidnap you."

"The money?"

"Possibly."

When it came to keeping her in the dark, he was as bad as her aunt Charlotte. They played their games and left her feeling like an idiot. She ripped off her sunglasses, took a tissue from her purse and confronted her image in the visor mirror. Her leaky tears had destroyed her eyeliner and mascara. "I should have figured out what was going on with Charlotte. But how could I? She was supposed to be dead. How could I guess that my aunt was on the run? What kind of crazy lady fakes her death and disappears?"

He guided the SUV to a stop at a red light and turned toward her. "She's not altogether different from you. Your plan is to run—to disappear by using aliases and disguises."

His comparison was accurate. Like Charlotte, she planned to leave New Orleans and move to a different location where she'd take on a new identity. She'd start over and find a way to survive, trusting no one, taking care of herself. For years, her identity had been based on those principles of self-sufficiency, but her plan had never felt so lonely.

Aunt Charlotte was a cautionary tale, and Alyssa didn't want to dive down the same rabbit hole.

Chapter Ten

Without a clear destination in mind, Rafe drove in a northeastern direction while he observed the traffic in his rearview mirror, making sure they'd escaped the church without picking up a tail. The similarities between Alyssa and her aunt had not been wasted on him. Though he suspected that Charlotte had always been a borderline criminal and Alyssa seemed to have a clear grasp of right and wrong, they were both stubborn, fiercely independent and determined to take care of themselves.

His thinking was colored by how much he'd come to like Alyssa after observing her for sixteen days. More than her green-eyed beauty, he appreciated her spirit and her intelligence. She could think fast, which was sometimes a blessing and sometimes a curse. Her impulse to chase after the skeletons had almost led to her capture.

Likewise, her independence held an element of danger. She trusted no one. He hated to think of the deep disappointments she must have experienced to build such a solid fortress around her heart. From the early abandonment by her father to the current debacle with Aunt Charlotte, Alyssa had been duped and discarded. No one stood beside her. Even her mom was gone. And Max Horowitz, her kindly boss who helped her through college, had disappeared.

Rafe couldn't expect her to trust him, but he had to keep her safe. Not only was that the job he'd been hired to do, but he cared for her. The real question was: Should he hand her over to the FBI? Law enforcement could protect her better than he could...if they hadn't been corrupted like Woodbridge.

After driving a few more aimless miles, he was certain that they were being followed. And he had a pretty good idea who was driving the bronze sedan with the tinted windows. Rafe cranked the steering wheel and made an unexpected left turn. The sedan dodged through traffic to follow.

Alyssa yelped from the passenger seat. "What are you doing?"

"Shaking a tail."

Any attempt to outsmart Jessop with defensive-driving techniques seemed futile. They had both been given the same training at the FBI. Each could anticipate the other's moves. The best way to escape was luck, the whims of traffic and skills Rafe had picked up when he was undercover as a race car driver.

"Is it Jessop?" Alyssa guessed.

"Probably."

"But that isn't a bad thing. Over breakfast, you mentioned setting up a meeting with him to get more information. What changed your mind?"

"It's hard to say."

During the few months Rafe had been part of the New Orleans office of the FBI, he was mostly undercover and out of contact with the other agents. He didn't know Jessop well, but he didn't want to poison Alyssa's mind against him in case it was necessary to transfer her into FBI custody.

She twisted her shoulders, craned her neck and peered

through the rear window of the SUV. "Is he still following us?"

"I don't see him," Rafe said, "but he could be behind that truck."

"You asked both me and Charlotte about Jessop and about Diamond Jim Davidoff. There's a connection between them, right?"

She was too intelligent to believe an ill-formed lie. "Yes."

"I'm guessing that Jessop—an FBI agent who knows you—was the person who referred Diamond Jim to you. That means that Mr. Davidoff is your client."

"Now that you've solved that mystery, I have another—"

"It's not solved," she said. "Not until I know why Davidoff hired you to be my bodyguard. His interest is probably motivated by the seven million, six hundred thousand dollars, but that doesn't explain why he wanted the decor to look like my bedroom."

"A talk for later." He set the conversation aside, hoping to distract her. "We have a different issue. Jessop is back."

"Which car?"

"The bronze Lexus."

"How can you tell? I can't identify the driver through the tinted window."

"An assumption," he said. "I remember the car from when we worked together, and I can't think of anyone else who could have followed us from the church."

With a sigh, she said, "There are just so damn many bad guys."

"As long as you trust me, we'll be okay."

He expected her response to be the oft-repeated statement of being able to take care of herself, and so he was surprised when she reached across the console and touched his arm. "Trust is important."

"It is, *cher*."

"That stuff Charlotte said about you and me wasn't true, was it?" Her fingers lightly squeezed his forearm. "I'm not interested in a relationship. Are you?"

"I'm French," he reminded her. "I'm always interested."

"Okay." She withdrew her hand. "How do you plan to meet with Jessop? If you pull over and let him catch up with us, he's going to grab me and sweep me into custody."

"You're right." And there was no one else in the local office that he implicitly trusted. Much of his undercover career had been in Florida until a long-term investigation into a smuggling ring had blown up in his face. That was one of the reasons he'd decided to quit the FBI.

"I don't want to go back to the house and hide. What if Jessop tracks us there?"

Again, he agreed with her reading of the situation. He couldn't leave her alone and unguarded at the house. But he couldn't allow her to meet Jessop in person. "I know a place where you can be part of the conversation but protected at the same time."

"And where is this magical place?"

"St. Louis Cemetery Number Three on Esplanade."

Over the years, Rafe had used the aboveground cemetery as a rendezvous for informants, suspects and—once or twice—girlfriends. His family had a mausoleum, and he knew his way around the place. As a kid he'd played hide-and-seek among the tombs during the interment of an aged uncle or a reckless cousin.

"Let me get this straight." Alyssa cast a skeptical gaze

in his direction. "You think a graveyard is a safe meeting place?"

A simple "trust me" wasn't going to ease her mind. "Allow me to explain with a short history of St. Louis Cemetery and my family."

"By all means."

"Cemetery Number Three opened in 1854, and the Fournier mausoleum was built two years later. My pirate ancestor, Jean-Pierre, had passed away in 1812, leaving his family with treasure but not respectability. His wife argued with the priests about burial for her husband in the existing cemeteries and decided on a more humble resting place. By the time Cemetery Number Three was laid out, the Fournier family was solidly established in New Orleans society, and one of my aunts wanted a big, showy, ornate monument."

"Your roots go deep," she said.

"*Oui.* There are so few of us left."

"I still don't know why you want to meet with Jessop in the cemetery."

"Every soul in New Orleans knows where the cemetery is located, and the Fournier mausoleum stands out. The walls are sun-bleached marble. Above the entrance is a peaked arch with a frieze of a sailing ship flying the Jolly Roger. Posed on top is a statue of a winged angel with a sword."

"Got it," she said. "It's easy to find."

"At the cemetery, I have an edge—an all-access parking sticker that allows me to drive onto the grounds. Also, most important, I have a key to the Fournier monument."

"Why's the key a big deal?"

"While I talk with Jessop, you will be safely locked inside the mausoleum."

"With dead people?" Her voice elevated several octaves. "Oh, I don't think so. Not that I believe in ghosts or zombies."

"At present there is no coffin in the tomb."

"If there's no coffin, who's buried there?"

Not wanting to give her another reason to be nervous, he decided not to go into details about the process of interment—waiting for the corpse to decompose, removing the coffin and returning the bones to the mausoleum. The remains of at least thirty-two people were housed in his family's mausoleum. "No need to be afraid, *cher*. The Fournier dead are very well behaved."

"Look at my face, Rafe. I'm not laughing."

She folded her arms across her middle and sank down in the passenger seat. With her long blond wig and pink dress, she looked like an angry sunbeam. He hadn't expected Alyssa—a down-to-earth accountant who planned for everything—to be superstitious. But he trusted her ability to cope. Meeting Jessop at the Fournier tomb was a good solution.

Without further discussion, he used his hands-free phone to connect with the number he had for Jessop. Rafe wanted to keep this conversation and the subsequent meeting short and simple. His plan was to use Jessop to find out who was after Alyssa and what they wanted from her.

As soon as Jessop answered, Rafe said, "Stop tailing me."

"Why would I be interested in following you?"

"In your bronze Lexus," he said. "In three blocks, I intend to merge onto the bridge. If you follow, we won't meet. If you do as I say, I'll arrange to sit down for a brief parley."

"Who's the girl, Rafe? Who's the blonde that followed

you out of the church? I know Alyssa is a brunette, but she could have been wearing a wig."

"Don't follow."

As Rafe disconnected the call, she pulled the blond curls off her head and combed through her sienna-brown hair with her fingers. "So much for my Baby Doll disguise."

"It served the purpose," he said as he drove onto the bridge. "Look through the back window. Can you see the Lexus?"

When she unfastened her seat belt and leaned over to look through the seats, her arm brushed his shoulder, and he felt an electric surge. Her crazy aunt had been strangely accurate when she predicted a relationship— not that he was looking for anything long term, but he wanted to go deep and know her in a meaningful way.

"I don't see Jessop," she said.

"If we're lucky, he's already stopped following us."

Rafe checked his rearview mirror, making sure they weren't being followed. On the other side of the bridge, he parked the SUV on a side street and called Jessop again. The FBI special agent answered quickly and started talking right away, issuing demands and threats. His technique failed to impress Rafe. They'd gone through the same interrogation training.

He cut through Jessop's chatter with a terse instruction. "Meet me at the Fournier mausoleum in St. Louis Cemetery Number Three at noon."

"That doesn't give me enough time."

"This is your only chance, *mon ami.*"

Rafe ended the call and turned to Alyssa. "You were smart to bring your backpack."

"I like to be well prepared and organized. It's what I do." She cracked open the passenger door. "I bet you want me to climb into the back and change out of this glaring outfit into something more subtle."

"S'il vous plaît."

As soon as she got into the back of the SUV, he redirected his route toward Esplanade Avenue. Situated between Lake Pontchartrain and St. John's Bayou, Cemetery Number Three had been badly flooded during Hurricane Katrina, leading to horror stories—mostly untrue—about floating coffins and decomposing corpses. These were not tales he'd pass along to Alyssa.

Glancing into the rearview mirror, he had a partial view of her shoulder and her lacy white bra before she slipped into a blue T-shirt and a denim jacket. Last night when he rescued her from the skeletons and had to remove her clothing, he'd seen more of her body. But she'd been unconscious. This glimpse was more exciting. Even the khaki shorts seemed sexy.

He tore his gaze away from the mirror and concentrated on what needed to come next. He had promised Davidoff that he would send a photo of Alyssa by noon today in order to prove that she was alive and well and not captured by Woodbridge or anyone else.

Davidoff remained a puzzle. His concern for Alyssa, the fact that he'd hired Rafe to protect her and his insistence on making her comfortable with a bedroom decorated like her own seemed like the actions of someone who cared about her—the father who had stepped out of her life but continued to love her? Charlotte probably could have explained Davidoff's interest in her niece, but she chose to keep her secrets.

"I'm ready." Alyssa poked her head between the front seats. "It took a million wet wipes to get the goopy makeup off my face, but I'm clean."

"I like your face without makeup."

She patted his cheek. "And I like your scruffy look. Are we almost there?"

"In a minute."

"Should I duck down and hide?"

"Couldn't hurt."

He'd taken the quickest route and doubted that Jessop could have arrived before him, but there was always the possibility that the FBI agent was working with someone else. Keeping Alyssa hidden from the feds, her crazy aunt and Davidoff was vital. If no one knew where she was, they couldn't hurt her.

Chapter Eleven

Crouched down in the back seat of the SUV, Alyssa tried to regain the emotional balance and determination she'd lost when she came face-to-face with her aunt…her dead aunt. *Impossible! Everything has turned upside down.* Her plan to leave town and start over seemed less positive and more futile. The example of Charlotte's wasted life reminded her that escape was impossible. The bad stuff would catch up, no matter where she ran.

What was her alternative? She couldn't stay here and wait for Woodbridge or Jessop or anybody else to grab her. She needed another plan, and that meant gathering more information and hoping that something would make sense. The meeting with Agent Jessop seemed like a good starting place, but she wasn't real happy about the idea of hiding out in a tomb.

"We're here," Rafe said, "entering the City of the Dead."

"You don't have to sound so cheerful about it."

She raised her head just high enough to peek out the window as the SUV turned at the entrance to St. Louis Cemetery Number Three. Outside the curlicue wrought iron gate, piles of bouquets from last night's parade were stacked in remembrance. The flowers were already starting to rot, giving off a pungent odor that penetrated the car and overpowered the air-conditioning.

She pinched her nose. "Why are the flowers outside instead of on the graves?"

"The cemeteries used to stay open for All Souls' Day and Day of the Dead, but the celebrations got too wild and destructive, especially in Cemetery Number One, where the voodoo queen Marie Laveau is interred."

That site was supposed to have voodoo magic. "I heard that if you mark three X's on her tomb, she'll grant one wish."

"And so the desecration became standard practice. *C'est triste.* It's sad. I regret the lack of access for the general public, but I'm glad there will be no graffiti to scrub from the Fournier monument."

Alyssa crouched lower and pulled the backpack over her head and shoulders while the official at the gate checked Rafe's identification and waved him through. He drove slowly, dropping casual facts like someone who had given this tour many times before. "The layout in Number Three is more organized than in the other two, and the statuary and tombs are more elaborate. If you look on the left, you can see a nearly life-size bronze of Padre Pio, who was famous for his stigmata."

She peeked through the window as they drove on a narrow street—Rafe referred to it as an aisle—between rows of tombs that were roughly the size of camping trailers but made of marble and stone. "How many crypts are there?"

"Over ten thousand burial sites and more than three thousand wall vaults," he said, "plus a Greek Orthodox section and mausoleums housing nuns and priests who had no other place to be buried."

Flowers had been left outside the doors to many of the

tombs, and the urns had been decorated with colorful displays of posies, feathers and beads. They drove past a woman and child who sat close together on a marble bench. Other people strolled along the aisle beside the grass border, not a crowd but a respectable number for a Sunday morning at the beginning of November. During her time in New Orleans, Alyssa had come to appreciate the city's acceptance of death as a celebration of the moment when a beloved person is freed from the bonds of earthly existence. Grief was inescapable, but Alyssa liked to imagine her mom at a wake filled with singing and dancing. Mom would have loved to have her coffin paraded in a jazz procession with trumpets, trombones and tambourines.

Carved stone tombs were much more interesting than being buried in the ground, but she still didn't want to be locked inside one. Peering through the car window, she nodded to a marble statue of a serene Virgin Mary with her hands outstretched and shot out a little prayer, asking for strength.

She cleared her throat. "How is Jessop going to find your family's tomb in the midst of all this?"

"As I mentioned before, it stands out." He parked the SUV. "Voilà!"

She sat up and stared. The Fournier tomb was, as promised, spectacular. Made of pale marble and rising several feet taller than either of its neighbors, the sepulchre had two slender columns flanking the double doors. The sword-wielding angel on top was ferocious with muscular arms and a mane of long, curly hair.

"That is some kind of tomb," she said as she emerged from the back seat.

"My great-great-great-great-aunt, who commissioned this monument, was red-hot furious when the priests excluded the descendants of the pirate Jean-Pierre Fournier from Cemetery Number One. She was determined to make a statement."

"She succeeded. Who's the angel on top?"

"Nana Lucille told me it's the archangel Rafael, my namesake. But I always thought it was Saint Peter. He had more to do with sailors."

She could easily imagine Rafe in the role of an avenging angel, diving into the fray with his flaming sword. If only she could trust him, life would be so much easier. But there had never been a time in her life when she had someone to lean on and be sure they'd support her. No doubt Rafe was as irresponsible as all the rest.

On the wall beside the door of the tomb, she noticed two vertical rows of engraved metal markers; there must have been more than thirty. Each marker had a name. "What do those names mean?"

"Those are the people buried in the tomb."

"Wait! You said nobody was in there." A flash of panic exploded inside her skull. "You promised there were no coffins."

"That's true."

"But all those people are buried in there."

"Try not to think about it, *cher*." He took her arm and moved her toward a poplar tree. "Stand here and act natural so I can take your picture for Davidoff."

"First, you need to explain." Her misgivings about entering the tomb had quadrupled. "After the coffins are removed, what happens to the corpses?"

"Nature takes its course," he said. "A body in a coffin sealed in a tomb and baking in the sun decomposes in a year or two. There's nothing left but the bones. In our family, we put the bones in a bag and return them to a marble ossuary at the back of the mausoleum."

Her throat closed, and she squeaked. "They're still in the tomb? Are we talking about the remains of thirty-something dead people?"

"You have nothing to fear, *cher*." He gestured for her to stand by the tree. "Don't look in my direction."

"I don't want to be locked up with a bunch of ossuary bones."

"Let's get this photo."

Inhaling a deep breath, she tried to ground herself. "Why don't you want me to turn toward you for the picture?"

"Davidoff doesn't need to know that we're working together. I'll frame the photo so none of the tombs are visible and the location isn't obvious."

She placed her hand on a low-hanging tree branch and gazed into the distance—a pose that was typical of a senior photo in a high school album. Lifting a slight smile onto her lips, she tried to look like she wasn't with Rafe and wasn't in a graveyard. His mention of Davidoff was a distraction from the unreasonable terror of being locked up in the tomb. Diamond Jim gave her a very tangible reason to be scared. He was interested enough in her to hire a bodyguard, and he seemed to want her to feel comfortable in the copycat bedroom. *But why?*

Davidoff had to be after the money. Like everybody else, he probably believed that she had a clue. But she didn't. The fact that she didn't have the secret knowledge that would lead to the missing millions was a problem more terrifying than if she could hand over a map showing the location of the treasure. If she was caught by any of these other thugs, she had nothing to give them, nothing she could use to bargain her way to freedom.

"The picture is taken," he said. "Now, come with me. It's time to hide."

"There's only one reason I'm going along with this plan," she said as she walked toward him. "Jessop might have useful information, and I've got to figure out what's going on. I also have questions for you, starting with an explanation about Davidoff and the weirdly decorated room."

"But of course."

"I hope you're taking me seriously," she grumbled. "Promise you'll tell me."

"Shall I cross my heart? Pinkie swear?"

"Listen up, Mr. Pirate or Avenging Angel or whoever, if you want my trust, you're going to have to start telling me the truth."

"I could say the same to you."

Taken aback, she masked her reaction. Did he know her secret? No way—he couldn't possibly know. She hadn't told the FBI or the US marshals or anybody. As long as she was on this tightrope, balancing for dear life, she wouldn't give away her safety net. She watched Rafe bound up the two wide stairs to the door of the tomb. When he fitted the old-fashioned key into the lock, twisted and pushed the door open, she could have sworn that she heard an ominous creak.

"Is this really necessary?" she asked. "Why can't I hide in the back of the car?"

"Inside this marble monument, you'll be safe. Nobody can reach you."

She swallowed hard, trying not to think of every horror movie she'd ever seen about being buried alive. "How do I get out?"

"You'll have this." He held the antique key toward her, and she noticed the skull and crossbones in the design at the top loop. "Not one of the originals, but it works just fine."

To illustrate, he leaned hard against the door on the left side. The carved wood appeared to be old and weathered enough to be part of the original 1856 construction. Sneaking around in this very old monument to the dead struck her as being somewhat irreverent.

Reaching into the pocket of his suit coat, Rafe lured her closer by holding up her cell phone. "You can have this back. I replaced some of the software and added encryption to make it impossible to trace your location. Don't turn it on unless you have to."

With a sense of satisfaction, she tucked the phone into the shoulder bag she'd brought from the car. Though she wasn't a person who spent every minute on social media, she'd felt naked without her phone. "Thank you."

He ushered her into the tomb and quickly lit three votive candles. The flickering light streaked against the roughened walls, where more than a century of dirt had accumulated. A small stained glass window in the rear wall depicted a sailing ship on the high seas. There were wrought iron candelabra and statues of saints and urns, but her full attention was captured by the carved stone ossuary where the bones of ancestors had found their final resting place—men, women and probably children, because the infant mortality rate was high in the mid-to-late 1800s during the yellow fever epidemic.

She clenched her fingers to keep from trembling. "Did your family lose anyone in Hurricane Katrina?"

"We were lucky," he said. "Our only loss was property and belongings."

"It's hot in here."

"When the sun beats down, it's like an oven. You won't be in here for long." He took a step toward the door. "I will leave this open a small crack. If you see Jessop

coming toward you or have any cause for alarm, give a
shove and twist the key in the lock."

When he stepped through the door, her heart leaped.
Her panic returned full force. She didn't want to be in
here alone. She struggled to hang on to her dignity. No
reason to be scared—this was only stone, marble, stained
glass and...bones.

The door closed, but not all the way. A pencil-thin
sliver of light cut through the darkness. She pressed her
face against the ancient door and peered into the cemetery, where she could see Rafe leaning against the front
fender of his SUV. The view was too narrow to be useful, but she could hear people outside talking and laughing. If she stayed here and remained unnoticed, she could
eavesdrop on Rafe and Jessop.

How long? Every minute seemed like an hour. She
tried to count and take slow, steady breaths, but the thick,
muggy air clogged her lungs. Generations of pallbear-
ers had entered this tomb to bid their final farewells. She
wondered if Rafe would be buried here.

Stepping away from her listening place, she paced to
the rear of the tomb and back again. *Damn, it's hot!* She
peeled off her denim jacket, fanned her hand in front of
her face and wiped away the sweat that had gathered at
her hairline.

When she looked through the crack again, she saw
Jessop saunter up to Rafe and shake his hand. The blond
special agent matched Rafe in height, but Jessop was
heavily muscled. He wore an untucked cotton shirt, snug
across his well-developed chest and loose around his hips
to hide his gun holster. He removed his sunglasses and
asked, "Where is she?"

"Somewhere safe," Rafe said. "Never follow me again,
my friend."

"Why not? What are you going to do?"

"A high-speed chase would not end well for you."

Jessop gave a short laugh. "I heard that you drove race cars in Florida."

"Perhaps," Rafe said. "Tell me about your connection with Charlotte."

"She's something else, isn't she? Don't let the silver in her hair fool you. That is one hot, sexy lady."

Alyssa tried to suck air through the crack between the doors. The tomb seemed to be sapping her energy. Quietly, she dropped to her knees, conserving her strength. Rafe and Jessop talked about the logistics of getting in touch with Charlotte and bringing her to New Orleans. Davidoff was involved. Her aunt's stated goal, according to Jessop, was to appeal to her niece and get her to open up.

Their plan was ill conceived. Anyone who knew Alyssa would tell you that she was extremely guarded and slow to trust. Having her lying, cheating, supposed-to-be-dead aunt pop up after all these years would strengthen her resolve to stay silent—not that she had anything to say.

She heard Rafe ask, "Do you think Charlotte has something to do with the money?"

"Not Charlotte. If she had millions, she'd be living an extravagant lifestyle. Alyssa is a different story."

"As a federal agent, you'd be obliged to turn that money over to the government."

"I deserve a taste." Jessop cursed and then he laughed "Don't get me wrong—I don't expect to be taking a bath in hundred-dollar bills, but there ought to be a nice little payoff for me."

Rafe asked the most important question. "What do

you and Davidoff want from Alyssa? What do you think she knows?"

Jessop glanced to the left and right as though looking for someone who might overhear. "I went over her files a dozen times and had the forensic accountants explain the details of the triple-entry system she and Horowitz used. Did she tell you about that?"

"Keep talking," Rafe said.

She appreciated that he wasn't giving anything away. Jessop didn't seem evil, but he was greedy. Under her breath, she murmured, "What does he think I know?"

"The reason everybody wants to talk to Alyssa," Jessop said, "is simple, and it doesn't have a damn thing to do with the accounting. Old man Horowitz wasn't smuggling, and his activity as a fence was minimal."

She was relieved to hear that her former boss wasn't a criminal. Her judgment about him had been accurate. He was a decent person.

"I'm losing patience," Rafe said. "Who was responsible for siphoning off the millions in cash?"

"You, more than anyone else, should be able to guess. You remember what happened in Florida when your undercover career was shot to hell by the Leone family. That's why I thought of you when Davidoff was looking for someone to be a bodyguard. You've got a reason to hate the Leones, and Frankie Leone—the warehouse foreman—was involved in the theft."

An involuntary gasp escaped her lips. She should have guessed. Frankie was involved in all the large transactions. He handled the inventory.

Rafe asked, "What does this have to do with Alyssa?"

"She held a dying man in her arms. With his last breath, he could have told her his secrets."

But he didn't. She struggled to suppress a sob. If Jessop overheard, he'd charge at the tomb and take her into custody. She pushed the door closed and twisted the key in the lock. Her only proof of innocence was her word. Why would anybody believe her? Through no fault of her own, she'd been condemned...might as well crawl into the ossuary and wait for her flesh to rot. Hopeless, she sank to the floor and wept.

Chapter Twelve

After confirming an appointment with Chance Gregory on his cell phone, Rafe watched Jessop walk down the aisle toward the wrought iron gates. The set of his shoulders and his athletic stride demonstrated the confidence befitting a federal agent. With his easy grin and the sunlight glinting in his blond hair, Jessop didn't appear to be a bad guy or a traitor, but Rafe could not consider him an ally. Jessop's motives were as tangled as the roots of the mangrove trees in the marshland. He liked his career as an agent but didn't mind getting dirty for the right payoff. He freely associated with Davidoff, a known criminal. Jessop didn't intend to hurt Alyssa but wouldn't hesitate to sacrifice her if she got in the way.

With these many contradictions and complications, nothing was certain. Rafe didn't know what to believe, but had to admit that Jessop was right about one thing: one of the reasons he'd agreed to work for Davidoff was a hint about the possible connection with the Leone family. Until Alyssa told her story about Frankie's murder, Rafe hadn't known how entwined she was with the family. He'd spent nearly a year working undercover with them and had never heard her name or any mention of the pawnshop in Chicago. His investigation had fallen apart, and he'd left too many questions unanswered. His time in Florida had ended in tragedy.

The Leones were not a topic he wanted to discuss with Alyssa, but he couldn't gracefully sidestep the issue. She'd been eavesdropping on his conversation with Jessop, and she'd demand an explanation, even if the story made him look bad.

As soon as Jessop was out of sight, Rafe climbed the marble stairs of the Fournier tomb. He kept his movements casual, trying not to betray his tension to other people who were walking in the cemetery. He tugged at the door handle. Locked! At some point during his conversation with Jessop, Alyssa had closed the door. Something must have spooked her. He called to her, "You can open up now, *cher*. He's gone."

He didn't hear a sound, not a peep. If he'd been the one sealed up in that cold, dank space, he would have gone mad. Alyssa was stronger, but she'd undergone a number of difficult situations in the past days, both physically and emotionally. Had she fainted? Was something wrong with her? His grip tightened on the handle, and he yanked hard. The old wood strained and jiggled but the door remained locked. He should have kept the key.

"Alyssa." He spoke into the place where the two doors met, hoping his voice would reach her. "You must unlock this door."

Logically, he knew she wasn't hurt. The time she'd spent in the monument was less than twenty minutes, not long enough to suffocate. The oxygen level was high enough to keep the votive candles lit. She was alone in the tomb. Nothing could harm her. Still, an unreasonable fear churned in his gut. He'd seen how nervous she was before he left her inside. Unmindful of the other people parading in the cemetery, he drew back his fist and hammered against the wood...once, twice, three times.

When he heard the sound of the metal key scratching against the lock, relief trickled through him. Silently, he assured himself again that she was all right. The door opened. He rushed inside and found her sitting with her bare legs sprawled out in front of her. Sweat glistened on her chest above her T-shirt. Her complexion had gone pale. Gasping, she said, "Frankie didn't say a word...just died. I tried to stanch the blood but couldn't help him."

"Don't worry, *cher*." She looked so miserable that he would have given the entire seven point six million bucks to make her feel better. He lifted her in his arms, carried her into the sunlight and sat her on the stairs. "Everything is going to be all right."

"Don't you understand?" Her green-eyed gaze searched his face. "I have nothing to tell Jessop or any of the others. I don't know what happened to the money, but they don't believe me. And they're going to keep coming after me until..."

"I won't let them hurt you." Rafe took the key and returned to the darkened tomb to lock up from the outside.

"You can't stop them," she said. "They think I'm holding out on them. But when they find out that I really didn't hear a dying declaration from Frankie Leone, I'm no use to them."

If these treasure hunters had been reasonable, he might have convinced them to leave her alone. But greed had transformed them into frenzied gators chasing swamp rats and gulping them down in one bite. If they questioned Alyssa and didn't learn anything new about the missing money, they'd demand revenge. And she would pay the price.

"We need a plan," he said. "First step is to get away from here. Can you walk to the car?"

She staggered to her feet, aimed a determined gaze at his SUV and lurched forward. "I'll make it. Crank up the air conditioner full blast."

BEFORE HE DROVE down the aisle toward the exit gates, Rafe glanced into the back seat, where Alyssa was curled up on the floor so no one could see her. Her T-shirt clung to her body, and her shoulders hunched. She looked like hell, and he didn't want to add to her woes, which meant he didn't tell her that if anybody had been observing them in the cemetery, her location had already been pinpointed. Plus, Jessop wasn't an idiot. While they talked in the cemetery, the fed had cast many suspicious glances toward the tomb and repeatedly asked about her whereabouts. He could have figured out that Rafe and Alyssa were together.

That conclusion was undeniable and unfortunate. She was not safe.

Their escape from those who pursued them would not be based on clever disguises or secret hideouts. In this moment, they needed to go on the run. Their survival depended on his detailed knowledge of the city where he grew up, and he was confident that his skill in navigating the detours and shortcuts and roundabouts would be enough. He could outsmart a bloodhound on the scent. Not to mention that his driving skills were exceptional.

After they left the cemetery, her disembodied voice rose from the back seat. "Where are we headed?"

"We're going to the home of my friend and colleague, Chance Gregory. He's a cyber genius. We can get more data from him in an hour than from talking to Jessop for days."

"And where does he live?"

"You'll be surprised, *cher*."

Though Chance lived with his mama, he wasn't a typical computer nerd who buried himself in a grungy basement and existed on a diet of cheese puffs and beer. He might best be described as an old-fashioned gentleman of the South. His family owned one of the classic antebellum plantations along the Mississippi River Road that ran between New Orleans and Baton Rouge.

"Speaking of surprises," she said as she popped up between the seats, "is there something you want to tell me about Frankie Leone?"

"How much did you overhear?"

"Jessop said you took the job offer from Davidoff because there might be a connection with the Leone family in Florida. How do you know them?"

"Through an extended undercover assignment," he said, fighting through his reluctance to talk about that time in his life. "Before I moved back to New Orleans, I was investigating their smuggling operation in Florida. Though I was close to several people in the family, I never met Frankie and knew nothing of his operation in Chicago."

"Is that true? You really didn't know the identity of the victim in my crime?"

"All I knew was that you witnessed a murder." Her skepticism frustrated him. Would she never trust him? "If I heard mention, the victim was referred to as a warehouse foreman."

"Did you enjoy undercover work?"

When she peeked around the edge of his seat and stared at his profile, he noticed that her wan complexion had returned to normal. "Covert operations can be *très difficile*, especially when they are long-term."

"You have to be a good liar to pull it off."

"I suppose." He tried to brush off the unfortunate direction of her questions. "It was my job."

"You were deceiving people for months at a time."

He stopped for a light and turned his head to confront her directly. They were close, almost nose to nose, and he was momentarily captivated by the facets of silver and hazel in her green eyes. He inhaled and regained his composure. "There are times for lies and times for truth. I know the difference, *cher*. I'm being straight with you. Ask me anything."

"I will." She pulled back. "In Florida, what was your cover story?"

"I passed myself off as a race-car driver."

His driving skills were nowhere near professional level, but he talked a good game. The Leone family accepted him as an eccentric Frenchman who had participated in several Grand Prix races in Europe. He recalled that ruse while he drove through New Orleans making unpredictable turns and dodging anyone who might be trying to follow his SUV.

Alyssa jostled backward as he slammed on the brake. "Watch it! You're not on a racetrack now."

"Put on your seat belt, *cher*."

He heard her rearranging herself behind him before she said, "Tell me more about the Leone family. What kind of smuggling did they do?"

"They owned a legitimate trucking company, but their trucks were sometimes filled with stolen merchandise, mostly appliances or electronics. They were considered small-time operators and too unimportant for the FBI to investigate."

"I don't understand. Why did you go undercover?"

"Information suggested that the Leones were expanding their operation into the smuggling of illegal weapons and possible drug trafficking." He guided the SUV through a sharp left turn. His goal was to evade pursuit until he left the city limits. At his friend's home, he could borrow another vehicle.

"Did Jessop give you any new information?"

"Currently, the FBI believes that Frankie was responsible for the missing millions."

"That's crazy!" Her disbelief exploded from the back seat. "I can't give you an accounting down to the penny, but I guarantee that the pawnshop wasn't making so much money that Mr. Horowitz wouldn't notice if seven point six million dollars went missing."

"Think about it, *cher*. Frankie's thieving was spread out for a very long time, all the way back to ten years ago when he was dating your aunt. And Horowitz was known to keep high-ticket items in his warehouse. Davidoff used to store some of his vehicles there, including a vintage Rolls-Royce that was worth close to three hundred thou."

For several long minutes, they were both silent. He imagined that she was remembering the many expensive objects that were housed in the Chicago warehouse. The locked safe was large enough for her to walk inside, and it must have held precious objects of great value. Over the years, it wouldn't have been difficult for Frankie to remove these artworks, jewelry, antiques and furs—especially since some of these items had been stolen in the first place.

"I can't believe it," she murmured. "Mr. Horowitz was careful with his inventory. He would have noticed."

"Not if Frankie was clever enough to replace the real objects with forgeries. He was in charge of the warehouse and had complete access. There would be no record of the pickup because he used trucks from his family's business to ship out the merchandise."

"If that's true, Frankie was a whole lot smarter than I gave him credit for. What was his mistake? What got him killed?"

"Greed." That seemed to be the underlying motive for everything that had happened. "Frankie deviated from the plan. Instead of funneling the merchandise to his family, he set up his own operation in Chicago."

"A double cross," she said. "He was stealing from the warehouse and double-crossing his family while building his private fortune. Then Ray McGill shot him. How does he fit into this picture?"

"The FBI has known for a long time about the connections between the McGill family and the Leones. They're criminals but still businessmen."

While she repeated and reviewed the twists and turns of Frankie's scheme, he checked his rearview mirror. After several blocks, he determined that they weren't being followed, and he set a course for the Mississippi River Road.

Under different circumstances, he would have enjoyed taking Alyssa on this trip, giving her a view of the more refined aspects of life in New Orleans. Not everything was about jazz and Mardi Gras and parades in the streets. The city was one of the oldest settlements in the country. Traditions ran deep.

"About the Leones," she said. "Jessop said something about how your assignment with them destroyed your career. I want to hear the whole story."

He'd hoped to avoid this painful memory. "My mistakes aren't relevant."

"I want to know the truth. You say that you aren't lying, but hiding the details is deliberately misleading."

She exhaled a powerful sigh that he heard in the front seat. "I want to trust you, Rafe."

And he wanted the same thing. "After several months with the family, I earned a place in their organization as a getaway driver."

"For bank robberies?"

"Never a bank. But there were meetings when it was necessary to make a swift escape. I kept the FBI informed, and they acted appropriately. Sometimes there were arrests. Other times, there were not. By the time my investigation was drawing to an end, I had become friendly with several in the family, including a young mom named Deedee who was routinely abused by her husband."

He remembered that slender creature with her long black hair and soulful eyes. Deedee looked older than her twenty-two years, except when she was playing with her two toddlers. That tiny glimpse of her happiness had touched his heart. One day, she'd confided in him, revealing that she was pregnant again and terrified of how angry her husband would be.

"My assignment had been a bust," he admitted to Alyssa. "I hadn't uncovered gun smuggling or drugs. The Leone family appeared to be small-time crooks and nothing more. I wanted my time with them to mean something."

"You tried to help Deedee," she said.

"I referred her to people who could protect her from her husband and help her establish a new life for herself and her children. I should have stayed with her, shouldn't have left her alone with strangers."

"I understand," Alyssa said. "You thought you were doing the right thing."

He should have known better. After the time he'd spent

in Florida, he should have realized that Deedee's loyalty to the family and to her husband was more important than her personal safety. She went back to her abuser.

As soon as Rafe heard, he'd raced to their house. Too late.

"He killed her."

Chapter Thirteen

Sitting in the back of the SUV with her seat belt fastened, Alyssa couldn't see Rafe's face, but she heard the intense pain in his voice, and she knew that he blamed himself for Deedee's death. "What happened to the children?"

"They were placed with a good family, and the arrangement seems to be working out. The foster parents are planning to adopt the boys. I send payments for their care."

"It sounds like you're doing the best you can to help out."

"Money is not enough. These babies lost their mama. I'll make sure that no one—especially not their father, who is incarcerated—will hurt them again." He jiggled his shoulders as if he could shake off the anger. "That's my story, *cher*. Have you heard enough?"

Though she appreciated how hard it was for him to talk about Deedee's murder, she had other questions. "Jessop said the Leones messed up your career. Is that true? Did you get fired?"

"The opposite," he said. "The FBI was very willing to sweep Deedee's murder under the rug and call it a case of domestic violence. They hoped I could continue undercover. But no, I couldn't stay in Florida. I had to come home to New Orleans and figure out what was the right course for the rest of my life."

"And you came up with being a private investigator?"

"For now, it works. I'm my own boss, I don't have to take orders from anyone else and I can use my training."

"Your special skills? Like beating up thugs in skeleton masks and escaping from a second-story warehouse window and tearing up the streets with your evasive driving? An interesting collection of talents, but I've got to admit that you're good at what you do."

"Merci."

"I'm guessing there's something else driving you. You're not a pirate—you're a hero. I think you enjoy helping people like me, doing the right thing."

Again, he shrugged. "I like being able to choose which jobs to take and which to turn down."

"Why did you choose me?"

He pursed his lips and scowled. "Now and then, everybody makes a mistake."

His little joke diverted their conversation from uncomfortable topics like honor and nobility. She was glad that he didn't take himself too seriously. Not everything that happened was about him. She hoped that Rafe didn't think Deedee's murder was his fault. If anything happened to her, he wasn't to blame.

He was a good man. But she didn't dare tell him so—not yet, anyway. Trusting him would be easy but risky. He might disappoint her. "Thanks for telling me about Deedee."

"You shared details about Frankie Leone's murder. Turnabout is fair."

"It's good to know that you're dedicated to your job—keeping me safe from the idiots who think I'm the key to finding their fortune."

"Was there any doubt?"

Outside her window, the landscape had changed. They'd left the city behind and were driving north on a divided four-lane road into a more sparsely populated area. "Where are we?"

"River Road." He pointed to the right. "Over that ridge is the levee, and beyond that is the Mississippi. This drive was once famous for the many plantation-style mansions."

The buildings they passed were far more mundane— gas stations, odd shops and tired-looking houses. Beyond the oaks, poplars and shrubs at the roadside, she glimpsed a ramshackle two-story structure with faded gray columns across the front. It looked like the great-great-grandmom to Tara. "What happened to the plantations? Were they destroyed in the hurricane?"

"Nothing so dramatic. The mansions grew old, required too much upkeep and were abandoned." At an intersection, he turned left and drove through a very small town. "We'll stick to back roads so no one can track my SUV."

"There's not much traffic," she pointed out. "We'd see anybody who follows us."

"I'm concerned about drones."

In spite of her massive paranoia, she realized that his knowledge of surveillance and tracking techniques was superior to hers. When she'd planned her getaway routes, she'd tried to consider every detail and contingency, but drones had never crossed her mind. If she hadn't been with Rafe, Alyssa doubted she would have survived the first assault by Woodbridge and his skeleton crew.

They drove along a two-lane asphalt road that curved through an overgrown area of streams, reeds, shrubs and ancient oak trees with long, twisted limbs that reached toward them like the grasping, gnarled fingers of witches. Spanish moss draped from their boughs. This close to the river, humidity thickened the air. "Your computer genius lives around here?"

"Chance Gregory is one of my oldest friends. We went to the same prep school. Across that field, that's his family's place."

In the distance, she spotted a two-story white mansion with pillars that reached from the veranda to the shingled roof. The carpet of grass on the hill leading to the magnificent entrance was neatly trimmed with autumn flowers planted in tidy beds. Two monstrous oak trees loomed behind the structure like sentries, and a weeping willow in the front completed the picture.

"I'm impressed," she said. "Keep in mind that I lived in Savannah, and I know what Greek revival–style architecture looks like."

"The best part about this place is the horse barn in the back. Chance raises thoroughbred race horses and Arabians."

She wished that she'd been wearing a more appropriate outfit. Her khaki shorts and sweat-soaked T-shirt seemed far too casual. Clothing shouldn't matter. People in Chicago didn't seem to pay too much attention, but Alyssa's mom had taught her about proper attire for a lady. *If you dress for the occasion, people take you seriously.*

"I must look a mess." She found a mirror in her backpack, slapped on a dab of blush and arranged her hair. "Can we explain to your friend that I was locked in a tomb for what seemed like hours?"

Rafe drove the SUV up the curved driveway leading to the Gregory mansion and circled around to the back. Outside a long garage, a slender man in jeans and a denim shirt stood waiting. He directed Rafe to pull into the last parking bay. Inside the garage, the SUV was completely hidden. Because of drones?

She slipped into her jean jacket, still musty from the tomb, climbed from the back seat and latched onto Rafe's arm. He leaned down and whispered, "No need to worry, *cher*. You're beautiful."

Outside the garage, Chance greeted her with a kiss on both cheeks that somehow didn't seem phony. His hair was light brown, his eyes were blue and he smelled like lemons.

After Rafe introduced her, Chance said, "I didn't believe it, but my old partner in crime was right as rain. You are Scarlett O'Hara come to life and ready to rule the bayou."

She opened her mouth and closed it again. "I don't know what to say."

"Come inside and have something to eat. Mama and Auntie are at church, but I have leftover jambalaya and corn bread from last night."

Rafe joined them. He was taller than Chance and broader across the shoulders. Rafe's features were more rugged, especially his chiseled cheekbones and the dent in his chin, but there was a similarity between the two friends. Maybe it was the cool assurance behind their eyes. Maybe it was the way they both had kissed her when they met for the first time. She couldn't say why, but she was a little bit fascinated by Chance.

She gave him a nod and said, "I'd love to taste your mama's jambalaya."

"Don't get too deep into hospitality," Rafe warned. "That goes for both of you. We've got work to do."

"I'm way ahead of you." Chance led them through the back door into the mansion. "I've already been digging into the business of Diamond Jim Davidoff and the Leone family. Which do you want first?"

"Davidoff," Rafe said.

They entered a well-equipped country kitchen that was big enough to prepare a sit-down banquet for a couple hundred people. It was obvious that Chance knew his way around food preparation, and he talked while he reheated the spicy, redolent rice and andouille dish, warmed the corn bread and threw together a light salad.

"Viktor Davidoff goes by the name Davis James or Diamond Jim, but his real name is a poorly kept secret. As far as I can tell, he has no family connections in the Chicago area, but he has links with the Russian mob in New York."

"Are you sure there's no family?" Rafe asked.

Chance set a plate of corn bread on the countertop, planted his fists on his hips and glared. "What's wrong with you, partner? You know better than to question my research. I'm never wrong."

Rafe scoffed. "Never say never."

"I'm curious," she said. "Why do you call Rafe your partner? Did you work together?"

"It's slang," Chance explained. "In Cajun, a pal is called partner."

"My pal Chance speaks crisp, clear English." Rafe gave him a nudge. "The true pronunciation is 'podnah.'"

Chance completed the thought. "Rafe is my podnah, and you are his boo."

For the second time today, someone had assumed that she and Rafe were in a relationship. Was this a conspiracy? "I'm nobody's boo."

He took a pitcher of lemonade from the fridge and handed it to her. "Please take this into the dining room."

When she stepped through the kitchen doorway into

a gracious room with high ceilings and tall windows, a sense of contentment settled over her. She recalled similar homes in Savannah when she was a child. This was how life was meant to be—civilized and genteel. The generous proportions of the dining room were balanced by a china cabinet, a linen cupboard and a long oak table with seating for five on each side. Two polished brass chandeliers over the table were unlit. There was no need for artificial light with all those windows.

At the end of the table, Chance had set three places with woven mats, plates, bowls and tall crystal glasses. The dusty-pink napkins complemented the centerpiece of orange and yellow blooms—mums, dahlias and carnations. She was beginning to understand what Rafe meant when he described his "podnah" as a gentleman. Chance appreciated the finer things in life.

After the two pals brought the rest of the food to the table, she relaxed even more. The jambalaya was delicious with spicy bites of andouille. The cold lemonade refreshed her throat and washed away the memory of being locked in the tomb. For the first time since the *Día de los Muertos* parade, she began to believe that everything might turn out all right.

"Can I get you anything else?" Chance asked.

"It's all good," she said, "really good."

"I hate to introduce an unfortunate topic," he said, "but I need to warn you, both of you. Mr. Davidoff—or Davis or Diamond Jim—is a very careful man. He dresses with precision, keeps his goatee trimmed and his jewelry polished. He hired a brilliant bookkeeper who can legally account for every penny even though Davidoff is most likely engaged in fraud, tax evasion and smuggling. Likewise, his attorneys are meticulous. Frankie Leone's murder caused a disruption in Davidoff's business."

"What kind of disruption?" Rafe asked.

"As near as I can figure, Davidoff had taken possession of three vintage cars that were worth over two hundred and fifty thousand dollars each. One went missing." Chance rolled his eyes. "The very thought of that Lamborghini V12 makes my mouth water."

A glance at Rafe told her that he was also captivated by that mental image. She would never understand why men loved pieces of machinery. Cars had never aroused her. As a teenager in Chicago, she preferred taking the bus or the L train so she didn't have to mess with parking. "Did Frankie steal the car?"

"It seems that he did," Chance said. "After years and years of carefully removing objects from the warehouse, Frankie Leone overstepped."

Her good mood began to crumble around the edges. "How do you know all this?"

"It took some serious hacking." He reached into his shirt pocket, pulled out a thumb drive and handed it over to Rafe. "The details are here, but I think you'll both agree with my conclusions. In the end, Davidoff was working with the Leone family in Florida, who were not real happy with their cousin Frankie double-crossing them for years."

"To the tune of seven point six million dollars," Rafe said.

"How did somebody like Frankie get away with this?" She sipped her lemonade. "I mean, this was a sophisticated operation using forgeries. He must have developed a network of criminal connections to fence the property. He couldn't just walk up to some person on the street and offer to sell them a Lamborghini. How did he pull it off?"

"By hiding in plain sight," Chance said. "Nobody paid much attention to Frankie Leone the warehouse foreman.

He didn't live a flashy lifestyle, didn't buy fancy clothes or women. There was only one time when he got in trouble. That was ten years ago."

"When Aunt Charlotte got involved."

"She could be in trouble."

"In danger?" Alyssa didn't want to care, but she did. Charlotte was the only family she had left in the world.

Chance made direct eye contact. "Your auntie isn't in as much trouble as you are. Rafe tells me that you're a woman who makes plans. I would suggest that you exercise that ability. You need to find a way to leave town and lie low."

Tomorrow, after she retrieved the necessary items from her safe-deposit box, she'd get away from New Orleans. "Is there anything I can do for Charlotte? She's working with Agent Jessop of the FBI, you know. How much danger is she really in?"

"I'll put it to you this way," Chance said. "The only way Frankie survived ten years ago was to put all the blame on her. That was why she had to fake her death. They were all after her—the Leones, other smugglers, Horowitz and everybody else."

Not her old boss! Of all the people she knew, he was the one she trusted the most. He'd helped her through the terrible time after her mom's death and had been nothing but kind. If anyone could rescue her from this mess, it was him. "Are you sure Mr. Horowitz was after my aunt?"

"I am," Chance said. "And I'm seldom wrong."

Chapter Fourteen

Cruising back to New Orleans on the Mississippi River Road in a Mercedes C63 sedan, Rafe almost believed his undercover identity as a Grand Prix driver was true. The ride was sheer perfection. Chance had insisted that they take his twin-turbo V-8 sedan to evade surveillance by drone, camera or any person who had the license plate for Rafe's SUV. It hadn't taken much convincing for Rafe to agree to the trade.

His first choice would have been Chance's racy red two-seater Porsche. But Alyssa pointed out that the car attracted too much attention. The sleek lines of the metallic-gray Mercedes didn't look all that much different from other vehicles on the road. But it was—oh yes, it was. Driving this high-performance vehicle was as satisfying as harnessing the power of a rocket ship and taking off for the moon.

"You're going over seventy," Alyssa chided from the passenger seat. "We don't want to get pulled over."

A typical police car could never catch this powerful vehicle, which, according to Chance, went from zero to eighty in less than four seconds, but she was correct. They wanted to escape notice.

Reluctantly, he eased up on the accelerator. "I didn't

realize I was breaking the speed limit. The suspension system is so good that I don't feel any bumps on the road."

"Very comfortable," she said.

He fondled the steering wheel. *"Magnifique."*

For a moment, they rode in comfortable silence. Their bellies were full, the ride was smooth and a bond was growing between them. He wanted this feeling to continue and deepen. Life would be easier if he aimed the nose of the Mercedes toward the west—away from Florida or Chicago—and kept driving until he found a safe place where he could sit with Alyssa and hold her without fear of attack.

"I like your podnah," she said. "Chance is different from any other computer nerd I've ever met."

"He's a mite crazy, but he's never let me down."

"He was right when he said I need to come up with a more detailed plan."

"First, you've got to make a big decision," he said. "Will you stay in New Orleans, or will you go on the lam?"

"On the lam? That sounds so…criminal. I guess I never thought about staying here. The plan was to run, and I made tons of arrangements from transportation and escape routes to fake identification. I never owned a lot of assets, but I inherited a bunch of cash when Mom died and got a hefty insurance payoff from Charlotte's death." She caught her lower lip in her teeth as she paused and considered. "If I know she's alive, is it fraud to keep the money? I should probably pay back the insurance company."

"You're going off track," he said. "Stay or go?"

"That brings up another set of questions. If I decide

to stay, should I contact law enforcement? The FBI and the marshals are out, so that leaves NOPD."

"I know some of the local cops—people who can be trusted."

"Even when there are millions on the line?"

The temptation to betray her would be tempting, even for the most morally upright officer. He didn't feel good about leaving her in the care of a system that had already revealed a rotten core. "Putting yourself in police custody means you give up on further investigation. You know how it works, *cher*. You aren't entitled to information or follow-up. The detectives ask questions, and you answer."

"And no one gets arrested." Her fingers curled into a fist, and she pounded on her thigh, emphasizing each word. "Just. Like. Before."

During his years in the FBI, he'd been on the other side and knew how hard it was to pry details from witnesses. "It's not always so bad."

"It's been three years since I went into WitSec, and nothing is solved. Turn myself in? No, thanks, I've already taken that route."

"You know the alternative," he said. "We do our own investigation."

Her mouth spread in a wide smile. "That sounds right to me."

He found her confidence somewhat disturbing. Their chances of outsmarting federal and local law enforcement weren't good. Not to mention Davidoff, the McGill family and the Leones. A lot of very motivated people were trying to solve this puzzle. What made her think she'd succeed when they all had failed? He had to wonder if she knew some detail that she hadn't revealed.

"That's your decision," he said.

"It is."

"Where do we start?"

"With Charlotte," she said firmly. "I don't owe that woman squat, but she's the only family I have left, and I'm concerned about her survival. Chance thinks she's in danger. At the very least, we need to warn her."

Contacting Charlotte wouldn't hurt their investigation. "She might give us leads on the missing millions. After all, she was Frankie's lover."

"She can tell us how he pulled it off. I know he wasn't smart enough. She must have helped him set it up." Enthusiasm rippled through her voice. "Maybe she can give us the names of her connections and we can follow up."

Rafe doubted that Charlotte had many secrets left untold. She'd probably shared the names of any contacts with Jessop and the FBI, which meant that Davidoff had the same information. Still, talking to her was worth a shot. "You have her phone number. Give her a call."

Sheepishly, she said, "I already tried. I called her from Chance's house. She didn't answer, so I sent a text."

He couldn't see her eyes behind her rhinestone sunglasses, but he could tell she was both excited and tense by the way she fidgeted and chewed her lower lip. "I wish I could tell you not to worry about Charlotte. She could be in danger. Keep in mind that she's not without resources."

"What does that mean?"

"The woman returned from the dead. She's been in hiding for ten years while appearing in public as a lounge singer. I'm not sure if she's on your side or is working for somebody else. Your aunt Charlotte is a wild card."

Alyssa bobbed her head in agreement. "She'd adore Chance. The gracious living, the charm and the manners are her favorite things. I wish we could have seen his thoroughbreds."

"We'll visit him again. I've got no choice about that. My podnah is going to want his Mercedes. In the meantime, I suggest you contact Sheila Marie. If anyone can find Charlotte, she can." He took his phone from his pocket and handed it to her. "I took a photo at the church. Send the picture of Charlotte and mention that she's a singer."

Approaching the city, he needed to be on high alert, watching for people who were looking for them. Rafe kept one eye on the road and the other on Alyssa as she put through the call to Sheila Marie. His phone was his lifeline containing information about the security at the house and his many contacts. He couldn't help worrying that she might scroll through and uncover something he didn't want her to see. No matter how many times he told himself to trust her, he couldn't set all his suspicions aside.

Unlike Jessop and Woodbridge, Rafe believed her when she said that the dying man hadn't told her any secrets. Her outrage when she'd confronted her aunt was genuine, which meant that Alyssa wasn't working a con with Charlotte. His misgivings came when he considered her skill as an accountant and her insider knowledge of how the pawnshop worked. Her familiarity with the place was second only to Horowitz's. Every time his name was mentioned, she bristled. Her feelings for her old boss went beyond the typical employee relationship.

Alyssa ended her call and turned to him. "Sheila Marie says hi. Her exact words were, 'Where y'at?' And I told her that you were happily driving a fancy Mercedes. She wants to take a turn behind the steering wheel."

"Not going to happen."

"She said that she'd look for Charlotte and let us know if she found her." Alyssa held the phone toward him. "You have a text from Davidoff. I didn't read it, but I think he wants you to call him."

That was exactly the kind of information he didn't want her to know. Davidoff was a topic he'd rather not explore in great detail. He pocketed the phone. "I'll check in with him later. Right now, we're headed back to the safe house."

Instead of the evasive driving he'd used when he knew Jessop and maybe Woodbridge were after them, he concentrated on obeying the traffic rules and blending in with all the lesser automobiles. Like a beautiful woman, the Mercedes didn't need to flaunt her superiority. Any fool who took a second look would recognize her value.

On a Sunday afternoon after a wild parade the night before, New Orleans felt lazy and comfortable. In the French Quarter, tourists meandered on the streets, carrying daiquiris and Bloody Marys in plastic cups. Music emanated from every little jazz club.

"I want to get started investigating," she said. "What can we do tonight?"

He would have liked to spend the evening getting to know her better. Not from what she told him or what he'd learned on the internet. He wanted to know her in a physical sense. When he thought about the natural heat from her body, his gut tightened. He could tell in a glance that she was in good shape, but he wanted to caress her arms and legs, to feel her strength. His arms ached to hold her. So far, he'd done a real good job of keeping his distance. They'd developed a certain level of trust, and he hoped she would let down the barriers that guarded her heart.

He cleared his throat. "We can review the case. I know

you've been questioned by dozens of professionals, but never by me."

"Do you think you can figure out something they missed?"

"Can't hurt to try."

"Fine." She spread her hands wide with her palms up. "Ask me anything. I'm an open book."

"Let's start by talking about Horowitz, *cher*."

The book slammed shut.

After all her demands that he tell her the whole truth, Alyssa was holding back. She had a secret, and her former boss was part of it.

As soon as they arrived at the safe house, Alyssa told Rafe she was tired and wanted to take a nap. He could hardly blame her. Though today hadn't been physically demanding, she'd been hit with one shock after another, from meeting up with her supposedly dead aunt to being locked in a tomb. Any reasonable person would need a rest.

In the room that was supposed to be a mirror image of her bedroom at home, she kicked off her shoes, peeled off her jacket and stretched out on top of the chenille bedspread that was a duplicate of the one she'd purchased several months ago. She liked being surrounded by her things—which really weren't hers, but looked like them. In spite of her tension, she relaxed. Soft afternoon light from the windows shone on her bedside table and the Toulouse-Lautrec poster on the wall at the foot of the bed.

Figuring out a plan for what they should do after the visit to the bank was going to take focus. A different concern was foremost in her mind. While they'd been driving here, she'd managed to evade Rafe's questions about Mr. Horowitz, but she wasn't sure how long she could keep from telling him the truth.

Her former boss had disappeared after the murder, and everybody—feds and criminals alike—had a stake in finding him. Horowitz was the most probable person to know where the money had gone. After all, he owned the pawnshop and handled all the merchandise. His awareness of the inventory was encyclopedic. How could millions disappear without his express knowledge and consent?

Over and over, she told herself that Max Horowitz was an honest man. She trusted him, believed in him and knew he wouldn't do anything illegal. Before he skipped town, he'd told her that she wasn't alone. If she needed him, he would be there. Then he gave her a phone number, which she memorized. If she called the secret number, he would know that she needed his help. But she could only call in the very worst-case scenario—worse than being pursued by Woodbridge or the feds, worse than being on Diamond Jim's enemies list and worse than meeting up with Charlotte. The threat had to be literally life or death. Even then, she wasn't sure she could bring herself to betray Max Horowitz.

When she closed her eyes, she remembered the pleasantly musty smell of his sweater-vests and jackets. When he chuckled, his mustache twitched. He was only a few inches taller than she was, but he was surprisingly strong—an ability that served him well when he had to move heavy merchandise. While he worked, he liked to hum, mostly old Beatles tunes.

Thinking of him soothed her nerves. Her eyelids gently opened, and she was pleased to see the pale yellow she'd chosen to paint the walls. She inhaled the vanilla and cinnamon scent from her homemade potpourri. She didn't mind being here. Maybe Davidoff had been on to something when he'd arranged for a duplicate bedroom.

Rafe tapped on the door. "Are you decent?"

"I'm dressed."

He stepped inside, carrying a tray with two tall glasses of iced tea and a small bag of Zapp's spicy potato chips. "The tea is sweet," he said.

"That's how I like it." Iced tea in Chicago wasn't typically sweetened, but her mom had clung to her southern habits, and Alyssa was fond of the sugary flavor. "Thanks, Rafe, but I have to ask. Are you buttering me up?"

"You insult me." He placed the tray on the dresser, handed her a glass of the tea and took the other for himself. Then he tossed the bag toward her. "Chips?"

"There's nothing yummier than the Cajun gator flavor." She tore open the bag. A sip of cold tea and a crisp bite of spicy heat made a perfect combination. "How did you know that I love these chips?"

"Remember, *cher*, I've been watching you for two and a half weeks."

The idea of having him stalk her had been insulting when he first told her, but now his constant observation felt like a compliment. "What else did you learn about me?"

"You like to go running in the morning and don't mind working up a sweat. The gym doesn't hold your attention as well, not even the swimming."

"Yeah, you're right. I never got into the lap swim. And I don't like diving into cold water."

"I guessed as much."

When she realized that he'd been watching her in the pool, she wondered what he thought of her sleek one-piece swimsuit with the high-cut legs. She didn't want to seem conceited, but she was proud of being fit. She nibbled another chip. "What about you? Do you work out?"

"But of course."

Their conversation was beginning to sound like pickup lines at a bar, which was crazy, because they ought to be past that kind of chitchat. "You know a lot more about me than I know about you. I don't have to tell you my astrological sign, which is Aries, by the way."

"I know."

"And you know that I'm terrible at crafts, except for making stinky potpourri. I've already told you about the places I've lived and the important things that have happened in my life. It's like we're jumping into the middle of a friendship instead of poking around the edges."

He cocked an eyebrow. "I think you'll like where we're headed."

Her pulse began to accelerate. He'd kissed her within moments of introducing himself at the parade, but that had been a polite kiss on the forehead. If she was reading his intention correctly, Alyssa knew she was in for the real thing. "You're in the driver's seat, Rafe. Where do you want to take me?"

Chapter Fifteen

Alyssa had lobbed the ball into his court. There was nothing to do but sit back and wait for Rafe to make the next move. Another kiss would be good—a serious, sexy kiss that was a whole lot more than a polite greeting. She made bold eye contact, staring deeply into the splintered facets of his gray eyes. Then she lost her nerve and looked away. Her breath tangled in her throat. Her heart beat faster.

Every passing second felt like an hour, and she mentally prepped herself for the possibility that he'd reject her advance even though she felt their attraction when they touched, heard it in the way he called her *cher* and saw his appreciative glances. He liked her looks, and she knew it. But other stuff stood in the way, like his need to protect her, the temptation of the missing millions, which he had to be thinking about, and—most importantly—trust.

She hadn't been completely honest with him. Did he know it? Did he sense it?

He reached toward her and took the glass of iced tea from her hand. Without a word, he carried both glasses to the dresser and set them down where they wouldn't spill. When he came back to the bed and sat close to her, her pulse was racing faster than a drumroll.

Gently, he took her hand and said, "I want you to trust me."

Had he been reading her mind? Were they on the same page? *Please don't ask about Horowitz, please.* She felt her lips quiver. "Same here."

"There's something I need to tell you, *cher.* This might be difficult to hear."

Was he married? He hadn't mentioned a wife or a girlfriend. Neither Sheila Marie nor Chance had brought up the topic. But that might be Rafe's big secret. She snatched her hand away from him. Darkly, she said, "There's another woman."

The expression of surprise on his face would have been comical if she hadn't been so ticked off. He rattled off a stream of French that was liberally punctuated by denial before he switched to English. "I am not a perfect man. For years, I made my living undercover, telling lies. But I have never betrayed a woman I love. If I were married or involved with another, I would have told you from the start. No, *ma chérie,* there is no one else."

"Then what is this big, fat secret and why will it be hard for me to hear?"

"I spoke to Davidoff on the phone."

Five minutes ago, those words would have sounded a disturbing note of fear in her belly, but not anymore. Compared to the idea that Rafe might be hiding a secret wife, the mention of Davidoff seemed trivial. She had to wonder if her priorities were askew. "What's up with Diamond Jim?"

"The photo of you that we took in the cemetery lit a fire under him. He thought you looked frightened, and he wants to meet."

"With me?" She flapped her hands, waving away the request. "That's not going to happen. Davidoff is a criminal."

"I'm not so sure that he wants to harm you."

"Because he hired you as a bodyguard? Ha! That's no reason." She scooted away from him on the bed, pulling her knees up and pressing her back against the headboard. "Did you forget about Jessop? He's after the money, and he is most definitely in Davidoff's pocket."

"And possibly Charlotte, as well."

Davidoff was the ringmaster, snapping his whip and directing the clowns, tigers and acrobats in this crazy circus. She didn't want to believe that Rafe was part of the show, but he'd done Davidoff's bidding. His orders had been to follow her and to decorate this room to match her own.

Moments ago, she'd thought the similarity was comforting. Was she falling under Davidoff's spell? "I don't understand what kind of game he's playing, but I want no part of it."

"He told me a secret that makes sense of everything," Rafe said. "I promised not to tell, but it's unfair to withhold this information. You need to know everything before you make your decision."

The anticipation was nearly unbearable. "Spill it."

"Viktor Davidoff claims to be your father."

She was stunned. All her life she'd fantasized about the identity of her father, praying he was a prince and fearing that he was a monster. Her mom told her that he'd spent time with her when she was an infant. He'd held her and sang lullabies, but she couldn't remember the words. There were no photos, no cards, not a single note from him. She had a hazy memory of her fourth birthday party, when he gave her the music box, and she seemed to recall him telling her that she was his favorite girl and he would always take care of her.

If Davidoff was that man, he hadn't lived up to the promise. "Why wouldn't he tell me?"

"Think about it," Rafe said. "He didn't want to put you and your mom in danger from his enemies. When he first moved to Chicago, there were clues that he was escaping from the Russian mob in New York."

"I heard those rumors but I never paid much attention." She shook her head. "He hasn't been my father for twenty-seven years. Why now?"

"I don't know."

In the back of her mind, a tiny spark of hope ignited. Was it possible? Having a father would change her core identity. If he truly was her father, Davidoff couldn't be such a terrible person. Her mom never would have fallen in love with him. Maybe if she got to know him, she could accept him. And then she remembered…

As quickly as hope had been born, the light was extinguished. She glanced at the bedside table, where the lamp with the fringed shade stood beside the potpourri. "Where's my music box?"

He went to the dresser and opened the top drawer. "After you threw the box at the wall, I figured you didn't want it anymore."

"Give the thing to me." As soon as she held the box in her hand, she knew it was a fake. The wood wasn't as smooth as the original, and the patina was lighter. "My father gave me a music box when I turned four. Not this box but another. Before I went to sleep, I'd rub the wood against my cheek. And I'd open the lid and listen to the music—my music, 'Lara's Theme' from *Dr. Zhivago*."

She flipped open the lid and heard "Twinkle, Twinkle Little Star."

"Davidoff never mentioned the tune," Rafe said. "Your

real father wouldn't have allowed me to make that mistake. He would have given specific instructions."

The trick Davidoff had tried to pull on her was beyond cruel. He had played on the emotional needs of a fatherless child who had also lost her mom. She had no family. Asking Charlotte to be part of her life was like trying to bond with a feral cat. "He's truly a bastard."

"His claim was strange but somehow made sense," Rafe said. "He hired me to protect you, which is what a father would do. When he talked about you, he seemed sincerely concerned about your well-being. And Lara is a Russian name, short for Larissa. Davidoff might have chosen that name for his daughter. Lara Davidoff?"

"Yuck! Mom picked my name because she thought it sounded pretty. And it's not like Davidoff is the only Russian I know. Lots of people come from that part of the world, like Mr. Horowitz. His first name, Max, is short for Maksim. And one of the McGill brothers married a Russian woman who blames me for testifying against her husband." Alyssa's temperature was rising, and the initial hurt she felt was turning to rage. She rose up on her knees. "Why are we talking about this? I'm not Davidoff's daughter. There's no way I'll agree to meet with him."

"I'll find a way to get rid of him."

Still angry, she climbed off the bed and stalked across the bedroom to the dresser, where she grabbed her iced tea and took a long drink. The cool liquid failed to quench the fire burning in her belly. "Why would he make up that particular lie? What did he hope to gain?"

"Your trust."

She steamed across the bedroom and back to the bed. After she placed her glass on the bedside table next to the Zapp's bag, she hopped onto the chenille spread. Rafe

watched her warily as though she were an exotic creature in a zoo.

"I'll never trust Davidoff," she said.

"Is there anyone, *cher*? Anyone whom you trust?"

Though she could have run down a long list of associates and friends who watered her plants when she wasn't
home, that wasn't really what he was asking. Rafe wanted
to know if she trusted him—a fair question. He'd proven
his loyalty many times over. Now that he'd told her about
Davidoff's grand scheme to pose as her absentee father,
she had the feeling that all his cards had been played. He
had nothing left to hide.

There were dozens of other questions she could ask,
teasing out the details of how he'd learned the colors in
her bedroom and if he'd followed her home after a party
at work when one of the servers tried to kiss her. She
could ask about his time undercover and his other FBI
assignments. But trust was a feeling, not an accounting.

She believed in him and didn't need proof. "I trust
you, Rafe."

He lowered his arms and crossed the small bedroom
in a few quick strides. First, he went to the two windows
near the bed and pulled down the blinds to block the late-
afternoon sunlight. The room dimmed, and she turned
on her bedside lamp with the fringed shade. The glow
was soft, soothing and intimate.

The first thing he took off was his shoulder holster,
which he hung over the wooden chair by the tiny desk.
Then he returned to the opposite side of her bed and held
out his hand as though asking her to dance. She was so
ready for this tango. When she grasped his outstretched
fingers, he pulled her toward him. Rising up on her knees
again, she closed the space between them.

His arm encircled her, and he gently rested his hand

at the small of her back. She hadn't felt her bruises for most of the day, but his nearness heightened her sensitivity. There was a twinge. Her nerves were humming. The surface of her skin prickled.

He leaned close and whispered, "I trust you, *cher*."

She didn't deserve his trust. She was still holding on to a secret. But she wasn't about to switch gears and talk about Mr. Horowitz. Not right now. She was ready for this special dance with him and had been expecting it from the moment he'd introduced himself as a pirate at the parade. She glided the back of her hand down his cheek and held his jaw. Her thumb traced his lower lip and explored the dimple in his chin.

Her head tilted back, ready to receive the kiss that she knew was coming. His mouth joined hers with a firm but gentle pressure that elevated her desire into the stratosphere. She suspected he'd be a skillful lover. The man was French, after all. If this kiss was any indication, she wouldn't be disappointed.

At just the right instant, the tip of his tongue tasted her lips and pushed inside to probe the interior of her mouth. Excitement pulsed through her. She wanted him to be closer, wanted to feel the weight of his body atop hers. Leaning backward, she pulled him off balance onto the bed.

Her maneuver wasn't exactly graceful, and they ended up in a tangle of limbs. When they got their bodies sorted out, she was on her back. She wrapped her legs around his hips and reveled in the full-body contact. Her need was maybe a little too aggressive, because he slowed the pace and separated from her.

Breathing hard and wanting more, she gazed up at him. She was so mesmerized by his smoldering, sexy eyes that she hardly noticed when he started unbuttoning his white shirt. He was using only one hand, and it was taking too long.

"I'll help." Her fingers trembled as she unfastened the buttons. "Is there some word for what we're doing in French? Some romantic phrase?"

"We call this sex," he said.

"Oh good, we're on the same page."

With the buttons out of the way, she opened his shirt. Though she'd seen him bare-chested in the morning before breakfast, being this close was better. His skin was darkly tanned, and the hair across his pecs and washboard abs made an intriguing pattern. She drew a line down the center of his chest with her index finger, pausing to swirl the hair and admiring the tight muscularity from his collarbone to the waistband of his trousers.

"Your turn," he said, interrupting her quest.

Within seconds, he'd removed her T-shirt and slipped off her bra. "Speedy," she commented. "I didn't even feel you unfasten the hooks. That must take years of practice."

"I like looking at you," he said. "You are *magnifique*."

He used that word a lot, and she liked being in the same category as the Mercedes. Before she could make a smart comment, he lowered his head and nuzzled her breasts, paying particular attention to her nipples.

Her back arched, and she closed her eyes. A low moan slipped through her lips and hung in the air. There was no time for comments or chatter. She abandoned herself to the pleasure he coaxed from her body with his light caresses and kisses that covered her torso. She wanted more.

Wordless, they tore off the rest of their clothing. She pulled him against her with all the strength she could muster. She wanted him inside her. Clinging to the last thread of conscious control, she felt truly alive. *More, more, more!* She didn't want him to stop, not now, not ever.

Vaguely aware of what was happening, she realized that he'd put on a condom. Where did he get it? Did he keep a supply in the bedside table? She didn't care but was glad that her bodyguard had taken the need for protection seriously.

He rose above her on the bed and spread her thighs. Shivering and shaking, nearly weeping, she endured gentle nips, licks and kisses that descended from her breasts to her belly to her groin. His fingers teased and manipulated, raising her level of arousal to amazing heights.

He covered her with his body. His heat flowed through her. His heartbeat synchronized with hers. Finally, he penetrated her. Her gasps became moans as he drove into her, harder and harder until she completely lost control and exploded like fireworks into a million sparkling pieces.

After the first glittering bursts, she lay back and enjoyed a rumbling earthquake of sensation that shook her from head to toe. It took a while for her breathing to return to normal and for her racing pulse to resume a sensible pace. Then another aftershock hit. She whimpered like a kitten.

He stroked her hair off her forehead. "Are you all right?"

"Fine, I'm fine. I'm fine." Another tremor rippled through her. "How about you?"

He spoke to her in French. Though she didn't know the language, she caught a few words about champagne and roses. "Translation?"

"It's poetry, *cher*. I'm comparing your mouth to a rosebud and the taste of your breasts to the sparkle of champagne."

She liked the musical French version better. "Whatever you're saying, thanks."

He lay back against his pillow and stared up at the ceiling. "At a time such as this, I hate to bring up unpleasant subjects, but we have an investigation that we might pursue tonight. Chance gave me a thumb drive with raw data from the accounts of the pawnshop and the inventory. I've glanced at the information. It means nothing to me, but you might be able to translate the numbers into leads."

She allowed another aftershock to chase through her body. Getting her feet solidly back on the ground was going to take a few minutes. "I can compare Chance's data with a copy of the accounts and inventory from the last few months before Frankie was killed."

"You have these accounts?"

She nodded. "There's a thumb drive in my safe-deposit box. I turned over the original to the feds, but it seemed prudent to keep a copy. I've studied the list but didn't notice anything out of the ordinary."

"Tomorrow," he said, "we will compare this paperwork."

"And tonight, what will we do tonight?"

He traced his finger across her lips, leaned close and whispered in her ear. "I want to thoroughly investigate every inch of your body."

She liked that plan.

Chapter Sixteen

They stayed in the bedroom until the sun set and the streets were dark. Rafe could have spent many more hours lying beside her—naked, happy and fulfilled. He laced his fingers with hers and brought her small, slender hand to his lips. She was lovely, delicate. Her apprehension was gone, erased by a sexual compatibility that surprised him. He hadn't expected them to be so good together.

Yes, she lacked experience. But she was graceful, enthusiastic and energetic. Alyssa held nothing back. She made him feel like he'd invented sex.

Cradled in the crook of his arm, she gave him a contented smile worthy of an otherworldly angel, then she reached up and booped the tip of his nose. "I'm hungry. What should we do for dinner?"

"I wish we could go out," he said. "New Orleans has incredible restaurants, but we don't want to risk the exposure."

"I guess that means we've got to cook."

He tossed aside the spread, rose from the bed and stretched his arms over his head. "Come with me to the kitchen."

"Whoa, podnah. You're not planning to make dinner in the nude, are you?"

He glanced over his shoulder. "There's no reason for either of us to wear clothes."

"Oh yeah, I can think of a few negatives, like not wanting to get grease spatters on the delicate parts of my anatomy. And we're still in danger. We should be prepared to run at a moment's notice."

He liked her intelligence and her wit. "You always think ahead."

"Which is why I'm still alive," she said. "Meet you in the kitchen."

He charged down the hallway to his bedroom, where he put on a pair of jeans, a black polo shirt and running shoes. He hadn't been planning to go out tonight, but it didn't hurt to get all the way dressed and ready to run. He even fastened his holster to his belt. Earlier tonight, he'd brushed his teeth but hadn't shaved. His stubble was heavier than usual. A shower would have felt good…a shower with Alyssa would be better.

In the kitchen, he took a couple of rib eyes from the fridge and threw brown rice in the cooker. On the table, he set up the laptop for Alyssa and loaded the thumb drive Chance had given him. After he made a marinade for the steaks, he gathered ingredients for a tomato and cucumber salad.

Alyssa seemed to be taking her time getting to the kitchen. When she finally strolled through the door, dressed in a coral blouse and shorts, he noticed her damp hair. He kissed her forehead and inhaled the peachy fragrance of her shampoo. "You took a shower," he said. "I would have been happy to join you."

"Not surprised." She stroked his jawline. "It's okay with me if you don't shave. I kind of like the unkempt look."

He knew that he couldn't spend every minute of every

day fondling her and he should set boundaries. But he couldn't resist another kiss. He yanked her tightly against him and realized that she hadn't bothered to put on her bra. Though tempted to sweep everything off the table and make love right here, he put on the brakes.

"Did I tell you how beautiful you are?"

She looked uncomfortable. "You don't have to compliment me every minute just because we, you know, did it."

"Not an obligation, it's my pleasure. But you are correct. Unfortunately, we have other concerns. Voilà! Here is the computer."

She sat in front of the screen, tapped a key and smiled when a row of numbers appeared. "Is this the data from Chance?"

"Ready and waiting for you."

While she scrolled through the pages, he finished preparing their meal. Though he wasn't a great cook, the arrangement pleased him. He liked taking care of her.

Apparently, she'd reached a stopping point, because she stepped away from the computer, helped him load the plates and placed them on either end of the table while he poured the chilled Chardonnay. "I can't believe Chance got access to all this info. Not only are there ledgers and receipts, but he found personal correspondence and FBI stats. He even tapped into a psychologist report about me. Guess what the guy said."

He sipped his wine and sliced off a juicy bite of rib eye. "Tell me."

"He claimed that I had abandonment issues because my father ran off when I was a little kid. Also, he called me fearful and tense and suggested that I might have some kind of anxiety disorder. Well, of course I was upset. A man died a violent death in my arms, and I'd been whisked into WitSec. Still, he should have noticed that I'm resilient, strong and brave."

"And sexy," he added.

"That goes without saying."

She dug into her food with her typical enthusiasm. Their conversation was replaced by a series of appreciative moans, which were not unlike the sounds she made in the bedroom. Finally, she paused to take a drink of her Chardonnay.

"Here's what I'm wondering," she said. "Obviously, some of Chance's data was uncovered through illegal hacking. Is there any database he can't get into?"

"I've never known him to be stumped."

"That's disturbing." She gestured to the computer and the kitchen and the house at large. "We're protected by your surveillance and computer firewalls, but there has to be someone—a hacker who is as talented and smart as Chance—who could break through and find us."

"I built this surveillance system using my FBI training and state-of-the-art equipment. Plus, you'll be happy to note that Chance added his very own special mojo to anticipate every kind of attack."

"Chance did that?"

"That's got to make you feel better. My podnah used his superior technology to make this place nearly impregnable and invisible."

"Any fortress can be broken into," she said, "because of human error."

"And so, we can't make mistakes."

He wanted to believe that was possible, but Rafe knew better than to count on perfection. Sooner or later, they might get careless. After they finished eating and cleaned up the dishes, they went into the small front room and had a cup of chamomile tea while they made tentative plans for the following day. Another glass of wine would have been nice, but that was an easy mistake to avoid. He needed to stay alert. In the morning, their first stop would be at her bank, where they would pick up her thumb drive and compare her data with the information Chance had provided.

"Then we should get my second car," she said. "The key is in the safe-deposit box."

"We could have gotten the car at any time, *cher*. I might not actually know how to win a Grand Prix race, but I know how cars work. I could have hot-wired the ignition."

"I'll keep that in mind in case things go south at the bank. There are tons of things in the trunk of that car—a computer, clothes, shoes, cash and credit cards in a different identity."

He hadn't forgotten how resourceful she was. "We can use all those things. With Davidoff coming to New Orleans, the city is even more dangerous than before. Moving somewhere else might be wise."

She sipped her tea and licked her lips. "Before we go, I want to figure out where the missing millions are hiding. Finding the money is the only way I'll be truly safe."

She seemed to be ignoring the threat from the families of the men who went to jail because of her testimony, but he didn't remind her. One horror story at a time was enough. Besides, her odds for survival were greatly improved because he would be at her side, constantly protecting her and ever vigilant.

His cell phone rang. The caller ID showed the call was from Sheila Marie. Rafe suppressed a groan, recognizing that she'd be calling with new information and they'd have to leave their cozy nest. He put the call on speaker.

After a quick hello, Sheila Marie said, "I done found

Missy Charlotte with the silver hair. She's at the Corner Oak Tavern on Bourbon Street."

He heard a bluesy saxophone wailing in the background. "Is she singing with the band?"

"Not a bit of it. This lady is slumped down and drinking hard. She looks sad."

"Keep an eye on her," he said. "If she leaves the Oak, let me know."

"Got it, boss man."

"Wait for me outside. I'll be there in a minute. Is there a place you can take Alyssa where she'll be safe?"

"No prob. I got a dozen hideouts."

He believed her one hundred percent. Sheila Marie knew the city better than anyone. "*Merci beaucoup.* See you in ten minutes."

Alyssa was on her feet. "Do I need a disguise?"

"Keep it simple."

He watched her dash down the hallway to her bedroom. Bringing her along might be a mistake, but he had no choice. She couldn't stay here by herself.

IN MINUTES, SHE joined him in the Mercedes. Instead of the fancy pink outfit, her disguise was to go minimal: no makeup and slicked-back hair tucked under a black baseball cap with "Mardi Gras" written across the front in letters of purple, green and gold. From a distance, she'd be unrecognizable. He had no disguise, only a blue windbreaker over his black shirt. They didn't have time for anything more complicated.

As she buckled her seat belt, she said, "Thank you."

"For what, *cher*?"

"Meeting with Charlotte. I shouldn't worry about her, but I can't help it. We need to get her to safety, which means far away from New Orleans."

His reasons for seeing her aunt weren't completely altruistic. She'd been in on Frankie's smuggling scheme from the start and might have helpful information. She had contacts in the criminal world. Someone considered her useful enough to pay her bills for ten years. Rafe welcomed the opportunity to question her without having her sympathetic niece standing by.

He approached the location of the Corner Oak and spotted Sheila Marie standing under a streetlamp. On a Sunday night, there were still tourists milling around but not a crowd. He pulled up to the curb.

His favorite confidential informant climbed into the back seat. With her long dreads, an embroidered turquoise blouse and a long paisley skirt with swirls of red, green and yellow, she was an explosion of color. The first thing she did when she got into the Mercedes was stroke her fingers—polished half red and half yellow—across the upholstery.

"Leather," she said. "Man, you oughta keep this fine ride."

"It belongs to Chance."

"Oh yeah, I like that boy, even if he does live on a plantation." She flicked her hand toward the windshield. "Go straight, turn on Bourbon Street and then left. We be paying a visit to Jolene's voodoo shop."

He knew the place. "Alyssa, wait for me there."

"Take your time," Sheila Marie said. "Alyssa should have a reading. Jolene can see the future. Dat's good, yeah?"

"Sure," she said. "I went to a psychic in Chicago after my mom died. She didn't tell me anything I didn't know, but she made me feel better."

Dropping her off in a voodoo shop felt like a bad idea, but meeting with Charlotte had the earmarks of a trap.

He wished he could take Alyssa home where they'd be alone and safe. But there were unavoidable hurdles they had to jump to reach the truth.

Before she left the car, she leaned across and kissed him on the lips. "Take good care of Aunt Charlotte."

"I intend to." He couldn't wait to get that woman out of town.

In moments, he'd returned to the Corner Oak Tavern, parked illegally and entered the dimly lit jazz club. The four-piece band followed their own jam, shifting from drums to piano to guitar and sax. A woman with bright red lipstick swayed and murmured a sad song about being left by the only man she'd ever loved.

Charlotte should have been on stage; she had a better voice and more presence. But she sat by herself at a small round table in the audience. Her two-tone rum cocktail looked like she'd barely taken a sip. When he pulled out a chair and sat, she shot him a sidelong glance, and he knew this would not be a friendly interview.

"Ten years ago," he said, keeping his voice low, "you were in love with Frankie Leone. The two of you ran a smuggling scam using the pawnshop warehouse."

"Who sent you? Was it Jessop? Or was it my snippy little niece?"

"Someone else could be looking for you."

Her head snapped up, and she stared. Now he had her attention. She spoke in a trembling whisper. "What are you talking about?"

Though he was tempted to tell her that Davidoff was on his way to New Orleans, Rafe didn't want to give away too much information without getting something in return. He gestured toward the stage. "I expected to see you singing."

"Not my gig."

"It could be. If you unleashed that voice of yours, people would clamor to hear more."

"That's a nice fairy tale, but talent doesn't get you far."

He added bitterness to the long list of her negative traits that included lying, cheating and stealing. "You know the business."

"I've got more talent in my pinkie toe than that singer has in her whole body, but singing doesn't pay my bills. That's why I'm sitting here, waiting for Jessop. He's half an hour late." She looked down into her cocktail and muttered, "He knows where I'm staying. I don't know why he wanted to meet here."

Rafe had a pretty good idea why Jessop would stage a meeting outside her room. "He wanted you out of the way so he could search your place."

She sipped the drink and set it down on the table. "You're not as dumb as you look."

"Neither are you," he said. "You didn't leave anything for Jessop to find. Being on the run for ten years means you know how to think ahead. Here's the irony. Your niece is the same way. She wanted me to come here to warn you."

Charlotte didn't bother to pretend that she was dumb or innocent. "What's the warning?"

"You need to give me something first. I'm pretty sure that Frankie didn't come up with the logistics of a lucrative smuggling operation, double-crossing his criminal family by using forgeries and fences. Frankie Leone just wasn't that smart."

"He wasn't, bless his heart. My Frankie was funny, sexy and devoted to me. But he was no genius. I came up with the basic plan, and I'd be happy to jot down the names of my contacts. Not that those names will do you any good."

"Why not?"

"It was ten years ago. My list is dated."

Unfortunately, she was right. "Anything you can tell me might help."

"Use your brain, sonny boy. There's only one name you need to know, only one person who can explain everything. That person is Max Horowitz. He knew everything that went on in his pawnshop and warehouse. I wouldn't be surprised to learn that he partnered up with Frankie after I left town."

Similar thoughts had occurred to Rafe. Siphoning off millions of dollars could be part of a scam to avoid paying taxes. Horowitz had something to hide. Why else would he skip town after the murder? He pushed back his chair. "Take me to your hotel room."

"What's in it for me?"

"Davidoff is on his way to New Orleans, and you need protection. Jessop can help and so can I."

The arrival of Davidoff was good motivation for her to move fast. She gathered up her huge purse—probably filled with the necessities of her life—and they left the Oak.

On the street, he didn't waste the effort to engage in conversation. She was Jessop's problem. For Alyssa's sake, Rafe would keep her aunt safe until she could be taken into protective custody. As they walked through the crowd, he scanned for threatening people who mingled with the cheerful tourists and bar hoppers. He spotted a pickpocket and a sinister drunk who yelled at anyone who crossed his path.

Her hotel was small but charming, located only a block off the main route. Instead of being trapped in the rickety old elevator, he climbed the staircase to her second-floor room. On the landing, he motioned to her. "Which room?"

She pointed to a door that stood ajar. Before going forward, Rafe pulled his weapon from the holster on his hip and held it ready. Charlotte stayed behind him, moving silently. Her attitude told him that this wasn't the first time she'd walked into danger.

Entering her room, he flipped on the overhead light. Everywhere was chaos—overturned chairs, drawers pulled from the dresser, clothing scattered on the floor. The mattress had been pulled off the box spring. In the tiled bathroom, he found Jessop, lying on the tiled floor in a puddle of blood. A head wound matted his blond hair.

Rafe squatted beside him and felt for a pulse. Jessop turned his head and groaned. He wasn't dead.

Chapter Seventeen

"Death comes close. He carries a sword. He rides the white horse." Jolene, the owner of Dragon's Blood Voodoo Emporium, held the tarot card toward Alyssa and jiggled the edges so the skeletal death figure looked like he was dancing. "He comes for you."

Sheila Marie reached over and patted Alyssa's hand. "Doncha worry, hon. Dat card is not so bad."

"Really? Are you telling me that death isn't a bummer?"

"Death don't always mean being buried in the cemetery—could be an end of things, like a bad habit."

"Truth," Jolene said. "Many smokers come to me."

Her gestures were quick, darting, almost birdlike. Her skinny arms waved emphatically when she talked, clanking her many bracelets and sending her necklaces twirling. She fluttered energetically in the back room of her shop, where a huge mural of dancing skeletons and a fire-breathing dragon decorated the walls. The shelves were lined with candles and jars filled with mysterious substances. Incense tainted the air and mingled with the scent of something bubbling in a pot on a hot plate. Alyssa hoped the stew was chicken.

She didn't really believe in voodoo or magic, but she found the practice interesting. Besides, getting a reading from Jolene was a good alternative to thinking about what was going on with Rafe and Charlotte. "Can you really use magic to get people to quit smoking?"

"If they believe in dragon's blood," Jolene said, "I can cure them."

"Where do you find dragon's blood?"

"Special formula. It comes from plants and trees." She held a small vial containing a crimson liquid. "Very precious. I use dragon's blood to make the gris-gris I sell in my shop."

"A gris-gris is a lucky amulet, right?"

"And so much more. My gris-gris wards off evil and turns away zombies."

She'd been in New Orleans long enough to understand that voodoo wasn't always about ugly little dolls to stick pins into and rituals to cast dark spells. Most of the magic involved love potions or ritual enchantments to bring fame and fortune. "Can I buy a gris-gris necklace from you? I need all the protection I can get."

"First, we talk of your future." Jolene touched the bill of Alyssa's baseball cap. "Take this off."

She removed the cap. "Now what?"

"Sit, my child."

Alyssa sank into the patterned cushions of a low rattan chair. Glancing at her phone, she checked the time. Rafe had been gone for eighteen minutes. She estimated eight to ten minutes to get to the Corner Oak Tavern and back here. That meant he'd been talking to her aunt for about eight minutes. Would he bring her here? Could he convince Charlotte that she was in danger?

Jolene combed her fingers through Alyssa's hair. "Clear your mind," she said. "Stop your worrying. Forget your woes."

Not necessarily good advice. Alyssa tended to suppress her negative emotions. A therapist had told her she needed to deal with all these issues: abandonment by her father, her mom's early death by hit-and-run, witnessing a murder and the whole WitSec thing. *No, thanks.* She'd rather do it the voodoo way. "Forget my woes."

Perching like a colorful canary, Jolene took a seat on the opposite side of a small round table draped in woven kente cloth from Ghana. She motioned for Sheila Marie to join them. "Alyssa, place your hands on the table, palms down."

She tilted her vial of dragon blood and allowed a drop to fall on the back of Alyssa's hand. While she murmured incomprehensible syllables, Jolene smeared the red liquid in a jagged pattern. She put on a good show. Alyssa's only other experiences with fortune tellers hadn't been half so dramatic.

"In your future," Jolene said, "there is a man."

Sheila Marie cackled. "Tall, dark and handsome, I betcha."

"Not this man. He is not tall. A nice smile…" She rubbed her upper lip. "And he has a mustache. A kind man and strong, he has many secrets."

She had to be talking about Max Horowitz. Ever since Alyssa learned that Davidoff was coming to town, she'd been thinking that it was time to make the emergency call to her former boss. "Will he help me?"

"He would do anything for you. He would die for you."

That wasn't what she wanted to hear. Dragging Mr. Horowitz into danger was the last thing she wanted. "If I call him, what will happen?"

"I cannot say." She leaned back from the table, distancing herself.

"That's not fair," Alyssa said. "What kind of fortune teller are you? I need answers."

"I'm not a carnival act." Quickly, Jolene leaped to her feet, ready to take flight. "I am a seer. I connect with the future and the past. I can advise you, my child, but there are too many variables to make an accurate prediction."

"Advise me. Should I contact this man?"

"The decision is yours," she said archly. "It's not my job to make you happy."

"Back it up," Sheila Marie said. "You got to tell her about the French man with the powerful mojo. He is important."

"When it comes to him, she doesn't need my advice," Jolene said. "They are already bonded, hand to hand and heart to heart."

Alyssa liked the way that sounded. She peered at the painted bamboo curtain that separated this small room from the outer store. Any minute, Rafe should be here.

In the meantime, she bought a gris-gris amulet that was marked with genuine dragon's blood and found a quiet corner to make her phone call to Mr. Horowitz. She punched the number she had memorized into her phone. After three rings, a mechanical voice answered and repeated the number back to her. She selected her words carefully, not wanting to give too much away.

"You told me to call if I needed your help, and I do. Everyone thinks I know where the millions are hidden, and I might have a clue if I can compare inventory with my accounting. At least, I'll know what was stolen. I miss you. All I want is for this to be over. Life used to be safe and calm, and I want that life back."

She stopped herself before she launched into a nostalgic memory of the Christmases he'd spent with her and her mom or the spring days when they strolled along the lakefront. This wasn't the time for sweet, soft memories. She needed to be strong.

"Charlotte came back from the dead," she said. "Seeing her makes me think of Mom."

Her comment was too personal. If anyone other than Mr. Horowitz was listening, they'd know she was the caller. "Anyway, please get in touch with me. I'm in New Orleans. Oh yeah, and I met a guy. You'd like him. 'Bye for now."

Before she put her phone away, she checked the time. Rafe had been gone for forty-two minutes. A lot of bad mojo could happen in that amount of time.

RAFE PERFORMED BASIC first aid on Jessop. The bleeding was minimal, and there were no deep lacerations from gunshot or knife wounds. Jessop had been beaten, and his head wound was beyond Rafe's rudimentary skills. He shouted over his shoulder at Charlotte, "Call 911."

"I can't. This is my damn room. The cops will think I did this."

He doubted there was anybody who'd suspect her of pistol-whipping a physically fit, well-trained federal agent. Charlotte was tall but didn't have the muscles to inflict this level of damage. "Just make the call."

"Can we move him out of my room?"

"He's unconscious and in bad shape. By moving him, we might make his injuries worse." Why was he even talking to her? He took his phone from his pocket and tapped in the numbers.

"Rafe, no. You don't understand. I can't go to jail."

"We'll wait for the ambulance, and I'll get you out of here."

"But the room is in my name."

An alias, he thought. After ten years on the run, Charlotte knew better than to use a name that could be traced. When the 911 dispatcher answered, he gave the important information. "We have a 10-999, officer down, immediate assistance requested. Send a bus to this address, second floor."

Instead of staying on the line as instructed by the dispatcher, he disconnected and looked over at Charlotte. "Bring me a pillow and a blanket."

"Why?"

"To prevent shock." Jessop was breathing steadily and groaning." Rafe leaned close and spoke with urgency. "Who did this to you? Give me a name."

Still, Jessop didn't open his eyes. If anything, he squeezed them shut, blocking out the overhead light in the bathroom. When he tried to move, it was apparent that his right arm had been injured. Likely, his shoulder was separated—an injury that Rafe could fix if Jessop moved into the right position. He decided to wait for the paramedics.

Jessop's eyelids fluttered as though he was struggling to regain consciousness, trying to wake up and name his attackers. Rafe encouraged him. "Tell me, *mon ami*. Who hurt you?"

There had to be at least two of them, maybe more. Rafe took the pillow from Charlotte and used it to elevate Jessop's head. Though he didn't wake up, Jessop responded with a gasp. His mouth opened. A thin trickle of blood spilled from the corner.

Rafe tried to reconstruct what had happened in this room. Jessop wasn't the sort of man who came up with elaborate conspiracies; his actions would be straightforward. He had arranged to get Charlotte out of the way, drinking at a blues club. While she was gone, he went to her room. But why? What was he looking for? She must have evidence in her possession. He remembered that

Jessop had a connection with Davidoff and might have been doing his bidding.

The thugs must have been waiting in the room to ambush him. If they'd interrupted Jessop midsearch, he would have pulled his weapon, and it didn't look like he'd had time to get off a shot. His holster was empty, and there was no smell of gunpowder in the air. The men who attacked were cowards and definitely not geniuses. Leaving a witness alive wasn't a smart move.

Charlotte peeked over his shoulder. "Is he going to be okay?"

This was the first time she'd showed concern. "With a head injury, his condition is unpredictable."

"He's a nice man. I hope he recovers."

From outside, he heard the scream of an approaching ambulance. "Do you know who attacked him? Can you take a guess?"

"You mentioned Davidoff," she said.

"Why would he come after Jessop? Does he want something from you, Charlotte?"

In an angry huff, she stamped away from the bathroom, returned in a shot and snapped at him. "Can't you just take my word? It was Davidoff."

"You're a liar and a scam artist. I wouldn't take your word for the time of day if you showed me a clock." The ambulance was louder. "You need my help, Charlotte."

"Get me out of New Orleans, and I'll tell you what Davidoff wants."

Not a great deal, but he had very little choice. The longer he stayed at this crime scene, the longer Alyssa was unprotected. "Listen to me, Charlotte. When the paramedics get here, stay out of the way. They'll have to use the staircase to move Jessop. The elevator is too narrow."

"Should we take the elevator to the ground floor?"

"Too obvious," he said. "The bastards who attacked Jessop are probably watching."

"What should I do?"

"Grab your necessary stuff. We've got to run."

He wiped his hand on a towel before sending a similar text to Alyssa. Be ready to go.

Moments later, they heard the EMTs coming up the staircase, dragging their equipment and complaining with every step. While Charlotte disappeared into a closet, Rafe directed them to the bathroom. "This man is a federal agent. Check his wallet."

"You should stick around, pal. The police are going to have questions."

"You got here fast, *merci*."

"Pas de quoi." The paramedic grinned. "It's our job."

Rafe stepped out of the way while they worked on Jessop. He was lucky that the ambulance arrived before the police A call of "officer down" usually brought an aggressive response. He heard their sirens approaching.

Charlotte came toward him. She had used her few minutes alone to prepare for flight, changing from a light dress to black slacks, black jacket and sneakers for running. She had a small backpack on her shoulders. He was glad to be wearing a dark-colored windbreaker to cover the blood. They would blend into the darkness, and they needed every advantage to evade the local police and the people who had attacked Jessop. "You need to do as I say," he told her.

"Absolutely."

Her quick agreement was something of a surprise. Alyssa never would have accepted his leadership without a fight. Maybe her aunt had something to teach her after all.

Without exchanging a word, they exited her hotel room

and rushed to the elevator. Instead of going down, he hit the "up" button, taking them to the fourth floor where they exited into an empty hallway. So far, so good. He motioned for Charlotte to follow and crept down the hall to a door at the end of the hall. He jiggled the handle, played with the lock. The door opened onto a fire escape.

Rafe went first. On the metal fire escape, he ducked and peeked through the bars at the chaos in the street below. Two ambulances and four police cars blocked traffic. A crowd of watchers gathered on the sidewalk, chatting and drinking.

He scanned until he saw a man who stood alone and didn't seem to be observing the police action. Instead, he stared at the building, watching. He tilted his head and looked up.

Though Rafe had only seem him once before from a distance, he recognized Woodbridge.

Chapter Eighteen

Nervous, Alyssa paced on the wood floor in the front shop at Dragon's Blood Voodoo Emporium. Moments ago, she'd gotten a text from Rafe, warning her to be on the lookout for Woodbridge and his buddies. Her thumb rubbed the leather of the gris-gris amulet that hung from her neck, and she prayed that Rafe was unharmed. Sending him to meet with her aunt might have been a mistake, but she couldn't ignore the signs of danger that pointed at Charlotte like daggers.

Sitting outside the door by the front window, Sheila Marie kept watch for Rafe and the luxurious Mercedes. The night shadows didn't dim her vivid clothing. If anything, she seemed more colorful. She held a wooden drum between her knees and tapped a rhythm on the tautly stretched head. More than once, she pointed tourists toward another shop and told them to come back in fifteen minutes. Jolene had asked her to keep people away until they knew Rafe was all right. Though the fortune teller couldn't really see the future, she didn't want to take a chance that a tourist would be injured in her shop.

Jolene poked her head around the bamboo curtain and flashed a too-bright, toothy grin that hinted at mischief. "May I introduce you to my dearest companion?"

Reluctantly, Alyssa said, "Okay."

With her arms spread wide and her hands gesturing gracefully, Jolene stepped into the front of the shop and slowly turned in a circle so Alyssa had a chance to admire the companion she'd mentioned: an eight-foot-long, brown-and-black-patterned snake. Alyssa didn't have a problem with reptiles. One of her friends in Chicago was a stripper who used snakes in her act.

"Burmese python," Alyssa said. "May I touch her?"

"She would enjoy being touched. Dominique is my sacred serpent, a creature of great wisdom and magic."

Alyssa stroked the smooth skin, marveling at the muscularity of the snake as it coiled around Jolene's arm. "Are snakes important in voodoo?"

"I don't use Dominique as much as I could," she confided. "But she's very helpful when it comes to warding off bad people. Many fear the snake."

"A matter of taste."

Carrying her drum, Sheila Marie bustled through the front door and charged toward the back of the shop. "I saw the fine Mercedes. Rafe is almost here. He gonna come through the back door, like I told him. Go, Alyssa. Wait for him."

"Hide in the closet," Jolene said. "Don't come out until I give you the signal."

Alyssa wasn't bothered by the Burmese python, but she didn't know how Rafe would feel. "Do you have any of Dominique's friends stored in the closet?"

"There's a cage full of food. Rats."

"Okay."

She ducked behind the curtain but didn't rush to get into the closet with the rats. Instead, she peeked into the front of the shop, where Sheila Marie had settled down with her drum. Jolene went out the door, chanting and dancing with her snake. When she returned, a few tourists came with her. Within five minutes, others arrived. They must have been locals, because they were carrying their own drums and singing their own tunes.

Woodbridge stepped through the front door. She immediately recognized his hatchet jaw. As she pivoted toward the rear of the shop, she saw Rafe enter. Charlotte was with him, but Alyssa barely noticed her aunt. Rafe was the center of her world.

She dashed across the room and leaped into his arms. He was here. He was safe. Everything would be all right. She wanted to indulge in a long, deep kiss, but now wasn't the time.

Though the drumming and dancing were loud, he kept his voice low. "What's all the noise from the front of the shop?"

"The voodoo dance of the sacred serpent." She grabbed his hand and pulled him toward the closet. "Jolene said to wait here. Aunt Charlotte, that means you, too."

Muttering under her breath, she followed them. "You two have really made a mess of things. I was doing just fine until I came to New Orleans."

Sadly, the feeling of disgust was mutual. Alyssa would like nothing better than to build a loving relationship with the only person left in her family, but Charlotte wasn't the happy, imaginative, loving aunt who'd played games with her when she was a child. This silver-haired woman with the beautiful voice was cold, bitter and deceptive.

"We didn't bring you here." Alyssa opened the door to the closet. "By the way, there's a cage full of rats in here. Don't scream unless you want to die."

"I'm too tough to scream. Why would I die? Who's after you now?"

She looked up at Rafe. "I saw Woodbridge come into the front of the shop."

He hustled them into the closet and pulled the door almost all the way closed. They could still hear the drumming and chanting. Jolene's voice was louder than the others'.

In a tuneless wail, she called out, "Death is coming, coming for us all. Feel his icy presence. Welcome him. The serpent will bring the truth."

A man gave a hoarse shout. "Get that thing away from me!"

"Death is very near to you."

"I mean it, lady. I'll kill that snake."

"And burn in the damnation fires for eternity." She let out a cry. "Look at him! People, look at his feet. He has blood on his shoes. Who did he kill?"

"Back off, voodoo bitch. I'm out of here."

In the closet, Alyssa looked up at Rafe. Just enough light leaked through the crack in the door for her to see the dimple on his chin. His head tilted down, and she knew he was looking at her. She asked, "Was Jolene talking to Woodbridge?"

"I wouldn't be surprised to find out that he has blood on his shoes."

"Who died?"

"Jessop was badly beaten. We called the paramedics, and I'm hoping he'll survive."

"And you suspect Woodbridge." In her mind, she'd placed Jessop into the bad-guy camp along with Davidoff and Charlotte. Still, it was possible that he was working for someone else. Double-crossing each other seemed to be standard procedure, which didn't explain the attack. "Why would Woodbridge take that kind of risk? Why assault a fed?"

"Don't be stupid," Charlotte growled. "They all want

the money. Until you tell them where it is or how to get it, they'll keep coming after you."

"I don't know anything, but that doesn't mean I'm stupid."

"Call it naive," Charlotte said. "Would you please change places with me? I don't want to be back here. The shelf with the rat cage is right next to my nose."

Alyssa ignored her aunt's complaint. "You're as bad as they are. You thought you could get me to talk. Well, guess what? The joke's on you. I'm not lying. I don't have a secret."

"But I do," Charlotte said ominously. "This is your last chance, sweetheart. If we put our heads together, we might figure this out. I can tell you about the contacts I made with Frankie."

"From ten years ago," Rafe said. "I expect we'll find that half of them are in jail and the others are dead."

"He's right," Alyssa said. "You don't have much to bargain with. Who are you working for, Charlotte? It is Davidoff?"

"Not a chance. That bastard crossed a line, and I can't forgive him. He's evil to the core."

Alyssa wondered what Davidoff could have done to exceed her aunt's very minimal threshold for bad behavior. Charlotte didn't have a problem with stealing, cheating and deception. Nor did she seem worried about Jessop getting beaten so badly that he had to go to the hospital. Did she draw the line at murder?

"Suppose I agree to work with you," Alyssa said. "Where would we start?"

"It's obvious. We need to sit down with your old buddy Max Horowitz."

Alyssa was glad they were in a dark closet where panic couldn't be seen on her face. The raucous noise from the other room covered the guilty tremor in her voice. "Mr. Horowitz disappeared. Why do you think I'd know where he is?"

"You're closer to him than anyone else."

And she couldn't betray him, couldn't even tell Rafe about the phone call she'd made less than an hour ago. "I don't know where he's hiding." *That much was true.* "And I can't think of a single logical reason he'd steal from his own pawnshop." *Also true.*

"I'll give you a tidbit of information for free," Charlotte said. "There's a forger in Chicago who has information about a murder. It's all about the paint. I've known about this for a couple of months, but I couldn't go to the authorities. You can."

"This cryptic thing doesn't work for me," Alyssa said. "Just tell me."

"Later," Charlotte said. "I've got to run. Goodbye, sweetheart."

"Wait," Rafe said. "The plan was for all three of us to leave together. We can drop you off at a hotel or at the airport."

"Plans change." She shoved her way past them to the front of the closet, stepped into the back room of the shop and shuddered from head to toe. "This place stinks. All that weird stuff in jars gives me the creeps."

As Alyssa watched her aunt stride toward the rear door of the shop, she wondered if she'd ever see the woman again. In memory, she flashed back to a summer day in Chicago when she was nine or ten. Her mom and Charlotte had just finished a set of tennis and were both wearing whites. She'd thought they looked like angels. "Goodbye, Aunt Charlotte."

Alyssa retreated into the closet with Rafe. Now that they were alone, she didn't hesitate to snuggle against his chest. His arms draped over her shoulders, and he pulled her closer. His warmth comforted her. She couldn't hear the beating of his heart over the loud drumming and chanting from the other room, but she felt his vitality and his pulse. While they'd been apart, she was terrified of losing him.

Gently, he kissed her forehead, probably not intending to be sexy, but her engine was already revved. After they'd made love, she couldn't go back to the way it was before when they were merely friends. They were lovers. He knew the secrets of her body and vice versa.

Taking advantage of that knowledge, she went up on her tiptoes and nuzzled against a sensitive place on his throat just beside his carotid artery. He gave a low moan that only she could hear.

"A question, *cher*. Why are we still in the closet?"

"Jolene said to stay until she gave the signal, and she has a very long snake." She kissed his throat again. "She understands reptiles. It only took a minute for her to pick Woodbridge out of the crowd."

"The blood on his shoes was a clue."

"What's our plan?"

"I suggest that we leave here, get into the car and return to the safe house."

More specifically, they'd return to his bed at the safe house. "Here's what worries me. How did Woodbridge know we were here? Did he follow you?"

"It's possible." He shrugged. "After we found Jessop, we had to wait for paramedics and didn't have time to plan a careful exit. We went down the fire escape, a messy retreat. He could have seen us."

She was beginning to know Rafe well enough that she could read between the lines. There was something he wasn't telling her. "Any other theory?"

"I suspect Charlotte is hooked into a tracking device, either voluntarily or someone slipped it into her handbag. Previously, I thought Jessop was monitoring her, but Woodbridge and his cohorts might be the ones keeping tabs on her."

"Too complicated." She nibbled at his throat, tasting the salty flavor of his skin. "I wish I had a scorecard that told me who was playing on which team."

Aunt Charlotte seemed adamant about hating Davidoff, but she was a liar.

If Jessop was Davidoff's contact in New Orleans, why was he beaten? Maybe Woodbridge was working for somebody else, like the Leones in Florida.

The Russian bride of Ray McGill might want revenge against Alyssa for her testimony against her sleazebag husband.

"In the future," she said, "I'll stick to juggling numbers. They're not as complicated as people. By the way, how did you know to go around to the back entrance to the shop?"

"Sheila Marie and I have been texting."

"She's wonderful. Whatever you pay her as a confidential informant, it's not enough. And I like Jolene, as well. Has she ever given you a reading?"

"Many times. After I left the FBI, she predicted a long journey across water and great wealth. What did she tell you?"

She hesitated, not wanting to confess her link to Mr. Horowitz but wanting to be completely transparent with Rafe. "There was something about a tall, dark, handsome man."

"I'm tall and dark. Two out of three is not so bad. *C'est moi!*"

He was also undeniably handsome, but she didn't need

to tell him. Rafe had a healthy ego. Her thoughts were interrupted by what sounded like a door being opened. Had Charlotte forgotten to lock it before she abandoned them? "Did you hear that?"

He peeked through the partially open closet door. "It's Woodbridge. He has a gun."

And the closet was the most obvious hiding place. After a cursory look at the rest of the back room, he would surely open this door and find them. They were in big trouble.

But then she had an idea. Woodbridge was afraid of snakes. Maybe rats would have the same effect. She took the mesh cage off the shelf and tried to squeeze past Rafe. "Let me by. This will freak him out."

"What are you doing? Setting free the rats?"

"Yep."

"If we were in a cartoon, I would agree to your plan." With his gun in one hand and his phone in the other, he peeked through the slit in the door. "Stay behind me."

Her adrenaline was already pumping, and her pulse raced. Her rational mind told her that she should be terrified. When Woodbridge opened that door, he'd start firing. Rafe would be forced to do the same. Either way, the result was a bloodbath. She ought to be scared to death, but she wasn't. She believed they'd get through this. Maybe the gris-gris protected her, or maybe she trusted Rafe. She tugged at his sleeve. "What's Woodbridge doing out there?"

"Poking around, touching things, handling the beads and jewelry. He keeps checking a small electronic device and looking toward the front of the shop."

"A tracking device that Charlotte was carrying?"

"That's my best guess."

The atmosphere shifted. The rhythm of the chants

sped up, and the volume turned up to high. Alyssa heard Sheila Marie shout, "Look here!"

She must have charged through the bamboo curtain. She continued, "People, do you see? The thief is here. He be stealing our treasures with his bloody hands."

Jolene joined in. "The sacred serpent sees all. Her poison will make his fingers wither into stumps, and he will die."

Alyssa appreciated the drama of Jolene's threat, even though she knew for a fact that Burmese pythons weren't venomous. No doubt Jolene was parading around with her favorite companion, Dominique, held high over her head. Alyssa heard the sounds of people running and dancing and drumming and singing.

"This is hot as the devil's fire," Sheila Marie shouted.

Alyssa thought of the mystery stew boiling on the hot plate. "What's she doing?"

"She's got a pot, and she's getting ready to throw whatever is in it." There was a scream. Rafe continued, "That was Woodbridge. He's running. A sensible move."

She heard the back door slam.

"The thief is gone," Jolene announced. "Come with me to the front. We will speak of the future and the past and these precious moments in between."

The crowd followed her instructions, which—Alyssa suspected—would lead to readings along with the sale of gris-gris and love potions. She looked up at Rafe and said, "This is the most amazing hideout."

"When I'm here, I never know what to expect."

Sheila Marie opened the closet door. "You okay?"

"How did you know that we needed help?" Alyssa asked.

"The magic of my cell phone. It is not as exotic as voodoo but more efficient. Your tall, handsome man sent a text." She tapped Rafe on the chest and pulled Alyssa out of the closet. "How come you're holding the rats?"

"I thought that if I released them from the cage, they might run after the bad guy."

"Attack rats?"

"It's not like I gave them tiny guns and helmets." She returned the rats to the shelf in the closet. "I like your way better. It sounded like you scared Woodbridge half to death."

"He won't be showing his ugly mug around here again."

Rafe gave her a hug and thanked her. "Give my love to Jolene. We'd better go while Woodbridge is still too scared to tiptoe into the voodoo shops."

On the street, she stuck to him like a shadow as he dodged the light and kept to the darkness. "We're almost to the car," he said. "I found parking on the street."

She couldn't wait to sink into the comfortable seat of the Mercedes, sit back and ride to the safe house. Only a few days ago, she'd risked her life trying to escape from Rafe. Now she thought of the house as her home, the place where they were surrounded by security and no one could find them.

Why had they left that sweet little nest? Oh yeah, they'd ventured out to warn her aunt that Davidoff was on his way to New Orleans, which was definitely the right thing to do, even though Charlotte hadn't paid much attention and had left them in the lurch.

They rounded a corner. Rafe took two steps and came to a dead halt.

"What's wrong?"

He gestured to an open space at the curb. "Your aunt stole my Mercedes."

Chapter Nineteen

Fuming, Rafe stared at the empty space where the Mercedes should have been waiting for him. There were no words sufficient for his rage. *I trusted that woman. I saved her from being arrested by NOPD.* And this was his payback?

He clasped Alyssa's arm and pulled her off the sidewalk into a nearby alley. Halfway down, he ducked into a darkened doorway, where they wouldn't be seen. His chest was tight, and his lungs constricted. He inhaled a gulp of night air, thick with humidity. Garbage from the seafood restaurant at the front of the alley reeked of onions and fish guts.

There had to be some mistake! He felt around in the pockets of his windbreaker and his jeans, searching for the key fob needed to start the Mercedes. He found his own keys, his Swiss Army knife, an extra clip for his Glock, his wallet and his phone, but the fob for Chance's car was gone. While they'd been jammed in the closet together, Charlotte must have picked his pocket—a skill he wasn't surprised to learn that she possessed.

"I guess we need a new plan," Alyssa said with a grin that was too cheerful for his current mood. "We could hop onto a streetcar and go back to the house."

He hated that solution. Trapped inside a streetcar,

they were vulnerable to Woodbridge and the men he was working with. Rafe knew there would be more thugs out on the street, looking for them. Even if Woodbridge had started the evening on his own, he would have summoned backup when he knew their location.

"No streetcars," he said.

"Maybe we can stay in the voodoo shop for the night," she suggested.

For a moment, Rafe considered returning to the Dragon's Blood and lying low, allowing Jolene's python to protect them. But he didn't want to bring more trouble to her doorstep. One encounter was enough.

"I've got a plan," he said darkly. "A simple plan."

She looked up at him expectantly. "What is it?"

He could track down Charlotte and tap her on the shoulder. When she turned around, he could drill a neat bullet hole into the center of her forehead. Ha! The plan gave him momentary relief. She deserved retribution. She'd put them in danger. Right now, she was probably at the airport buying a ticket to an unknown destination. But of course, he wouldn't take such drastic revenge. "Never mind."

Alyssa's eyes were bright. Her attitude determined. In spite of the constant threat and betrayal by her aunt, she remained hopeful. He doubted that she thought of herself as courageous, but the description was apt. He needed to focus and to find the best way to protect her.

"Here's another plan," he said. "Where do you keep your getaway car?"

"A long-term parking structure over by the docks." She pumped her fist like the winner of a tennis match. "I knew that car was going to come in handy."

"Do you have the key?"

She bobbed her head. "In my backpack, I've got the

car key and the card to get into and out of the parking garage. I'm so happy we're going to get it. I can really use all the clothes and shoes packed in the trunk."

"I'm guessing that you selected a parking garage that stayed open late."

"Twenty-four-hour access, and there are two night watchmen on duty." She beamed a radiant smile that lit up the dingy alley. "I know which streetcars to take to get there. We'd only need one transfer."

Hadn't he already told her that he wasn't going to hop onto a streetcar like a schoolboy headed to classes? "We'll take a taxi. With all the hotels around here, it won't be hard to find one."

Hand in hand, they walked to the end of the alley. Before they stepped into the comparative light of the street, she pulled her cap down on her forehead—a minimal disguise but better than nothing. All he could do was hunch his shoulders to look shorter and blend in with the other people on the street.

He glanced across the street, looking for the people who were looking for them. In this touristy area, most of the pedestrians were walking in couples or groups. The car traffic on the narrow streets of the French Quarter was minimal, limited mostly to taxis and rickshaws and scooters. The lack of vehicles suited Rafe very well. With the glare from neon streetlights bouncing off windshields, it was difficult to see the interior of a car.

She nudged his shoulder. "Lighten up. You're supposed to be a happy tourist."

Taking on that undercover role, he splashed a smile onto his face. "Do you think we should pretend to be lovers?"

"Pretend?" She threw her arm around his neck and pulled him down for a kiss. "Was that convincing?"

"That was a start."

Though he enjoyed the sensations that came when her body pressed against his, Rafe maintained his surveillance. He noticed two men standing at the street corner who didn't cross when the light changed from red to green. One of them spoke into a phone. The other wore sunglasses.

Smoothly, he guided Alyssa into an open storefront packed with colorful souvenirs: postcards, scarves and T-shirts. He pretended to admire a bottle of Tabasco sauce. "Check out the men on the corner."

"I see them. Sunglasses at night are a dumb disguise." She dangled a string of Mardi Gras beads from her fingers. "They're just standing there, not moving."

"We should double back."

They didn't have to wait for a distraction. A casual four-piece brass band, including a tuba, marched down the sidewalk, pausing to give a shout every few steps. *Gotta love New Orleans.* Rafe tugged her hand, and they went back the way they'd come.

Though he didn't actually see Woodbridge, he felt the pursuit as surely as a chipmunk senses the approach of a hawk. On these streets, people were watching them and listening for the sound of their voices. They needed to escape the French Quarter.

Rafe directed their route closer to the Bourbon Street hotels, where he had no problem hailing a black-and-white cab. He told the driver to take them to Louis Armstrong Airport. When the cabbie—a woman with curly red hair and a derby hat—set out, he watched through the back window, trying to spot suspicious characters on the street and the sidewalk.

"Why are we going to the airport?" she asked. "Are you going to look for Charlotte?"

He was still too angry to face that woman. "I want to get away from the crowd in the French Quarter. On the open road, we'll be able to see if we're being followed. I expect to change cabs at least twice more before we go to your parking facility."

In his mind, he laid out a grid of the city, fitting together the unique parishes of New Orleans like pieces of a puzzle. In addition to the residential streets and areas dedicated to business and commerce, there were historic structures and government buildings. Throughout this map of irregular shapes were slivers of the tourism industry, restaurants, art venues and an amazing selection of music, ranging from smooth jazz to Samoan war chants. Visitors had a wide choice of activity, and the people who lived here had it all.

He gazed through the window as the streets unfolded around him. His city. He never wanted to leave again. Somehow, he needed to convince Alyssa to stay here with him.

After reversing their route to the airport, he directed their taxi to the neighborhood around Tulane, where he'd grown up, then to a Marriott on Canal Street. Anyone following them would be confused. The red-haired taxi driver told him that he was *couyon*, crazy.

He heard Alyssa's ringtone. She took her phone from her backpack and checked the identification. "Anonymous," she said. "It's not the same number Charlotte had before, but I'll bet it's her."

He agreed. When Charlotte stole the Mercedes, she had recommitted to her life on the run. The first thing she needed was a new disposable phone. "Put her on speaker."

Alyssa answered. "Who's this?"

"I need to explain something," Charlotte said.

"If you're planning to make some kind of lame excuse for taking the car, don't bother. That was just plain wrong. It's not even our car."

"I'll get the car back to you."

Rafe didn't believe a word that woman said, not a word. He could have warned her that Chance was the kind of guy who had electronic alerts installed on his Mercedes. At the stroke of a few computer keys, he'd know her location.

"Are you at the airport?" Alyssa asked. "We could come and pick you up."

Slowly, Rafe shook his head from side to side. *No more favors for Auntie Charlotte.*

"Listen to me," Charlotte said. "Remember when I told you about that forger who had evidence about a murder?"

"I remember."

"This evidence is actually one of the reasons I wanted to find you in New Orleans. It's important, sweetheart. I guess I should start by telling you that this guy isn't a great forger, but he's an excellent tattoo artist."

"How would you know?" Alyssa asked.

"I've had some work done. There's an angel on my heart and a butterfly on my bottom. Also, this guy has a reputation for doing amazing custom paint jobs on fancy cars."

Rafe felt himself being drawn in to her story. Angry as he was at Alyssa's aunt, he admired her ability to spin a web of deceit. She'd have made a good undercover operative.

"This artist," Charlotte said, "came into possession of a couple of paint chips from a custom job on a Beamer that had been in an accident. The front end was all caved in. At the time, my artist friend was working in a chop shop where they break down stolen cars and—"

"I know what a chop shop is," Alyssa interrupted.

"So you understand when I tell you that the car was completely refurbished and is unidentifiable as having been in a hit-and-run accident."

Like the accident that killed her mother. The blood drained from Alyssa's face. Her arm went limp, and Rafe scooped the phone off the seat of the taxi. Alyssa stared straight ahead, clearly devastated.

If this was some kind of scam, he'd have to revisit his revenge fantasy about shooting Charlotte. He kept his voice low. "What else do you know?"

"By the way, Rafe, I really do feel bad about taking off with the Mercedes."

He didn't believe her. "Tell me about the paint chip."

"I can do better than tell you," she said. "Is Alyssa all right?"

"She's in shock."

"I'm glad you're with her. She needs someone to support her."

He wasn't going to let himself get thrown off track by Charlotte's phony concern. "When did the tattoo artist find this paint chip?"

"About five years ago."

That fit the time frame for her mother's death. "Where did he find it?"

"The chop shop belongs to Diamond Jim. I can't say for sure who was driving, but Davidoff has information that I'm guessing he never shared with the police."

In itself, a paint chip—even an exact match to the hit-and-run vehicle—didn't prove anything. "I need more information."

"How about this for a headline—Alyssa has the chip. It's in a plastic baggie, and I tucked it into her backpack. That's why I called. I didn't want her to accidentally throw it out."

She still wasn't telling him everything. Pulling information from her was harder than wrenching a snack from the jaws of a snapping turtle. "Why do you believe this is evidence?"

"I forgot the most important part." With some frustration, he imagined her sly, Cheshire cat grin. She was playing with him. "There's blood on the paint chips. I didn't have a way to test DNA, but if someone had friends in law enforcement, they might get those tests done, which would give the identity of the victim."

And provide a link between Davidoff's chop shop and the victim of a hit-and-run from five years ago… Alyssa's mom. "That's good stuff."

"Damn right," she said.

"I might have to forgive you, after all."

"Essentially, I'm a good person. Give my niece a big hug and keep me posted." She made kissy noises. "Adieu, Rafe."

"*Au revoir*, crazy lady."

He gathered Alyssa in his arms and held her without speaking while he sent the cabbie on another wild ride through the Treme parish and up to Gentilly. The music from the radio was oldies and Elvis. The ride wasn't unpleasant.

Finally, Alyssa spoke. "I should be pleased. I might find out who killed my mom. But I feel…empty."

"You need time to think," he said. "Here's a new plan. Instead of hanging around in the city, trying to piece together clues while the bad guys are after us, we leave town. From a distance, I might be able to work with my FBI contacts and find someone we can trust."

She nodded. "Maybe that's for the best."

After returning to Canal Street, they disembarked, picked up another ride and went on a circuitous route before switching to yet another cab outside another hotel in the central business district. Tucked into the rear of that taxi, he kissed her cheek. "Are we close to your parking garage?"

"Less than a mile away." With her thumb, she stroked the leather surface of the voodoo gris-gris. Her eyelids drooped, and she yawned. "I'm so tired."

He might have pushed her too hard. "If you want, we can stay at this hotel."

"I'd rather get this done." She sat up straight and shook herself. "We have a plan, and I want to follow through."

In the warehouse district near the docks, they left the taxi outside a parking garage with a straggly palm tree and a vertical neon sign that said Park. The homely four-story blond-brick structure with windows marching in horizontal lines on each floor reminded him of her storage warehouse near Café du Monde.

He asked, "Do you have a thing for ugly brick buildings?"

"I spent most of my life in cities, so I guess the answer is yes."

"What does the garage look like inside?"

"Totally organized. The exit ramp is in the middle, and cars are parked on each side. Mine is on the fourth floor." She pointed to the double entrance and exit with wooden arms blocking each side. "The night watchman's booth is over there. We need to check in with him."

She paused to dig through her backpack, mumbling something about her alias for this garage. "Don't call me Alyssa or Lara. This car is in the name of Wanda Wilson. I need to show her ID to the guard."

"The name doesn't fit, *cher*. I think of Wanda as a taller woman, maybe a blonde."

"You're wrong," she said. "When I choose my aliases, I usually stick to something related. Lara is short for Larissa, which sounds like Alyssa, which led to another fake name of Alice. Wanda came to me by surprise. I don't have friends or family named Wanda, don't know anybody named Wanda. Wanda Wilson reminds me of a mermaid. Am I babbling?"

"A bit."

"I'm excited, Rafe. This is almost over, which means we have a chance to try a normal life." She hesitated. "Is that something you want?"

He didn't think life with Lara/Larissa/Alyssa/Wanda would ever be considered normal. "When this is over, I want to be with you. We don't need a label. It doesn't have to be normal or exotic or anything else. Just you and me."

She planted a quick kiss on his mouth then dug deeper into her pack and pulled out the plastic baggie containing the precious chip of evidence. "It's hard to believe this little scrap of old paint could change my life. I want you to hold on to it, then you can give it to your DNA people."

The chip had been protected by bubble wrap before being placed in an envelope and tucked into the baggie for safekeeping. He tucked the small package into the inner jacket of his windbreaker, hoping it could actually be useful as evidence. Off the top of his head, he could think of dozens of reasons a defense attorney would object to a paint chip that had been passed from one person to the next without maintaining chain of evidence. But it was a starting point for reopening the investigation.

Retrieving her Chevy station wagon presented no particular problems. The twelve-year-old vehicle didn't have the horsepower or the luxury suspension of the Mercedes, but it was a decent ride. He drove carefully onto the city streets. At this hour on a Sunday night, the traffic was light, and he was ninety-nine percent sure that they weren't being followed. "I'm tempted to get on the highway right now."

"We need to wait until morning when I can go to the bank," she said. "I need the cash and credit cards from my safe-deposit box…and the thumb drive."

Though he wasn't anxious to pursue the investigation any further, he knew she wouldn't be safe until they found the missing millions. "We'll go early tomorrow, *à demain.*"

When he drove the Chevy onto the street where the safe house was located, he didn't feel the sense of relief that usually accompanied a return to home base. A lamp in the front room was lit, and the porch light was on. That was the way he'd left the house, and he hadn't received any security alerts on his phone.

He parked on the breezeway and unlocked the back door. As soon as he stepped inside, he smelled freshly brewed coffee. Something was wrong.

Alyssa charged past him. "I should unload some of the boxes from the car, but that can wait. Right now, I want to rest."

He turned on an overhead light in the kitchen.

Three men with guns drawn stood in the corners of the room. They had the drop on him. He couldn't react without putting Alyssa in mortal danger.

Sitting at the kitchen table, and cradling a mug of coffee in his beefy hands, was Viktor Davidoff.

Chapter Twenty

Her heart stopped beating. Alyssa felt her lungs shut
down. Drained of strength, her arms and legs went limp,
and yet she remained standing, held in place by invisible
strings while she stared into the face of the man who had
probably killed her mother. She barely knew Davidoff,
had only met him once or twice before. He hadn't made
much of an impression on her. Though his grooming
was sheer perfection from his shaved head to his neatly
trimmed black goatee and tailored suit, he had the rough,
thick hands of a peasant farmer.

His lips were moving. He seemed to be talking, but
the inside of her head filled with a static buzz, and she
couldn't hear his words. *I have to answer, can't just stand
and wait for these people to kill me. I have to be smart.*

Desperately, she wanted to survive, to escape this situation in one piece and bring Rafe along with her. After
all they'd been through, they deserved a chance.

She inhaled a huge gasp of air and immediately started
coughing. Trying to keep from falling, she grabbed the
back of one of the kitchen chairs and collapsed onto the
seat. A glass of water appeared on the table in front of her.
She took a sip and looked over the rim at the man who
sat opposite her. He wore a dark blue suit with a yellow
ascot fastened in place with a flashy piece of jewelry—a

diamond pin for Diamond Jim. His wristwatch was platinum. He wore one large ring on each hand, probably to inflict maximum damage when he was beating on some poor soul who dared to cross him.

She forced herself to keep looking at him, hiding her disdain. He didn't deserve pretty things. This man had played a part in killing her mother—he didn't deserve to live. Dark thoughts hammered inside her skull. She hated him, wanted revenge. Whatever she had to do, she was ready. He wasn't going to beat her.

"I almost fainted." She kept her tone low, soft and non-threatening. Since she didn't have the power to threaten Davidoff, she wanted to get inside his head. "I was shocked to see you, surprised and happy."

Like a grizzly bear watching his prey, he cocked his head to one side and focused intently. "Explain yourself, girl."

She glanced over her shoulder at Rafe, who was handcuffed with armed guards on either side of him. Anger clenched inside her, but she pushed it aside. "Please don't be upset with my bodyguard. He didn't mean to tell your secret, but I begged. I can be very persuasive."

"What is this secret?" Davidoff demanded.

"You know," she said, daring to be flirtatious. Her ploy was to be cute and seductive and make him like her enough to let her and Rafe live, at least until morning. "All my life, I've dreamed of this moment when I'd meet the man my mom loved so much that she left her beloved home in Savannah and moved to Chicago. I can't wait to get to know you, Father."

One of his thugs grunted in apparent disbelief, and she bolted to her feet to confront him. "You don't believe me? Well, let me show you the room he arranged exactly the way I like it. My father was worried about me. He hired a full-time bodyguard. That's true, isn't it?"

"She is correct," Davidoff said.

Gritting her teeth so she wouldn't vomit, she took a step closer to him. "May I embrace you, Father?"

He opened his arms. "Come to me."

When she touched him, her stomach curdled. Not only was the man a disgusting liar, but he wore too much aftershave. "Now that you're here," she said, "we can work together to find the missing millions."

"And how will we accomplish that?"

"Rafe can tell you our plan," she said. "Please take off the handcuffs."

Davidoff gestured, and his minions did as he indicated. The cuffs were removed, and Rafe was welcomed to the kitchen table. If there hadn't been three men with guns plus Davidoff, she thought Rafe might have lashed out. But he was smarter than that. In a few words, he explained how they needed to go to her safe-deposit box at the bank and compare her accounting data with the other information they had.

"What was your source for the original data?" Davidoff asked.

"Let's just say that I still have friends in the FBI."

"Friends like Jessop?"

"He was on your payroll," Rafe said. "Now he's in the hospital."

"Not on my orders," Davidoff said. "I was pleased with Jessop. He's a skilled agent, and there's always room for such a person in my organization. He managed to do the impossible and find this safe house."

"How?" Rafe asked bluntly.

She knew how proud Rafe was of his supposedly impregnable security. He had to be curious about how Davidoff and his thugs had found this place and managed to get inside without setting off the alarms. When she recalled the events of the day, she realized that Rafe's first encounter with Jessop was at the cemetery. Could he have planted a tracking device on Rafe's SUV? Even if he had, it wouldn't matter because they'd left that car with Chance before they returned to the house. If not a tracking device, then what?

She spoke up. "Can I guess?"

"You?" Davidoff sounded amused. "A pretty girl like you has no need to know about equipment and electronics."

"The way you bypassed security has to do with Rafe's phone," she said. "Jessop figured out how to break through the protective firewalls and read the security system on Rafe's phone."

Rafe groaned. "He cloned me. The FBI has been working on this technology for years. When Jessop was near my phone in the cemetery, he transferred my data to another phone."

"A clone," she said.

Davidoff reached over and patted her cheek in a parental gesture that would have been sweet if he really had been her long-lost father. "You're very bright," he said.

"I must take after you, Father."

"Call me Papa."

She suppressed her revulsion. "You're too kind, Papa."

"I found you in time," he said, claiming all the credit. "I saved you."

Apparently, Woodbridge and his thugs—the guys who beat up Jessop—were part of another faction. She needed to get away from Davidoff, needed to have time alone with Rafe to plan their escape. She stretched her arms over her head. "I'm so tired. May I go to bed, Papa?"

"Of course, my dear one. We can take care of the safe-deposit box in the morning."

Now came the tricky part. She decided on the brazen approach, taking Rafe's hand and giving a proprietary tug. "Come on," she said to him. "We should get some sleep."

"Not in the same room," Davidoff said.

"But, Papa, I like him. I mean, I really like him." She was shocked by her innate ability to act like a spoiled daughter. Was teenaged whining part of her DNA? "You want me to be happy, don't you?"

"I will decide if this man is good for you. Now, off to bed."

One of the thugs escorted her down the hall toward her bedroom. She had to stop in the bathroom first, where she locked the door, went to the toilet and puked. She was playing a dangerous game, and the stakes were literally life or death.

She splashed water on her face and looked at herself in the mirror over the sink. Her panic wasn't readily apparent, and she wondered if her DNA also included some of the deceit that made Charlotte such a good liar.

Alyssa needed an edge. She took out her phone and punched in the secret number for Mr. Horowitz. When the mechanical voice answered, she whispered the address of the safe house into the receiver. "Davidoff is holding me and Rafe here." She rattled off the address. "I need your help. Please."

He had to respond. Mr. Horowitz was her only chance.

As SOON AS Alyssa left the room, Davidoff turned toward Rafe. Stroking his goatee with his full lips curved in an evil grin, he looked like a villain from the old-fashioned movies his mama used to watch. Rafe missed his family; they would have liked Alyssa.

"You didn't tell me about the data she has hidden in her safe-deposit box," Davidoff said. "And you neglected to mention that you and Alyssa are intimate. These things seem disloyal, Rafe. I'm your employer."

"My relationship with her is very much to your advantage," Rafe said.

"How so?"

After Alyssa's Oscar-winning performance as the prodigal daughter, he needed to present a cover story of his own. Davidoff would never believe that he was a minion, but he might be able to work a deal. "If she trusts me and knows that I trust you, she'll cooperate. If you had told me from the start about the money, I might have gotten further with her instead of following her around for two weeks."

"You would have taken the millions for yourself," Davidoff said as he pushed the coffee mug away. "Where do you keep the vodka?"

"I don't actually live in this house. And I don't entertain."

"No vodka? I'll take care of it." He snapped his pudgy fingers at a very large man with an equally huge weapon. "Two bottles. We'll toast to our success in retrieving the money I lost at the pawnshop warehouse and the profit I will earn."

When Rafe reviewed Alyssa's work on the information Chance had given her, he'd noticed several expensive cars unaccounted for. "You lost a Lamborghini V12 when Frankie Leone was killed. That must have hurt."

"What do you know of cars?"

It was the perfect opening. Rafe slipped into his undercover identity as a former Grand Prix race car driver.

They talked until the vodka came. And then they talked some more.

When they were three shots into the bottle, Davidoff pinned him with an icy stare and said, "I like you, Rafe. I'll be sorry if I have to kill you."

Chapter Twenty-One

In spite of her fears and anger, Alyssa managed to sleep. It helped that she'd convinced one of Davidoff's minions to bring in her suitcase from the car, and she had a soft, comfortable nightshirt to wear in bed.

When her mattress bounced, she awakened instantly. If this was one of Davidoff's boys, she'd have to beat him to death with her crystal potpourri bowl. She heard murmuring and the word *cher*. There was only one person who called her that. "Rafe?"

"C'est moi." When he stretched out in the bed beside her, she couldn't believe it was really him. He smelled like booze. "You've been drinking."

"That's the vodka, *cher*." He got very close to her ear and said, "Gotta be careful. Watch out for hidden microphones and cameras."

"I found two devices, one under the table lamp and another on the dresser."

"Look at you, being so smart." He planted a sloppy kiss on her cheek. "Can I turn on the lamp? I want to see your pretty face."

"Does Davidoff know you're here?"

"I told him I was going to the bathroom." He turned on the light and gazed down at her. "You're beautiful, the most beautiful woman in the world."

"Do you still have your phone?" she asked. "In case I need to call you?"

"Nope, Davidoff took my cloned phone." He repeated the words. "Cloned phone, cloned phone. I wish I'd remembered that technology before I got within twenty yards of Jessop."

"You should leave before we get caught."

"I want to spend every minute with you. We don't have much time left."

This wasn't what she needed to hear. Alyssa was already disgusted with herself for pretending to be the daughter of a man she hated, a monster. But she'd been feeling that things were under control. "Does he know I'm…"

He shushed her before she could finish the sentence. "They could be listening."

"True."

"He's a businessman," Rafe said. "It's all about the bottom line."

"So if we find the money for him, he'll let us go."

He got close to her ear again. "If we deliver, he has no more use for us. On the other hand, we're expendable if we fail. A classic case of damned if we do and damned if we don't."

"How do we get out of this?"

"Look for a miracle," he said.

"That's not reassuring."

"It could happen. For example, what are the odds of a woman like you and a man like me getting together? Yet, here we are. When it comes to Davidoff and these guys who work for him, we stay alert and wait for something to turn up. Then we take advantage."

He swept her into his arms for a deep, passionate kiss that was better than she expected, given the amount of vodka he'd been drinking. Then he staggered to his feet and went out the door, leaving her with miserable thoughts about her own mortality. *Wait for a miracle.* Not the most useful advice—she needed specifics. Did miracles carry guns? Would the cavalry come riding over the hill?

Again, she took out her phone. This time, she sent a text to Mr. Horowitz with the address of the safe house and pertinent information. Why hadn't he answered her? He was her only chance, and he wasn't paying attention. She didn't want to imagine that something bad might have happened to him. She couldn't bear to lose another person she loved.

THE NEXT MORNING, Alyssa showered and dressed in a beige linen suit for her trip to the bank. Though she had the platform sandals that went with the outfit, she opted for more comfortable loafers that would be good for running. Instead of taking her huge backpack, she put selected items in a much smaller shoulder bag that contained her phone, her wallet with the necessary identification in her current name, keys and miscellaneous things, like lotion, sunglasses, a notepad and pen.

In the kitchen, Davidoff greeted her with a cup of coffee. "Not chicory," he said. "I hate that stuff."

Rafe sat at the kitchen table. In spite of his bloodshot eyes and stubble that was beginning to look like a beard, he was cool and handsome. He greeted her quietly.

In contrast, Davidoff boomed, "Your boyfriend can't handle his vodka."

She took advantage of another opportunity to remind Davidoff of their supposed connection. "He's not Russian, Papa. He's not like us."

He patted her shoulder. "You're a good girl."

"Are we going to the bank this morning?"

"Very soon," he said. "I'll go inside with you. After you open your box and take out the contents, we'll return to the car and come back here."

"I'm frightened," she said. "Do you know what happened to the guys who were after me, the ones who beat up on Jessop?"

"You have no need to worry. My men will protect you."

She tried a different tactic. "I'd feel a lot better if Rafe came along."

"You must be brave, little sparrow." His grin looked sinister, as though he'd just tasted something unpleasant. "Let's go. Take your coffee."

Before leaving, she gazed at Rafe, trying to communicate silently and tell him that she wasn't giving up hope. Something miraculous would turn up.

She and Davidoff sat in the back of a vintage Lincoln Town Car—a spacious, gorgeous vehicle. Two of his henchmen were in the front: one was the driver and the other held his semiautomatic weapon on his lap. She considered jumping out of the moving car but decided against it. If she ran, Rafe would pay the price.

While Davidoff talked about New Orleans as though he knew his way around this complicated city, she gazed at him with the kind of adoration a daughter reserves for her father. She nodded and smiled at every dopey thing he said. How was she going to escape? How could she get a message to the authorities?

At the bank in the central business district, they entered the dimly lit underground parking lot. Davidoff ordered his men to wait and then took her arm to escort her. She could feel the endgame approaching. Her pulse accelerated, and she began to sweat.

"You're trembling," Davidoff said.

"I told you I was scared."

"You'll be fine. I will be standing close beside you."

And that was the problem. She didn't want him anywhere near her. If she could put some distance between them, she might make a break for it. Her opportunity came when the bank official—a tall, lean black man with an officious manner—escorted her into the private room beside the safe-deposit vaults.

"I'll leave you alone," the official said. "If you need help, my name is Mr. Morgan."

Davidoff was right behind him. "I need to get into the room with her."

"I'm sorry, sir. That's against our rules."

"Your damn rules must be changed."

While Mr. Morgan called his supervisor for permission, she took the notepad from her shoulder bag and scribbled three words: *I'm. Being. Kidnapped.*

There was no time for more explanation. As soon as Morgan opened the door, Davidoff charged into the private room, roaring like a bull. Though she tried to placate him, he wasn't accustomed to having his will thwarted. Quickly, she emptied her box into a shopping bag she'd brought for the purpose.

As they left the room, she pressed the note into Mr. Morgan's hand, and she almost got away with it. Her miracle crashed and burned when Davidoff pounced. He snatched the small scrap of paper, opened it, read it and turned his large, shaved head toward her. "This is not funny, little sparrow."

"I wasn't making a joke."

"Please excuse her," he said to Morgan. This time when he grabbed her arm, his grip tightened like a vise. "Don't try any other stunts or Rafe is dead."

She wanted to scream her lungs out, but she couldn't take the chance. There might be a way to talk him back into a good mood.

In the underground parking lot, he slammed her against the rear left fender of the Lincoln. "Why?"

"I want to get away from you. Just let me go."

"But you are my beloved." He sneered. "My long-lost daughter."

"We both know that's a lie. You tried to scam me but made a mistake. The music box played the wrong tune."

He signaled to the driver. "Open the trunk."

Before she had time to object, the other thug shoved her into the extra-large trunk space and closed the lid. Davidoff issued one more order, and he spoke loudly enough that she could hear.

"Call the house," he said. "Kill Rafe."

RAFE SAT UNCOMFORTABLY on the kitchen chair. After Davidoff left with Alyssa, the two guys who stayed behind replaced his handcuffs so he wouldn't attempt an escape. He watched as the supersize thug took a call. The only word he said repeatedly was "yeah."

He ended the call, gave Rafe a wink and drew his semiautomatic. The bore of the gun barrel pointing at Rafe's belly gaped as wide as a cannon's maw. He hoped death would be fast.

The back door crashed open. Three guys in lace-up boots, helmets and military garb charged inside. Taking advantage of the element of surprise, they disarmed Davidoff's thugs in a few minutes. One of them unlocked Rafe's handcuffs. He had just enough time to stand up before their leader entered.

He was slightly below average height, white-haired with a walrus mustache to match. He wore baggy khakis, a short-sleeved white shirt and a plaid sweater vest. He held out his hand to Rafe and said, "I'm Max Horowitz."

"And I'm Rafe Fournier. Thank you for saving my life."

"Lara mentioned meeting a fellow. Is that you?"

"I hope so," he said.

"Where is she?"

"On her way back from the bank, but she should have been here by now."

Horowitz took his phone from his pocket and punched in a number, leaving the phone on speaker. "I told her to call me if she ran into trouble. She's the only person with this number." Impatiently, he tapped his foot on the kitchen floor. "If she doesn't answer, how will we find her?"

"Mr. Horowitz, is that you?" Her voice was a little choppy.

"It is, and I'm here with Rafe. Where are you?"

"In the trunk of a vintage Lincoln Town Car," she said. "Davidoff is really mad. I've got to get away from him."

"I don't know my way around the city as well as Rafe," Horowitz said, turning to him.

She gave a small cry. "Rafe is still alive! Thank God! Davidoff told them to kill him."

"We'll talk later, *cher*. Do you know where you are?"

"Definitely not headed back to the house. The driver seems to be lost. I kicked out part of the taillight, and I can see bits of scenery as we go past."

"Tell me what you see."

"We were wandering around by the docks and warehouses. Now the houses look like Treme. We're heading toward Canal Street."

Last night's tour of the city was proving useful. While she described various landmarks, he and Horowitz and two of his three paramilitary guys got into an SUV and tried to follow her directions.

Back and forth and around, it felt like they were on Mister Toad's Wild Ride until she came up with a definitive location. "We're in the Ninth Ward."

"That's a lot of real estate," said one of the men working for Horowitz.

Rafe spoke gently into the phone. "Alyssa, try to see some of the houses. We need more clues to tell us where you are."

"I can't."

She went quiet, and he thought he heard gentle weeping. "Don't give up. It's time for our miracle."

"Purple with yellow stripes," she said. "I remember seeing this house when we were here before. It's not far from the church. And we're stopping."

He barked directions at the guy who was driving, and they whipped through the streets of the Ninth Ward. The big, beautiful Town Car wasn't hard to spot. Was Alyssa still in the trunk? Was she okay?

They approached the location with military precision. Rafe didn't know where Horowitz had found these guys, but they were top-notch. Davidoff and his men weren't expecting an assault and were easily overpowered. Before they had time to react, they were disarmed and cuffed. Their leader flipped open the trunk of the big car, and Alyssa popped up.

When she ran to him and threw her arms around his neck, Rafe had never felt so fulfilled and complete. He wasn't ready to declare his intentions, but he felt love in every fiber of his body. He wanted to be with her forever.

She showered a half dozen kisses on his face. "You told me there would be a miracle. And you were right."

For a few moments, she transferred her affection to

Horowitz, who was absolutely delighted to see her. Then she leaped back to Rafe.

Her beige linen suit was ruined after being in the trunk. She had smudges on her cheeks, and her eye makeup was a mess. Still, he thought she was beautiful, prettier than Scarlett O'Hara and all the other southern belles combined.

"Do you know the worst part of this mess?" she asked her two men. "I had to pretend that Davidoff was my father. That could never be. He's a monster."

"You're right," Horowitz said. "I know, because I'm your father."

Rafe wasn't as shocked as he might have been. Max Horowitz had taken care of her for many years, giving her a job and sending her to college. Those considerations went far beyond the duties of an employer. Max had trusted her with his secrets.

The old man reached into his pocket and produced a photograph. "Here's proof."

Alyssa held the picture in both hands. "This is you, but your hair isn't gray. And that's Mom, and she's looking at you like you're her whole world."

He nodded. "That's the way you look at Rafe."

"And the child in the picture?"

"I'm sure you recognize the teddy bear," he said.

"It's mine. Bobo Bear. This is crazy. We look like such a normal family."

"Your mother and I were soulmates. We tried so hard to protect you and make a good life that we lost track of what was truly important. Don't be foolish like we were. Put your love first and foremost, and then everything else will fall into place."

"I agree with every word you say."

"Your father is wise," Rafe said.

She took his hands in hers. "You are my pirate, my bodyguard and my dearest love. I never want to be apart from you again."

He cinched his arm around her slender waist and pulled her close for the first of an eternity of kisses.

Epilogue

Drinking sweetened tea on the veranda outside Chance's plantation home, Rafe finished telling the story to his friend as they watched Alyssa ride across the front field on a prancing Arabian mare. She was laughing with her head thrown back, and she looked like the embodiment of freedom.

"A mostly happy ending," Chance said, "especially since I got my Mercedes back."

"More than mostly happy," Rafe said. "This was perfect. Woodbridge and his friends got picked up by the cops and will rot in jail for many years."

"What about Davidoff?"

"On trial in Chicago," Rafe said. "The paint chip was enough to reopen the investigation into the hit-and-run murder of her mom."

"Here's a big fat flaw in your story—you and Alyssa didn't get your hands on the millions of dollars."

"And neither did anybody else. Frankie Leone had been pilfering little bits and pieces over the years, nowhere near millions. That big payoff never really existed except on paper, which is something Alyssa would have found when she compared the data from her records and the stuff you got on your computer hack. Horowitz set up the lure to draw out a bunch of smugglers. The FBI and ATF moved in and scooped them up."

"I guess you're right," Chance said. "What are you going to do to top this story?"

Rafe took a small box from his pocket and flipped open the lid. "Five carats, flawless, canary yellow."

"Nice. That should lead to another extremely happy ending."

* * * * *

EXPOSING COLTON SECRETS

MARIE FERRARELLA

To
Melany Yee,
If There Was A Catalog
Featuring The Perfect Daughter-In-Law,
You Would Have Been On The Cover

Prologue

All in all, Brooks Colton felt that he was doing rather well for himself. Oh, nowhere near as well as he might have done had he gone into the family business the way his father had wanted and expected him to, but he definitely wasn't falling on his face the way his father had predicted he would.

As a matter of fact, he was rather successful in his chosen field and building up a solid reputation.

Still, Brooks sensed that his father, Fitz Colton, the head of Colton Construction, which was currently doing extremely well in its third generation of existence, was waiting for him to stop "playing PI" and get serious about his life. Colton Construction was a large and generous employer, having built many of the offices and factories in Wichita as well as in Braxville, which was where the Colton family resided.

His father, a solid workaholic, couldn't accept that he was very serious about being a private investigator, just like he couldn't understand why all of his six children had gone into vocations that had to do with some form of public service rather than become part of the family business.

As far as Brooks could tell, all five of his siblings seemed rather suited to their career choices and were quite happy with their lives. And as for him, well in true detective form, he was blessed with that little voice in his head, the one that would occasionally raise points that seemed to defy logic, but nonetheless existed, nudging at his conscience and telling him that something just didn't seem "right."

Sometimes it was just a small thing. Other times it seemed to involve his whole case.

That was what he was feeling at the moment.

Something was "off."

For the most part, his cases fell under three categories. He worked missing persons cases. Those, on occasion, required working with the Braxville Police Department as a consultant. Brooks also worked cases of identity theft. And, once in a while, he took on cases that involved cheating spouses.

Truth be told, Brooks didn't like working those, but they did help to pay the bills on the few occasions when he found himself short on funds and needed to fill in the gaps.

But right now, he was hearing something from his prospective client that wasn't sitting right with him.

"Let me get this straight," Brooks said, interrupting the man on the other end of his phone who seemed enamored with the sound of his own voice. "You're not currently married to this Gwen Harrison?"

"No, I never was," Daniel Shelton snapped, obviously irritated that he was being interrupted by "the help."

"But—"

"And you're not even engaged to this woman?" Brooks asked, wanting to make sure he hadn't accidentally missed something.

"No, I am not engaged to Gwen," Daniel retorted, his irritation growing by leaps and bounds. He was unaccustomed to being interrupted *and* having to explain himself. "Now, one more time. Gwen moved to Braxville after I expressly told her that I didn't want her to leave."

The man's high-handed tone was really beginning to irritate Brooks, but more than that, he didn't care for his character. He was not about to help Shelton track down his former girlfriend or whatever the woman was to him.

"And she didn't live with you or have you paying the rent for her apartment?" At this point, Brooks was certain he was just going over what he felt was established fact.

"What the hell difference can that possibly make to you doing your job?" Shelton demanded angrily.

It was obvious to Brooks that the man expected to be obeyed, not get into a debate over this with someone Shelton obviously considered beneath him.

"The difference is that if you didn't enter into any sort of an arrangement with this woman, then you have no expectations of her obediently coming when you call," Brooks informed the man, biting back a few choicer remarks. Most likely they would have been lost on someone like Shelton.

"What the hell is that supposed to mean?" the angry voice on the other end demanded.

"It means, Mr. Shelton, that I'm not taking the case, which in turn means I won't track down this woman for you. A woman who is within her rights to go off and live her life as she sees fit, not as *you* see fit," Brooks concluded.

"You're turning me down?" Shelton asked, his voice rising and growing shrill. "Listen, you sanctimonious, two-bit jerk—"

"Goodbye, Mr. Shelton. Very nice *not* doing business with you," Brooks said just before he disconnected the call.

Brooks took a deep breath as he put his phone back down on his desk. He wasn't so well-off that he could afford to just turn down jobs at will, but he had his principles. Besides, there was just something about this particular one that told him it was all wrong.

So much so that he did feel he needed to track down this Ms. Gwen Harrison, not for Daniel Shelton but to warn her that the man was looking for her. Brooks was certain that Shelton could very well go on to hire someone else to find her. And then, who knows? He didn't want that on his conscience.

From the information he had gotten from the overbearing man, Brooks was confident that he could find this woman with a minimum of effort. After all, he knew Braxville like the back of his hand. Ordinarily, since he had turned down this job, he would have walked away. But that same little voice that told him something was off about Shelton's scenario also made him realize that if anything did happen to this Gwen Harrison, a newly transplanted elementary school-teacher, he would wind up feeling guilty as hell because he hadn't warned the woman.

And considering the impatient urgency he'd heard in Daniel Shelton's voice, Brooks figured he didn't have that much time to lose. Daniel Shelton had struck him as an angry man who didn't just let matters drop if they didn't go his way. Instead, Shelton gave every indication that he focused on getting revenge.

This Gwen Harrison needed to be warned.

Chapter One

Gwen Harrison had forgotten how totally draining keeping up with a classroom full of third graders could actually be. In the last elementary school where she taught, she had only temporarily taught a class until their regular teacher returned from maternity leave. Ordinarily, she taught fifth graders who seemed, on reflection, calmer to her. But when she decided to move to Braxville, this was the only position open to her.

Today had just been an introduction to what was ahead in the coming school year. Teachers and students had briefly mingled, getting to know one another.

The thinking behind that was forewarned meant forearmed. Oh well, it would get better—she hoped.

What she wanted more than anything right now was to catch a quick nap, but she needed to run a couple of errands first and after that, she needed to prepare for a teachers' orientation session the next day.

Not only that, but she also needed to update her grandmother, Rita. She wasn't all that eager to do that because, although she dearly loved the woman who had raised her, she didn't have anything to report so far and she knew that although she wouldn't say anything, her grandmother would be very disappointed.

That makes two of us, Grandma, she thought.

The search she was conducting—when she had time to conduct it—was turning up nothing.

That was nothing new, except that she'd really hoped being in the town where her mother had disappeared all those years ago might lead her to eventually pick up her mother's trail. Gwen was fairly certain that something had to have happened to her mother. Something fatal, because otherwise Olivia Harrison would not have completely abandoned her only daughter and her mother for more than two whole decades.

Her grandmother was certain of that, as well. That was the main reason Gwen had picked up and moved to Braxville after living her entire life in Kansas City.

When Gwen had packed up her life and moved here, she was so sure she had done the right thing. Now she wasn't all that sure about it.

She knew what she was doing, Gwen thought. She was stalling.

"Might as well get this over with," she murmured, planting herself on her sofa and taking her cell phone out of her pocket.

She just hated hearing the disappointment in her grandmother's voice. Rita Harrison had raised her from the time she had been an infant, taking care of her while her mother was at work. The woman had taken over completely when Olivia had decided to come to Braxville on some secret mission, although Rita confided that she believed Olivia had gone to talk to the man who was her father to find out why he'd stopped sending her child support payments.

At least, she thought that was why her mother had gone to Braxville, but she wasn't sure. Her grandmother hadn't been very clear about that. The only thing that Rita Harrison *was* sure of was that her daughter wouldn't have just up and left both her daughter and her without a single word of explanation.

Olivia wasn't the type.

Gwen had just turned on her phone and tapped in two of the numeric keys that would eventually connect her to her grandmother when she heard the front doorbell ring. She stared at the door for a second, at a loss as to who it could be. She hardly knew anyone in town yet, certainly not anyone who would take it upon themselves to just come over at this time of day.

"Only one way to find out," the redhead murmured as she slipped her cell phone back into her pocket and rose to her feet.

Walking up to the front door, Gwen looked through the peephole.

She was no more enlightened now than she had been a minute ago.

Standing on the other side of her door was a tall, ruggedly built man who had to be at least six feet tall, possibly even a little taller. He had close-cropped, dark brown hair and had what appeared to be only a very casual relationship with his razor. He had a five-o'clock shadow that appeared to be quickly approaching its sixth hour. He was also well-dressed.

Another teacher? she wondered.

The bottom line was that she had never seen him before in her life and that was definitely not a man who was easily forgotten, Gwen thought.

"Yes?" she asked, thinking that maybe the man, who looked as if he was about her age, might have rung the wrong doorbell.

"Are you Miss Gwen Harrison?" the man on the other side of her door asked.

The fact that he knew her name and seemed to be looking for her took Gwen by surprise. For now, until he gave her more to go on, Gwen left her door just where it was—locked.

"Yes, I am," Gwen answered, then decided to take the lead and ask a couple of questions of her own. "Who are you—and why are you looking for me?"

Brooks cast about for a way to answer her questions without scaring her or putting her immediately on the defensive. The private investigator dug into his pocket for his wallet. After finding it, he took his ID out and held it up close to the peephole for the woman's perusal before putting it away again.

"I'm Brooks Colton and I'm a private investigator," he told her, reinforcing what he knew she had already determined from the license he had just shown her.

The moment she heard his last name, Gwen was instantly intrigued. Her grandmother had told her that her mother had been involved with a married man who worked for Colton Construction.

Could this good-looking man standing on the other side of her door somehow be related to that man who her mother had known?

Don't get ahead of yourself, Gwen, she silently warned. Things didn't just come together this easily or this quickly.

Maybe this was a risk, but then, so was moving to Braxville. Gwen decided to unlock her door. She swung it wide-open, a silent invitation to the man who had just rung her doorbell.

"Come in," Gwen told him, stepping back.

He looked even taller without the door in the way, she couldn't help thinking, looking up at the private investigator as he crossed her threshold. He had to be at least six foot one, maybe even six foot two, she decided.

The woman's apartment had all the signs of someone who had just moved in within the last month, possibly even within the last couple of weeks, Brooks noted, doing a quick survey of the area.

There were unopened boxes scattered about and a pervading feeling that her possessions were still looking for their final resting place.

Accustomed to speaking her mind at all times, Gwen spoke up now. "If you don't mind my asking you, Mr. Colton, why are you looking for me?"

Brooks decided that maybe now wasn't the time to ease the young woman into this or try to sugarcoat the situation for her. He had come here thinking that time was of the essence. The woman needed to be warned.

"Strictly speaking, I'm not the one who's looking for you," he told the young schoolteacher. Believing that the man who had called to hire him could very well be a stalker, Brooks asked, "Ms. Harrison, do you know a Daniel Shelton?"

At the mention of the man's name, the pretty woman before him turned slightly pale and her posture grew a little more rigid than it had been a moment ago.

Oh no, it couldn't be, Gwen thought. She had assumed, gratefully so, that everything was over since she hadn't acknowledged Shelton's texts or answered any of the dozen or so messages he had left on her phone.

Obviously, the man did have trouble taking no for an answer.

"Yes, I know him. *Knew* him," Gwen deliberately corrected herself. "Why did you just ask me that?" Her eyes pinned the other man in place. "If you don't mind my asking, exactly what is this all about?"

Brooks had walked into her apartment at her invitation, but he was not about to take anything for granted, which was why he was still standing just a couple of feet into the apartment. He was prepared for her to tell him to get lost.

Still, in an effort to get her to relax a little, he asked, "Would you mind if we sat down? This might take a minute or so to explain."

Braced, Gwen gestured into her living room, specifically toward the large sectional sofa that was in the middle of the room.

Indicating that Brooks should take a seat first before launching into his explanation, she waited for him to do so. "All right, I'm listening," she said.

He sat down on the edge of the sofa rather than appearing to make himself comfortable. He didn't want the woman getting the wrong impression about this. He was strictly here out of his concern for her safety, not to intimidate her.

Brooks watched as Gwen seated herself, as well. He noticed that she appeared to be somewhat more on edge now than she had been a moment ago. He was right to come warn her, he thought, silently grateful for that little voice in his head.

"All right, I'm listening," Gwen repeated, waiting for the detective to start explaining.

"Like I said, I'm a private investigator. My specialty is finding missing persons, but I also work on cases involving identity theft and occasionally, I take on cases involving gathering evidence against cheating spouses."

The last, he realized, tasted rather bitter in his mouth as he said the words. Maybe he needed to look into rewording his job description in the future. For now, he pushed that to the back of his mind.

Gwen shook her head, wisps of red hair moving almost seductively about her cheeks. "I still don't see what any of this has to do with me."

"Daniel Shelton called me yesterday, looking to engage my services as a private investigator. He wanted me to covertly follow you around and take photographs. In general he wanted me to report back to him on whatever you were up to."

He could see by the completely stunned expression on the teacher's face that she hadn't seen *any* of this coming.

"What I was 'up to'?" she echoed, flabbergasted. "What I'm 'up to' is relocating and teaching third grade." This wasn't making any sense to her. "Are you sure he said that?"

"Completely sure, yes," Brooks answered.

Gwen was having trouble trying to put all of this together.

"If you're working for Daniel, then what are you doing here, talking to me? Shouldn't you be skulking in the shadows with a camera pointed at me?" Gwen asked.

Her mind was scrambling as she searched for a way to get this man out of her apartment and on his way before this whole situation escalated into something really terrible with her ending up as the victim.

"That's just it," Brooks explained. "I'm not working for Shelton. I turned him down because I found something rather odd about his request."

"Odd?" she repeated. She thought it was odd, but she wasn't sure exactly what the detective meant by that.

Brooks nodded, then thought the best way to explain things to her was by asking further questions. "How long were you two together?"

She shrugged. To be honest, she hadn't actually thought of them as *being* together. They dated and then, when he became more possessive, they didn't.

"Not long," she answered. "Certainly not long enough for him to think we had some sort of a serious relationship going on." Looking back, she had seen warning signs and she should have taken note of them. But to be honest, she thought she was just imagining things. Obviously not.

"When I told him that I was taking this job in Braxville, he actually forbade me from taking it—which was when I decided that it was time to end things between us," she told Brooks.

"Was there anything else?" the private investigator asked.

Gwen pressed her lips together and then nodded. "He was getting too controlling," she admitted, shaking her head at the memory. Taking a deep breath, she continued. "I thought that if I just ignored him once I was here, he would get over things and just move on. He did leave several messages and texts…well, several dozen messages and texts. But I never answered any of them and I thought he'd just take the hint that whatever we had—which wasn't very much of anything," she qualified, "was over. I certainly didn't think that ignoring him told him to try harder."

Gwen ran her hands up and down her arms, as if to try to warm herself and ward off the eerie chill she felt.

"Apparently, Daniel thought otherwise." Gwen raised her eyes to meet the detective's. She found Brooks's blue eyes to be kind, sympathetic and in a strange way, they made her feel almost protected. And then she thought of what Daniel had wanted to hire him to do. "You know, what you just told me about Dan is positively creepy," she told him. For a moment, she was at a loss as to what to do.

"No argument," Brooks agreed. "You know, you could get a restraining order taken out against him."

Gwen blew out a breath, nodding her head in response. But it was that empty sort of reaction that put the person talking on hold and it wasn't really meant to be an actual agreement to what was being suggested.

As if on cue, the redhead seemed to suddenly come around and she looked directly into his eyes again. "Look, I have somewhere I'm supposed to be right now, but I'd like to continue talking to you when I'm done. Could you meet me at this little coffee shop on the next corner in about two hours from now?" Gwen asked.

Her request, coming out of the blue the way it did, caught Brooks off guard, but only in that it reinforced what he was already experiencing. From the moment he had laid eyes on her, Brooks had felt this rather intense attraction to the lively-looking redhead.

The attraction went beyond his initial damsel-in-distress reaction. No, it was more than that. There was just something about the young teacher that seemed to all but reel him in.

Obviously it wasn't one-sided, he thought, silently congratulating himself. Unless he hadn't heard correctly, she had just subtly asked him to meet him for coffee, which could be construed as asking him out on a date.

Just to be certain that he'd meet her there, Gwen began to rattle off the coffee shop's address. Brooks stopped her before she could finish. "I'm familiar with the place," he assured her.

With a nod of her head, Gwen rose to her feet and crossed over toward the breakfront where she'd left her purse hanging when she'd walked in.

"Fine. Then I'll see you there in about two hours," Gwen confirmed.

Brooks nodded, then followed her out the front door. "It's a date," he told her, then immediately realized what he'd just said. "I mean, it's not a date, but I'll see you there in two hours."

Feeling a blush working its way up the sides of her neck, then up to her cheeks, Gwen avoided his eyes and nodded.

"Right," she agreed, thinking it best to leave it at that.

BROOKS WASN'T THE type to trip over his own tongue. Usually, he was right on top of things, able to think on his feet and say what was on his mind without stumbling. But he had to admit this woman had thrown him off his game.

He was intrigued by her, drawn to her the way he hadn't been drawn to anyone in a long, long time.

Actually, he couldn't remember the last time he had felt this way about a woman. He knew what that meant. That left him prone to making mistakes, Brooks silently upbraided himself. That meant he needed to be twice as careful.

He looked around the small coffee shop, which was apparently Braxville's latest stab at being trendy.

Given the fact that it was not quite the time when most businesses let out, the shop was still fairly empty, and there were plenty of seats available. He had come in early and had deliberately chosen a table for two off to the side where he could watch the door and keep track of whoever entered. That way, he was able to see the subject of his non-investigation the moment she entered—provided that she hadn't used the excuse of meeting him "later" to just blow him off, he thought.

Where the hell was this coming from? he wondered.

Besides, he decided, she wouldn't do that. Unless his ability to read people had gone entirely haywire, she didn't strike him as the type of person who would just blow someone off by making up unfounded excuses. She was coming. She was just a little late, that was all, he told himself. But she was definitely going to be here.

The opening front door immediately caught his attention.

And then he smiled when he saw who walked in.

Gwen.

He was right, Brooks congratulated himself. He still had the ability to read people.

Chapter Two

Brooks half rose in his chair as he waved his hand to catch Gwen's attention.

She was scanning the area, hoping to locate Brooks quickly—provided he was still here. After all, he had said he'd be here, but she didn't know him. Maybe he had changed his mind.

Gwen felt a little self-conscious just standing there, searching for the private investigator.

And then she saw him. Without realizing it, her smile grew wider.

Brooks hadn't taken his eyes off the shapely redhead since she had walked in. No doubt about it. The woman had the most beautiful smile he had ever seen.

Relieved to have found him—and happy that he had actually come to the coffee shop to wait for her the way he'd said, Gwen quickly cut the distance between them and made her way over to the table.

Brooks caught himself thinking that her eyes seemed to sparkle as she declared, "You're here."

"I said I would be," Brooks reminded her, adding, "I don't know about the kind of people that you're used to, but I don't say things just to hear myself talk. I mean them."

Gwen slid into the seat opposite him and Brooks sat down again, as well. "Sorry I'm late. My errands took longer than I expected," she apologized. "I didn't keep you waiting long, did I?"

She sounded sincere, he thought. And she had kept him waiting just long enough to build up his anticipation, but he knew better than to say something like that to her. The poor woman already realized that she had a stalker, he wasn't about to say anything to make her think that he was potentially one, too.

"No, not long. Besides, the coffee here is pretty good," he said, looking at the container in front of him, "and the pastries are in a league of their own instead of the heavy, gluey things these places usually sell. You know the kind. They seem to sink like lead in your stomach the second you swallow them."

Gwen laughed. "You've never been here before, have you?" she asked, surprised by his comment. She had only been in Braxville less than a month and she'd already come to this coffee shop several times.

"Well, I've been *by* here a number of times," he told her. "But I have to admit that I've never actually gone into the shop until now." He raised his half-empty container of coffee as if toasting her. "Thanks for the introduction. By the way," he said, "I went ahead and ordered something for you. Feel free to get something else though if the latte doesn't meet with your approval."

"The latte is fine," Gwen assured him, touched that he had been so thoughtful—and that he was willing to admit he might have chosen the wrong thing. "But I have to tell you that I had an ulterior motive for asking you to meet me here."

Whenever he found himself in an awkward situation, Brooks had always resorted to humor as a way of saving face. Now was no different.

He leaned back in his chair, studying Gwen over his coffee container. "So I take it that it wasn't my mesmerizing blue eyes that brought you here?"

For a moment, his comment caught her off guard. Did the handsome PI suspect that she was attracted to him? She couldn't tell by his expression if he was kidding or serious.

Even so, Gwen rallied quickly, telling him, "You do have beautiful eyes, especially for a man, but no, I didn't ask you to meet me because of your eyes." Pausing, she grew serious. "You said you were a private investigator."

"I did and I am," Brooks replied, watching her and waiting for the woman to get to the point.

Gwen took a breath, as if bracing herself for possible disappointment. "Then I need your help."

Brooks had no idea what to expect. Was she going to say something to the effect that turnabout was fair play? Was she going to ask him to spy on Shelton for her so she could be prepared just in case the man still intended to come after her?

"Go on," he said, waiting to hear where this was going.

Gwen was outgoing and friendly, but this was extremely personal to her. She paused, trying to find a way to word this correctly.

"I didn't come out here because I was looking to change schools," she confessed. "Or even to get away from Dan, although now that I have, I realize that was the right move to make," she commented, more to herself than to Brooks. "I came to Braxville so I could find out more about my mother, who came out here when I was three. She went missing shortly after that."

"When you were three," Brooks repeated, absorbing the information. "That was how many years ago?"

"Twenty-five," she answered without any hesitation. When Brooks opened his mouth to make a comment, Gwen quickly continued. "I know what you're going to say next. You're going to ask me why I'm only looking into this now, after all these years. Well, this isn't the first investigation into my mother's disappearance. I mean, it is for me," she quickly clarified, "but my grandmother actually hired a private investigator to look for my mother shortly after she first went missing."

Good, a piece of information he could work with, Brooks thought. "Would you happen to know the guy's name?" He assumed that her grandmother might have mentioned it to her.

"As a matter of fact, I do," Gwen said. "The investigator's name was Felton Crane. I remember because his name would come up with a fair amount of regularity in the beginning. My grandmother would say it, then call the man a lot of choice words that she would then quickly tell me never to use. When I would ask her why she used them, she said it was only because she was so angry at the man for taking her hard-earned money and running off with it."

"I take it that this Crane guy never managed to find your mother," Brooks guessed.

Gwen shook her head. "Not only didn't he find her, but he never reported back to my grandmother about the case one way or another." She frowned. "Crane just took my grandmother's money and ran."

"And your grandmother never tried to follow up on this guy?" Brooks asked. It was shoddy investigators like this Felton Crane who gave the rest of private investigators, himself included, he thought, a bad name.

"Believe me, if she could have, she would have," Gwen assured him. "Grandma Rita isn't just a pushover who would meekly accept things without questioning them. But as it turned out, that investigator was nowhere to be found and eventually, my grandmother had to give up.

"But she never bought into the idea that my mother ran out on me or her because she didn't want to be saddled with the responsibility of being a single mom raising a daughter or having to eventually take care of an aging parent." Gwen raised her chin proudly as she told him, "According to Grandma Rita, everyone knew that my mother was better than that."

And then she leaned forward across the small table, instantly creating a very intimate setting between them as she looked up at him with the greenest eyes he had ever seen and said, "And there's just one more thing."

The woman's tone completely captivated him. Brooks realized that he could go on listening to that melodic voice forever without hardship.

He hated to admit it, but he was beginning to understand why Shelton was so drawn to this woman, although he definitely didn't approve of how possessive Gwen had said he was. That seemed to be especially bad since Gwen maintained that she hadn't given Shelton any reason to believe they were in a relationship, exclusive or otherwise.

"Go on," Brooks said, his curiosity definitely aroused.

"You said that your last name was Colton," Gwen began haltingly, her eyes on his.

This wasn't going where he had expected it to, but he remained encouraging. "It is."

He had already shown her his identification when he had come to her door. Was there some sort of a problem with his being a Colton? he couldn't help wondering.

"Are you related to the people who run Colton Construction?"

"The man in charge of the company is my father. Why? Is that a problem for you?" Brooks decided that it was better if she explained why she'd asked about his connection to the company instead of his taking a guess at the reason.

"No, not a problem. It's just that the only thing that Grandma Rita said she knew about my father was that he was a married man who lived in Braxville—and that he worked for Colton Construction," she said, her eyes never leaving his face. "I thought that since you're the company owner's son, you might be in a better position to do a little more digging into the matter than a complete stranger could," she told Brooks, already treating him as if he had agreed to take on her case.

Brooks had dealt with his share of clients who had

come to him needing his help. At least half of them had been women. Many of those had approached him with hope in their eyes, but he didn't recall any of them ever looking at him with quite this amount of hope brimming in their eyes.

"So what do you say, Mr. Colton? Would you take on my case and find my mother—or what happened to her—for me?" Not wanting to take a chance on having the man turn her down, Gwen decided to add a little bit of ammunition on her side.

"My grandmother's not in the best of health and not being able to find out what happened to my mother has really taken a great deal out of her over the years. Finding my mother, or at least what happened to my mother, would go a long way in helping my grandmother get closure and help give her a better lease on her remaining years."

"I—" Brooks started to tell Gwen that he would be happy to take her case.

But he got no further than that because, afraid he would turn her down, Gwen quickly interjected, "I can't pay you much to begin with. I'm a schoolteacher and we don't exactly earn very much, but whatever I have is yours. And as for the rest of it," she continued, guessing that Brooks's fee would probably be high because the trail was so cold, "I can make regular payments to you until the entire amount is paid off. How about it?" Gwen pressed. "Will you take on the case?"

"It's not a matter of the money," Brooks began, wanting to assure her that money was never the motivating factor in whether or not he took a case. If it had been, the money that Shelton had offered him right up front to take his case would have been more than enough for him to say yes.

Again, Brooks didn't get a chance to say anything further. But this time, the attractive redhead sitting across from him wasn't the one to interrupt him. The cell phone in his pocket was guilty of that. It rang just at the wrong moment.

Habit had Brooks taking his phone out and glancing at the screen. He had every intention of telling whomever was calling that he would get back to them—in his line of work he couldn't afford just to ignore an incoming call without saying anything.

But then he saw who it was. The incoming call was from Jordana, one of his sisters. A year older than he was, Jordana had risen through the ranks of the Braxville Police Department and was currently working on the force as a police detective.

It was Jordana who had used her influence to get him hired on to act as a part-time police consultant. He worked on some of their more complicated cases, the ones that could use someone thinking outside the box rather than being restricted by the need to toe the line and obey all the rules. As a private investigator, Brooks was able go places and do things that a police detective couldn't—as long as that fact wasn't broadcasted.

Brooks held up his hand, stopping Gwen before she could continue. "I really need to take this," he told her apologetically.

Gwen nodded. "Of course. Go ahead," she said, gesturing toward the phone in his hand.

"Thanks," he murmured. With that, he rose and made

his way over to a corner of the shop that was currently unoccupied. Opening his phone, Brooks said, "I'm with a client, Jordana."

"Well, you're going to have to tell the client that you'll get back to them, Brooks," Jordana replied, her solemn tone leaving no room for argument. "Right now I need you here."

Brooks glanced over his shoulder, looking in Gwen's direction. He felt himself wavering, but he knew that his sister wasn't given to arbitrarily calling him in for a case, not without a very good reason. But he was just about to get into Gwen's case and he had to admit that she had managed to pique his interest, not to mention the fact that he wanted to have an actual reason for getting closer to the woman.

"You sure this can't wait, Jordy?" he asked his sister. "I can swing by later—"

"No," Jordana said, cutting him short. "I need you to swing by *now*. This case can't wait. It's already waited for about twenty-five years as it is. And don't call me Jordy," she told him, not for the first time.

That little voice in his head instantly came to life the second he heard how long it had been. Twenty-five years. The same number that Gwen had mentioned just a couple of minutes ago in reference to her mother's disappearance.

This couldn't just be a coincidence. But he needed more information before he allowed himself to get carried away.

"What's waited for twenty-five years?" he asked pointedly.

He heard his sister sigh before answering him. "Dad's

company is in the middle of a new project. They were just demolishing an old warehouse building."

"And?" Brooks asked, glancing back at Gwen again. His potential client looked as if she was growing restless.

"And they found a body buried in the wall," his sister told him.

He felt as if he had been punched in the gut. It couldn't be that easy—could it? He had to ask. "Was it a woman?"

"No, a man," Jordana answered. "Why would you think it was a woman?"

So much for easy, Brooks thought. "I'll explain later when I get there. Do you have any idea who this man is?" he asked, although he had a feeling he knew what her answer probably was.

"No, but he hasn't been completely unwrapped yet," Jordana answered.

"Unwrapped?" Brooks thought that was an strange way for his sister to put it.

"Yes, it's the oddest thing," Jordana continued. "Turns out that the body is in surprisingly good condition, given when the wall was actually built. Whoever killed this man painstakingly wrapped the body up really well and in this instance, that somehow managed to preserve it, although I doubt that even entered the killer's mind when he, she or they did it. Do you want to come down and take a look?" she threw in since Brooks hadn't already told her he was on his way.

"Do I want to come down?" Brooks repeated incredulously. "Try and stop me."

"I kind of thought you'd have that sort of reaction,"

Jordana said, although it certainly had taken him longer to arrive at this reaction than she would have expected. "Well, then, get a move on. The world isn't going to stop turning, waiting on you," she reminded him. And then she told her brother exactly where they were in reference to the warehouse. "You can't miss it. We're the site with all the debris, surrounded by police cars."

"Very funny. Okay, hang on, Jordy. I'm on my way," Brooks told his sister.

Now he just needed to put Gwen and her technical missing persons case on hold, he thought, terminating the call from his sister before she could tell him for the dozenth time not to call her Jordy.

The little voice in his head was telling him that there was a connection between the body that was just found and Gwen's missing mother, but he wasn't going to say anything about that to Gwen quite yet.

He didn't want to risk disappointing her in case he was wrong.

Besides, he reasoned as he crossed back toward Gwen, a grown man responding to a little voice in his head wasn't exactly the easiest thing to sell or explain.

Chapter Three

By the time Brooks returned to the small table, Gwen was on her feet, as if she anticipated that their impromptu meeting was over.

He wasn't about to keep her wondering. "I'm afraid I have to go."

"Another case?" she asked.

The private detective had looked rather interested in her mother's story until his cell phone had taken him away. Now he seemed to be in a hurry to go somewhere. She could only assume that it had to do with a case he was probably working.

"Something like that," Brooks answered, keeping the specifics vague.

"You're not at liberty to say," Gwen guessed. It wasn't a question.

Brooks smiled at her, glad she wasn't pressing him for any information on the call he'd taken. "You've read the bylaws."

Gwen lifted one shoulder in a half shrug. "Confidentiality is an important cornerstone in building trust and I assume that if a person hires a private investigator, they want to be able to trust him—or her," she added as an afterthought.

Her eyes held his, searching for some indication that she was right.

He would have liked nothing more than to go on talking to this woman and to take on her case, which he had to admit intrigued him. But Jordana had that urgent sound in her voice and he knew better than to keep his sister waiting unless it was unavoidable, which, in this case, it wasn't.

Jordana was the reason he had gotten his consultant's gig with the department in the first place, although her new captain wasn't happy about the situation and was looking for any reason to change it. Hopefully the man wasn't a permanent fixture.

Reaching into his pocket, Brooks took out his business card, a very plain card with his name and business number proclaimed in bold, black letters.

Brooks Colton: Private Investigator.

His cell phone number was directly beneath that. He held the card out to her.

"I'd like to talk more about your case," he told her. "If I don't get back to you by tomorrow afternoon, call me."

Gwen looked at the card he had handed her with interest, then turned her eyes up to his. There was amusement in hers. "You need to be nagged?"

"No," he laughed. "It's just that right now there's a lot on my plate and I wouldn't want your case to get lost in the shuffle."

"Does that happen often for you? Things get lost in the shuffle?" she specified, curious as to how this man operated and if she was possibly making a mistake, hiring him.

He knew better than to give her a definitive answer. He didn't want to risk her changing her mind. It wasn't every day that he got an intriguing cold case.

"Always a first time," was all he was willing to admit.

Gwen wavered. Maybe she *was* making a mistake. But the man was a Colton, which could be handy, and besides, he was really charming.

More important than that, he had gone out of his way to warn her about Daniel, confirming the uneasy suspicion that had been in the back of her mind. Daniel had turned out to be a stalker in the making.

"All right," Gwen finally said, slipping Brooks's business card into her purse. "You have two days to get back to me."

They began to walk out of the coffee shop together. "Make it one," Brooks told her, fairly certain that whatever Jordana needed wouldn't take him longer than that to handle.

Gwen inclined her head. "All right," she agreed, "one it is."

They separated right outside the coffee shop entrance, with Gwen going to her car while Brooks went in the opposite direction toward his.

He was already looking forward to seeing her again.

THE SITE OF Colton Construction's current project was located on the east side of town, some twenty minutes away by car, as long as the driver obeyed the speed limits that were in force.

Brooks made it there in less than fifteen, zipping through yellow lights about to turn red. The company was demolishing one of their own old warehouses. The building was earmarked to become part of the Crest View Center, which in turn was to be even more modern than Ruby Row, the former shopping center, had ever been.

Brooks had never been part of the construction company, not even summers to earn extra money when he was going to school. But he was still a Colton and he kept up on his father's projects if for no other reason than because there were times when someone might ask him about them. He didn't want to sound as if he and his father hadn't spoken, which on occasions was truer than he was happy about.

But Fitz Colton had always put his company first because he found work to be more interesting and rewarding than family life.

It wasn't so much a failing on Fitz's part as just the way he was built. Brooks and his siblings had accepted that fact a long time ago, just as their father had grudgingly accepted the fact that none of his children had any intentions of working with him in the company.

As Brooks came closer to the actual demolition site, it felt as if there was a cloud of dust still hanging in the air, a leftover residue thanks to his father's people having brought down two of the warehouse walls. Those walls, or what had been found in those walls, was ultimately the reason he was here.

After parking his vehicle in an as out-of-the-way space as he could find, Brooks got out and made his way to the center of the debris. That appeared to be where most of the uniformed men and women had gathered.

One such uniformed police officer instantly snapped to attention when he saw Brooks approaching.

Spotting the officer, Brooks caught himself thinking the young man in the crisp uniform had that fresh-out-of-the-academy look about him. He began silently guessing just how long it had been since the police officer had actually graduated.

Brooks realized that the officer had now put himself directly in his path, keeping him from going any farther.

"I'm sorry, sir, but you can't be here," he announced.

Brooks looked beyond the young officer's shoulder. Not more than ten feet away he could see the body his sister had called him about. It was lying on the ground like some sort of prized trophy. And, just as Jordana had said, the body was entirely wrapped in transparent plastic from its head all the way down to its feet.

Fascinating, Brooks couldn't help thinking as he quickly circumvented the rookie.

"Hey, I said you can't be here!" the police officer shouted, growing indignant that he'd been disobeyed. "Stop right now or I'll have to restrain you!" he threatened, turning around.

"It's okay, Officer… Madison," Brooks said, pausing to read the name on the young man's badge. "You're new here. I'm Detective Colton's brother. She asked me to come here," he explained.

The boyish face, which seemed to be utterly devoid of the slightest hint of facial hair, scowled at him. "Yeah, right. Now get back or I'm going to have to—"

"It's all right, Madison. I asked him to come," Jordana told the young officer, weaving her way over to him and her brother. "This is my brother Brooks Colton. He's a private investigator and on occasion, he acts as a consultant on some of our more…unusual cases," she said, settling on that word even though other, more descriptive ones occurred to her.

Brooks flashed a quick smile at the officer.

The officer flushed a little, obviously embarrassed that he had made a mistake.

"Oh sorry. I didn't know," Madison apologized.

Brooks had no desire to torture the young man. Who knew, the officer might come in handy down the line in this case or some other one. He liked maintaining positive relationships whenever possible.

"Why would you?" he asked charitably. He turned his attention back to his sister. "You found him like this?" he asked her, nodding at the body.

"Wrapped up neat and tidy like a serving of fish that was prepared this morning," she commented.

"Remind me not to have dinner at your place," Brooks quipped.

"He came tumbling out of the north basement wall. Nearly scaring one of dad's people half to death," Jordana told him. "Poor guy couldn't stop shaking."

Crossing over to the body, Brooks was about to bend down for a closer look when Jordana put her hand on his shoulder, stopping him.

"Something wrong?" he asked her.

"You can look, but don't touch. The captain is lurking around here somewhere. He's trying to be more hands-on," she explained, and it was obvious that she didn't welcome the watchful attitude. "I just wanted you to see the body for yourself. Any ideas?"

"Well, the guy definitely hung out with the wrong crowd," Brooks joked, straightening up.

Jordana sighed. "Any ideas that haven't occurred to the rest of us already?"

"Not offhand," he told her honestly. He looked at his sister. "I take it the guy had no ID on him."

"We haven't checked yet, but I'm betting that if someone went through all the trouble of wrapping his body like this, they weren't about to leave any telltale evidence in his pockets," Jordana said. She frowned, looking down at the plastic-cocooned body. "Whoever he is, he obviously got on someone's wrong side."

His interaction with Gwen still fresh in his mind, Brooks had another take on the crime. "Or he could have walked into something that someone else was trying to hide and paid the ultimate penalty for it," he conjectured.

Jordana eyed her brother sharply. "Why? What are you thinking?"

Brooks didn't like to offer half-formed theories without first thinking them through. "Nothing yet. But his body had to be in obviously great condition to look that preserved after being dead for twenty-five years." He looked back at the body, specifically at the dead man's hands. "I'd say that there's a good chance you can lift a set of viable fingerprints off your victim."

Jordana had already thought of that as well as the possible outcome of the search.

"It won't do us much good if the guy wasn't in the system," she pointed out. "Twenty-five years ago, only a limited number of people were fingerprinted. It's not like it is today."

Brooks didn't believe in coincidences, and the story that Gwen had told him about the private investigator her grandmother had hired who wound up vanishing just seemed like too much of a coincidence to him. From where he stood, it almost seemed like fate dealing him a hand.

He could be wrong, he thought. But that little voice in his head didn't think so.

"True, but there were still other databases with fingerprints that could be accessed. Noncriminal," he stressed.

"Like?" his sister asked.

"Like people who went into the armed forces." Brooks paused for a moment, letting that sink in before adding, "Or licensed private investigators like yours truly."

The latter thought obviously hadn't occurred to his sister. "You think he might be one of yours?"

"Only one way to find out," he told her.

Jordana watched him for a long moment. He wasn't fooling her. Her eyes narrowed. "You know something, don't you?"

"I know many things," Brooks answered vaguely, refusing to be pinned down. "Some of them might even be pertinent, others might not."

Growing impatient, Jordana blew out a breath. "I hate it when you play games."

"Not playing a game, big sister. Just playing a hunch—but hunches," he added quickly before Jordana could ask him anything further, "don't always pan out and I'd rather not be caught with egg on my face."

"Risk it," she ordered.

His sister was about to say something further to him along the lines of how irritating he could be, but then she saw a familiar face walking their way and survival became her main objective—mainly Brooks's not hers.

"Uh-oh, maybe you'd better make yourself scarce, Brooks. I see Captain Hastings heading this way and you know how he feels about private investigators horning their way into police cases."

"I didn't horn my way in," Brooks reminded her. "I was invited."

That had been the old captain's doing. This new captain had yet to work out his overall policy when it came to private investigators. Jordana was quick to point that out to her brother.

"And if you ever want to be invited again," she told Brooks, "leave now."

"Going," he said accommodatingly. "But don't forget to check his prints against the registered private investigators from that time period."

Jordana nodded. She had one final question for him before he left. "Any particular private investigator you have in mind?"

Brooks paused for a moment as he looked at her.

Amused, he pretended to keep a straight face. "You want me to do all your work for you, is that it?"

"You want me to ever call you in on another case?" Jordana countered.

"Touché," he responded, inclining his head as if bowing to her. The captain had almost reached them by now. Brooks knew that in order to keep the peace, it was time for him to go. "You might try Felton Crane."

"Felton Crane," Jordana repeated. The name meant absolutely nothing to her and she always tried to remain current on police investigations, ongoing as well as cold cases. "Who's Felton Crane?"

"Very possibly the man who had the misfortune of getting wrapped up in heavy-duty plastic wrap and stuffed into a basement wall," Brooks said as he left the crime scene.

The next moment, Captain Hastings was on the scene and he was frowning. Deeply.

"Detective, did I just see your brother leaving our crime scene?" the captain asked as he walked up to Jordana. The man's dislike of civilian interference was the first thing he had made known when he took over his present position.

Jordana knew the futility of lying so she didn't even attempt to. Instead, she verified the man's suspicions. "Yes, sir, you did."

"What was he doing here?" the captain asked.

Jordana searched for a believable excuse to use. Nothing came to mind at first. She grabbed at the first thing that did occur to her. "He just came by to tell me that he was most likely going on vacation next week."

The expression on the captain's face was highly skeptical. "And why would he be doing that?"

"Going on vacation?" Jordana asked innocently.

"No," the her boss snapped. "Why would he be coming to tell you about it?"

"He just wanted me to know. We're all close in my family, sir." And then an idea hit her. "But he did have an interesting suggestion," she said, thinking that this might put the captain in a more favorable mood when it came to her brother.

"I'll just bet," Hastings almost growled. "All right, what was it?"

"He said if our victim's prints can't be found in the regular database from that time period, maybe we could try seeing if they match any prints from a private investigator."

"Because they're always sticking their noses where they don't belong?" the captain guessed. And then his scowl abated as he looked at Jordana. "For once, your brother actually might have had a good idea. Follow up on it—if it turns out that our vic's prints aren't in the usual database," he qualified.

"Yes, sir," Jordana replied, doing her best not to let the captain see her smile.

Chapter Four

Brooks couldn't get past the fact that it was just too much of a coincidence, finding a body that had been buried in a basement wall for the last twenty-five years. He knew that if he had killed someone and wanted to get rid of the body without leaving a telltale trace behind, he couldn't have thought of a better place to hide it than within the walls of a building under construction.

That meant that the killer, or killer's accomplice if there was more than one person involved in this man's murder, had to have some sort of connection to his father's construction company. Or, barring that, at least knowledge about the construction business.

His father's company had built the original warehouse that they had just knocked down. So the Colton Construction Company had been involved in some way on both ends of this.

And now Jordana had been called in to discover who the person in the wall was and who had killed him as well as why.

Talk about it being a small world, Brooks marveled. This had to be the very definition of that.

Well, with Hastings hovering around the crime scene, Brooks knew that he obviously wasn't welcome there. If he showed up, he was fairly certain that he could, in all likelihood, be given a bum's rush back out.

But that didn't mean that he couldn't attempt to find some answers. Jordana wasn't the only Colton on the police force. His youngest sister, Yvette, was a lab technician who was part of the crime scene investigative team. Hastings might have made his displeasure known about seeing him at the scene, but as far as Brooks knew, the captain hadn't said anything about his asking a few questions after one of the technicians had finished examining the dead man's body.

With that in mind, Brooks drove over to the Braxville police precinct. Once there, he headed straight for the investigative lab, which was located, appropriately enough, in the building's basement.

Yvette's door was open, the way it usually was during work hours. He knocked on it, anyway, so she couldn't accuse him of barging in. Only then did he peer into the large room.

"Hi," he said, addressing the back of his sister's head. "Mind if I come in?"

The pretty lab technician's long chestnut-colored hair was securely bound and piled up on her head, employing an army of pins to make sure that no hair could come loose and accidentally contaminate anything she might have been examining.

Surprised by the fact that someone was there, Yvette glanced toward the doorway to verify her visitor's identity.

"Brooks." She should have known, she thought. Her brother had a habit of popping up when he was least expected.

"What are you doing here?" she asked him.

"Well, it looks like I'm paying my incredibly intelligent baby sister a visit," he answered glibly.

Yvette's eyes narrowed, giving him a penetrating look that told Brooks he wasn't fooling her. "Okay, now what are you *really* doing here?"

He decided not to waste any more of either of their time by beating around the bush. "I hear that you've got a really interesting case on your hands." He held up his hand to stop the onslaught of questions he sensed were coming. "Jordana asked me to come down to the crime scene. Seems that when Dad's company was demolishing an old warehouse they had put up twenty-five years ago, they found something that wasn't supposed to be part of the original structure."

"A body, yes, I know," she said. "But that still doesn't explain what you're doing here." What she did was usually considered to be of secondary importance in the grand scheme of things. "So if she called you down to the crime scene, why aren't you still there with Jordana?"

"Because her new captain is still having trouble trying to wrap his head around having a civilian at his crime scene, 'gumming up the works,'" Brooks explained, using the description that he had heard Hastings retort when he complained about his presence.

"So what is it that you want with me?" Yvette asked, jotting down a few notes to herself regarding something she had just done.

"Can't I just want to see my little sister?" he said innocently.

"You can, but I'd say that it's hardly likely," Yvette answered, letting him know that she saw right through his excuse. "What do you really want?"

Rather than attempting to snow her, Brooks merely grinned. "Clever girl."

Yvette inclined her head in what seemed like a little bow. "That's why they hired me," she quipped. "Now are you going to answer my question seriously, or do I have to have someone official escort you out of here?"

"So young and so cold," Brooks pretended to lament. And then he shifted gears, getting serious. "Did the medical examiner call you in to take a set of fingerprints from our well-preserved mystery man yet?" he asked his sister.

"From what I hear, they're in the process of unwrapping the man." She shook her head. She had only been on the job for a short while, so she was still being surprised by the usual kinds of cases that came up. "Why are you so interested in this case?"

"Mysteries are my life," Brooks told her flippantly. "If you don't get a match from the criminal database from around that time period, see if you can match his prints to ones that were in the licensed private investigator file."

His suggestion surprised her. "Well, that's pretty

specific," Yvette commented, giving him a penetrating look. "What makes you say that?"

He didn't want to get too specific. "Call it a hunch that may or may not pan out."

Yvette didn't have time to waste on games, so she let the matter go. "Okay, Sherlock," she said, humoring him. "If and when I manage to lift the victim's prints and they're viable enough to run, I'll let you know what I come up with." She frowned slightly. Brooks was casting a shadow across her work area. "Now you're standing in my light, so either make yourself useful or leave."

Brooks saluted his sister. "Yes, ma'am," he responded as if he were a lowly recruit and she was in a position of authority over him instead of a lab technician who had only been on the job for a short amount of time. "I'm going to hold you to that," he told her as he approached the doorway.

"Never expected that you wouldn't," Yvette murmured under her breath, already back to focusing on the task at hand.

LEAVING THE POLICE LAB, Brooks thought of calling Gwen to tell her that he was going to take on her case. But then he decided to see if he could find anything out about the private investigator her grandmother had hired.

The name she had used wasn't familiar to him, but he knew someone who might be able to give him some useful information about the man. Namely Richard Stanhope, his old mentor who had, for a short while, taken him under his wing to show him the ropes. In the process, Stanhope had taught him what it really meant to be a private investigator.

Brooks had heard, via the grapevine, that technically the man was now retired. In Richard Stanhope's case that meant that he was slowly losing his mind and most likely was on the path to going stir-crazy.

He had also heard that in order to deal with the boredom, Stanhope was currently working part-time at his cousin's bar, a place that saw a fair amount of business and looked decidedly much more inviting at night than it did in the light of day.

Brooks found his old mentor sweeping up in anticipation of the evening crowd to come.

A tall, burly man who looked as if he could still take care of himself in a fight if it came down to that, Richard Stanhope's florid face lit up when he saw Brooks walking into his cousin's establishment.

Temporarily retiring his broom up against the wall, Stanhope crossed over to his old student, flashing a large, genial grin.

"Well, look what the cat just dragged in," Stanhope said with a laugh, offering Brooks a hearty handshake. "How have you been, Colton?"

"Surviving," Brooks answered without any undue fanfare.

"Yeah, I'll bet." Stanhope laughed again, then nodded toward the bar. "Would you like a drink? On the house," he added.

"Not right now, thanks." He didn't have the time to wait for the alcohol to metabolize before he got back behind the wheel. "But you can answer a question for me," Brooks told the older man.

"If I can," Stanhope qualified. Gesturing toward a chair for Brooks, he sat down on one himself.

Brooks took the chair opposite his old friend. "When you were still working cases," he began.

"Oh, so this is a trip down memory lane," the man guessed. Stanhope settled in, getting comfortable. "Go on."

Brooks asked his question. "Did you ever work with or come across a private investigator by the name of Felton Crane?"

"Crane," Stanhope repeated. His tongue wrapped around the name easily. "Now there's a name I haven't heard in a long time."

"Then you did know him?" Brooks asked, happy he had thought to come by.

Stanhope raised his hand, not wanting his old trainee to get ahead of himself. "Just to nod at," the older man qualified. "Crane liked to work alone and he kept to himself mostly. He was good, though," Stanhope recalled. He had always believed in giving a person their due. Blackening reputations had never been his thing and Brooks was well aware of that. "He worked one case at a time and his clients really got their money's worth."

"Would you happen to know where I could find him?" Brooks asked hopefully. "I want to ask him about an old case of his that has suddenly fallen into my lap in the last twenty-four hours."

Stanhope shook his head, looking genuinely sorry.

"Haven't a clue," he confessed. "The guy up and disappeared from the PI scene years ago."

"Would you happen to remember how many years ago?" Brooks prodded, trying to get as much information as he could out of the former private detective. Every little bit helped, he thought.

Stanhope nodded. "*That* I can answer," he said. "I think it was about twenty-five, maybe twenty-six years ago. I remember because that was when Ginny, my wife, walked out on me. Said she couldn't put up with my 'unorthodox' hours anymore." Stanhope leaned in a little closer. "I think what really bothered her was that she thought there were other women."

Brooks studied his old mentor. "Were there?" he finally asked.

Stanhope merely smiled. "A gentleman never tells."

Rising from the chair, he crossed over to his broom and picked it up again. "Anything else?" he asked before he resumed sweeping.

"No, but if anything occurs to you, give me a call," Brooks told him. As he said that, he gave the older man one of his business cards.

But Stanhope merely looked at the offered card and then, still blessed with amazing vision, he shook his head. "I've already got one of those," he said.

To prove it, Stanhope took out his wallet and pulled a bunch of cards out of it.

It appeared that the former private investigator never threw anything out once it went into his wallet. A thought suddenly occurred to Brooks. "Would you happen to have Crane's card in that collection?"

Stanhope grinned. "As a matter of fact, I do," he said, beginning to thumb through the collection until he managed to locate the card. He plucked it out of the collection. "But why do you want it?" he asked. As far as he could see, the address wasn't going to do Brooks any good. "I already said Crane disappeared."

"Yes," Brooks agreed, gingerly taking the card from Stanhope once he had a handkerchief in his hands, "but his fingerprints haven't."

"O-o-kay," Stanhope agreed, drawing the word out as he waited for Brooks to give him more of an explanation than that.

However, Brooks wasn't about to offer one at this point.

"Thanks," he said, carefully tucking Crane's business card away.

Stanhope desperately wanted something to sink his teeth into. "You'll get back to me if you find out anything," he asked, calling after Brooks as the latter began to walk out of the bar.

Curious if the older man had anything specific in mind—Stanhope could be incredibly closemouthed when it suited him—Brooks turned around and asked, "About?"

"Anything," the former PI answered. "Toss me a bone. I feel like I'm fermenting here."

"Will do," Brooks promised as he finally left the establishment.

He decided to go back to see Yvette with the card he'd just obtained from Stanhope. Who knew, if there were any clear prints on Crane's business card, they just might be useful in clearing some things up.

"TWICE IN ONE DAY, huh?" Yvette questioned.

"Hey, what can I say? You just keep me coming back." And then he became serious. "I've got something for you," Brooks told his sister just before he took out the business card and laid it down, still in his handkerchief, on her work area.

"What is it?" she asked, nodding at the card.

"Something that just might help identify the Man in the Plastic Overcoat," her brother said.

"English, please?" Yvette requested.

"Felton Crane's business card, which may or may not have viable prints on it." His eyes met Yvette's. "Call it a hunch. I think the prints might match the guy currently cooling his heels in the morgue."

Yvette sighed. "I won't ask where you got this," she told him.

"Well, it's complicated, but I didn't steal it if that's what you're thinking," he said.

Yvette slipped Felton Crane's business card into a plastic evidence bag, sealed it and after labeling it, set the card aside.

"Call me if you come up with any sort of a match," Brooks instructed.

Yvette nodded. "That was already understood."

BY THE TIME Brooks picked up some take-out dinner and got back to his place, the hour was getting late. In all likelihood, he reasoned, it was probably too late to call

Gwen. They certainly didn't have the sort of relationship where he could just call her at will, anytime night or day. And he didn't want her thinking that he was injecting himself into her life, even though his reason for calling was perfectly aboveboard and strictly honorable.

In the end, he didn't call her, telling himself that he could call her in the morning. Since she was an elementary schoolteacher, he figured she would be used to getting up at about six thirty, so that, he reasoned, would be a good time to call.

He was up at six, staring at his phone. Last night he was worried that if he called her, she might think he was stalking her. This morning he was concerned that she might think he had forgotten about her, or at least about her case.

Maybe he should have called last night.

This was new for him, Brooks realized. He was definitely overthinking the situation and he *never* had been guilty of something like that. When there was something to do, he just went ahead and did it, the way he had yesterday when he decided to find Gwen and warn her about Shelton.

Damn it, Colton, get a grip, he ordered himself. *It's just a case.*

He input Gwen's number into his cell phone, then listened to it ring on the other end. Five rings later, he was listening to her voice mail greeting telling him to leave a message and she would get back to him as soon as she was able.

Belatedly, he started talking. "Good morning, Gwen, this is Brooks Colton. I said I'd call you back and here I am." Lord, that sounded so lame, he thought. She was going to think he was a nerd. "Anyway, I've decided to take on your case if you're still interested in my looking into your mother's disappearance. You've got my business card with my number, but just in case you've misplaced it, here it is again." He rattled off his number. "Give me a call when you get a chance and we'll discuss the case further," he told her.

With that, he terminated the call and slipped his cell phone back into his pocket. He decided to take a quick shower before he had his breakfast and applied himself to seeing if the identity of the man in the wall had come to light yet.

Brooks was halfway to his bathroom when his cell phone started to vibrate in his pocket.

Chapter Five

Glancing at the cell phone screen, Brooks saw that the caller was listed as unknown. He debated letting the call go to voice mail, but all things considered, it had been a pretty crazy couple of days so he decided to answer his phone and see who was calling him.

"Colton Investigations," he declared, waiting for whomever it was on the other end to identify him-or herself.

"Mr. Colton? This is Gwen Harrison," the voice on the other end told him. "I'm returning your call." She sounded almost eager as she asked, "You've decided to take my case?"

"Yes, but why did your call just come in as Caller Unknown?" he asked. "Your name and number were both listed on my screen yesterday."

"I decided that maybe it was safer for me to use a prepaid burner phone," she answered. "To be very honest, I was afraid that if Dan could try to hire you to keep tabs on me, he could also hire someone to hack into my phone and use what he found there against me somehow."

He had no idea what to say to that and he knew that as the private detective who had initially tracked her down, he was undoubtedly part of the reason she was so spooked now.

"I'm not a very technically oriented person," she continued, "and I'm probably letting my imagination run away with me, but like my grandmother always says, better safe than sorry."

"Your grandmother sounds like a very wise lady," Brooks told her, sensing that Gwen both needed and wanted his validation in this case.

"She is that," Gwen agreed. "Not to mention selfless. That's why I want to be able to give her some closure about what happened to my mother." She paused for a moment. "Are you really going to take on the case?"

"Absolutely. And I might have some information for you about that private investigator your grandmother initially hired."

"You found him?" He heard Gwen all but whisper in awe.

She sounded so hopeful, Brooks really hated having to shoot her down. "No, but it's the next best thing."

Gwen sounded confused as she responded. "I don't understand."

"I'll explain more when I see you," he promised. "When can we meet?"

"Well, I have to go into school for a meeting. It's about the upcoming school year, but the meeting should be over by one o'clock. Are you able to meet me then?" she asked him.

One o'clock, he thought. That should give him

enough time to check in with Yvette to find out if there'd been any progress made identifying the body that had been buried in the basement wall.

"Just name the place," he told Gwen. "I'll be there. And if you're really worried that Shelton might turn up, I can arrange for you to have protection," Brooks offered.

"Are you talking about hiring a guard?" Gwen asked uncertainly.

She knew she should really jump at the idea of having someone protect her from the likes of Dan, but the thought of bringing yet another stranger into this less than ideal situation did make her feel somewhat uneasy.

"No, actually I was talking about me," Brooks told her. "I could set myself up right in front of your apartment if it'll make you feel safer."

That solution did put a different spin on it, but she didn't want him thinking she was some frail woman who was afraid of her own shadow. Especially since until this thing with Dan had turned so weird, she had considered herself to be a very independent woman. Her grandmother had made it a point to raise her that way.

Torn, she told Brooks, "Let me think about it, all right?"

"Absolutely. It's entirely up to you. But just remember, there is no shame in taking precautions to keep yourself safe," he told Gwen, sensing that she might be worried that accepting his help in this case made her appear needy or vulnerable. And then there was the matter of her feeling she couldn't afford him. He wanted her to know he wasn't going to charge her since this was his idea. The case intrigued him. "Actually, it's rather smart."

Gwen didn't comment on that. Instead, Brooks heard some shuffling in the background, as if she was gathering papers together, preparing to leave. And then she confirmed his suspicions by saying, "I've got to get going. I'll see you at my place at one."

"One o'clock," Brooks repeated. "You got it." He was about to tell her that he was taking the case pro bono but he heard the connection on her side terminate.

Pocketing his own phone, Brooks finally hurried into the bathroom for that shower, mentally giving himself fifteen minutes to shower, shave and get dressed. Since he wasn't slated to meet with his new client until one, he thought he could get a few things squared away before he went to see Gwen.

The woman hadn't seemed all that unnerved yesterday when he had first met her and told her about Shelton wanting to hire him to keep tabs on her. He couldn't help wondering if something had come up between the last time he'd seen her and this morning.

Maybe, he thought, as he got dressed, Gwen had had time to think about the full implications about what being stalked by someone really meant and that might have been what frightened her.

Well, she wouldn't be the first one, Brooks thought. He knew that for a fact. He intended to go out of his way to reassure her.

Dressed and ready to go in under the time limit he had set for himself, Brooks followed that up by going to his favorite fast-food restaurant. He picked up a serving of breakfast for himself as well as one for Yvette. He wasn't above using bribery to get his answers faster and he knew for a fact that his youngest sister was always far more approachable on a full stomach.

Brooks got what he wanted from the restaurant and was on his way to the Braxville precinct in less than twenty minutes.

Nodding at a few people he knew by sight as he passed them on the first floor of the police station, he made his way to the elevator and took it down to the basement.

As he expected, Yvette was already at her workstation.

"First one in, last one out," he declared by way of a greeting as he walked into the lab.

Brooks set down the container that contained sausage, egg, cheddar cheese and finely chopped chives, red pepper and green onion in front of his sister.

Yvette eyed the container, then looked up quizzically at her brother. She made no move to draw the container closer to her, or open it, even though the aroma was exceedingly tempting.

"What are you doing here, Brooks?" she asked.

"I thought I'd drop off some fuel for you so you don't wind up passing out facedown on your work," he told her cheerfully.

Yvette frowned. She was still trying to find her place here within the crime scene lab. Having her brother say something like that wasn't helping.

"For your information, I'm not about to go facedown," she told him frostily. Then, finally breaking down, she opened the container and took out what was inside. Weakening, she stopped trying to resist and took a healthy bite. "But thanks," she added as an afterthought, nodding at the packed breakfast bagel. Lowering her guard, she smiled. "You remembered."

"It wasn't exactly rocket science," Brooks pointed out. "Remember, I grew up with you and some of that time, we did sit near one another at the breakfast table." Very little escaped his attention, even at that young age. "Well, enjoy," he said, nodding at the bagel in her hand.

"Thanks, I intend to," she responded, already making short work of what he had brought for her.

Watching her, Brooks had to laugh. "You never cease to amaze me. You put food away like a real live Pac-Man character—"

"That's Ms. Pac-Man," Yvette corrected her brother with a grin.

"Whatever. The point is that you never seem to gain an ounce," he marveled. "How is that possible?"

"Clean living," she quipped without a trace of amusement in her voice.

Brooks shrugged. "If you say so," he responded. "Well, I'll see you later—"

Yvette looked up him, surprised that her brother was just walking away like this, without asking her anything. Especially after he'd just brought her breakfast in an obvious attempt to get on her good side regarding a case whose intel was supposed to be strictly limited to department personnel.

Yvette spoke up by the time her brother reached the

doorway. "Aren't you going to ask?" she said just before he crossed the threshold.

Turning around, Brooks looked at her, his expression the very epitome of innocence.

Brooks secretly congratulated himself for having played his cards just right. "I figured you'd tell me if you had something to tell."

Frustrated, Yvette blew out a breath. She had obviously fallen for her brother's act.

Again.

But now that she had, Yvette decided she might as well tell him what she'd discovered a little earlier today. "I have something."

Brooks quickly retraced his steps to his sister's workstation. His smile was wide, and he projected the very picture of satisfaction.

"Talk to me," he encouraged.

"Okay, but first answer a question for me," Yvette told him.

"If I can," he replied, being completely serious. He waited to hear what she had to ask, although part of him was certain that he already knew.

"How did you know the guy's name?" Yvette asked.

"So it is him?" Brooks was aware that there was still a small chance that the body belonged to someone else.

"Don't play innocent, Brooks. You know that innocence isn't your strong suit. You can't pull it off," she added. "Now, how did you know who our mystery man was?"

"I didn't," he told her. "It was just a hunch on my part."

Her eyes narrowed as she studied her brother. "That's

a hell of a hunch," she said skeptically. "Since when did you become so clairvoyant?"

"I didn't," Brooks said. "I'm just lucky I guess."

"With that kind of luck, I'd say that you should go to Las Vegas," she said.

He smiled at her. "My luck only works on cases. Getting back to the man in the plastic wrap, you're sure it's him?" he pressed.

"You're the one who provided the card with his fingerprints—after I eliminated someone's more recent prints. A Richard Stanhope," the lab tech said, glancing at the paper where she had written down the name. "*His* were on a database for licensed private investigators." She looked up at her brother again. "Friend of yours?" she questioned.

Brooks nodded. "Yes, he is, actually." He never mentioned the man back when he first took up being a PI. That would have caused too much turmoil at home. "Rick and I go way back," he said now, then got back to his subject. "And Crane's time of death?" he asked.

"What, you want the exact time and date?" Yvette asked incredulously.

"You can do that?" Brooks feigned surprise.

"No, I can't," she responded flatly. "Best I can do is estimate that it was twenty-five years ago—and that figure's not based on decomposition, which he obviously didn't do at the usual rate because he was gift wrapped."

"So how did you come up with it?" Brooks asked.

"Actually, I based it on the state of the cement that was found on the plastic wrap," she told him.

It amazed her the number of tricks she had managed

to have learned in the short amount of time she had been working at the lab.

Brooks was heartened by what he'd just heard. "Terrific." Kissing his sister's cheek, he told her, "I owe you dinner, Yvette."

She frowned, undoubtedly thinking of all the work she had to push aside so she could process the dead man's prints quickly after Brooks had provided her with that business card.

"No, Brooks, you owe me your firstborn," she corrected.

He laughed under his breath. "All things considered, I think you have a better chance of getting dinner out of me than that."

She knew what Brooks was referring to. It was a given that her brother didn't believe he was ever going to get married. Well, she thought otherwise.

"Someday, some woman is going to decide to set her sights on you and you won't even know what hit you," Yvette told him. "You'll just go down like some kind of a lead balloon."

"Someday," he repeated. "But definitely not today and not tomorrow, for that matter."

"You know, annoying confidence like that is just begging to be taken down," Yvette informed him. "Now get out of here and let me do my work for the boatload of people who *hadn't* thought of trying to bribe me with food."

"Their loss," he told her with a wink. And then something suddenly occurred to him. "Hey, can I be the one who tells Jordana that you found out the identity of the guy in the wall?"

"Any particular reason why you want that honor?" Yvette asked.

Actually, he did have a very particular reason. "Yeah, her new boss doesn't think much of private investigators—and yours truly specifically."

"Well, this isn't exactly going to make you look ten feet tall in his eyes," she predicted.

"No, but it just might make the good captain a tad more respectful of what I can bring to the table," Brooks told his sister.

"Maybe," Yvette agreed, then she gestured toward the doorway. "Be my guest, go tell Jordana," she told him, adding, "Good luck."

He looked at Yvette over his shoulder and winked just before he left.

BROOKS FOUND JORDANA on his first try. She was in the squad room when he walked in.

His older sister didn't see Brooks immediately. When she finally did, the pleased look on his face gave her pause.

"I was about to tell you that I was busy so I don't have time to talk," she told him. "But I know that look on your face. It's that cat-that-swallowed-the-canary look, otherwise know as your 'I was right' face."

"That's a lot of words to describe what I'm feeling—but I was," he confirmed.

"I'll bite," Jordana said. "About what?"

"About the identity of the man you found moored in the wall," he replied.

"You're kidding. That was fast," she marveled. "It was Crane?"

"It was. I was just down in the crime lab. Yvette verified it." He still couldn't believe how the pieces had come together. "I thought you might want to be the one to tell your boss that private investigators do have their uses."

"Oh, I definitely will," she promised with feeling, more than happy to be the one to give Hastings the news. "Do you have anything else for me?" Jordana asked.

For the time being, he decided to keep the details of his new case to himself. "Not at the moment. Don't get greedy on me, Jordy."

She rolled her eyes. "I told you, don't call me Jordy."

But Brooks merely grinned as he turned to leave. "Can't hear you," he told her. "I've got to go."

"Stay out of trouble, Brooks," Jordana called after her brother.

"Don't I always?" he asked, tossing the question over his shoulder.

"Unfortunately no," she murmured to herself because Brooks was already gone.

Chapter Six

Gwen just couldn't seem to shake the feeling that someone was following her. This feeling had been going on
for most of the morning.

She was probably being paranoid and there very well
wasn't *anyone* following her, but all the same, she could
have sworn every time she glanced behind her or turned
unexpectedly, she saw someone ducking out of sight.

Just your imagination, Gwen, she upbraided herself.
This was something entirely new for her. She wasn't
normally like this. She certainly didn't usually see people hiding in the shadows as they tried to tail after her.

She supposed that this was the result of everything
hitting her all at once. In a short amount of time she
had moved to another town, changed jobs and now she
was being told that the man she had only been casually
dating had turned out to be a full-fledged stalker bent
on having her tailed.

Had she really been such a poor judge of character?
She couldn't help wondering. And if that was the case,
how was she going to change that? Because if she didn't

change that, she was going to be doomed to repeat her mistake in the future.

Gwen sighed as she took a very roundabout way back to her apartment. No matter how she sliced it, she felt she really needed to adhere to her grandmother's old adage about it being better to be safe than sorry. That was why, when she left the meeting at school, she drove defensively with one eye on her rearview mirror so that she made sure she wound up losing whoever might be following her.

To that end, Gwen had already shut off her regular cell phone before she left the apartment this morning. She had also turned off the prepaid cell phone she had used to call Brooks back earlier today. Neither phone was giving off a signal now.

Even so, she worried that there was still some way she hadn't thought of for someone to be able to track her. Technology seemed to be twelve steps ahead of her, she thought unhappily.

Gwen knew she'd told Brooks she would meet him at one o'clock, but it was closer to one thirty by the time she finally pulled up before the apartment she had recently rented.

As she approached the rental unit, Gwen saw that Brooks was standing outside her door. She had the impression that he had been there for quite a while now. Parking her car, she quickly hurried toward him.

She was apologizing even before she managed to reach Brooks. "I'm so sorry that I've kept you waiting."

He didn't look put out, but that might just have been because he was good at keeping his feelings hidden.

"I was beginning to think I got the time wrong. Either that, or you changed your mind and decided to go with another private investigator," he told her, really relieved to see her.

Was it possible that this woman got better looking every time he saw her? Brooks wondered.

Gwen shook her head. "No, none of the above."

"But?" he asked. He had caught something in her tone that implied there was something else going on that had caused her to be late. He had a feeling it had something to do with the case.

Gwen stalled as she unlocked her door.

"You're going to think I'm paranoid," she began, walking into her apartment. She wasn't happy about admitting this, but if he was going to be working for her, he needed to know everything.

"Just because you're paranoid doesn't mean that they're not after you," Brooks said—only to see her suddenly growing pale right before his eyes. "That was a joke," he told her quickly. He was trying to lighten things up for her, to keep her from being nervous.

It obviously wasn't in this case, he thought, but he certainly didn't want her getting any more spooked than she already was. He'd noticed the way she had glanced over her shoulder—not at him but just at the general area itself. She was looking for someone.

"I'm a little shaky," she said.

Gwen quickly closed and locked her front door. The fact that she treated it like the first line of defense wasn't wasted on Brooks. This wasn't an act on her part. She was really frightened, he thought.

"Did you happen to see anyone following you?" he asked her.

Gwen shook her head, feeling foolish and at the same time uneasy. "No, it's just a feeling."

He didn't want her thinking that she had to apologize. "Hey, I'm the last one to knock a feeling," Brooks assured her.

Taking a can of soda out of the refrigerator, she popped the top, then paused suddenly. "Can I offer you one?" she asked before taking a sip.

Brooks smiled as he shook his head. "No, I'm fine," he answered. "Why don't you just sit down and catch your breath?"

Gwen crossed back to the sofa in the living room. She didn't want Brooks making a big deal out of what she'd just told him or think that there was something wrong with her, for that matter.

"I'm okay." Trying to redirect the conversation, she said, "You mentioned something this morning about having some news about that private investigator my grandmother hired." She waited for him to take it from there.

Sitting down next to her, Brooks nodded. "The good news is that Crane didn't just take your grandmother's money and run off."

"Then you did find him," she cried, making no effort to hide her excitement. This was the first positive information she'd had about her mother's case since Olivia Harrison had disappeared all those years ago.

Brooks qualified his statement. "Only in a manner of speaking."

"I don't understand."

He decided to give her a little background information first. "Colton Construction is currently demolishing a number of old buildings to make way for a new shopping mall that will be built on the same site. When they brought down an old warehouse yesterday, they found a body that had been hidden in one of the basement walls."

Without realizing it, she had leaned in toward Brooks and had caught hold of his hand when he told her about the body. Gwen was squeezing it now, all the emotions that were rushing through her managed to manifest themselves as her grip became more pronounced.

"Was it my mother?" She asked the question in a breathless whisper.

He should have told her who it was immediately, Brooks thought. He could have spared her this awful moment.

"No, but thanks to our conversation yesterday, I could tell my sister to try to match the man's fingerprints to those of Felton Crane. Her department did and they turned out to be a match," he told her. "The man in the wall was your 'runaway' private investigator."

But something he had previous said caught Gwen's attention. "Your sister?"

"My sister Jordana is a detective on the Braxville police force," Brooks told his new client. "And, in the interest of full disclosure, I also have another sister Yvette—the youngest one in the family. She works as a lab tech in the crime scene investigative department."

Gwen was impressed. "That must come in handy," she couldn't help commenting.

"At times," Brooks admitted, then added, "But at other times it's more of a hindrance than anything else. Anyway, finding Crane's body in that building tells me that he must have stumbled across something about your mother that no one wanted to have become public knowledge—which was why Crane was killed."

But Gwen had been disappointed so many times before, thinking that she was close to finding out what happened to her mother, it was hard for her to become enthusiastic about this latest discovery. This, too, could just be nothing.

"Or maybe some other case Crane was working got him killed," she speculated.

He was surprised by Gwen's negative attitude. Here, at least, he could offer her something positive.

Brooks shook his head. "I don't think so."

More than anything, Gwen wanted to cling to the investigator's version of things. But it was going to take more than just a PI with a gut feeling to convince her.

"Why not?" she asked, secretly ready to believe any half-decent theory Brooks could advance that told her otherwise.

"I spoke to someone yesterday who knew Crane. The guy said that Crane would only work one case at a time. My friend maintained that that was what made him so good at his job, his laser-like focus on a case, seeing it to the end until he found a way to solve it."

"So whatever he found that got him killed was connected to my mother," Gwen summed up, finally giving herself permission to grow hopeful.

Brooks nodded. "That's it in a nutshell."

She sat there, letting the words sink in. They were actually getting somewhere, she thought. Turning her eyes toward Brooks, she asked, "So now what?"

"Now, with your permission," he qualified, "I tell my sister about your mother's disappearance so that Jordana is aware of this piece of the puzzle and the investigation officially has legs."

"Does that help?" Gwen asked hopefully, not certain if it did or not. This was a whole new phase for her.

Brooks nodded. "It's now considered to be a cold case." He knew that sounded bad from her standpoint. "A slightly warm cold case," Brooks qualified. "So, do I have your permission to tell my sister? Keep in mind that my loyalty in this case is to you and you do have a right to privacy. So if you don't want me telling my sister that Crane was investigating your mother's disappearance when he suddenly disappeared himself, I'm going to have to find another way to let Jordana know that."

Finished with the elaborate statement, Brooks sat back and waited for Gwen's final say on the matter.

It was immediate in coming. "By all means, tell your sister. FYI, my grandmother went to the police when my mother initially went missing, but at the time whoever she spoke to at the station just thought my mother didn't come back because the burden of being a single mother who was also saddled with an aging parent was just too much for her. He didn't look into the matter any further.

"That was why my grandmother hired Crane to begin with, because the police weren't interested. Someone told her about Crane, so she went to him with the story. Crane said he could find my mother, but he wanted to be paid up front." She had heard the story a number of times. "Somehow, she scraped together the money and she pinned all her hopes on him."

Gwen frowned. She'd been a little girl at the time, but certain things left an impression, like the way her grandmother had been devastated by what she believed happened.

"When my grandmother thought that Crane had run off with her money, she tried going back to the police. But her second attempt to engage them didn't fare any better than her first attempt had. Since there was nothing to suggest that there had been any foul play—to my mother or to Crane, the investigation into the matter was dropped and we never heard anything further about it."

"Until you decided to do some investigating of your own," Brooks guessed, referring to her reason for being in Braxville.

Gwen nodded. "I had to see if I could find anything, even if it has been twenty-five years." She lifted a shoulder in a half shrug. "I thought maybe I'd get lucky. After all, this is my mother and there are a lot of unanswered questions involved. I thought my personal stake in the case would make a difference…" Her voice trailed off.

"No need to explain," Brooks told her kindly. "In your place, I'd feel exactly the very same way," he assured her with feeling.

"I really am grateful," Gwen told him without any

preamble. "About you taking on this case as well as you coming to warn me about Dan."

She didn't want to seem as if she was just taking all that for granted. He didn't have to put himself out like that for her initially. After all, he had no way of knowing that she would hire him.

"Hey, no need for thanks. Just common courtesy on my part," he explained, then told her his own philosophy when it came to life in general. "We all need to look out for one another, otherwise the situation becomes intolerable."

That intrigued her. "You really believe that?" she asked.

"Yes I do. Down to my toes," he told her in all sincerity. And then he flashed a grin at her. "Now why don't you tell me everything you can about your mother—unless you don't have time now," he qualified. "Then we can do it some other time, but I do need to know anything you can remember."

"No, now is fine," Gwen assured him. "This is why I came to Braxville in the first place, to look for her and see if I could find any sort of a trace of her. Or, barring that," she said solemnly, "at least what happened to her." Aware that this meeting was going to take some time, she asked Brooks, "Can I get you anything to eat or drink?"

"Coffee would be good," he said, then added a disclaimer, "Unless you have decaf."

She picked up on his dismissive tone. "No, no decaf." Gwen made a face. "What's the point in drinking something intended to be a stimulant if it doesn't stimulate?" she asked.

Right now, he thought, looking at this woman who had just hired him, he felt as if he was definitely stimulated enough. There was something about Gwen Harrison that made his blood rush and the rest of him stand up and come to attention.

Still, he couldn't say any of this, even in a kidding manner, because then he could very well wind up spooking her. Just the way Shelton had, even though he intended to be strictly honorable and Shelton's intentions were most likely the exact opposite.

"Ah, a woman after my own heart," he told her, then quickly added, "I'm talking about how you feel about your coffee."

She flashed him a quick smile as she made her way into the small kitchen. "I understand what you mean."

As her old-fashioned coffee maker went through its paces and prepared a fresh pot of dark roast coffee, Gwen excused herself and disappeared into her bedroom.

When she emerged, Brooks saw that she had changed into a pair of worn jeans and a comfortable-looking light blue peasant blouse. She had on sandals instead of heels and gave the impression of being more petite than she actually was.

He couldn't help thinking that even dressed like that, she looked like a goddess.

Brooks saw that Gwen had a small covered shoebox in her hands.

She placed the shoebox down on the coffee table

before she returned to the kitchen to pour two cups of coffee.

"Do you take anything in your coffee?" Gwen asked.

A glib line flashed through his mind about asking Gwen to stick her finger into the black liquid in order to sweeten it. It was a lame line he recalled hearing someone once say in junior high school, or maybe that was in elementary school. He recalled that it was a know-it-all kid who thought he was being incredibly clever.

Why that ridiculous comeback occurred to him now was beyond him, but Brooks pushed it out of his thoughts as quickly as it had shown up.

"No," he told her, "I like it black."

She nodded her approval, oddly content that they thought alike in this minor matter, although she couldn't have explained why that pleased her. But it did. "I do, too."

"No foam, no sweeteners?" Brooks questioned.

Gwen shook her head. "Just black, like nature intended."

That was the moment, Brooks realized, that, odd as it seemed, he began to fall in love with Gwen Harrison.

Chapter Seven

Rather than bring the two cups of steaming black coffee over to the sofa, Gwen decided that it might be better to have the coffee at the kitchen table.

Since it made no difference to him one way or the other, Brooks saw no reason to offer any sort of protest. He took a seat opposite his client at the small table for two.

Taking a sip of his coffee, the private investigator nodded his approval.

"Strong coffee," he told her after the sip had ample time to wind its way through his system.

"It's not too strong, is it?" she asked, concerned that she might have been too heavy-handed while preparing the coffee. It was the way she liked it, but maybe he didn't.

Brooks appeared mildly amused. "I believe this is the part where one of the three bears proclaims their serving to be 'Just right,'" he told her, adding, "Your coffee is the kind that makes every bone in my body stand up at attention."

He took another sip, a bigger one this time, and then

placed his cup back down. After a momentary pause, he said, "So, are you going to tell me, or are you going to make me guess?"

Gwen looked at him, perplexed. "Guess about what?"

"About what's in the box," he elaborated, nodding at the shoebox she had placed on the table.

Gwen turned to where Brooks's attention was focused and immediately flushed. In trying to get her coffee just right for her visitor, she had temporarily forgotten all about the box she'd brought out of her bedroom. He needed to see what was inside.

"I'll show you," she answered, getting up from the table.

Gwen brought the shoebox over to the kitchen table. Removing the lid, she tucked it underneath the box and tilted the shoebox toward him so that he could see the contents for himself.

"These are all the photographs I have of my mother," she went on to explain. "Some of them were taken of the two of us, others have my mother and my grandmother in them. There's also a handful of photographs of my mother just by herself."

As she spoke, she took out photos to illustrate her point. "I thought if you knew what she looked like, these might help you find her. I realize that they're at least twenty-five years out of date, if not more, but it's the best I can do."

"No need to apologize," he told her as he carefully looked over the photographs. "I can ask Yvette to age a couple of these for me so we can get more of a realistic idea of what your mother might look like now.

"Oh, and Yvette's the sister who works as a lab tech," he added as an afterthought, anticipating that was going to be the next question that Gwen was going to ask him.

But Gwen was focused on something else he had said, a comment Brooks had made in passing. "Wait, then you think my mother might still be alive?" she asked him.

There was no missing the hopeful inflection in her voice.

"Hey, anything's possible," he said, not committing himself one way or another. At this point, he wasn't about to rule anything out. Hope was a precious commodity and he wanted her to be able to hang on to it for as long as possible.

"But if that's true," she questioned, "then why, in twenty-five years, hasn't she attempted to get in touch with me?" Gwen was really hoping that this investigator could tell her something believable to get her through this trying period of time.

Practicing his trade, Brooks had gotten very good at reading people. He could sense now what this new client of his was looking for. Something plausible she could believe. He did his best to supply it without actually lying to her.

"There are all sorts of reasons why your mother didn't try to get in touch with you," he told her.

She wanted to believe that, but she needed convincing. "Such as?"

"Such as your mother grew embarrassed that she had let this much time go by. And that fed on itself. The more time that went by, the more her embarrassment grew. Or maybe she'd been in an accident that prevented her from coming home. And now she feels it's better for you to just continue living your life rather than having her disrupt it."

Gwen frowned. She wasn't buying that. "That's ridiculous."

"To you, yes, that might sound ridiculous," he agreed. "But maybe it doesn't sound so ridiculous to her." He went on to tell her something that his mentor had once told him. "Fears that haven't consciously been dealt with can grow to huge proportions until they just about overwhelm us."

For a second, she was putting herself in her mother's place. "Well, that's just not true," Gwen protested. "You have to make my mother see that—" And then she abruptly stopped, a surprised expression in her eyes as she realized what she was doing. "I'm talking as if my mother is still alive and you're going to zip right out and bring her back to me."

He really did want her to hang on to hope, at least for a little while. "You know how you said your grandmother has this saying that you live by?" he asked her. "The one that you said went 'better safe than sorry'?"

Gwen had no idea where the investigator was going with this. "Yes?"

"Well, my grandmother had a saying, too. Hers was, 'Prepare for the worst but hope for the best.' I always found those to be very good words to live by," he told his client. "Now why don't you take me through these photographs so I can start to get to know your mother?"

Gwen's lips curved, forming a heartened smile that

he found completely captivating. It took effort to tear his eyes away as she began to take her treasured photographs out, one by one. She spread them out on the table, giving him a narrative as to what was in each of the photographs as best she could. There weren't all that many and she couldn't possibly remember all the circumstances she was now reciting for him. His guess was that, as a child, Gwen had had her grandmother repeat the stories that were behind the photographs over and over again.

From the state the photographs were in, he didn't doubt that they had been pored over countless times and she had memorized all the circumstances that went with each photograph until she probably believed that she could actually remember back that far.

When Gwen had taken the last photograph out, one depicting what appeared to be a lovely young woman and her three-year-old daughter, she looked up at Brooks, clearly wishing there were more photographs to show him.

"I guess that's not much to go on, is it?" she said ruefully.

"It's more than I had before," Brooks kindly pointed out. He watched as Gwen neatly gathered the photographs together and returned them to the shoebox that had housed them. "You mentioned the other day that your mother left Kansas City and came to Braxville to find out why your father had stopped sending her money to support the two of you," he began.

"That's what my grandmother surmised because

there was money coming in, and then she saw that there wasn't," Gwen maintained.

"Do you have any idea who your father was or where he lived in Braxville?" Brooks asked. He knew it was a long shot, but at bottom, he was an optimist.

However, Gwen shook her head. "No. All my grandmother could tell me was that the man who fathered me worked for your father's construction company."

"Do you think your grandmother knows the man's identity," Brooks asked, "but for some reason she's just not telling you?"

Gwen paused for a moment, thinking. "I suppose it's possible, but I really doubt it. I mean, why would she be trying to protect that man? She made no secret of the fact that she didn't approve of him not stepping up and doing the right thing. And don't forget," she told Brooks, "he's the reason that my mother took off in the first place."

Brooks had his own thoughts on the matter. It could very well be possible that Rita Harrison knew the man's identity but for some reason, she wasn't saying anything because she was trying to shield Gwen.

There were too many unknowns in the case right now, Brooks decided, for him to be able to say anything for certain.

What he needed was more information. "Would you mind if I talked to your grandmother?" he asked.

Brooks really needed to talk to the woman so he could get more input. But he didn't want to have Gwen thinking that he was planning on just barging into Rita Harrison's life and firing questions at her point-blank, especially since he had gotten the impression from Gwen that her grandmother wasn't doing all that well healthwise.

"Well, like I said previously, my grandmother's not here. She's back in Kansas City. I can take you to her," Gwen volunteered. "But I'm not free to go anywhere until the weekend. Right now, I'm the new kid on the block," she said, referring to her new job at the elementary school, "so I can't just suddenly take off for a few days." And she didn't want him talking to her grandmother without her.

"Understood," Brooks assured her. "I can look into some things from here. And there's also the matter of finding out just who killed Crane. I'd like to see if I can come up with a working theory to give Jordana."

Gwen nodded. She understood where Brooks was coming from.

Sensing that the private investigator was getting ready to leave, she rose to her feet. She was going to accompany him to the front door.

"You'll call me if you find anything?" she asked just before she opened the door.

"Count on it," he promised. "I mean, it's your case that helped me to identify Crane in the first place," he reminded her, thinking again what a small world this actually was.

When Gwen began to go out the door with him, Brooks turned to her one last time. "I realize that people aren't restricted by gender roles anymore, but you still don't have to walk me to my car," he joked. "I can get to it on my own."

"I'm not walking you to your car," she told him. "I did, however, forget something in mine. By the time I got to my apartment complex, I knew that I was running late and when I saw you standing in front of my door, all I could think of was getting to you so I could properly apologize for the fact that I'd kept you waiting."

"Oh, well if that's the case, I'll walk you to yours," he said good-naturedly, adding, "It's on the way to mine, anyway."

"Well, that seems fair enough," she teased.

Walking beside him now, it felt somehow right as well as comfortable. It was as if they had always been doing this, walking together this way.

As they came to her car, Gwen turned toward Brooks and told him, "This really means a lot to me."

"Being walked to your car?" A teasing smile playing on his lips even though he knew what she meant.

"That's just nice," she said honestly. "But what I was referring to was you taking on my case like this," she explained. "You still haven't actually said anything about what you're planning on charging me," she reminded the investigator.

"Well, if it makes you feel any better, I'm not looking to retire after I finally close this case." And then Brooks smiled down into her face as he looked into her eyes. "Don't worry, I intend to be more than reasonable about the charges for my services." He shared something further with her in hopes that it would reassure her. "I like taking on cases that challenge me and this one certainly promises to be a challenge."

"You really mean that?" she asked, hoping he wasn't just stringing her along, trying to placate her.

"I never say anything I don't mean," Brooks assured her.

Maybe she was being gullible, Gwen thought. But heaven help her, she believed him. And believing him gave her hope.

Standing here like this, so close to him that she could feel the warmth coming from his body, was making her very skin tingle, she thought.

Tingle and heat up, she realized.

She couldn't help wondering if what she was experiencing was due to the fact that in some way, she was on the rebound after having been with Dan. After all, Dan had been charming in the beginning. It was only after some time had passed that she realized there was no substance there and eventually, his true colors began to show. But she hadn't known any of that in the beginning.

Heaven knew that the tall, sexy private investigator certainly fared exceedingly well when it came to a comparison with the other man. All in all, it was like comparing a filet mignon to a fast-food hamburger.

The unexpected comparison had Gwen smiling to herself. She had always had a real weakness for filet mignon.

"That looks good on you," Brooks observed, his voice breaking into her thoughts.

Surprised by his comment, Gwen looked up at him. "What does?"

"That smile of yours. It seems to light up your whole face," he told her.

His words stirred up something in her stomach. For a second, she was tongue-tied. And then, because she had no real comeback to offer him, she murmured, "You have to say that."

"No, I don't," he protested. "In taking on your case, I have to solve it. But I don't *have* to say anything even remotely flattering to you—unless I actually want to and mean it. Which I do. In both cases."

Without actually being aware of it, Brooks drew closer to the woman before him, cutting the distance between them down to absolutely nothing.

He told himself that he had to get going. There was no actual hurry, but he sensed that by standing here like this beside her, he was playing with fire and he wasn't certain that he was carrying the kind of fire insurance that was necessary to prevent a fatal burn.

Even if he was, he was certain that it definitely wasn't sufficient enough to bank down any flames that were now leaping up in his veins, threatening to completely incinerate him.

Her eyes were melting him, Brooks thought. They were going to be his undoing, turning him into a puddle.

He knew he shouldn't be mixing business with pleasure, shouldn't be giving in to this feeling that was sweeping over him, but it was getting really, really hard to resist.

And when she turned her face up to his like that, his ability to resist went from a vague possibility down to zero—and even that number was dropping quickly.

Before he knew what he was doing—certainly before he could stop himself—Brooks found himself framing her face with his hands and then lowering his mouth down to hers.

His fate was sealed.

As he kissed her, he could have sworn that he felt fireworks erupting and zipping right through his veins. His kiss immediately intensified, making everything that much hotter than it had been only a few moments ago.

And then, just like that, the explosion came. Not a figurative one, but a literal one. The explosion turned into what sounded like a series of explosions, like the kind emitted by high-pitched automatic gunfire.

Brooks only had time to react. Grabbing hold of Gwen's shoulder, he pushed her away from her car, then down on the ground. He flung his own body over hers, effectively covering it in its entirety.

She didn't even have time to be afraid.

The unnerving noise continued, echoing in her head.

Chapter Eight

It was over as quickly as it had started. The high-pitched crackling, shooting noises faded away as if they had never happened.

The second they did, Gwen became even more intensely aware of the fact that Brooks's hard body was still covering hers. She became aware of other things as well, like the fact that every breath she took seemed to bring her body up, touching his.

Not to mention that somehow, they were now facing one another and his eyes were on hers. In addition, one of his hands was cradling the back of her head, keeping it from hitting the sidewalk.

"I think it's over," she finally managed to say out loud.

"Yeah," he responded.

Then the next moment Brooks realized that the woman beneath him was giving him more than a status report. She was telling him that it was safe to let her up now.

"Oh." Brooks all but sprang to his feet, then took her hand so that he could help her up, as well.

The first thing she did was look at all the car windows to make sure none of them had been shot out. They hadn't been.

"Well, at least the windows are still intact," she told Brooks.

"I don't think that was gunfire we heard," he said, doing his own survey, both of her vehicle and the surrounding area. The cars parked around hers all seemed to be intact.

"If it wasn't gunfire, what was it, then?" She had to admit that once she played the sound back in her head, it didn't seem as if it actually *was* gunfire.

"I'd say it sounded more like firecrackers going off," he told her.

"Firecrackers?" Gwen repeated. This was August. She associated firecrackers with the Fourth of July. Maybe a couple of weeks before and after the holiday. But not in August. "Are you sure?"

Brooks had crouched down beside her vehicle, doing his best to peer under it and assess the damage. He was not about to use his hands to pull out anything he might have found just in case one of the firecrackers were still live and could go off.

"Yep," he declared. "Those were firecrackers." He pointed toward the area on the ground that was just beneath the center of the automobile. There was a cluster of spent firecrackers right there.

Gwen eyed the firecrackers uncertainly. "They're not going to go off any more, are they?"

"Doesn't look likely," he replied, "but I think we

should have this checked out by the police, just to be safe." He already had his cell phone out.

Not bothering with a middleman, Brooks placed a call in to his sister. Once he explained what had happened, and assured her that neither he nor Gwen had been hurt, she told him that she and her partner would be there as soon as they could.

Putting his phone back in his pocket, Brooks looked Gwen over again carefully. She had insisted that she was all right, but he wanted to make certain for himself. She appeared to be unhurt.

"Are you sure that you're okay?" Brooks asked her again.

"I'm sure. I'm just shaken up—and really annoyed," Gwen admitted. She looked back at her car and frowned. "Why would someone do something like this?"

"To make a point. Maybe for the effect." He was just guessing now because he had no real answers for her—yet. But he could see that there was something on her mind, gnawing away at her. "Why? What are you thinking?"

Ordinarily, she might have just waved this away. But since he was technically in her employ, running an investigation for her, she should tell him everything.

"All morning I had this uneasy feeling that there was someone following me." She blew out a breath. "I know I'm probably just imagining it, or being paranoid, but still…" Her voice trailed off, as she looked up at him, frustrated.

"Did you actually see anyone?" he pressed her in all seriousness.

"Then you *don't* think it was my imagination?" she questioned.

"At this point, we can't rule anything out yet," he told her. And he said what he knew they were both thinking. "If Shelton wanted to hire me to follow you around and keep tabs on you, he could have just as easily turned around and hired someone else to do it."

Gwen frowned uneasily. She knew he was right. Still, she almost wished he had lied. "I thought your job was to reassure me."

"No," he contradicted. "My job, among other things, is to make sure that you stay safe."

She forced a smile to her lips. She had to admit that hearing him say that those were his intentions did reassure her to some degree.

"How long do you think it'll be before the police get here?" she asked, glancing in the direction she knew they would be using in order to get there.

"It shouldn't be that long, but it's hard to say," he answered honestly.

She nodded. "Then maybe we should go back to my apartment and wait there."

His smile was warm, comforting. He really wanted to set her at ease. "Sounds like a plan."

As Gwen turned away, ready to cross back to her apartment, he suddenly stopped her. *Now what?* she wondered. As she looked at him quizzically, he proceeded to take a couple of curled-up leaves from her hair. Brooks held them up for her to see as if to silently explain what he was doing, and that he wasn't just pretending to groom her.

She cocked her head, amused at this bit of normalcy amid the chaos.

"Anything else?" Gwen asked him.

"No, you look just as perfect as you did before we wound up diving for cover," he assured her.

"Uh-huh," she murmured. "You don't need to flatter me."

"I wasn't," he told her innocently. "That was just me, exercising my keen powers of observation."

"You do realize that I've already hired you," she teased. "There's no reason to keep complimenting me."

"I know," he replied. They'd reached her apartment by now. Brooks waited for her to unlock her door again, then he moved her gently aside so that he could enter first and look around.

She picked up on that immediately.

"What, you think someone slipped into my apartment while we were out there, ducking for cover?" she questioned.

The possibility made her feel *really* uneasy.

"That would be one explanation for why there was a diversion," he told her.

"You're making me nervous," she confessed. "Very nervous."

"Well, if it's a choice between having you nervous and having you compromised, I pick nervous every time," he told her without any qualms.

Gwen had to admit, if only to herself, that part of her was beginning to regret having come here to find out what happened to her mother.

The moment the thought occurred to her, Gwen instantly regretted it. She'd never been the type to just fold up and run. She had always been the type to stand her ground and dig in. If someone was attempting to spook her or make her back off, then maybe she was actually closer to solving her mother's disappearance than she thought she was.

And if this was just Daniel's way of getting to her, she wanted to know that, too.

SURPRISINGLY, IT TURNED out they didn't have long to wait. Jordana and her partner, a six foot tall, shaggy-haired detective named Reese Carpenter, arrived at her door and rang the doorbell within the half hour.

"Slow day?" Brooks asked her, kidding because he knew that lately, the opposite was true.

"Actually, I just thought we'd come by to take a look and eliminate this from our to-do list," Jordana told her brother. "Cold cases are pretty far down on our list of things to investigate, seeing as how the clues are all buried in the past and ice-cold. Show me where this firecracker 'attack' happened."

"Follow me," Brooks said.

"To the ends of the earth," Jordana quipped.

"Luckily, that won't be necessary," Brooks told his sister, leading her as well as her partner over to Gwen's car. Gwen came with them. "We thought you'd like to be the ones who pulled the firecrackers out to examine them."

Jordana began to bend down, but her partner stopped her. "I'll do it. You won't want to get oil stains on those slacks of yours," Reese said, snaking his way under the car.

Using a handkerchief to secure it by one edge, Reese looked the string of firecrackers over carefully. All of them had gone off and no longer offered any further danger. He held out the spent firecrackers for Jordana to look at.

Jordana in turn examined them carefully. She found nothing unusual or suspicious about them.

"They're just run-of-the-mill firecrackers," she pronounced. "They were probably tossed under your car by some kids playing a prank," was her best guess. "Or maybe the kids thought they were being clever. After all, the Fourth of July was just last month and there are probably a lot of unused firecrackers lying around in this town," she pointed out, then turned to face Gwen directly. "You haven't irritated any parents, have you?"

Gwen shook her head, rejecting that idea. "I'm too new to have irritated anyone," she told the police detective. "Besides, my only goal is to educate the kids in my classroom, not lock horns with their parents."

"Admirable. I can't see any parent taking exception to that and prodding one of their kids to make his or her displeasure known by throwing live firecrackers underneath your car. For one thing, they'd have to know what sort of car you drove. That would have to take a bit of surveillance work.

"No, I'd say that this is back to being just a random, senseless prank." She offered the woman beside her brother an encouraging smile. "Anything else I can resolve for you?"

Gwen wanted to say that the situation wasn't really resolved, but she kept that to herself. "No, I'm fine."

"Then we'll be going," Jordana said. "Nice meeting you, Ms. Harrison. Sorry the circumstances had to be this unsettling."

Gwen nodded. "Yes, me, too," she agreed. She stood beside Brooks as his sister and Reese got back into their car.

"She looks like you," Gwen commented.

"You think so?" he asked, turning toward her as he accompanied her back to her apartment. "I don't see it."

"That's because you're too close," she said.

He shrugged. "If you say so." He had something more important on his mind to take care of right now. "Are you going to be all right if I leave you?"

"A week ago, I didn't even know you existed and Dan was just this guy I had broken up with who was lurking in the shadows, although I didn't know that at the time. Point being," she said as she returned to her apartment, "is that I was all right in my ignorance. Now that I've been informed, I'll be on my guard. Don't worry, I'll be all right."

"I'm sure you will be." He didn't want her thinking he felt she was this fragile flower. He just wanted to be sure she was going to be okay. "But I'm still going to swing by after I finish up what I intend to do."

Gwen smiled at him. Knowing he was going to be back again later made her feel better, although she wasn't going to say so. "Okay, I'll keep a candle burning in the window," she told Brooks.

"Just don't put it near the curtains," he warned, amused.

"I won't," she replied, doing her best to try to keep a straight face. She realized that he wouldn't get paid if anything happened to her, but it was still nice to think that he was looking after her.

"Keep the door locked," he said as he left, then realized that had just slipped out. When he turned to look at Gwen, he saw that she looked amused rather than indignant.

"Can I talk to strangers?" she asked him, suppressing a smile.

"Use your judgment," he answered.

"I always do."

Flipping the lock into the closed position after Brooks departed, she leaned against the door for a moment. This was an interesting development, she thought.

Well, she reminded herself the next moment, she had paperwork to look over and review. That was the packet she had gone back to her car to retrieve. If she hadn't gone back, she wouldn't have been there when the firecrackers had gone off.

And, she thought the next moment, she wouldn't have had her own private fireworks display either. Because if she hadn't gone back to her car, incidentally accompanying Brooks as he left, he wouldn't have taken the opportunity to kiss her.

She thought about that now as she sat down on her sofa, curling her legs under her, closing her eyes and slowly reliving that moment—just before all hell had broken loose.

Gwen sighed as she opened her eyes again. She felt almost cheated because if it hadn't been for those stupid firecrackers, she would have been free to slowly relive that moment, that exquisite moment when he kissed her and actually made the immediate world momentarily fade out of sight.

She certainly wasn't a novice when it came to being kissed. She'd had her share of men in her life, both the kind who were just passing through and the kind that had lingered for a while until they had mutually gone their separate ways. But she had to admit that not a single one of these men—in either group—could have been accused of setting off fireworks in her veins when they'd kissed her.

Looking back, Gwen couldn't help wondering if that had ultimately been a mere fluke. If what happened right after that kiss had affected the way she'd reacted to it. Maybe it had even heightened the experience somehow.

No doubt about it, Gwen decided. She was definitely going to have to revisit that situation in order to get her answers.

Although he said he was leaving, Brooks didn't immediately drive away once he got into his vehicle. Instead, he lingered where he was, watching Gwen's ground floor apartment. He wanted to assure himself that no one was going to turn up and attempt to get her to open her door to them. Or worse, attempt to break into the apartment.

Now who's being paranoid? the private investigator asked himself.

But in all honesty, he didn't really see this as being paranoid. He saw it as being careful and not taking any unnecessary chances when it came to Gwen's safety.

Brooks remained there for a good thirty-five minutes before he finally decided he should be on his way.

He also decided that for now there was a change in plans. Rather than look further into Felton Crane's untimely murder and who had caused it, Brooks would instead get in touch with a few people he knew in order to check on Daniel Shelton's current whereabouts. The man could very easily have paid someone to plant those firecrackers beneath Gwen's car. But even that indicated that Shelton knew where she lived—information that the man hadn't been able to provide when Shelton had initially attempted to hire him to follow Gwen around and keep tabs on her.

If the man knew where his ex-girlfriend lived, that meant he had hired someone to find that piece of information out for him. Who knew what else Shelton had hired that PI to do?

Brooks needed to either talk Gwen into letting him sack out on her sofa, or he needed to have her agree to relocate and stay in his house. Although he had to admit, of the two places, staying in his three-story house actually made more sense. His was a great deal larger and there was a good chance that Shelton had no idea where he lived, or even that he had decided to provide Gwen with protection.

That missing piece of information, he decided, would enable him to keep Gwen safe, at least until this whole case was resolved.

Chapter Nine

Gwen made a conscientious effort to keep busy so that her imagination wouldn't be able to just run away with her, conjuring up frightening thoughts.

She'd always had a very strong, vivid imagination which not only enabled her to dream big dreams, it could also create things out of nothing. But until now, those things hadn't been scary. So although she had the TV on louder than she usually kept it, filling up the emptiness with the sound of people talking, when she heard the doorbell ring she was sure she had jumped at least three feet in the air—if not more.

She remembered that Brooks said he would swing by later when he was finished. But she also knew that the man did have a life apart from her. Maybe he had even forgotten that he told her he would come by, which meant that whoever was at her door wasn't anyone she knew.

She needed a weapon.

Gwen looked around for something to use in order to defend herself. But there were no handy fire pokers because she didn't have a fireplace. And there was no bat around for her to use because she didn't play base-ball. She didn't play *any* sports.

Ready to give up, she spotted the large carving knife sticking out of her butcher block. Relieved to have some kind of weapon at hand, Gwen gravitated toward that. Although she doubted she could actually use it, it did look intimidating and at least it was better than nothing.

The doorbell rang for the third time, accelerating her heart rate up another level. Taking a deep breath—whoever was at her door obviously wasn't going to go away—she made her way over to the door and looked through the peephole. It actually took her a moment to focus her eyes so she could see who was standing on the other side of her door.

Brooks!

Exhaling a deep sigh of relief, Gwen undid the locks on the door and opened it wide so he could come in.

"I think I'm going to have to get a dog," was the first thing she said to him.

Finding that a strange greeting, he asked, "Why would you do that?"

"So I can feel safe," she told him honestly.

"Hold off on the dog," Brooks advised as he walked inside the apartment. "You have me for that for the time being." He was about to elaborate when he turned around and finally really looked at her. That was when he saw the thick carving knife in her hand. "Did something happen?" he asked seriously.

Gwen was still clutching the knife like a weapon. She put it down on the counter. "No, just my imagination going into overtime," she admitted ruefully. Still, the idea of having a dog—a big dog—to protect her had its merits.

"So nobody rattled your doorknob or even knocked on your door?" he questioned, still scrutinizing her. If she attempted to lie, he knew he'd be able to see right through it.

"No, nobody rattled or knocked. Really," she told him. "I guess those firecrackers going off spooked me even more than I actually thought."

Gwen didn't want to talk about her anxiety anymore. Being afraid like this didn't exactly cast her in the kind of light that she was used to thinking of herself.

"Well, nobody could blame you for that," Brooks said. His voice was gentle, kind and completely understanding as he set down the large bag that he'd brought in.

She opted for a change in subject. "What is that?" she asked, indicating the bag. "It smells wonderful."

"What you smell is Chinese food," he answered. "Four entrees." As a thought suddenly hit him, he looked at her, slightly chagrined. He should have checked first. "I hope you like Chinese food."

"I *love* Chinese food," she told him with feeling, already getting dishes from the overhead cabinet. "But you really didn't have to do this. It's not part of the private investigator package, right?" she asked facetiously, still trying to cover up how nervous she had seemed when she'd opened the door.

"No, it's not," he agreed, joining her in the kitchen. He began to distribute the plates she had taken down. "It's part of the Brooks Colton Package. You get me, I come with food. I think better when I'm not hungry," he explained, then asked, "How about you?"

Gwen nodded. "Me, too." She took out two glasses and then grabbed two cans of soda. She placed one down at her customary place setting, but stopped when it came to the opposite space. "Would you rather have wine? Or a beer? I've got a couple of cans of beer in the refrigerator as well as a bottle of unopened wine."

He could see her with a glass of wine. "You don't strike me as a beer drinker."

"Good call," she commented. "I'm not."

Then the contents of her refrigerator didn't make any sense to him. "Then why—?"

"I thought maybe if I ever got to the part where I had company coming over, or maybe even by some miracle, found my father, he'd like to have a beer—or wine." Gwen shrugged. "I guess I just like being prepared."

"Apparently," he said with a laugh. "I'll have the beer," he told her. "Unless that winds up setting your plans back."

"No problem. I can always buy another one," she said, sitting down. "So—" she picked up the carton labeled fried rice and opened it "—did you find out anything?" Gwen distributed a heaping spoonful of rice on her plate. "Or am I not supposed to ask?"

"I'm working for you," he reminded her, taking the fried rice carton from her and helping himself. "So feel free to ask me anything you want."

"Okay. *Did* you find out anything?" she asked him again.

"Well, what my sources told me is that Daniel Shelton is still just where he was a couple of days ago, in his house clear across the state."

"So he really wasn't the one who threw those firecrackers under my car," Gwen surmised.

She sounded almost disappointed, Brooks thought.

"No, not personally, although, like I said, he could have paid someone to do it for him." They were still dealing in possibilities and he knew how frustrating that could be. So he decided to tell her what he did have. "But I did find out something interesting."

He saw Gwen immediately look alert as she sat up a little straighter. "What?" she asked eagerly.

"This is verified fact," he prefaced, then told her, "Several of the women Shelton had any sort of a relationship with wound up in the hospital. They had everything from deep cuts and bruises to fractured ribs and a broken nose."

"Daniel did this?" she asked, stunned.

"I have my sources and yes, he did," Brooks confirmed.

Lord, she had certainly dodged a bullet there, she thought. If she had stuck around, who knew? She might have joined the ranks of those women. She had only seen his temper flare up once, when she refused to stay in Kansas City. That was when she had broken off their relationship.

"He was brought up on charges, wasn't he?" she asked Brooks. It seemed odd to her that she had never heard anything about that.

"No, he wasn't," Brooks answered flatly. The words left a bitter taste in his mouth.

She didn't understand. "Why not?" Gwen asked. It didn't sound right.

"Because none of the women involved would press charges against him. As far as I could determine, Shelton either paid them off, or he threatened to drag their names through the mud. They were all young women, just starting out. They couldn't risk the embarrassment or suffer from any repercussions."

A few choice names for Shelton flashed through her mind, but Gwen refrained from uttering them. Instead, she just shook her head.

"How could I have been so blind?" she marveled in disgust. "I mean, I didn't think he was exactly Mr. Wonderful, but I did think he was a nice guy—until he started trying to control me," she added. "But when it started turning ugly, I just told him it was over between us and I ended it."

"Apparently, he didn't think it was over, that's why he tried to hire me to follow you." Brooks paused for a moment, putting down his egg roll. "I think what we have here is a two-pronged problem. On the one hand, we're trying to find out just what became of your mother after she came to Braxville. On the other hand, we need to make sure that Daniel Shelton knows to stay out of your life. Permanently."

Heaven help her, Gwen thought, but she did like the fact that Brooks had used the pronoun *we* in both cases, as if they were a united front. It definitely made her feel that she wasn't alone in this.

To be honest, that was a rare feeling for her. It was

one, Gwen thought, that she could really get used to if she let herself.

Don't get ahead of yourself. Remember, you're paying the man for this. He's not being motivated by some form of selflessness. The bottom line here is that the man is motivated by money.

"Did I forget anything?" Brooks asked, his voice breaking into her thoughts.

Gwen snapped out of her mental reverie and forced a smile to her lips. "Not a thing," she assured him. And then, as one thought blended with another, she just shook her head. She was disappointed in herself.

"Something wrong with your food?" Brooks asked, saying the first thing that came to his mind.

"Oh no, the food's terrific," she told him with feeling. And then her smile faded a little. "There's something wrong with my perception," she confessed, then explained why she was so down on herself. "The man's a predator. How could I not have seen that? How could I have missed all the signs? I'm usually so good at connecting all the dots."

"Your 'fault' if you want to call it that," Brooks said, "is that you seem to see the best in people. However, in Shelton's case, there is no 'best.' There's only an illusion of that. Just be glad he wound up going to the wrong private investigator to do his dirty work for him."

Pausing again, Brooks looked at her over the half-finished portions of lobster Cantonese and made a decision. "I'm not going to let anything happen to you," he promised Gwen. "After we finish eating, you're going to pack a few things and you're coming to stay at my place."

Gwen paled slightly, and then pulled her shoulders back. Was this a case of going from the frying pan into the fire? She honestly didn't know. "I don't think that's a very good idea."

He could practically read the reasons behind her misgiving on her face. "Relax, this is strictly for practical reasons," he told her. "You can have one of the guest rooms. Most likely, I'll wind up camping out on the living room couch. I usually sleep with one eye open, anyway, so if you're thinking about having your way with me, it's not going to happen."

Gwen stared at him for a moment, then began to laugh. She laughed so hard, the booming sound just filled the air.

Brooks hadn't heard the full scope of her laughter before and he had to admit that the full-bodied sound really surprised him. It occurred to him that the sound should have been coming out of someone at least one and a half times her size.

But there was a genuineness about the sound that made him smile, as well. "Feel better?" he asked her.

She took a breath as she wiped away the tears from her eyes. It had been a long time since she had laughed until she cried and she had to admit that it felt really good.

"Yes," she answered. "Thank you."

"No thanks necessary," Brooks said, then added with an amused smile playing on his lips, "It's part of the package deal."

Gwen finally began to relax.

IT TOOK THEM a while to finish the impromptu dinner. There were still leftovers and to Gwen's surprise, Brooks put what was left back into the containers, then repacked them in the bag he had initially brought.

When she looked at him quizzically, he explained, "You might want to have the leftovers tomorrow. Leftover Chinese food for breakfast is my favorite."

"Then we really are going to your place?" she asked. For some reason, she had thought that he would change his mind once he had time to think about it.

He nodded. "I think it'll be safer for you right now."

Gwen frowned slightly to herself. "Just how much should I pack?" she asked. She had no idea how to gauge how long she would be gone.

"Just a few changes of clothing for right now. It's not as if we're leaving the country. We can come back for more clothing later—or I can," he suggested, thinking that might be less conspicuous.

She wasn't about to agree to anything wholesale at this point. "Why don't we just play it by ear?" she told him.

Brooks inclined his head. "You're the boss. I'm just here to advise you."

She doubted he really believed that, but she had to admit that for the time being, it was nice to hear him going along with what she said.

When she was finally all packed up, Brooks took her suitcase and the remainder of the Chinese food out to his car. But it was then that Gwen raised an objection.

"I want to bring my car," she told him. "I'm going to

have to be going in to school and you have things you said you're going to need to take care of. We're going to need both of the cars."

She had expected Brooks to try to talk her out of taking her car. When he didn't, she had to admit she was surprised.

"Okay. But let me give you my address in case we wind up getting separated," he offered. Taking his business card out of his pocket, he wrote his home address on the back of it.

The expression on her face told him that she didn't think that was necessary.

"Unless you plan on driving like a maniac, which would be out of character for you, we're not going to get separated." She tucked the card he handed her into the back of her cell phone case.

Brooks smiled at her. "It's called covering your bases," he said.

The more she learned about the private investigator, the more she thought they had things in common. "Very admirable."

"I thought the same thing about you," he said just before he walked to his car. Starting it up, he drove it over to where she was parked. Leaning his head out the opened window, he told her, "Okay, let's go."

Gwen started up her own car. A minute later, she fell in behind him, ready to follow him home.

The journey seemed painfully slow to her. Because of his slow speed, it seemed to her that they caught every single light. She had been in the car with him a couple of times before and he had *never* driven this slowly.

Was he just being cautious, or was this for her benefit? she couldn't help wondering. Maybe he thought she had been so rattled by what happened today, she couldn't focus properly and would wind up losing him if he went any faster.

She had mounted her cell phone on her dashboard before they'd started and she hit his number now. She listened to it ring twice on her end before she saw him hit his own phone just up ahead.

The second she heard him say "Hello?" she said, "You can go faster, you know."

"Yes, I know," Brooks answered.

She expected him to speed up. But he didn't. He continued going at the same speed he'd been going up to this point.

"Okay, have it your way," she told him between clenched teeth, terminating the call.

She was so intent on following the back of his car—and not running into it—that she really didn't take that much notice of the neighborhood they had entered, other than to think it seemed exceedingly nice.

When Brooks pulled his car up in front of a three-story, very modern-looking house, she assumed he was stopping his car to take care of an errand.

But then he got out of his vehicle, pocketed his key and walked up to hers.

"You can park your car right over there," he informed her, pointing out an area to the left of the imposing structure.

She didn't understand. "Why would I want to park

my car?" she asked him. "I thought I'd just stay in my car while you do whatever it is you need to do."

"Well, that might wind up being a long stay for you," he told her.

She didn't understand. "Why?"

"Because we're home."

Chapter Ten

"Home?" Gwen repeated incredulously as she slowly got out of her car and walked up to the three-story building. After staring at the house for a full two minutes, feeling as if she was looking up at a castle, she asked, "You really live here?"

Brooks tried not to laugh at the stunned expression on her face. He supposed despite his last name, most people didn't associate this sort of a house with something that a private investigator would be living in, unless he was a fictional one.

"Yes," he told her. There was no arguing with his tone. "I live here."

"Alone?" She turned around to look at the building again. How was it that he wasn't married yet or at least in a permanent relationship? she wondered as she followed him up to the front door. The man was beyond handsome and the house he lived in was gorgeous.

"Well, business has been fairly good for a while now so I don't have to take in boarders," he said, amused by her question. Brooks unlocked the door and then held it open for her. He waited until she crossed the threshold before he addressed her question seriously. "Yes, I live here alone. So you can see, there's plenty of room for you. You're definitely not going to feel cramped," he added.

"Cramped?" Gwen echoed, taking in the wide, open first floor with its winding staircase. "I might need a compass to keep from getting lost."

"Compasses will be provided upon request. You're probably tired," he guessed, looking at her face. "Just let me drop this off in the kitchen." Brooks referred to the leftovers that he'd brought with them. "And then I'll show you to your room."

Her room. That sounded so permanent. She wasn't sure how to react to that. "You mean the guest room."

"Well, it is a guest room," he pointed out. "And you're a guest so if A equals B and B equals C then A equals C—thereby making the guest room your room," he told her. He looked at her and made a judgment call. "Would it make you feel better if I added the word *temporary* to the sentence?"

"You think I'm being paranoid, don't you?" she said, a little embarrassed.

Brooks was going out of his way to be kind to her and she was acting as if she'd just stepped into a serial killer's lair. He was going to assume that she was ungrateful.

"I think that after finding out that Shelton hadn't quietly disappeared into the night but wanted to keep track of your every move, you have every right to be gun-shy." He considered how to put her mind at ease. "I could ask my sister to send over one of her police officers to stand watch outside the house. Or even inside the house if that would make you feel more secure."

He really *was* nice, Gwen thought, instantly feeling even more guilty about how she must have come across to him.

"No, I'm just being silly—and you're being incredibly understanding," she told him. "This arrangement will be just fine, really. Thank you for opening up your house to me."

Brooks shrugged, willing to play this any way she wanted. "Don't mention it. Actually, having some company for a change would be nice." He gestured around. "This is rather a big house to rattle around in on my own."

Going into the state-of-the-art kitchen, Brooks put the leftover containers of Chinese food into an over-size refrigerator. He picked up her suitcase that he'd brought into the house, then said, "Okay, let me take you to yo—the guest room." He corrected himself at the last minute. He had almost said "your room" again.

Gwen flashed a grateful smile at the PI. It wasn't everyone who would take someone else's idiosyncrasies in stride the way Brooks just had and she knew it.

The bedroom he was having her stay in was located at the top of the stairs on the second floor. Upon reaching it, he opened the door for her, then stepped aside to allow her to look around and get her bearings.

"Wow," Gwen finally said once she had found her tongue and could form words. She looked at him with wonder etched into her features. "I think my whole apartment could fit in here."

"I think that's a bit of an exaggeration," Brooks told her.

"Maybe, but not much," Gwen countered with feeling.

Brooks put her suitcase down next to the queen-size bed. He couldn't help thinking that she appeared a little helpless.

"What time do you have to be up tomorrow?" he asked, lingering in the room a little longer.

She thought his question over, factoring in that she was now farther away from the school than she had been. "Well, I have to be at the meeting at eight and it'll probably take me a little longer to get to the school because of where your house is located, so I'd say I need to be up at six."

"Six, then," Brooks said with a nod. "I'll make sure I wake you up at six."

She didn't want to continue to impose on him, or get in the way of his regular schedule.

"That doesn't mean you have to be up at six," she quickly said.

"Well, I'll have to be if I'm going to wake you up," he told her in all seriousness.

"But you don't have to do that. I've got an inner clock," she explained. "And I've been waking up at the same time for years now, so my waking up at six doesn't present a problem."

Brooks smiled at her. "Tell you a secret. I've been getting up at six myself now for a long while. It'll be nice to see another face sitting across the table from me."

About to leave, Brooks stood in the doorway for a

moment. "Is there anything more you need or that I can do for you?"

"You've already done more than enough for me," Gwen replied.

"All right, then I'll leave you alone so that you can get some sleep. By the way, if you can't fall asleep right away, the remote control for the TV is on the night-stand," he said, indicating the one that was closest to him.

Until just now, Gwen hadn't even realized that there *was* a TV in the room. It was mounted on the opposite wall. The full scope of the bedroom had taken her breath away and left her somewhat dazed.

"Brooks," she called after him.

About to close the door, he quickly doubled back and stopped at the other side of the threshold. "Yes?"

"Thank you," Gwen told him.

The man's smile was almost shy. "Don't mention it," he replied just before he left, closing the door behind him.

Gwen blew out a breath as she scanned the room again. Each time she did, the room just seemed to grow larger.

"I have a feeling we're not in Kansas anymore, Toto," she murmured to herself, repeating the famous line from the iconic movie.

Geographically, she was actually in Kansas, but it definitely didn't feel like that anymore. This was a part of Kansas that she had never seen before.

Gwen felt completely wound up and unable to go to sleep so she decided to call her grandmother that night instead of in the morning. It had been a couple of days since she'd touched base with the woman and she wanted to let her know about this latest development. Her grandmother liked being forewarned.

"Gwen!" Rita Harrison responded with pleasure at the sound of her granddaughter's voice. "What a nice surprise. How is everything, darling?" she asked, adding, "When you didn't call for a couple of days, I started to worry."

"You know, Grandma, you could always call me," Gwen reminded the woman.

"I know, but I didn't want you to feel as if I was crowding you," her grandmother replied.

"Grandma, you could never crowd me," Gwen said. "You have been the one constant in my life since I was three years old. You've been nothing but kind and loving to me my entire life." Then she reminded the woman of something she had never taken for granted. "You raised me when you could have just as easily placed me up for adoption—"

"I could *never* do that," her grandmother protested vehemently.

"I know that," Gwen responded, adding, "I also know you would never *crowd* me. I like talking to you. How do you feel about my talking to you in person?"

Rita picked up on her granddaughter's meaning immediately. "You're coming home?" the woman asked. There was no missing the hopeful note in her voice.

"Temporarily," Gwen stressed. "Do you remember that private investigator I told you about? The one who showed up on my doorstep to tell me that Dan had wanted to hire him to follow me around?"

"Of course I remember. I also remember that you wound up hiring him to try to find your mother," Rita said. "Colton something, right?"

"Brooks Colton, Grandma," Gwen supplied. "He'd like to come by your place so he could ask you some questions about Mom. Is it all right?"

"What kind of questions?" Rita asked before giving her consent.

She really didn't know any specific questions he had yet. "The kind that might be able to help him find what happened to her, Grandma," was all she could tell her grandmother. "He's a good man, you know."

Rita read between the lines. She had always been able to do that with Gwen. "You like this Brooks, don't you, Gwennie?" She waited for her granddaughter to respond. When she didn't, Rita said, "You're not answering me. That means you do. All right, yes, by all means, bring him with you when you come by for a visit. And make it soon."

"Sooner than you think, Grandma. I'll call you as soon as I know when we're going to be there."

"I'll hold you to that," Rita told her, then said with feeling, "You're a good girl, Gwennie. You would have made your mother very proud."

Hearing that, Gwen smiled. Being told that meant the world to her.

THE MORE TIME Gwen spent with Brooks, the closer she felt to him and the more she trusted him. When she wasn't at the school, preparing for the coming school year and the new curriculum, she would return to the beautiful house where the private detective lived.

To her surprise, he had given her a key the second day she was there.

"In case you come home when I'm not there," he explained.

"Are you sure you want to do this?" she asked, looking down at the key in her hand. She was surprised that he would trust her this way. After all, he hardly knew her. "I mean, this is the key to your house."

"I know what it is. I just gave it to you. I trust you," he told her honestly. "Besides, if you planned to make off with the furniture, it would take you a long time to load it onto a van. I'd undoubtedly be back before you could steal it." Humor sparkled in his eyes.

"I wasn't planning on robbing you," she said. "It's just that, well, nobody except for my grandmother has trusted me this much. And she always believed in the saying, 'trust no one.'"

He laughed. "I am really looking forward to meeting your grandmother." He felt that the older woman would be able to fill in some of the more important blanks that Gwen wasn't able to because she'd been so young when her mother had disappeared. "Speaking of your grandmother, have you spoken to her yet about my coming to see her so I could ask a few questions?"

Gwen nodded, pocketing the house key. "I told her all about you and she's looking forward to meeting you."

"I guess, then, this is all working out," he said. "We

can leave for Kansas City as soon as you finish with your meeting tomorrow. As a matter of fact, why don't I drop you off at the school tomorrow?" he suggested. "That way, when I come to pick you up, we can head out straight to Kansas City from there?"

"That sounds like a plan," she agreed. She couldn't get over how much they seemed to be on the same wavelength when they talked, not to mention the fact that he was really easy to talk to. "Are we going to stay there overnight?" she suddenly asked as the question occurred to her. "I want to know because if we are, I have to pack a bag."

"That all depends on whether my questions wind up bringing up more questions," he said. "If past experience is any indication, I'd say yes."

Gwen nodded. "Then I guess I should pack for a couple days," she said. "But I'll have to be back before Monday morning. I can't afford to miss Monday's meeting."

"Understood," he replied. And then he paused, curious. "I don't get something. Isn't this still part of summer vacation?"

Gwen smiled at him. His question took her back. She'd thought like that once herself—until she had learned differently.

"If you're a kid, it is," she explained. "However, the school year doesn't just magically fall into place, fully drawn up and structured. There are teacher schedules to finalize, lesson plans to draw up and so many things to take into account that if I start telling you about them, your head would probably explode."

"I guess I never thought of it that way," Brooks admitted.

"Neither did I when I was on the outside," she agreed. "But once I started teaching, everything suddenly changed. Don't get me wrong," she said quickly, "I really love teaching and I really love kids. It's the prep work that I find a little overwhelming and at times daunting.

"Anyway, let me just throw a few more things into my suitcase and you can drop me off at the school. I should be all done by one o'clock so you can pick me up at the school then."

"It's a deal. You did tell your grandmother that I'm coming and I want to ask her a few questions, right?" he said, wanting to make certain of his facts.

"Absolutely," she told Brooks, about to leave the room.

"And she *is* all right with that, right?" Brooks pressed.

Gwen stopped walking. "You're investigating my mother's disappearance and you haven't even taken any money for it." That point hadn't been wasted on her and she'd told her grandmother about it. "Or pulled a disappearing act yourself, so my grandmother is more than all right. She's close to being overjoyed about you."

He smiled at the information. Looking at his smile really warmed her.

"Well, I do aim to please," Brooks said. He glanced at his watch. "We'd better get going, Teach, or you're going to be late. You don't want the principal making you take a time-out." Humor curved the corners of his mouth.

When he looked at her like that, she had this over-whelming urge to feel that mouth pressing against hers again.

This was no time to give in to her urges, she up-braided herself. And if she stayed here for even another minute she would find herself really weakening.

"No," she agreed, responding to what Brooks had just said, "I certainly wouldn't want that to happen."

With that, she went to the room she was staying in and quickly packed a bag. Within five minutes, she was back and heading for his car.

It occurred to her that with very little effort, she could definitely get used to living like this. With Brooks.

The next moment, she completely blocked the thought out of her brain.

Chapter Eleven

"She can be a little sharp-tongued at times," Gwen said suddenly, wanting to warn the man in the driver's seat about her grandmother. They were just pulling up in front of the woman's home. "But that's just because she's so used to being protective of me."

Brooks found Gwen's warning to be rather sweet. "I promise I won't cry if she hurts my feelings." He then laughed. "It's all right. Don't worry so much. I've dealt with an awful lot of people in my career and many of them didn't care whether or not they said cutting things about me or about my family."

"Well, just so you're prepared," she told Brooks as she rang the doorbell. When there was no answer, Gwen rang it again.

Still nothing.

"Maybe she's out," Brooks suggested, although it was getting late and in his experience, women her grandmother's age were usually home at this hour.

"No, I know she's home," Gwen said. "She's expecting us."

Just then, to prove her right, the front door opened and Rita Harrison was in the doorway.

"Grandma!" Gwen cried, putting her arms around the woman. She was careful not to throw her grandmother off-balance. Rita had been using a cane to get around for the last few years.

The woman who was happily greeting her granddaughter was a slightly heavyset woman in her late seventies. She wore her white hair in a carefully styled hairdo that surrounded her face like a fluffy crown.

Rita was shorter than her granddaughter, although she did have the same luminous green eyes. And when she smiled, Rita Harrison resembled her granddaughter a great deal.

Releasing Gwen, the older woman asked, "Why didn't you use your key, Gwennie?"

"I didn't just want to walk in on you and wind up surprising you," Gwen told her. "Especially since I wasn't alone."

"No," Rita agreed, turning to look at her granddaughter's companion. Her eyes slowly traveled along the young man and closely scrutinized him. "You certainly are not. Is this the young man you were telling me about?" Rita asked, her sharp green eyes taking an extremely full measure of the private investigator. "The one with all the questions?"

Brooks stepped forward, politely extending his hand to the older woman.

"Brooks Colton, ma'am," he said, introducing himself. "I'm very happy to make your acquaintance."

"Well," the woman said as she glanced toward Gwen,

"he's got manners, I'll give him that." Rita shook his hand. "Come into the living room, young man, and sit down," Rita invited, turning slowly around so she could lead the way back.

But for the moment, Brooks remained where he was. "May I?" he asked, offering his arm to the woman on the side that was not leaning on the cane so that she could get into the living room more easily.

Rita didn't say anything, but she did smile as she took his arm and there was, Gwen noticed, just a bit of a twinkle in her eyes.

"You have a lovely home, Mrs. Harrison," Brooks told the woman as they walked into the living room.

"I don't know about lovely, but I keep it clean. With Gwen gone now, there isn't much to do these days," she said with a note of resigned sadness. "Can I offer either of you something to eat or drink?" Rita asked before she began to sit down in the straight-backed chair facing the sofa.

Brooks assumed that Gwen could get herself something to eat if she was so inclined, so he just answered for himself. "No, ma'am. Just some answers if you're feeling up to them."

"Oh, I've been feeling up to them for the last twenty-five years," Rita assured him with enthusiasm. "The only problem is that nobody wanted to take the trouble to ask. Except for that private eye, Crane." She said the man's name with disgust. "And he was just interested in taking my money and making off with it."

"Well, that might not have been the case, Mrs. Harrison," Brooks told her, easing into the subject.

"Please," she requested, "call me Rita. And what do you mean that might not have been the case? The jackass never came back to tell me if he found anything."

"That's because he couldn't," Brooks said. He was glad to see that the woman didn't just dismiss what he was saying. She appeared to be willing to listen. "Someone killed him."

"Killed him?" Rita echoed, looking from the private investigator to her granddaughter. "Who? Why?"

"We don't know that yet," Gwen told her grandmother. "His body was just discovered this week. He was found buried in one of the walls of an old warehouse that was built twenty-five years ago," she said, repeating what Brooks had told her. She watched as shock passed over the woman's lined face.

"Did his death have something to do with my daughter?" Rita asked, gazing directly at the private investigator. "Was he killed because he found out that someone did away with my little girl?" the older woman asked, emotion all but choking off her voice.

"We don't know yet, Rita," Brooks answered. "But I can tell you that the Braxville Police Department is looking into it."

"The police department." Rita said the name as if it was a dirty word, following it with a dismissive snort. "I'm not going to hold out much hope there. I went to them when my daughter first disappeared and they told me that she had probably just run off, that she'd be back again when she ran out of money.

"They didn't know my girl," she said, tears filling her eyes. "My Olivia would have never done that. She would have never left Gwen—or me." For a moment, she was overcome with emotion and she took a few moments to pull herself together before she could speak again.

Brooks studied the older woman for a second, then turned toward Gwen. "Gwen, why don't you get your grandmother something to drink? Maybe make her some tea."

"Would you like that, Grandma? Would you like some tea?" Gwen asked the woman.

Her grandmother exchanged glances with Brooks. "Yes, I would. That would be very nice," she told Gwen. "You know where everything is. I haven't moved anything since you left to move into your own place—and then moved to Braxville after that."

Gwen nodded. "I'll be right back," she promised, then slipped out of the room. She went to the small kitchen to prepare the tea.

Brooks turned toward the older woman. There was something about her expression and her body language that tipped him off. Rita Harrison had something she wanted him to know.

"What aren't you telling me, Rita?" he asked Gwen's grandmother.

Gripping the armrests, the woman shifted in her chair. She seemed rather uncomfortable. But it wasn't her sciatica causing her discomfort, it was the topic she was trying to broach and talk about with the young stranger in her living room.

"This isn't easy for me to say," Rita said haltingly.

"Take your time, Mrs. Harrison—" Brooks began.

"Rita," she corrected him pointedly.

Brooks inclined his head, smiling indulgently at her. "Take your time, Rita," he said, rephrasing his statement and adding, "I'm not going anywhere."

"I know, but I really don't want Gwen to hear this," she explained. Rita took a deep breath, knowing she didn't have much time before her granddaughter returned. "My daughter didn't talk much about Gwen's father. I don't even know that man's name. But I do know that he worked for your father's company," she told him.

Gwen had mentioned that the first time he'd met her, he recalled. This gave him the opportunity to verify that information. "And you're sure about that, Rita?"

"Absolutely," she replied without hesitation. "I also know that the man was married, which was why Olivia was so secretive about him." Her face clouded over. "She did say that the worthless scum told her that he intended to leave his wife for her as soon as he could, but we all know that part was a bald-faced lie he used just to string her along."

Rita's disgust grew as she added, "Every married man with a little something extra on the side swears he's going to leave his wife, but that never happens." She sighed, shaking her head. "I don't know anything else about the worthless, lying vermin, but I believe he had money."

She took in another long, deep breath and then, looking into Brooks's eyes, she said, "My daughter was a kind, hardworking, sweet soul but like so many other highly impressionable young women, she fell in love with the wrong person.

"Oh, for a while he lived up to his responsibilities.

He even sent Olivia money for the baby and for her, although she never said as much. Though it pains me to say it, my daughter was a kept woman," the older woman admitted, unshed tears shining in her eyes. "And then, just before Gwen turned four, the money suddenly stopped coming with no explanation, nothing.

"Olivia kept trying to reach him to find out why he wasn't sending any more money—or even telling her why—but she didn't get anywhere. Finally, she decided to go to Braxville herself in order to confront Gwen's father. I had a bad feeling about it and begged her not to go, but she told me not to worry. That when she came back, everything would be fine again. She sounded so sure…" Rita's voice broke.

Tears spilled down her cheeks as she gazed off into the distance. She struggled to collect herself so she could finish her narrative.

"That was the last time I ever saw my daughter." She looked at Brooks with tears still shining in her eyes. "I *know* Olivia wouldn't just leave us this way. Something awful had to have happened to her, I can feel it," she insisted. Rita put her hand on his arm. "Please find out what happened to my daughter. I have to know."

Brooks didn't usually make promises. What he would say to his clients was that he would try his best to do what they asked of him and he would leave it at that.

But seeing the look on the woman's face, seeing the utter anguish in her eyes, he just couldn't help himself. He made Rita Harrison a simple promise.

"I will, Rita. I'll find out what happened to your daughter," he told her. "You have my word."

Blinking back a fresh onslaught of tears, Rita responded, "Bless you," and gave his hand a squeeze. "Please don't say anything to Gwen about our talk. She doesn't know her mother was a kept woman."

Brooks took out his handkerchief and handed it to Rita. Her impromptu confession as well as her request put him smack in the middle of this situation, Brooks couldn't help thinking.

But the woman was clearly distressed and it meant a great deal to her to shelter her granddaughter from this information and to also protect her daughter's good name. He arbitrarily decided that Gwen didn't need to know and that allowing Rita to keep her secret was beneficial to the older woman.

So, at least for now, he saw nothing wrong in agreeing to keep this a secret from the woman who had initially hired him.

The subject was instantly tabled because at that moment Gwen returned carrying a steaming cup of hot tea on a tray. Right beside it were containers with cream as well as sugar.

Her grandmother was given to using either both, on occasion neither, but usually one or the other depending on her mood so Gwen was prepared for any choice.

She set the tray down on the coffee table right in front of her grandmother, then glanced from the woman to Brooks and then back again.

Something was up, Gwen thought.

"Everything okay?" she asked, addressing both of them.

Rita never blinked. "Everything's fine, dear. Your

friend and I have just been talking and getting to know one another." The older woman slanted a look toward Brooks, silently asking for a confirmation from him.

"Your grandmother told me a lot of useful things about your mother," Brooks told Gwen. "Hopefully, it'll help us pick up her trail, although at this point, that trail is rather cold. Still," he theorized because he sensed that both grandmother and granddaughter needed to hear this kind of reassurance, "there are people to talk to, places to look into as well as trails to follow."

"So it's not hopeless?" Gwen asked.

"Nothing is hopeless unless you give up," Brooks told her. Looking at Rita, he could tell that she was tired although she was struggling to look alert. "Now, we've kept your grandmother up long enough," he said to Gwen, then told Rita, "We're going to go now, Rita."

"Go? Go where?" she questioned. "Are you going back home?"

"No, we're not leaving Kansas City yet. We're just going to see if we can rent a hotel room for the night. Hotel rooms," Brooks corrected himself, knowing how each woman would wind up taking that unfortunate slip of the tongue.

"Hotel rooms?" Rita echoed incredulously. "Nonsense. You two can stay right here." Then, thinking she was just keeping up with this charade that she assumed was being played out for her benefit, Rita said, "Gwen can sleep in her old room and you can sleep right here on the sofa. Gwennie," Rita said, turning toward her granddaughter, "go get the extra bedding from the linen closet and bring it here so that you can make up the sofa for Mr. Colton."

"That's all right," Brooks told the woman, still attempting to veto the idea, "I don't want to put you out."

"You're not putting me out," Rita told the private investigator. "And I'll be very insulted if you walk out on me now." She looked at him plaintively. "You wouldn't want to hurt an old woman's feelings now, would you?"

"No, but I don't see an old woman anywhere," he replied, then looked at Gwen. "Do you?"

Rita laughed, delighted. "Oh, Gwennie, I do like this young man of yours," she told her granddaughter with a wide smile.

Gwen opened her mouth to correct her again, then decided that there was no point. Once her grandmother got a notion in her head, it stayed there and she didn't want to waste any time trying to dislodge it when every moment she had to spend with the older woman was very precious to her.

So instead, Gwen just nodded. "I'll go get the bedding, Grandma."

"That's a good girl," Rita said with pride and then the woman turned toward Brooks. "She is, you know," Gwen's grandmother told him, and emphasized again, "A very good girl."

Brooks had a feeling he was being put on notice, although for the life of him, he really didn't know exactly what sort of notice it was.

Chapter Twelve

Gwen returned in a few minutes carrying a pillow, a couple of sheets as well as a blanket, although since it was August, the blanket was strictly to use for padding in order to make sleeping on the sofa more comfortable for Brooks.

Once she set the items down on the coffee table, Gwen proceeded to make up the sofa with them so that Brooks wouldn't feel as if he was sleeping on a board.

"You don't have to put yourself out like this," Brooks told her. He tried to get between Gwen and the sofa but she shifted, blocking his attempt to get at the bedding. "I can do that. I do know how to make up a sofa."

"I know you can, but it's the least I can do," Gwen said. She paused, looking at the bedding and reconsidering. "Actually, why don't I take the sofa and you can have my bed?"

She could see that Brooks was about to turn her down and guessed at the reason for that. He probably thought her bedroom was decorated with pink and florals.

"I promise that it looks like an adult bedroom, not

something that looks like it's still inhabited by the average preteen girl if that's what you're worried about," she assured him.

"I wasn't worried at all," he countered, then amended, "At least not about what the room looks like."

Gwen thought that was a very odd way for him to put it. "All right, I'll bite," she said gamely. "What are you worried about?"

Well, since he'd started this, he might as well be honest with her, Brooks thought. "I'm worried about staying on my good behavior if I'm in your old bedroom and you should come into it."

"Oh?"

He couldn't read her expression, but he had his suspicions. "Okay, I'm going out on a limb here, but—" The only way to say this was to say this, he thought, pushing ahead. "Tell me I'm imagining the chemistry between us."

Gwen bit her lower lip. "You're imagining the chemistry between us," she said, then reversed herself immediately because that wasn't true. "I'm also lying," she admitted, and then looked into his eyes and went for broke. "You feel it, too, huh?"

"Crackling from across the room," Brooks said. "Even before I kissed you that first time." He smiled at the memory of it. Heat forged through his body. "If I had been wearing glasses, you would have fogged them up. As it was I think my eyes actually got cloudy for a couple of seconds there."

His admission warmed her heart, but she still didn't understand why he was telling her this. "What does this have to do with you sleeping out here on the sofa instead of taking my room?"

"Out here I have to be on my best behavior because your sweet old grandmother is liable to walk in on us at any time. If I'm in your room and you should stop by for any reason…"

Brooks didn't bother finishing the sentence. Instead, he merely raised his eyes heavenward, then looked back at Gwen.

She supposed he was right. It was a lot easier keeping their distance if he had to be the one who was out in the open in the living room instead of her. He was probably thinking that if their positions were reversed, she could always use any excuse to slip back in her room. From there, one thing could easily lead to another. And if it did, she was certain neither one of them would hear her grandmother if she came in for some reason.

"Point taken," Gwen agreed. "But if you find you have trouble sleeping…" she began to say.

He stopped her before she could get any further. "I'll be all right. If you remember, I said that I'm used to sleeping with one eye open. I've done it for so long, I'm not sure I know how to sleep any other way," he told her.

Gwen knew when to withdraw. "All right, then, sleep tight—or however you do actually sleep when you keep one eye open," she said, leaving the description up in the air.

She went back to her bedroom and got ready for bed.

Once she changed out of her clothes and crawled into bed, she found herself lying there, staring at the ceiling and watching shadows cast by passing cars chasing each other.

It felt really strange being back here in her old bedroom, Gwen couldn't help thinking, reflecting on how things had changed. She had grown up in this house, in this room, she thought. She had slept in this bedroom until she graduated from Donnelly College. Since the college was located in Kansas City, in order to save money she lived at home.

That meant a lot of traveling back and forth over the years, but she wouldn't have had it any other way. Living at home instead of a dorm allowed her to be there for her grandmother when the woman needed her.

Once she did graduate and she got her first teaching job, she'd moved out into her own very small studio apartment.

But even so, she still came by to see her grandmother at least once a week, if not more. Rita had never been one to complain, but as she got older, her grandmother had had her share of medical problems. Gwen wanted to stay close by.

If it hadn't been for the fact that her grandmother had asked her to find out what happened to her mother, Gwen knew she would have never moved to Braxville.

Of course, Dan's growing possessiveness had been an added factor to get her to move, but until the day that Brooks had turned up on her doorstep, she hadn't thought it was *that* much of a factor.

But it should have been.

With her brain insisting on reviewing everything, Gwen found herself tossing and turning for almost half the night. It took her a long time before she finally fell asleep. And when she did, it turned out to be a restless sleep filled with half dreams she couldn't really grasp or remember two seconds after they faded away to make room for another dream.

If anything, she felt less rested when she finally got up the next morning than when she'd gone to bed.

Despite feeling like something the cat had dragged in, Gwen was determined to look happy when she walked into the kitchen to face her grandmother.

Her plans to make breakfast for Rita died a quick death when she came into the kitchen and found that her grandmother was already preparing one of her large breakfasts. Not only that, but she was talking to Brooks as she did it.

"Did I miss the wake-up call?" Gwen asked, looking from her grandmother to Brooks and then back again. This was her home base and she wasn't accustomed to being odd woman out.

"We thought we'd let you sleep in, dear." Rita paused as she looked at her granddaughter's face, making it sound as if it had been a joint decision that had been discussed. "Obviously that didn't quite work out the way we had planned," the older woman observed, glancing toward her guest to see if he agreed. She decided that he did and proceeded to ask her granddaughter, "Did you have trouble sleeping, dear?"

Gwen's immediate response was to deny that there was a problem. She didn't want her grandmother to worry and the woman would. But then she decided not to bother with the denial.

Rita Harrison had always been able to see right through her, even when she was a little girl. Saying yes just saved time.

"I guess I had a lot of things on my mind, Grandma. It made it hard for me to fall asleep," Gwen said.

Rita glanced over toward Brooks, then smiled knowingly. "I'm sure it did. Anything you want to talk about?"

"Not really," Gwen said, avoiding both sets of eyes that were looking at her.

To her relief, her grandmother let the matter drop, at least for now. "Well, take a seat, dear. I'm making your favorite breakfast—a western omelet with French toast on the side."

Still feeling restless, Gwen really wasn't hungry. "If it's all the same to you—"

Her grandmother was quick to cut her off. "It's not. I haven't had anyone to cook for or fuss over for a long while now, so hear me and hear me well. Neither one of you are getting up from the table until your plates are clean. Do you understand?"

He didn't know if she was being serious or not, but it cost him nothing to go along with the older woman's edict.

"Yes, ma'am," Brooks answered, not bothering to keep the grin off his face.

"Yes, Grandma," Gwen replied.

Rita nodded, satisfied. "Good. Breakfast is almost ready," she replied.

Despite the fact that she moved slowly, far slower than she had in years past, the woman was definitely in her element and looked quite happy to be making breakfast for her granddaughter and the man Gwen had brought with her, a man whom Rita found she liked a great deal more than she would have ever thought she would.

"Coffee is on the counter if either one of you is interested," she told them, knowing that they would be. Gwen had started drinking coffee at a young age and one look at the man with her told Rita that the private investigator liked his coffee without any frills or fancy additives.

Breakfast turned out to be a surprisingly relaxed, pleasant event.

Her grandmother appeared happy, Gwen thought, and that observation warmed her own heart. She was well aware that this was all Brooks's doing. He had managed to charm her grandmother, something she knew for a fact was not easily accomplished. Rita had always been suspicious of strangers and on her guard, but Brooks had managed effortlessly to get her to open up to him. They acted as if they were old friends.

Maybe it had to do with his promising to find out what happened to her mother, or maybe the older woman had sensed that something was going on between her and Brooks and had put her own interpretation to it.

Whatever the reason, her grandmother had really taken to Brooks and from where she stood, Gwen thought it was a really good thing because this was the happiest, most hopeful she had seen her grandmother looking in a very long time.

After breakfast Gwen cleared off the table and then

washed the dishes. Brooks had insisted on helping her while he made Rita sit and savor a second leisurely cup of coffee.

"I want you to know that I really enjoyed our time together," Rita told them as she brought her empty cup to the sink to rinse out. "No matter what the outcome of your investigation is," she said to Brooks, "I want you to know that you're welcomed back here at any time. Maybe if you come, *she'll* come more often," Rita concluded, indicating her granddaughter with a wide smile and a wink.

"Grandma!" Gwen cried.

"Am I wrong?" Rita asked, her tone challenging Gwen to dispute what she'd just said.

"We can talk about that later," Gwen said, clearly embarrassed by what the older woman was saying without any qualms right in front of the private investigator.

Brooks was quick to come to Gwen's rescue by changing the subject. "Look, before we leave, why don't you show me around your neighborhood?" he suggested to Gwen.

He was also furthering his own agenda. Familiarizing himself with the neighborhood where she had grown up allowed him to see what elements might have gone into forming the woman Gwen had become.

When Gwen hesitated answering him, he told her, "I'd *really* like to see where you grew up."

"Well, I think that's a lovely idea," Rita said, seconding the suggestion. "As a matter of fact, why don't the two of you do that now and then you can come back and spend a little more time here before you start back for Braxville?"

Gwen wiped her hands on the dish towel and then slipped it back onto the oven handle where her grandma usually kept it.

"All right," she agreed. "That sounds good to me. Brooks?"

"Hey, I'm the one who asked you to show me around this city in the first place. Sure. Let's go," he urged, then paused for a moment to tell Rita, "We shouldn't be gone too long. Right?" he asked Gwen.

She laughed. "How big a neighborhood do you think this is?" To her, by definition, neighborhoods were small.

"To be honest, I have no idea," he answered.

Rita patted him on the back. "Take as long as you want, Brooks, and when you've had your fill, just come back."

He smiled at the woman. Brooks had already grown very fond of Gwen's grandmother. "Sounds like a plan."

"You know," Gwen said once they walked out and closed the door behind them, "my grandmother *really* likes you. I've never seen her react to anyone else this way or take to someone this fast."

"Well, that's good because I really like her," Brooks said quite honestly. "I also intend to deliver on that promise I made to her."

"About that," Gwen began as they continued walking down the block, then crossing the street at the light. "Thank you for giving her hope. But between you and me, I know she doesn't really expect you to deliver. She is aware of how difficult it is to solve a murder, much less one that's over a quarter of a century old.

"She just wanted someone besides her—and me—to act as if they cared about what had happened to my mother. I know that, after all this time has passed, she thinks my mother's not among the living. Because if she was still alive," Gwen stated with feeling, "my mother would have found some way to get in touch with us. The fact that she didn't—" Gwen sighed in resignation "—speaks volumes."

Stopping at yet another crosswalk, Gwen saw that the light was green. She stepped out into the street just a step ahead of Brooks.

She was looking at him as she continued talking about her mother, but luckily, Brooks caught a movement just out of the corner of his eye.

There was a car speeding up and it was heading right for her.

He reacted in an instant. That was why he managed to pull Gwen back, out of the way, just in time. Otherwise, the speeding silver sports car would have completely flattened her.

Brooks pulled Gwen to him so hard, she collided with him, sending them both stumbling backward until they both fell to the ground just out of the way of oncoming traffic.

Brooks was on his feet immediately. He ran after the car but it flew down the street and was almost immediately out of sight. He didn't think he could catch up with it, but he did try to get the vehicle's license plate number.

"Damn it!" he bit off, then immediately turned on his heel and doubled back to Gwen.

She was on her feet, shaken but angry as she dusted herself off.

"That was awfully close," she cried just as Brooks reached her. She was breathing hard and would have been even more frightened right now if she hadn't been so furious.

And then she looked at Brooks, her eyes widening as what she had just seen registered belatedly with her brain.

"I think that was Dan!" she said. "It wasn't his car, but I'm sure it was him. You ran after it. Could you make out the license plate?" she asked. By the time she was on her feet, the car had gotten too far away for her to be able to read the plate.

"No, I didn't." There was disgust in his voice. "Whoever was driving, this *wasn't* an accident," he told Gwen.

There was something in his voice that made her nervous. "What makes you say that?"

"The driver had mud on his license plate, blocking out the numbers. This was done deliberately," Brooks said. "Let's get you back to your grandmother's place so you can pick up your things. The sooner I get you back to my house, the better I'm going to feel."

Chapter Thirteen

Rita sensed there was something different the moment that Gwen and Brooks returned. For one thing, since her granddaughter had said she was taking the private investigator around the neighborhood, Rita expected them to be gone a great deal longer than they were. Moreover, she could feel the tension in the air despite the fact that they both appeared to be smiling. She concluded that whatever was going on, it wasn't because of an argument they'd had.

Still, she felt the need to ask, just in case. "Is anything wrong?" She directed the question to both of them.

"No, we just decided that we should get an early start going home," Brooks explained, taking the lead.

Gwen and he had discussed what they would say to her grandmother. Neither one of them wanted to alarm the woman by telling her about the car that had almost run Gwen down.

"We completely forgot that Brooks had a family commitment to attend," Gwen added to give the sudden change of plans more plausibility.

Rita nodded, going along with what she felt in her heart was a manufactured story.

Her sharp eyes swept over her granddaughter's apparel. "Better find something else to wear," she advised. "Your skirt has a streak of dirt on it. Or that could even be mud. In any case, it doesn't look as if it's about to come off easily."

Gwen looked down at her skirt. She thought she'd managed to get everything off, but obviously she had missed a stubborn patch. Leave it to her grandmother to home in on that.

"I guess I'll have to send this to the cleaners," she said.

Rita nodded her agreement. "And be more careful in the future."

"That, too," Gwen replied. She went to hug the woman. "I'll see you soon, Grandma," she promised.

"You'd better," Rita said. And then she looked at Brooks over her shoulder. "Both of you," she added, putting him on notice.

"WE DIDN'T FOOL HER, you know," Gwen said after they'd left her grandmother's house and were on their way back to Braxville.

"I know. That is one very sharp old lady," he told Gwen with admiration. "I think she would probably get along very well with my mother. As a matter of fact…" His voice trailed off for a moment as he stopped to roll something over in his mind. He liked the idea and decided to bounce it off Gwen. "How would you like to meet my mother? For that matter, how would you like to meet my whole family? The ones who live in Braxville at any rate," he qualified because Bridgette, who comprised one-third of the triplets in his family—he and Neil being the other two-thirds—currently lived in Kansas City thanks to her job with the State Department of Health.

For a second, the air stopped moving in Gwen's lungs and she looked at him, stunned. Brooks had just said he wanted to introduce her to his family. This was a huge step. Or it would be if it meant the same thing to Brooks that it did to most men.

But Brooks wasn't most men, she reminded herself and consequently, bringing her around to meet his family was probably just a convenient way for him to fulfill a family obligation, she thought. Most likely it had nothing to do with her at all.

A small wave of disappointment washed over her, but she pushed it away.

"Well, you met my entire family," she said, referring to her grandmother. "I suppose that turnabout is only fair play," she told him. Gwen shifted to study his profile. "When?"

"My mother is always saying how she doesn't see enough of her children now that they're all grown and so busy with their careers, so my guess is she'll be more than happy to have us all over at the house as soon as possible. Like today," he added with emphasis. "Would that be all right with you?"

Well, she had set herself up for that one, Gwen thought, so it would have to be all right with her. For the time being, she turned her attention toward something else. "And by 'house' you probably mean mansion, right?" Gwen asked him.

"Well, technically," he told her with a bit of reluctance, "it's referred to as an estate. It's a custom-built house in the Lakemont Estate development. That was also the first development that my father built."

There was no pride in his voice, she noted. He was just stating a fact. If she actually knew who her father was and he had done something so outstanding, she would have been proud enough to burst.

But if he didn't seem to care for the man, then why was he orchestrating this meeting to take place—and so quickly?

"What's the hurry?" she asked him out loud.

Brooks had his eyes on the highway, but he spared her a quick glance. "What do you mean?"

That sounded so artificial, she thought it could break into little pieces. "Wow, you're probably an excellent private investigator, but I'd say your 'innocent act' definitely needs a bit of work."

"Okay, you want to know why I thought meeting at least my mother was a good idea? You had a pretty close call today and that had to have shaken you up." He knew for a fact that it did. "I'd say a dose of normal would really be in order. My mother, Lilly, is the closest to normal and nurturing that I know. She'll definitely make you feel welcomed and just better in general," he said. "Meeting the rest of my family—if they happen to be there—will just add color," he told her.

All this talk about his mother made her wonder about his father, "Would your dad be there?"

"This is the weekend, chances are that he will be," Brooks said as he sped up and made his way around a vehicle he felt wasn't doing the speed limit. "Why?"

This had been at the back of her mind now since she had first met Brooks. "Since he's the head of Colton Construction, maybe he could tell us something about my mother. About the man she had gone back to meet with." Brooks noticed that she had deliberately avoided using the term "my father," but he knew that was who she was talking about.

Brooks read even further between the lines. She needed to have that notion squashed right now. "My dad is all about business, that's all he has ever had time for. If you're thinking that he might have had an affair with your mother—that he might be your father— I honestly don't think that he did. All he has ever cared about since I can remember was his construction business. If he had an iota of extra time to spare, he spent that time at home."

"But maybe he knew my father," Gwen said, not ready to let go of the idea.

"Maybe he did know your father—but most likely he didn't know he knew, at least not this part of it," he assured her.

Brooks looked up into his rearview mirror and saw a car swerving from one lane to another. It narrowly avoided crashing into him, but at the last minute, Brooks went into another lane. Even so, he never dropped the thread of his conversation with Gwen.

"My father's relationships were all strictly focused around his construction business. I doubt if he even knew that the people who worked for him *had* personal lives. To know that would have meant getting involved with them, and he didn't. *Ever.* Trust me," he told her.

She did. Heaven help her, she did trust this man. And part of her was worried that she was being *too* trusting. Worried that the attraction she felt toward Brooks was coloring her perception of the man and making her block things out that might have ordinarily been a warning signal to her.

"You're sure about that?" she asked him, just wanting him to say it one more time.

"I'm sure. But that doesn't mean I'm not going to continue to follow up on the details. Trust but verify," he said with what Gwen thought of as a sensual smile. Brooks was quoting an edict that he had lived by not just in his work but for most of his life.

She pressed her lips together. "What if the details lead you somewhere that you don't want to go?" she challenged.

"My first allegiance is to you," he said simply. "I promised you answers and I intend to get you answers. But right now, I need you to relax and I really can't think of a better way to get that to happen than to bring you over for a visit to the old homestead—after I get you checked out."

"Hold it. Checked out for what?" she asked, confused. Was he telling her that he was worried she had some sort of infectious illness she could transmit to his family?

Working his way around another slow-moving vehicle, he glanced at her. Was she serious? "You were almost run over by a maniac behind the wheel of a car."

Oh, he was talking about the near accident. Now it made sense. And he was being overprotective, she thought. "The key word here is *almost* and I wasn't."

"No, but the back of your head did meet the pavement rather unceremoniously. I just want to make sure there are no bad aftereffects, like a concussion or you fracturing something. It's possible," he emphasized when Gwen made a dismissive noise to show what she thought of that.

"I'm not even limping. I'm not seeing double and everything is fine. Stop worrying," she said.

He wasn't exactly keen on her powers of observation right now. "You didn't even realize that you got mud on your skirt."

"That can easily happen without a concussion," she insisted.

This woman sounded as if she was prepared to argue until the cows came home, Brooks thought. "Just humor me," he told her, pointing out, "This is just for your own good."

Gwen frowned as she blew out a breath. "Since when did you become my parent?"

"Not a parent," he answered patiently. "Just being a concerned friend."

"So we're friends?" she asked him, a skeptical tone entering her voice.

"Aren't we?"

"Well, most of my friends aren't this annoying," she retorted. To be honest, she didn't think of him as a friend. She was setting her sights on something a lot more than that.

Maybe she had made a mistake and misread the signals she thought he was giving off—although she doubted it.

His smile was warm, charming—and driving her utterly crazy.

"I consider being in a class by myself."

She rolled her eyes. "No argument there," she told him.

"Good, hold that thought. No argument," Brooks repeated with emphasis.

Something about his tone set off warning signals. Exactly what was he telling her? "Wait, you lost me, Brooks. What thought am I supposed to be holding?"

"The one about you not giving me an argument," Brooks answered.

She still didn't understand. "Wait. What am I not giving you an argument about?" she asked, back to being leery.

"Getting checked out," he said without any fanfare.

"Oh no. No, no, no, no. I am *not* going to a hospital to get checked out," she informed him adamantly, her bantering tone entirely abandoned.

He had actually anticipated her digging in her heels and was prepared for that. "All right, we'll compromise. I'll take you to see a doctor."

Okay, he was just kidding then, she decided. "In case you haven't noticed, it's the weekend. There's no doctor around who has office hours on a weekend," she told him with finality—or so she thought.

"I know one."

The way he said it, she suddenly knew that he had to. "Of course you do," she cried with resignation. "Why did I even doubt that for a minute?"

"Beats me," he said cheerfully, his mouth curving again. "In case you're wondering how I know a doctor whose services are available to me on a Sunday…"

She shifted in her seat, giving him a piercing look. "Oh yes, please tell me," she urged in a less than sincere voice.

"Sarcasm isn't really a good look on you. But since you asked," Brooks continued, tongue in cheek, "he was a client of mine. I tracked down his daughter Heather a few years ago. She had run off to Abilene with this guy she had met on the internet. When I found her, she was more than willing to go back home—the guy turned out to be a serial abductor with a weakness for teenage girls.

"Heather just graduated from college this June. Her father told me he was in my debt for life and if I ever needed anything…" His voice trailed off and Brooks let his sentence hang there, confident that Gwen could easily fill in the blanks.

"You might as well stop fighting this," he concluded, "because I'm bigger than you are and if I have to, I can carry you in to see him."

"That's not fighting fair," Gwen protested.

"So who said anything about fighting fair?" he asked. "Fighting fair is for people who have time to argue and go back and forth until one of them is exhausted and gives up. We're up against a clock here. You'll submit to a quick exam, he'll clear you if you're as okay as you claim to be and we're on our way to see my mother. I'm happy, you're happy and my mother's happy," he added as if that was enough to tip the scales in his favor.

"Fine," Gwen declared, throwing up her arms and giving in. "If it really means that much to you…" She didn't get a chance to finish.

"Atta girl!" Brooks said, genuinely happy. "If I wasn't driving, I'd kiss you."

She looked at him. Her skin was growing hot again, she realized. She needed to get better control over her reaction when it came to this man, Gwen thought. "You can owe it to me."

He glanced in her direction. The way he said, "I always pay my debts," sent a really hot tingle dancing up and down her spine before it settled into the pit of her stomach.

DR. WILLIAM WALTERS would have been the kind of doctor she would have picked out for herself had she been in the market for an all-round family doctor. There was something about the tall, smiling mild-mannered man that instantly inspired confidence, Gwen thought.

Brooks brought her over to the physician's house. It was obvious that they'd interrupted a family lunch. But, Gwen noticed, neither the doctor nor his wife appeared upset or even put out once they saw that Brooks was on the other side of their front door, making the request.

"I'll be right back," the doctor told his wife. "Come this way," Dr. Walters urged his visitors, leading them to a small office in the rear of the first floor. "I don't use this very often," the amicable man explained to Gwen. "It's just for emergencies, or when friends want a second medical opinion. Think of this more as a pre-exam to assess whether or not you'll need to see someone for further evaluation or treatment." Opening the office door, he asked her, "Did Brooks here tell you how we met?"

"He gave me a brief summary," she replied.

The doctor nodded. "He's not the type to beat his chest about the things he does. What you have here is a really good man," Walters concluded very simply. It was obvious that he meant every syllable.

Gwen didn't exactly know how to respond to the doctor's statement. She was at a loss as to what to say without sounding as if she'd already formed an opinion about Brooks, which she had.

Luckily, she didn't have to. The doctor spared her the trouble. Instead, he focused on the exam. "All right, take a seat." Walters indicated the exam table that was over to one side. "What exactly am I looking for?" he asked.

Rather than have Gwen answer, Brooks took over, giving the older man a quick thumbnail summary of this morning's events and how the back of Gwen's head and the sidewalk had a quick, unplanned meeting.

"Well, to rule out a concussion completely, you'll need an MRI and I don't have the equipment here for that," Walters told the duo honestly. "However, there are signs to look for and if they're completely absent, I'd say that your chances are rather good that you don't have a concussion." With that, he smiled at Gwen. "All right, shall we get started?"

She nodded. "I think both of us are rather eager to be on our way," Gwen responded. "Do whatever you need to do to make that happen."

Walters had a kind bedside manner, but he was nothing if not thorough. He executed a battery of tests on Gwen and when he was finished, he called Brooks back into the room so he could talk to both of them.

"Well?" Brooks asked. The eagerness in his voice was hard to miss as he waited for his friend to tell them his findings.

"I'm happy to say that apart from a few bruises," he momentarily glanced toward Gwen, "your lady is in perfect health, Brooks."

Brooks didn't bother to correct the doctor's mistake about their relationship. Instead, he said, "Great." Then, taking out his wallet, he asked the man, "What do I owe you?"

"Your money's no good here," Walters informed him. "I'm the one who owes you far more than I can ever repay. Now, if you'll excuse me, I have to get back before Marjorie decides to raise Cain that we never get to eat in peace anymore." Walters inclined his head. "Nice meeting you," he told Gwen.

With that, the physician withdrew, leaving them to do the same and be on their way.

Chapter Fourteen

The closer they came to his parents' house, the more nervous Gwen became. How many times had she heard people say that the Coltons weren't like other people? To her, that meant that not only were they exceedingly rich, they were also unapproachable. Yes, Brooks had turned out to be the real deal and didn't give himself any airs, but what if he was the family maverick? There was always one in every family as long as there were enough members in it. In this case it meant that he was the only normal one.

"Are you sure that your mother won't mind having me just show up with you like this?" Gwen asked him as he turned down a very impressive winding road that led to the two-acre estate overlooking the lake.

"Are you kidding?" he asked in disbelief. "My mother will be thrilled to death to meet you. Her main complaint is that she doesn't see enough of any of her children. She's gotten used to my father being at work twenty-three hours a day, but with the rest of us off on our own, nothing makes her happier than having us all gather together, no matter what the reason."

Glancing Gwen's way, he saw the concern on her face. "My mother doesn't bite. I promise." He laughed quietly to himself. "Even my father doesn't bite. He's just removed and doesn't talk much, but that's the way he is with everyone, family or strangers." Brooks pulled up into the driveway. "Come to think of it, he's a little politer with strangers. Okay, take a deep breath," he advised, stopping his vehicle and pulling up the brake. "And remember, I've got your six."

That didn't mean anything to her. "My six?" she questioned.

"Fancy talk for 'your back.' I've got your back—which also means you can't run away," he pointed out with a grin.

Circumventing the car, Brooks was at the passenger side door, opening it before Gwen could come up with a way to beg off.

"I've never met anyone who didn't immediately like my mother," Brooks said as he took her hand to coax her out of the vehicle.

She highly doubted anyone would actually tell him that they found his mother off-putting or offensive. It just wasn't something a person would admit to unless they were attempting to draw blood. But she couldn't very well argue with him about this.

"Tell you what," he said as they walked up to the massive etched and beveled glass entry door. "If you start feeling uncomfortable, just give me a signal and we'll leave. All I ask is that you give my mother forty-five minutes. You can last forty-five minutes, can't you?"

She supposed that she couldn't begrudge him that, Gwen thought. Brooks was being more than accommodating.

Pulling back her shoulders, she said, "All right, let's do this."

He flashed Gwen a smile as he leaned over her and rang the doorbell. "Whatever you say."

He had barely gotten the words out when the front door flew open. Instead of a servant standing there the way she expected, Gwen saw a tall, attractive woman of about her height with dark auburn hair piled fashionably up on her head. The woman's kind blue eyes reminded her of Brooks. This had to be his mother.

"Brooks!" Lilly Colton cried, delighted as she embraced her son. "You came." Stepping back she turned to look at the young woman standing beside her son. "And this must be Gwen." It wasn't really a question. "Welcome to my home," Lilly said, giving Gwen just as warm a hug as she had just bestowed on her son.

Releasing Gwen from her embrace, Lilly took the opportunity to look at her a little more closely. Her eyes narrowed just a touch. "You know, dear, you remind me of someone. What did you say your last name was?"

"She didn't," Brooks told his mother. He had only used Gwen's first name when he'd informed her that he was bringing someone with him today. "Gwen's last name is Harrison."

"Harrison," Lilly repeated, digesting the name. She shook her head. "No, I don't believe I know anyone by that last name, but there is something so familiar about you." She cocked her head. "We've never met before, have we, Gwen?"

"No, ma'am. I would have definitely remembered meeting you," Gwen told the woman.

"How sweet," Lilly said, pleased. She slipped her arm around the younger woman's shoulders. "Come on in and meet the others. Just to alert you, my husband might look right through you," she warned Gwen. "But don't take it personally. He's been ranting about the mayor's campaign to put a stop to 'urban sprawl' ever since he walked in the door an hour ago. In a perfect world, it's a lovely idea, but Fitz is approaching it from a financial point of view and taking it like a punch to the gut," Lilly confided, guiding her young guest into the main sitting room. The room had a stone fireplace that ran all the way up to the top of the twenty-one-foot ceiling.

Gwen felt as if she was walking into a palace. "It's beautiful," she breathed.

"Everyone," Lilly announced warmly, "this is Gwen Harrison, Brooks's friend."

Everyone turned her way and Lilly proceeded to go around the room, introducing her children and husband to their guest.

"Gwen, these are two of my daughters, Jordana and Yvette. They both work at the police station. Jordana is a detective and Yvette is a crime scene investigator."

"We've met," Jordana told her mother as she smiled at Gwen.

"But we haven't," Yvette said, leaning forward to shake Gwen's hand.

"All right, then," Lilly drew Gwen over to a young man who looked as if he could have been Brooks's double. "This handsome young devil is Neil, a criminal attorney who enjoys butting heads with Jordana and Yvette on a regular basis. By the way, in case you feel like you're seeing double when you look at him, that's because he and Brooks are two-thirds of the triplets in the family. Just to keep it interesting, Bridgette is the third—she's not here, by the way," Lilly added. "She's in Kansas City working in the State's Department of Health.

"And this young man is Tyler or Ty as we tend to call him. He's my firstborn." The latter barely had time to say "Hello" before his mother was taking their guest over to the last member in the room. "Last, but definitely not least," Lilly concluded, "this distinguished, brooding man in the corner is my husband, Fitz. You came at a rare time, dear. Fitz isn't usually home until close to midnight."

There was no recrimination in Lilly's voice. She had resigned herself to this reality years ago.

Feeling as if she might have stumbled across a family argument, Gwen glanced at the woman's face. But she realized that Lilly hadn't meant what she had just said as a dig. If anything, she was extremely happy to be able to introduce her visitor to her husband.

Gwen had no idea what to make of it, so for now she didn't try.

As for Fitz, he stepped forward and shook Gwen's hand. "Nice to meet you," he said in a voice that sounded as if it had been preprogrammed. Turning toward his wife, he told her, "I can't stay, Lilly." He looked toward Jordana. "Your daughter over here is threatening to have my worksite shut down, so I need to get back over there to make sure that as much work as possible is done before she makes good on her threat." Fitz cast a very irritated glance toward Jordana.

Jordana, Gwen saw, was not happy about being the target for her father's anger.

"It's not up to me, Dad. The order came from on high." To make her point, the police detective said, "It's not every worksite that has a body falling out of its walls."

"That body was buried there twenty-five years ago," Fitz reminded his daughter stiffly of her own department's findings. "Stopping my men from doing their jobs isn't going to tell you who put that body in there in the first place. And thanks to your brother over here—" he nodded toward Brooks "—your dead man has been identified." It was obvious that he felt the argument should end right here.

Lilly stepped in, taking her husband's arm and patting it as if she was attempting to soothe an unruly child. "Hush, Fitz. I'm sure Gwen didn't come here to hear you berate your daughter for doing her job. If Jordana worked for you, you'd be happy that she was being so efficient," Lilly said, attempting to mediate between the two sides.

Instead, she had accidentally hit a nerve. "But she doesn't work for me, does she?" Fitz said. "None of them work for me. They just enjoy living off the fruits of my labor," he stated none too happily.

"Fitz," Lilly warned sharply.

To Gwen's surprise, the tall, distinguished-looking patriarch turned and addressed his apology to her rather than to his wife.

"I'm sorry, miss. I'm not at my best right now. Dead bodies and setbacks have this way of affecting me. If you'll excuse me, I have to be getting back. Sorry, Lilly."

Whether it was a sincere apology or for show wasn't quite clear, but he did brush a kiss against Lilly's perfectly made-up cheek before he turned to go. "Nice meeting you, Gwen. Enjoy dinner," he said as he walked out.

The sound of a door closing was heard a moment later.

"And that was my father," Brooks said, turning toward Gwen.

"He looks like he's got an awful lot on his mind," Gwen commented, feeling sorry for the man as well as for Brooks and his mother.

"He's always had a lot on his mind as far back as I can remember," Brooks replied.

Gwen saw Lilly nodding toward someone in the hallway. She presumed it was a maid.

Lilly turned to address her children and her guest. "Well, it seems that dinner is finally on the table, so shall we adjourn to the dining room?" she suggested.

Rather than leading the way, Lilly hooked her arm through Gwen's. "You can sit next to Brooks. I had the housekeeper put an extra chair next to his for you." She smiled over her shoulder at her son.

His mother was playing matchmaker, and none too subtly, Brooks thought. He debated warning his mother not to go there. Her efforts might be pointless.

He could very easily let himself fall for Gwen, he mused as he followed behind his mother and Gwen to the dining room. But he had been on that route more than once. Coming to a woman's rescue, solving whatever problem was threatening her at the time and once the problem was dealt with and in the past, that woman would express her gratitude and then disappear out of his life, leaving him holding his heart in his hands.

He didn't want to be in that position again if he could help it.

But to deliberately move his chair away from Gwen's was far too rude a move, so he let his mother continue to think that she was doing a good thing. After all, Gwen was his client and there was nothing to say that he shouldn't be sitting next to his client.

He promised himself to set his mother straight when he got the chance and was able to talk to her—alone so that no one else could hear. He definitely didn't want to be the subject of his siblings' pity.

BETWEEN EATING AND catching up with everyone's life, it was late when he and Gwen finally left his parents' estate.

Driving to his house, Brooks glanced toward Gwen. At least the visit had gone well. Better than he'd even expected.

"You know, if you smile any harder, you might wind

up cracking your face," he warned, not bothering to hide his own smile.

She looked in his direction, clearly happy. "I had a really nice time."

He still had his reservations about that. "Sorry about my father," he said.

"There's nothing to be sorry about," she told Brooks. She certainly hadn't been offended. "I mean, he wasn't being rude to me. It was obvious that he was just very stressed." As had always been her habit, Gwen pointed out the positive side of the situation. "At least you know who your father is and he does come home most nights." She looked straight ahead at the road. "I don't even know who mine was—or is. And I don't even know if he's dead or alive."

"Gwen," he began, searching for something to say that could take the sting away from her remark. But at the moment, he had nothing.

"I really like your mother," Gwen said, thinking about her visit today.

"What a surprise," Brooks said, not bothering to keep a straight face. "I told you that you would."

Gwen laughed. "Yes, I believe that you did."

"It's mutual, you know. It's obvious that she likes you."

Gwen was a wee bit skeptical about his conclusion. "Well, she couldn't very well throw me down the stairs and tell me to get lost, now, could she?" she asked Brooks.

"No, I'm serious," he insisted. "I know when my mother is just being polite and when she absolutely means what she says." For a second, in the face of Gwen's skepticism, Brooks debated what he was about to say next—then decided to dive in. "When she had your chair put next to mine, that was her way of saying she approved of the arrangement."

"Arrangement?" Gwen questioned, hoping her voice hadn't risen too high and given her away. She knew what she was hoping for, but was afraid of getting too far ahead of herself.

Well, he only had himself to blame so he might as well finish what he'd started. "My mother was playing matchmaker."

She really doubted that was the case, but she had to admit that it was still nice to hear no matter what.

"Well, whatever she was doing, let her know that I'm grateful because for the space of a little while today, I managed to forget about almost being run over by that homicidal maniac that I made the mistake of letting into my life."

Now, of course, the thought was back and she couldn't get it out of her head no matter how hard she tried.

"First thing tomorrow morning, I'm going to show you a few self-defense moves you can use to protect yourself," he said, attempting to offer her confidence and make her feel more prepared. "Just knowing what to do and how to defend yourself will make you feel better about the situation."

"What would really make me feel better is if that lowlife was in jail and the key to his cell was dropped into the ocean," she told Brooks.

"Don't worry. Until we can make that happen, I'm not going to leave your side," he promised her.

"You can't be at my side 24/7," she argued. That wouldn't be fair to him. "You have a life and other commitments."

"As of right now," Brooks informed her as he pulled up in front of his house and turned the ignition off, "*you* are my only commitment."

Gwen shifted in her seat and looked into his eyes. "Believe me, I would love for that to be true, but I'm not that self-centered. Besides, this is the twenty-first century," she continued as she got out of his car and followed him to the front door. "Helpless damsels in distress are supposed to be passé."

"Yes," he agreed, pressing the combination on his security lock. "This is the twenty-first century and as such *everyone* needs help at some point. No one is invincible," he stated emphatically, "and it's okay to accept help."

"But I'm the only one who needs help here," she pointed out.

"Let me think about it," he responded. "I'll come up with something you can help me with."

"I'm not an idiot, Brooks. You're just saying that," she told him as she walked into the house ahead of him.

"No, I'm not," he insisted, locking the door behind them and pressing the button to engage the security system again.

She turned to face him. "All right," she challenged. "Tell me just one thing I can help you with."

He wasn't about to get distracted. Maybe she needed

to learn those moves he had mentioned sooner than later. "Right now, you can let me show you a few self-defense moves and tomorrow, we can go into your training much more fully."

"All right," she said, watching him set down their suitcases on the floor. When he did, she presented herself in front of him like a willing student and spread her hands in a silent invitation. "Go ahead. Show me what to do, Brooks."

Why did that sound like an invitation for far more than just self-defense lessons to him?

And why in heaven's name wasn't he saying anything that would just put her off?

Chapter Fifteen

"Well? I'm waiting," Gwen said to Brooks as she moved a little closer to him. And then closer still until she was almost standing in his space. "Show me something, Brooks."

"On second thought, it's late," he told her. "Why don't we wait until tomorrow, when we're both fresh? I'll call Ty and ask him to come by so he can give both of us a proper demonstration."

"Tyler?" she asked, not really following him. "Why Tyler?"

"My older brother is a security expert who picks up bodyguard gigs on the side. What that means is that he's up on all the latest self-defense techniques. He's also the one who can show you what to do in an emergency."

She appreciated Brooks offering her his family's expertise, but she wouldn't presume to take advantage of any of them. Brooks was the one she had an actual relationship with, not any of the others, as nice as she thought they all were.

"But you're a private investigator. You can't tell me

that you don't have a few handy moves at your disposal," she said.

Damn, Brooks thought. Gwen was standing much too close to him for him to be thinking clearly. Even so, he did give it another try.

"Again, tomorrow would be a much better time for this. We'll both be more clearheaded then."

Gwen inclined her head, looking up into his eyes. Suddenly, she really wanted to feel his arms around her. "You know, clearheadedness can be highly overrated at times."

He felt himself growing progressively attracted to Gwen, and that was dangerous. "Gwen, you and I have a professional relationship," he explained. "I can't disrespect that relationship by stepping over the line."

He could only hope that he sounded more convincing that he felt because he was weakening by the moment.

"It takes two to overstep," Gwen told him. Her heart was racing at an ever increasing speed, causing her throat to throb.

Brooks could feel her breath on his face, could feel his own desire growing to such proportions that he was having a very difficult time being able to manage it.

"You know, you're making this very hard, Gwen," he murmured.

"How hard?" she asked, her voice hardly above a whisper. It was drawing him in quicker than he would have ever thought possible.

"Damn near impossible to resist," he told her in all seriousness.

"Then maybe you shouldn't be trying so hard to

resist," Gwen advised just before she brushed a kiss against his cheek.

"Gwen…"

His intention was to warn her off, to make her back away from him. How he wound up pulling her to him in a crushing embrace was something he couldn't quite understand. All he knew was that it happened, anyway. And once it did, once he was holding her against him, the resulting flash of desire that shot through his veins made it impossible for Brooks to walk away from her.

But for the sake of his conscience, he gave it one last try. He put the situation into her hands. "Damn it, Gwen, don't you know that you're supposed to run?"

"I am," she breathed against his mouth as she kissed him again.

He drew his head back to look at her. He felt as if he had stepped into quicksand and was sinking incredibly fast.

"Run away *from*," he emphasized. "Not *toward*."

Gwen smiled at him. "I've never had a very good sense of direction," she answered, every word separated from the next by more and more passionate kisses.

Good intentions only went so far before they completely disintegrated. He could feel that happening right at this moment.

Catching her up in his arms, Brooks began to kiss her in earnest, abandoning himself to the passion that was alive and well and raging through him like a wildfire that had gotten out of control.

His bedroom felt as if it was a million miles away, Brooks thought. The sofa was a great deal closer, especially in light of the fact that their clothes were quickly being shed and meeting the floor at a breathtaking pace.

This continued until there wasn't a shred of clothing separating their bodies.

Gwen's breathing grew more rapid and harder as she felt his hands gliding along every curve.

His touch was gentle.

She hadn't expected that. She would have thought that once they were at this point, Brooks would have moved quickly to satisfy the urges she was certain were raging through him.

Instead, his focus seemed to be entirely centered on her pleasure.

Brooks had gently pressed her against the light gray sofa cushions and rather than just take what was so willingly, so completely available to him, he took his time making love to every part of her.

He caressed her, stroking her body as if that, for the moment, was enough for him. That in turn led to more and more activity, more time devoted to making every area of her body respond and almost sing in reaction to his gentle touch.

Brooks feasted on her lips, the slope of her throat, the heaving area just above her breasts.

Each and every part was carefully addressed, carefully worshipped before he continued moving on to yet another part and doing the very same there that he had done to the area before.

This was different, Gwen thought, her head all but spinning out of control. Different from any of the other times she'd been with a man.

She would be the first to admit that her experience was limited, but never in her wildest dreams would she have ever thought that lovemaking could approach something this wonderful. The other times had been just whistled tunes in the dark while this, this was an entire symphony.

And it continued.

Though Gwen truly loved absorbing what was happening to her, she didn't want to be just a passive recipient in this lovemaking. She wanted to be able to make Brooks as crazy as he was succeeding in making her.

With a mighty effort, she pulled together the last of her ebbing strength and turned the tables on easily the most passionate lover she had ever had the good fortune of encountering.

Stunned, Brooks found himself on his back, his shoulder blades sinking into the deep pile cushions as the amazing woman he had thought he was bedding was working her lips along his pulsating body. Her warm lips were anointing it and making him desperately yearn the way he couldn't recall ever yearning before.

Definitely not anywhere near to this extent.

And then her fingers feathered lightly along the most intimate part of his body, making him ache for her so badly that he was afraid all this would be over before it ever had a chance to reach culmination.

To prevent that, he caught her hand, wrapping his own around it and drawing her hand away from him.

Executing a quick move, he caused her to change places with him. With her body below his, Brooks linked his fingers through hers and raised her arms above her head, all the while kissing her with slow, passionate deliberation.

Melting her.

He could feel her responding, feel her breathing hard against him, her body causing his own desire to grow in ever greater proportions.

Brooks moved his lips slowly, ever lower along her body, worshipping every part of her until he had managed to work his way down to her very core.

His tongue darted in and out at a very deliberate pace, causing her to cry out in mounting ecstasy as she arched her back, bringing her body even closer up against him. She greedily absorbed every delicious nuance that he was offering.

Suddenly surprised, she cried out his name as the first deep, intense climax seized her body and then exploded.

Exhausted, she sank back against the cushions only to feel him beginning a second round.

When that, too, took her prisoner and crested, she gasped, all but dissolving in a veritable puddle. She immediately felt almost contrite because she'd had this wondrous experience, but he had yet to join her.

The next moment, she felt his body moving up along hers. And then she was looking up at him.

His eyes were locked on hers and she knew what was coming.

Her mouth curved in an open invitation. "Just in time before I ran out of energy," she whispered.

"The trick," Brooks said just before he entered her, "is to conserve your strength."

With that he began to move.

At first slowly, lyrically. And then faster and faster until they both found themselves racing together to the very highest part of the mountain looming ahead of them.

Their hearts racing, their souls all but intertwined, they took the plunge together. They were wrapped up in each other's arms and experiencing the very height of this most exquisite experience.

Together.

They held on to each other tightly, savoring every nuance, every bit of the fireworks that were going off within them until the very last of the experience was nothing more than a fading memory.

Gwen desperately tried to hang on to the euphoria until there wasn't anything left of it.

Very slowly, she let out her breath, waiting for her heart to get back to normal.

That took longer.

"And just how," she asked breathlessly as she turned her head toward Brooks, "is that maneuver supposed to protect me?" Her eyes sparkled in amusement as she waited for his response.

"Well, for one thing, whoever's trying to put you out of commission will be too damn tired to make a single move after something like that," he answered her, trying to keep a straight face.

It was hard, considering the euphoria still going on inside of him.

She raised her head just a fraction in order to look at

him. "So, do you have any other moves to show me?" she asked.

"Any other moves?" he repeated. "I'm damn lucky I'm still drawing breath. I'd say let's go to bed, but I'm not sure that you left me enough strength to make it up the stairs."

She pretended to be surprised. "You mean you're actually tired?"

"Tired?" He laughed at the understatement. "Lady, I'm halfway past exhausted, on my way to dead."

Gwen laughed softly. Then, before he knew it, she was drawing her body up along his very slowly, very seductively, creating another wave of excitement that Brooks felt he was unprepared to handle.

"Really?" he asked in wonder. "You could actually go another round?"

"Well, you never know what you're capable of until you actually try," she told Brooks, punctuating each word with a quick, fleeting kiss that seemed to grow in dimension and breadth until it turned into a passionate, fiery meeting of two souls.

"You are the devil, Gwen Harrison," he declared, surrendering to what he felt was happening deep within him. "But heaven help me, I can't think of a better way to go than this," he rasped, giving himself up to the flashes of passionate desire that were going off inside of him.

They made love again.

This time it was even more energy absorbing than the first time and every bit as exciting and stimulating. Brooks had no illusions that what was happening between them would be something that lasted. But while he was caught up in its grip, he intended to make the very most of it and enjoy being with this woman. Enjoy making love with her until there was nothing left inside of him to give.

And when it was over this time, they fell asleep in each other's arms, holding one another as if to keep the dream from fading.

BROOKS WOKE UP suddenly the next morning to the feel of her hair brushing against his chest. It created a warm, fuzzy feeling that he savored for as long as he could.

He opened his eyes reluctantly, searching for a way to make the feeling continue, if only for a moment longer although he yearned for more than that.

But he was nothing if not a realist and he knew that he had already exceeded his personal limit when it came to his happiness quota.

Hell, he was probably in arrears by half a century because of what he and Gwen had shared last night.

Still, aware that he was likely risking everything, he moved his head, leaning in and kissing the very top of hers.

Gwen stirred against him, making murmuring noises that told him she would be awake any moment now.

Even though she was still asleep, he was already missing this moment, missing the warm, pliant woman in his arms and most of all, missing making love with her although he knew he was being incredibly selfish.

Last night might just have to last him a lifetime, he

thought, trying to come up with a way to somehow make that happen.

He was being greedy but something about all this had made him feel that maybe, just maybe, making this last could be possible if he only went about it in the right way.

That was the moment that it suddenly hit him. And the second that it did, he tried to block it, to deny it because it only happened that way in country songs and low-budget movies.

But even recognizing that, he couldn't talk himself out of it.

Like it or not, he had fallen in love with Gwen Harrison.

Chapter Sixteen

Without realizing it, he had fallen asleep again. When he woke up again, Brooks wasn't exactly sure what to expect. He anticipated that there would be some awkwardness, but to his relief, Gwen acted as if nothing had changed between them.

Up before him, she had breakfast on the table when he came into the kitchen.

The meal was accompanied by small talk. When it was over and the dishes had been put into the dishwasher, Brooks turned toward her and told her, "I'm going in with you. To your meeting," he clarified, then quickly added, "Don't worry, I'm not going to actually walk into your meeting with you so you won't have to try to explain my presence to the principal. But I'll drive you over there and then I'll just sit in the car out in the parking lot. And when it comes time, I'll take you home."

"But don't you have your own work to do?" Gwen asked.

"Until I find out what happened to your mother and get at least some answers for you, *you* are my 'work,'" he told her. He saw her frowning in response. "Something wrong?"

"I can't afford to pay for that kind of service," she said.

"Don't worry. There's no extra charge," he said, then teasingly added, "You won my once-a-year deluxe package."

That didn't sound right. She didn't feel good about making him lose money. "But—"

"Don't bother questioning it, just consider it a stroke of good luck," he coaxed as he glanced at his watch. "You want to argue about this and be late for your meeting or just accept that I'm going to be your shadow for the next few weeks and get to your meeting on time?"

"Few weeks," Gwen repeated. "You think all this will be over in a few weeks?"

"With any luck," he speculated. "Now, about your meeting…" Brooks looked at his watch again.

"You're right," Gwen agreed, picking up her purse and slinging the strap over her shoulder. "Let's go."

"ABOUT LAST NIGHT—AND this morning," Gwen began a few minutes after Brooks had started up his car and they were on their way to her school.

Okay, here it comes, Brooks thought, anticipating what she was going to say. He had been braced for this and worried about it at the same time. "You're not one of those, are you?"

"One of 'those'?" she questioned, her train of thought suddenly pulled up short. She wasn't sure what he was referring to. "Just what 'those' are you talking about?"

He needed time to think this thing through in order to decide if there was another ending waiting for him. He didn't want to risk setting himself up just to be disappointed when this case was behind him. He had played the hero too many times just to have the rug pulled out from under him once his services were no longer needed.

"What I'm talking about are women who immediately want to know 'where is this relationship going?' when it's only been on the road for a few days instead of an actual considerable amount of time." He took a breath, looking straight ahead. "Personally, I don't think a relationship has to be going anywhere. It can just be enjoyable going nowhere."

Gwen slanted a look at him, putting her own interpretation to his words. He was regretting moving so fast last night and was putting distance between them, she thought.

In a way, she supposed she could almost understand that. She certainly didn't want him doing anything against his will no matter how spectacular last night and this morning had been. And the last thing she wanted was for him to feel as if their lovemaking had all been a big mistake.

"I totally agree," she told Brooks.

"You do?" he asked, completely surprised.

"Sure," she said. "We were just two people caught up in the moment. That doesn't mean that either one of us should feel that they're trapped in a situation they didn't sign on for. That's only common sense," she stressed, doing her best to sound cheerful. "Don't you agree?"

Damn, he would have to be extra careful, he silently upbraided himself. The next moment he heard himself murmur, "Completely," although he didn't mean it.

"Make a left over here," Gwen prompted, pointing in that direction.

She had been so caught up in what he was saying—or not saying as the case was—she hadn't been paying attention to where he was driving. He had almost missed the turn.

There was just too many things crowding her brain, Gwen thought as if to excuse her oversight. First and foremost was the ongoing search for her missing mother, then there was Daniel. He had turned out to be totally different from the man she had taken him for, not to mention that she was certain that he had been the one who had tried to run her over. Added to that she was trying to adjust to a brand-new work situation in a new city.

And on top of all that was the unnerving discovery that the private investigator her grandmother had hired over two decades ago to find her mother had turned up dead.

Why was the man killed? Did his death have anything to do with his looking for her mother? And did that, by some wild chance, put Brooks's life in jeopardy as well because *he* was now trying to find out what happened to her mother?

The thought undulated before her like a snake, frightening her.

"Well, here you are," Brooks announced, pulling his vehicle into the parking lot that stood in front of Braxville Elementary School. "I'll be right here, waiting for you when you get out," he reminded her.

Nodding, Gwen swung her legs out and then got out of the vehicle. But instead of going to the school's front entrance, she circled around to the driver's door and told him, "Be careful."

He thought that was rather an odd thing for her to say to him. She appeared concerned, so he tried to treat the situation with humor to lighten the moment.

"I promise I won't engage with any marauding first graders."

He probably thought she was crazy, Gwen thought. Maybe she was, it was just that this man had suddenly become very important to her. That would undoubtedly scare him off if he knew.

So she forced a smile to her lips. "See you in a while," she said, stepping away from his vehicle and then turning toward the school.

Within moments, she was gone.

Brooks had just watched Gwen disappear into the school when his cell phone rang. He had assigned different ringtones to each member in his family so he didn't have to bother looking at his screen to know who the caller was.

"Hello, Mother. What's up?" he asked, answering his phone.

"She's a lovely girl, Brooks," he heard Lilly Colton tell him.

"Did you call to tell me that you're giving her your stamp of approval?" he asked, amused by what his mother considered to be subtle behavior.

"I just wanted to find out if your friend had a nice time last night."

His mother's question startled him until Brooks realized that the woman was referring to the family dinner, not to what happened between Gwen and him afterward.

Relaxing, he replied, "She told me that she really liked you, but then, who wouldn't?"

"You don't have to flatter me, Brooks."

He could just picture his mother on the other end of the call, beaming. "Oh, I kind of felt that I had to, you being the picture of insecurity and all."

"Very funny. But Gwen did have a good time, didn't she?"

"I'd tell you if she didn't, Mother," Brooks answered.

"No, you wouldn't," Lilly countered. "You're much too polite to hurt my feelings that way. Well, I just wanted to call and tell you that I approve."

"Approve?" he echoed, radar going off in his head. He'd teased his mother about her stamp of approval, but this actually sounded serious. Maybe he was misunderstanding her. "Approve of what?"

"*Who*, darling. Approve of who, not what. I approve of Gwen, although I really wish I could remember who she reminds me of," his mother lamented. "I feel like it's right on the tip of my tongue, but then it just disappears. It's maddening."

"Don't force it, Mother. It'll come to you when you least expect it," Brooks promised. "And since when do you feel you need to weigh in on my clients?"

He heard his mother sigh. "Don't act dumb, Brooks. It doesn't become you."

"I'm not playing dumb, Mother. I genuinely am dumb," he told her. "Enlighten me, please."

"All right, have it your way. I saw the way that you looked at her and the way that Gwen looked at you," Lilly pointed out.

"Yes, we know each other." Brooks was trying to curb his impatience, aware that he was being unreasonable. "I told you that."

Lilly sighed again. "Have it your way, dear. Just know that when the time comes for you to stop playing games, I approve."

"Always nice to have your approval, Mother, even if it makes no sense. I've got another call coming in. I have to take it," he told her.

"No, you don't," Lilly contradicted knowingly. "But I've said my piece and I'll let you go. You're welcome to bring her by anytime, dear," Lilly said by way of ending the discussion.

"Nice to know, Mother," Brooks said formally. "I'll see you."

"Soon, dear." It wasn't a question, it was a statement.

"*Soon* is a relative term, Mother," Brooks said.

He heard his mother chuckle. "Make sure that it is, dear."

He sighed. "I am terminating the call now, Mother," he announced just before he did.

Preoccupied, reflecting on what his mother had just said, Brooks didn't know what he was looking at, at first. It just seemed like another sleek silver automobile, just like hundreds of other silver automobiles that were out on the road these days.

But there was something about the way it was cruising through the parking lot that triggered red flags.

Leaning forward, Brooks tried to make out who the driver was. He could tell it was a man driving the vehicle, but beyond that, whoever was behind the wheel was too far away for him to be able to make out the man's features.

Brooks debated starting up his car and following the silver one, or at least getting out of it so that he could get a better look at the driver. But either course of action put him at a disadvantage. The last thing he wanted to do was to tip off the driver and put the man on the alert.

Something in his gut told Brooks that the driver cruising by was Daniel. While he couldn't get a clear view of the his face, there was something about the way the man held his head that set off alarms for Brooks.

After Shelton had tried to hire him to follow Gwen and spy on her, he had looked the man up and learned everything he could about the smarmy individual. He'd learned that rich, entitled Daniel Shelton owned several vehicles and as he had already told Gwen, the man had a habit of pushing himself on the women he was seeing at the time, feeling as if they owed it to him for taking the time to bestow his attention on them.

All in all, Brooks thought, Shelton was a reprehensible individual who didn't like taking no for an answer—so he wouldn't.

Taking out his cell phone, Brooks took a picture of the vehicle, then another of the license plate, enhancing it. This plate didn't have mud on it, obliterating the numbers and letters on it the way the first vehicle had. Either the man was getting bolder, Brooks decided, or he felt he wouldn't be identified.

Brooks sat where he was and watched the other car, but the driver apparently lost interest and the man finally drove away. When he did, Brooks pulled up the photograph again and wrote down the number, then called Ty.

His older brother didn't pick up immediately but just as his call was about to go to voice mail, Brooks heard his brother's familiar deep voice on the other end.

"Twice in two days. If I didn't know any better, I'd say that we were bonding, the way we used to when we were kids," Ty said with a laugh.

"We didn't bond when we were kids," Brooks corrected Ty. "You enjoyed torturing me too much."

"In my defense, I thought that was what older brothers were supposed to do," Ty said. "Did you feel like going down memory lane or is there another reason you're calling me so soon after the family get-together?"

"I need you to use your connections and track down a license plate for me."

"You can't track it down yourself?"

"I am tracking it down," Brooks pointed out. "I'm bringing it to you."

"Very funny. This wouldn't have anything to do with that cute little honey you brought to the house yesterday, would it?"

"I see Mother's been putting a bug in your ear," Brooks noted.

"What's Mother got to do with it? I've got eyes, Brooks," Ty said. "But if I'm wrong, if you've decided not to declare dibs on the pretty little lady, then let me know and I just might consider throwing my hat in the ring. Hell, forget about *considering*. I'll do it the minute I hang up."

Brooks snorted. "See that you keep that hat of yours where it belongs—on your head. I just need you to track down this plate number for me—pronto."

"Uh-huh, thought so. Okay, give me the number," Ty said. He listened as Brooks rattled it off. "Okay, got it," he told his brother. "I'll get back to you when I have something. Out of curiosity, why do you want to find out who this license plate number belongs to?"

"Because the driver of that car just might be this creep who tried to run Gwen over yesterday while we were in Kansas City, visiting her grandmother," Brooks answered.

"Yesterday?" Ty echoed incredulously. "Was that after you two left the homestead?" his brother asked.

"It was before then. I brought her over to Mother's to get her mind off the incident. Now, can you do it, or should I go find someone else?"

"Of course I can do it," Ty informed him just before he ended the call, presumably to get started.

"I sure hope that you're as good as you think you are, Ty," Brooks said under his breath as he closed his phone and put it away in his back pocket.

Chapter Seventeen

Brooks had no sooner tucked the cell phone into his pocket and shifted in his seat, trying to get comfortable, than he heard his phone ring again. This time he heard the beginning notes of a classic old song whose lyrics were "I am woman, hear me roar." He had assigned that particular song to Jordana.

This can't be good, he thought as he looked at the screen. It was too early in the day for a social call, he reasoned.

That meant that something was wrong.

No time like the present, he thought, pressing the button that connected him to the caller. "What's up, Jordy?" he asked cheerfully.

Rather than Jordana's usual, annoyed retort about what she considered to be the butchering of her given name, Brooks heard his sister say, "Under the circumstances, I'll let that go."

He was right. This wasn't good. Jordana never walked away from the opportunity to express her annoyance at his glib nickname for her.

"What circumstances?" he asked, still anticipating

the worst. However, he wasn't expecting what Jordana said next.

It sounded as if she was clenching her teeth as said, "I had to tell Dad to shut down his worksite until further notice. Needless to say, he is *not* happy."

Brooks wouldn't have been in his sister's shoes for anything in the world. It also struck him that it wasn't like Jordana to build things up this way. He braced himself for what was coming, although he wasn't entirely sure what it was that he was bracing for.

"You're burying the lead, Jordana. *Why* did you tell Dad to shut down the worksite? What happened today that didn't happen the other day?"

He could hear his sister hesitating. "I don't normally notify civilians—"

"Damn it, Jordana!" Brooks raised his voice. Adopting an exasperated tone, he cut through the rest of her rhetoric. "*What* happened?"

He heard irritation framing each word she uttered. "Dad's men brought down another wall and another body fell out of the debris."

"Another…?" He couldn't bring himself to finish the thought. Instead, he marveled in total disbelief. "You're kidding."

"Do I sound like I'm kidding?" she asked as frustration echoed in her voice. "My ears are still ringing."

He assumed that it wasn't from the explosion at the site, but due to another source. "When did he stop yelling?" Brooks asked, referring to their father.

"When he ran out of breath," Jordana told him. "And then our father stormed away, presumably to call his lawyer to find out how he can get an injunction against the work stoppage that was slapped on his company's worksite."

He could almost envision the verbal battle that had ensued between his father and Jordana. And then, out of the blue, another thought all but smashed into his brain.

What if…?

"Were you able to identify the body?" he asked his sister, hoping against hope the body didn't belong to Olivia Harrison.

"Not yet. This body isn't nearly as well-preserved as the first one was," Jordana said, not sounding particularly hopeful about their chances. "Best guess, it's going to take our medical examiner a good long while before he can determine *anything* to help us try to home in on who this victim was."

"Were you there on the site at the time it happened?" Brooks asked.

"No, but I got there pretty quickly," she replied. "Half the victim's teeth were missing and what was left would have to be matched against dental records, which means we'd have to know where to start in order to find said dental records—if they still exist." All in all, his sister didn't sound very optimistic about their chances of a good identification.

Brooks took a deep breath. He might as well go for broke, he thought. "How about the dead person's sex?" he asked. "Was the ME able to tell whether it was a male or a female?"

There was a pause before Jordana told him. "The pelvic area was in bad shape, just like the rest of the victim was. But the ME was able to tell that." His sister paused again, managing to make Brooks use up the last of his patience.

"Damn it, Jordy, don't toy with me. What was it, a man or a woman?" Brooks demanded.

"It was a woman," she told him, then quickly added, "but that doesn't necessary mean it's the woman you're looking for. More than half of the victims of a homicide turn out to be women. You know that."

"Yeah, I know that," he said with a sigh that came from deep down in his chest. "I also know that my gut is telling me that if what I think turns out to be true, I'm going to have real trouble telling this to Gwen."

"Then don't tell her," Jordana counseled. "Not until we can make some kind of a positive identification. If you want my advice, let the poor girl cling to some kind of hope for as long as she can."

"Don't you think that's kind of cruel?" Brooks asked.

"No. Sometimes allowing a person to hang on to hope, if just even for a little while, is the kindest thing you can do because for that time frame, the person they are looking for is still alive, can still be found." And then he thought he heard someone in the background calling to his sister. The next moment Jordana confirmed that impression. "Look, Brooks, I've got to go. I just thought you'd want to know."

"I do," Brooks answered her with feeling. "And thanks." He knew she was bending the rules. "Tell me the minute you know anything more about that body you just turned up. It's not looking very good, is it?"

Instead of giving him an immediate answer, she asked, "Honestly?"

"I'd expect nothing less," he said.

Her tone sounded disappointed—and resigned. "No, it's not."

Brooks found himself staring down at a silent cell phone in his hand. He sat there for a long moment, looking at the screen and waiting for his phone to ring again the way it already had twice before, but it didn't. This time it continued being silent.

One thought led to another and he found himself debating how to break the news to Gwen, how to prepare her for the news he was certain down to his very toes was coming.

Granted Gwen had lived most of her life with her mother absent from the scene. But being absent was a great deal different than knowing someone was never going to be coming back.

He tried to put himself in Gwen's place. How would he feel if this was his mother who was never going to be back? The thought was too painful even to entertain.

Well, if the second body in the wall did turn out to be her mother, the best thing he could do for Gwen was to find out who was responsible for the murder. And while he was at it, maybe he could track down who her father was, as well.

One thing at a time, Brooks cautioned himself. First he had to find a way to tell Gwen about the second body that had been discovered—and prepare himself for the questions he was certain were going to follow.

He glanced at his watch. It seemed to him like the

fashionable timepiece on his wrist was stuck in place. He did his best to be patient, but thirty minutes was his absolute limit.

He called Yvette.

As he listened, the phone rang five times, then went to voice mail. Rather than leave a message, he called again. After the same result, he called a third time.

On his fourth attempt, he heard the other end being picked up.

"I'm a little busy here, Brooks." He could hear the impatience in his sister's voice. She was obviously holding the phone against her ear using her shoulder. Her voice wasn't all that clear.

"I know. That's why I'm calling," he told her.

"You called to bother me because you knew I was swamped?" the lab technician questioned. "I don't remember you having a cruel streak."

"It's not a cruel streak. Jordana told me that a second body was found at the worksite," Brooks began to explain.

"I haven't got a clue yet as to the body's identity."

"From what Jordy told me," Brooks began, "I wouldn't have thought that you would. And I'm not trying to rush you—"

Yvette laughed shortly. "Could have fooled me."

Brooks continued as if she hadn't said anything. "I'd just appreciate a heads-up whenever you *do* make an identification."

"Brooks—"

She was going to warn him off, or worse, tell him

she couldn't release that sort of information about an ongoing investigation.

He appealed to her emotions.

"That body could turn out to be Gwen's mother. Put yourself in her position," he told his sister. "What if it was our mother who had disappeared a quarter of a century ago? Wouldn't you want to do everything you could to find her?"

For a moment, there was silence on the other end of his call, but then he heard his sister quietly tell him, "All right. Don't say anything to anyone, but I'll see what I can find out and when I do, I'll let you know."

"Thanks, Yvette," Brooks said. "You're just the best."

"About time you figured that out, big brother. Now let me get back to my job before I get hauled out on the carpet for getting sidelined by a personal phone call," she said right before she terminated the call.

For the first time since he'd begun working cases, he found himself fervently hoping that a body that had been unexpectedly discovered would be identified as belonging to someone other than the person he was tasked with finding.

But even so, deep down in his gut, Brooks had this awful feeling that the body that had turned up belonged to Gwen's mother, Olivia Harrison. Otherwise, it was just too unbelievable a coincidence, having the second body turn up buried in the same building that the first body had been.

He was still contemplating how to tell Gwen about this newest development and *when* to tell her when he heard a quick rap on the window right next to him, startling him.

The next moment, he turned the key in his ignition to the first position and had the window on his side rolling down so he was able to talk to his visitor.

"Everything all right?" Gwen asked him, concerned. "You looked like you were in another world," she said to Brooks.

Because he hadn't been able to prepare anything to tell her yet, he decided to keep the information Jordana had told him under wraps for the time being.

"Just working something out in my head," he replied—which was true. And then the private investigator deliberately brightened. "You're out early. Is that for good behavior, or are you just out because you're on a break?"

"No, the meeting's over." Gwen opened the passenger side door and slid into the seat next to him. "Just how involved is this thing that you're working out in your head?" she asked.

"Why?"

"Because you had this really strange look on your face."

Brooks waved his hand, as if brushing away her question as well as the observation she'd made, for the time being.

"I have a tendency to get really caught up in things. But that doesn't matter right now." He got back on topic. "So the meetings over for the day?"

She nodded, then informed him, "Actually, the meetings are over for the week. I don't have to come in until two days before the students come back to start the school year. That leaves me free to help you," she announced, pleased.

"Help me?" he questioned.

"Yes. With the investigation. I just figured that two minds are better than one."

He got that she was eager to be part of the investigation, but right now, until he knew who Jordana and her team had found, he didn't think that having Gwen joining in on this investigation in any way was such a good idea.

"Well, that's not always the case," Brooks told her cautiously.

She looked at him, confused. "What's that supposed to mean?" She wasn't being belligerent, she was honestly asking a question.

He grasped at the first thing that came to his mind. "I'm used to working alone. You might get in my way."

"I don't want to get in your way, I want to help you," she said in all sincerity. After all, it was her mother they were looking for, she thought. "I'll do whatever you tell me to."

She was doing it again, he thought. She was making a perfectly innocent statement sound incredibly suggestive and stimulating.

His new closeness with this woman was causing all sorts of thoughts to run amok in his brain.

"Um, Brooks?" she began, shifting in her seat and turning toward him.

When she looked at him that way, he was afraid that he would wind up baring his soul to her. That would mean saying things to her that he didn't know quite how to say or break to her.

"Yes?" he finally asked, telling himself he was ready for anything when in fact he knew that he wasn't. That was because he was experiencing this overwhelming desire to shelter her, to keep her heart from breaking at all costs. Unfortunately, at the same time he was feeling totally inadequate for the job.

"All right, I'm no expert," Gwen began, but got no further.

"Don't worry, I'll take that into account," he told her. Right at this moment he was desperately trying to stall, or even better than that, to divert her from asking the one question he didn't want to be faced with answering. "Unless the question you're about to ask makes you too uncomfortable, in which case it's all right if you want to take your time in asking it—or come back to it at a later time."

"No," she said. "I really think I should ask this now."

"All right," he replied, bracing himself.

"Well, like I said, I'm no expert when it comes to things like this, but, well—" she nodded at the front of his car "—you've got your key in the ignition and I was just wondering, wouldn't the car make better time if you actually *turned* the key in the ignition and have the car actually go?"

Brooks found himself breathing a sigh of relief, at least doing it in his head if not physically.

"Right again," he told her as he started up his car. The next moment, he was driving them out of the school parking lot and toward his home.

Chapter Eighteen

Gwen promised herself that yesterday's lovemaking was not going to be a repeat performance tonight. What happened last night had been wonderful, but there was nothing to suggest to her that this was anything but a onetime thing. The last thing she wanted was to have Brooks thinking that she was some sort of a clingy, needy creature who once she wrapped her tentacles around someone held on for dear life.

That wasn't her. She knew very well that coming across as if she was trying to hang on to a man was a surefire recipe for disaster, not to mention the very best way to lose that man completely. Look at what had happened to her mother. Olivia had gone looking to have it out with her ex-lover and she was subsequently never heard from again.

Gwen kept hoping that they would find her missing mother, or, barring that, some clue as to what happened to her. But worst-case scenario might just lead her to a conclusion she didn't want to acknowledge: that loving a man, be it her father or in her own case, Brooks, was asking for disappointment, pain—and perhaps even worse.

DESPITE ALL HER best intentions and resolutions, by the time the end of the day had come around—a day filled with running less than successful errands that led nowhere—Gwen wasn't feeling quite as noble as she had been when she'd first started out this morning.

This morning, she thought. That felt like it had been a million years ago.

Gwen had almost succeeded in convincing herself that nothing was going on between her and Brooks.

Almost.

She was busy putting dishes away in the dishwasher and he was coming over, carrying a second pile of plates and silverware. His intent was to rinse everything off and then stack them in the dishwasher. But somehow, she found herself the main focus of his attention rather than the plates he was stacking.

Brooks blamed his reaction to her on the lighting.

Gwen was dressed simply and the light seemed to hit her just right. It seemed to almost be making love to her. The way he wanted to.

Brooks gave up trying to be strong.

Looking into her eyes, he thought that Gwen literally looked like the most beautiful woman he had ever laid eyes on.

"Is something wrong?" she asked, her voice barely a whisper.

His eyes caressing her, Brooks replied softly, "Not a thing."

Taking the dish out of her hand, Brooks placed it on the counter, then took her face in his hands and brought his mouth down to hers.

That one simple action was all it took. His fate was sealed right then and there because he not only wasn't strong enough to fight what was happening between them, he didn't want to be.

Flashing red lights went off in his head, warning him that he was on a very slippery slope, trying to find his way to safety.

He ignored the lights. All he wanted to do was be with Gwen for one more night. To lose himself in her and pretend, just for a little while, that he wasn't a Colton, that he didn't have a reputation to uphold. And that he was free to make love with someone without worrying about what tomorrow would bring.

"GUESS I'D BETTER cross out stacking dishes in the dishwasher as being a safe activity," Brooks commented, when the lovemaking was over and he was holding Gwen in his arms.

He heard her laugh softly to herself. "Who knew?"

She traced the outline of his lips with her fingertip. Pulling herself up into an almost semi-sitting position, she kissed him quickly. "You make me feel happy."

Guilt filled him instantly. Here he was, making love with her and she had no idea he was keeping a secret from her. No idea that that there was a body lying in the morgue this very instant that could very possibly be her mother.

He needed to get this off his chest and let her know.

"Gwen?" he began, turning into her, ready to stumble through a narrative and tell her about the call he had gotten from his sister.

The words died in his throat without ever being uttered.

Gwen had fallen asleep.

He released the breath he'd drawn in order to make a full disclosure.

He stroked her hair from her face, feeling warm affection stirring within him. "Guess it'll keep until the morning," he told her softly.

BUT THE MORNING brought its own set of circumstances.

Brooks was in the kitchen, unloading the dishwasher when he heard his cell phone ringing. The ringtone belonged to Ty.

"Did you manage to find out who that car belonged to?" Brooks asked as he answered his phone.

"Well, hello to you, too, little brother," Ty said to him.

"Sorry," Brooks apologized, starting over. "Hello. Did you manage to find out who that car belonged to?" He nodded a greeting to Gwen as she walked into the kitchen.

"I said I would," Ty reminded him. Like the rest of his close-knit family, Ty prided himself on always keeping his word. "I just got a little sidetracked by my *paying* job," he explained to Brooks. "There was a slight hiccup there, but to answer the only question in your mind, yes, I managed to track down the car that almost ran your friend over."

He was about to correct Ty and tell him that Gwen was just his client, not his friend in the actual sense of the word, but that would have left him open to fielding questions on two sides—from Ty, who would have questioned the truth behind that statement, and from

Gwen who, after making love with him two nights in a row, might be hurt by the fact that he was hiding what he was feeling behind a professional relationship.

So Brooks found it safer to say nothing, other than "And?" as he attempted to coax the rest of the information out of his brother.

"And you were right," Ty said. "The car does belong to Daniel Shelton. It's one of three silver cars that are registered in his name. Do you want to file charges against him?" his brother asked. "I can get you the proper forms to fill out, but in the absence of any surveillance camera records—I checked, by the way and there weren't any—it's just a matter of he said/he said," Ty warned his brother.

"This is all I wanted for now," Brooks told him. "Thanks for getting back to me so soon."

"Hey, don't mention it," Ty replied. And the very next second, he'd hung up.

The moment he did, he saw Gwen looking at him. "That driver, it was Daniel, wasn't it?" she asked.

"It was." He tried not to frighten her too much. There was nothing to be gained by that. "Shelton's either stepped up his game, or he just wanted to scare you. Listen, I can get a few off-duty police officers to hang around outside my house if you're worried about Shelton. We can also get a restraining order in place."

She considered the latter for a moment. "I guess it wouldn't hurt to take out a restraining order," she told him. "But between the two of us, I don't think he's the kind of person that a restraining order would stop from doing what he intended on doing."

"I think you're right," he agreed.

Again, it was on the tip of his tongue to tell Gwen about the second body that had been discovered at his father's construction site, but then his phone rang again.

This time it was Yvette calling him.

Gwen's mouth curved. "You certainly are popular."

"At least with my own family," he responded, his eyes on hers. Brooks pressed the on button and immediately began talking. "This is a rare surprise, Yvette. I'm the one who usually has to try tracking you down to talk. What's up?"

He expected her to say something cryptic. He wasn't ready for what she told him.

"I think you should come down to the lab, Brooks," Yvette said. "You're going to want to see this."

"See what?" Brooks asked, but the call had already terminated.

Putting his phone into his back pocket, he noticed Gwen looking at him, an unspoken question in her eyes.

"Yvette wants to show us something," he told Gwen.

He was extrapolating on what Yvette had just said. He was well aware that she hadn't included Gwen in the invitation, but since he was certain that this was somehow connected to the case he was handling for Gwen, he wasn't going to let this be yet something else that he wound up keeping a secret.

"Now?" she asked, thinking it was still rather early.

Brooks nodded. "She certainly made it sound that way."

"All right," Gwen responded. "Let's go." Grabbing her purse as they approached the front door, Gwen had a confession of her own to make. The words weren't easy for her to say. "I don't know whether to be excited or scared."

He really felt for her, but that wasn't going to help her get through this. He gave her what advice he could. "How about you put both emotions on the back burner until we find out why Yvette wants to see us," Brooks suggested to her.

"How do you do it?" she asked as she got into his car a beat after he did.

"Do what?" he asked, not quite clear what she was asking him about. He put on his seat belt.

"How do you stay so removed from everything? You act as if you're just going out for a leisurely drive."

He gave her an honest answer. "Someone once told me that if I was going to get into this game, I was going to have to learn how to keep a cool head—or at least look like I'm keeping a cool head."

"So this cool head you're projecting right now, it's just a facade?" she asked Brooks, reading between the lines.

He smiled at her, his eyes sparkling just a little. "I'm not about to give away any trade secrets," Brooks told her.

Finding out that he wasn't just going through the motions, that he actually might be feeling at least a little of what she was feeling, made her feel better about things, Gwen thought as she settled back in her seat.

YVETTE HAD JUST finished photographing pages in small notebooks and loading those images into her computer when Brooks walked in with Gwen.

A fleeting look of surprise passed over the lab technician's face before it faded away again.

"I didn't realize you were bringing company," she told her brother, then smiled and nodded at Gwen. "Nice to see you again, Gwen."

Gwen returned the smile. "You, too, Yvette."

The air was pregnant with things unsaid, Brooks thought. He could feel it. He just hoped that it wouldn't be too devastating for Gwen.

"What did you want to show me, Yvette?" he asked, trying to get this interaction between them back on track. Then, before his sister could answer him, he pointed to the image she had just pulled up on the computer screen. "What is that?"

"What you see before you are the very faint notes— if you can actually call them that—made by the late private investigator Felton Crane. This," Yvette said, switching to a close-up of what looked like a tiny, very faded notebook, "was found in the lining of a torn breast pocket in his sports jacket. I presume we're looking at an old-fashioned notebook. Mr. Crane obviously took notes to help him stay on top of things. As near as I can make out, this page was the last entry that he made," she added.

"What does it say?" Brooks asked, squinting at the faded, small writing.

"I'm not really sure," Yvette confessed. "My best guess is that it says 'Meeting suspect MD at site noon' which I take to mean that our dead man was meeting someone somewhere at noon," she concluded with a shrug.

"The suspect he was meeting was a doctor?" Gwen

questioned, referring to the two initials the private investigator had used.

"I'd say that it looks that way. Were any of Crane's clients doctors?" she asked her brother.

"Not that I know of. Besides, the man had a reputation of only handling one case at a time. From what we know, he was supposed to be tracking down what had happened to Gwen's mother." He looked at Gwen. "Do you remember your grandmother mentioning any doctors in connection to your mother's case?"

Gwen shook her head. "No. She never mentioned anything to me about a doctor."

She looked at the photographs on the screen. It almost appeared as if the private investigator had written using invisible ink. Either that, or he'd used that old kid trick she'd once read about where notes were written with a pen dipped in lemon juice.

"Can I have the notebook?" she asked.

"No, I'm afraid not. That's still part of evidence, so I can't let you have it. I shouldn't even be showing it to you," Yvette said—and then she reconsidered what was happening. "But I can give you copies of the pages I photographed. I took photos of practically all the pages that were in the notebook. Will that do?"

"That would be wonderful," Gwen cried with genuine enthusiasm.

There was the very real possibility that the notes the murdered private investigator had made could wind up being a bridge across time and they would finally have some clues as to what happened to her mother.

"All right, just give me a minute," Yvette told Gwen

as well as her brother as she stepped away from her work area.

Gwen could feel her fingertips tingling. She glanced at Brooks. "We're getting closer, Brooks. I can *feel* it," she said. She was so excited, she found that she was having trouble keeping her voice under control.

"Don't get carried away just yet," Brooks cautioned. "You still don't know how this is going to wind up turning out."

Just looking at the hope on her face was making his heart ache for her.

"I know, I know," she said, realizing that he was only trying to shield her, to prepare her for what could be a bad outcome. "But, Brooks, you have to understand. This is the first positive turn this whole long, drawn-out investigation has taken in literally *years*," she cried. And then she beamed at him. "And it is all because of you."

Impulsively, Gwen threw her arms around Brooks, pressing her face against his chest as she hugged him. "Everything good that's happening right now is all because of you."

He carefully stripped her arms away from him. "Gwen, don't."

If this whole thing went the way he was afraid it was going to go, Gwen would be so terribly disappointed in the end that she might not be able to rally. He didn't want that for her. Didn't want to see the light go out of her eyes.

"Don't what?" she questioned. "Don't thank you for casting some light into that very dark world I've been

living in? Don't ask me to do that. Don't ask me to ignore the first ray of sunshine that actually penetrated
my world since I was a little child. Smile, Brooks," she
coaxed, silently begging him not to make her have to
face something terrible. "I just said a nice thing to you.
Why don't we just leave it at that for now?"

In her own way, he thought, she was saying the same
thing to him that he had previously told himself.

Chapter Nineteen

Gwen immediately saw the change in his expression. She couldn't explain why, but she felt a sudden chill. "Brooks, what is it?" she asked. "What's wrong?"

Okay, here goes, he thought. "My sister called me yesterday. As a matter of fact, she called while I was sitting in the school parking lot, waiting for you."

Her eyebrows drew together as she tried to understand what he was telling her—and why.

"I thought we were here because she called you today," Gwen said.

"We are," he answered, then tried to clear up the confusion. "I'm talking about my other sister Jordana. She was the one who called yesterday."

The chill she felt became more intense and unnerving.

"What did Jordana have to tell you?" Gwen's voice almost sounded hollow to her ears. "Brooks, what aren't you telling me?"

He pressed his lips together, then forced the words out. "They found a second body at the site."

"Was it—" Gwen's voice cracked and she tried

again, her voice so low it was hardly audible. "Was it my mother?"

"The medical examiner wasn't able to make any sort of an identification."

He heard a noise escape Gwen's lips. If he had to put a name to it, he would have said that it almost sounded like a keening. Brooks immediately felt that maybe he'd made a mistake. He should have waited before he told Gwen about the second body.

But he knew that every minute he delayed telling her, he ran the risk of having someone else release the information. That meant that Gwen would wind up hearing the information somewhere else, even on the news. He couldn't think of a worse way for her to find that sort of news out.

So you sprang it on her here, in the bowels of the police station. Nice going, bright boy, Brooks silently upbraided himself.

"Why couldn't he make an identification?" Gwen asked.

"Unlike the first body they found, this one wasn't wrapped up in plastic or nearly as well-preserved as Crane had been. The killer just seemed to stuff the body into the wall any way that he could. His main objective was to get it out of sight." She looked so crestfallen, Brooks wanted to give her at least a little hope about being able to make an identification. "After the body is cleaned up, Yvette is going to try to do what she can to reconstruct the victim's face. That way she might be able to come up with some sort of a composite."

Gwen filled in the missing words. "So right now you don't even know if the victim's a man or a woman?"

"Not yet." It was Yvette who answered her question, walking back into the lab. "Here are the photos I made of Crane's notebook," she told Gwen, handing her the photocopies she'd just taken. "As for the second body, right now it's in pieces, like a giant jigsaw puzzle. Once we get everything cleaned up and relatively matched, we should have better luck with identification."

"Could you call me—us—as soon as you know?" Gwen asked the lab technician. She sounded like she was almost begging.

Yvette squeezed her hand. "As soon as I know," she promised.

"You know, that's the first time I ever heard Yvette offer to go against the rules," Brooks told Gwen as they left the lab several minutes later. "I think you've managed to unearth my brainiac sister's kinder side," he said, hoping to get a smile out of Gwen.

She merely nodded, making a murmuring noise. He decided to just let that pass, thinking that perhaps Gwen needed the space.

But when Gwen continued to remain silent even as they walked out of the precinct and headed toward his vehicle, Brooks became concerned. This really wasn't like Gwen, he thought. She was usually more talkative.

"Talk to me, Gwen. Don't just keep everything bottled up inside like this," he said. When she still didn't respond, he pressed, "What are you thinking right now, this minute?"

She stood next to his car, making no effort to get in or even to open the passenger door.

When she turned to look at him, he could see the anguish in her eyes.

"I don't know what I'm thinking right now," Gwen admitted. "My mind's all over the place like a Ping-Pong ball that's still in play. I don't know whether to hope that whomever that second body belongs to, it isn't my mother so I can go on hoping she's still alive somewhere, or that it *is* her and this awful business of not knowing is finally over with."

And then she thought of what Rita had been going through all these years. "My poor grandmother probably feels exactly the same way," she said. Tears slid down her cheeks.

Brooks unlocked the passenger door and then held it open for her, but Gwen made no move to get in.

"Gwen," he said her name softly.

When she still remained standing there, frozen in place, he took her in his arms. That was when she completely dissolved in tears, sinking into his arms as she sobbed her heart out in pain.

Brooks held her until she was all cried out.

He held her for a long time.

"Let me take you home," he said when she finally seemed to be all cried out, at least for the time being. Comforting her was his first thought.

Taking the handkerchief he offered, she wiped her eyes. Gwen eyed him uncertainly.

"My place?" she finally asked.

"No," he answered, "mine. You're definitely in no

shape to be alone right now. And besides, that creep Shelton is still lurking out there somewhere and although he might be harmless, most likely he's not and I'm not taking the chance of underestimating him."

But as Brooks began to usher her into the car again, Gwen suddenly shook her head.

"I don't want to go to your house," she told Brooks. "Not yet, anyway. I want to see the body."

"Gwen, there's been no positive identification yet," he reminded her. "Yvette told you that the body is still just a pile of bones that haven't been joined together yet."

Gwen shook her head. "I don't care," she insisted. "I want to see the body, even if it isn't all together."

"Gwen, please," Brooks insisted, "don't put yourself through this."

But she remained adamant, even if her insides felt as if they were quivering. "Trust me, I'm better off seeing those scattered bones than letting my imagination run off with me."

Brooks frowned. "I'm against this."

Gwen nodded. "Duly noted," she told him. "Now, can we please go to the morgue?"

He closed the passenger door and turned away from his car, knowing all along that he was going to wind up giving in to her. "What is it you hope to get out of this?" he asked, escorting her up the stairs again.

"I'm not sure," Gwen admitted. "Maybe closure." She speculated, then added something unexpected. "At the very least, I can tell the medical examiner where he can find my mother's dental records."

Stopping at the top of the stairs, Brooks looked at her in surprise. "Wait. You actually know the name of your mother's dentist?" The next moment, he questioned, "How is that even possible? You were, what, three when she went missing?"

"That's right," she confirmed. "But my grandmother insisted on going to the same dentist my mother had. Dr. McClellan. She said it helped her feel connected to my mother. When it came time to take me to a dentist, she took me to the same one.

"And when Dr. McClellan retired," Gwen continued, "his son took over the practice. My mother's dental records are still on file there," she concluded, happy that she had something positive to contribute.

"How do you know that?" Brooks asked. He would have assumed that once everything went digital, the old, terminated records would not have been converted and very possibly just thrown away.

Gwen walked in front of him back into the building. "The answer to that is because my grandmother got involved," she explained, her voice returning back to its normal cadence as she became more positive. "After a while, she started to give up hope that my mother would turn up alive. But she still wanted to be sure there was some way to identify her if she was ever found.

"So," she continued as Brooks pressed for the elevator, "my grandmother persuaded the original Dr. McClellan to continue to keep my mother's records on file. When the practice changed hands, she offered his son money to keep the records on file. He turned down her money, but assured her that the records would continue to remain on file as long as he lived."

Brooks laughed quietly under his breath, totally impressed. "Your grandmother is a very resourceful lady," he told Gwen.

"And stubborn," she said, getting into the elevator. "Don't forget stubborn."

This time Brooks laughed out loud. "No way I could do that."

"ARE YOU REALLY sure you want to do this?" Jeffrey Robbins, the medical examiner, asked uncertainly, looking at Gwen. "I mean, I've had seasoned cops get really queasy—one of them all over my floor—the first time they have to view an autopsied body. And this one looks like some sort of really macabre Halloween puzzle," he told the two people standing in his morgue.

Robbins sighed. "Having you here is already bending the rules," he told Brooks. "And there's no justification for having her here." The doctor nodded his head at Gwen.

"A member of the deceased's family is allowed to come in and view the body, in this case the scattered bones," Gwen said, speaking up, "for identification purposes."

"How do you know you're a member of the deceased's family when I haven't even made an ID yet?" Robbins challenged.

"Just call it a hunch," Gwen answered the man in a low voice.

Gwen had certainly managed to pull herself together

rather quickly, Brooks thought, impressed. She no longer looked like the woman who had almost gone all to pieces on him.

He saw the medical examiner looking at him for some sort of guidance in this. There were times when being a Colton did come in very handy. Although a lot of people had less than kind things to say about the Coltons, very, very few of them put themselves out there by crossing anyone in the family.

Brooks nodded at the balding man, silently backing what Gwen had said.

Robbins sighed deeply again, then beckoned for his visitors to follow him. He brought the pair to what looked like metal filing doors.

Opening one of the doors, he pulled out a drawer. Instead of a body, there were disjoined legs and arms, a head and several bones that didn't appear to have been placed in the proper region yet. There were also numerous items sealed within a plastic bag.

"This is what you came to see," Robbins told Gwen.

Gwen stared at the collection of bones, her heart quickening even as she did her best to seal herself off from what those bones might have represented.

She looked at the bones that might have belonged to her mother for what seemed like a long time.

"Can I close the drawer now?" the medical examiner asked with a touch of impatience.

"Yes," Gwen replied, stepping back. But as Robbins began to close the drawer, Gwen suddenly put her hand on his arm and cried, "Wait."

"Now what?" the medical examiner asked, sounding irritated.

"What's that?" Gwen asked, pointing to the items that in the plastic bag.

"That?" Robbins asked, picking up the bag. "Those are what fell out along with the body parts when they knocked down the wall. Detective Colton thought they might have belonged to the deceased and could help identify whomever this is," he said, gesturing toward the bones. "She told me to keep it with the body until after I managed to put all those bones together into one big whole."

"Could you take them out, please?" Gwen asked the man.

"Now you want to *look* at them?" the ME asked. His tone indicated that he felt she'd already wasted enough of his time with this.

"Yes, please," she told the man.

When he made no effort to comply, Brooks stepped in. "Do you think you recognize something?" he asked Gwen. The expression on her face made him think that something had triggered this request.

"I don't know. I'm not sure," she admitted quite honestly.

"Look," the medical examiner said, finally losing his last bit of patience, "I've got work to do and I just can't be—"

"A couple more minutes isn't going to make a difference," Brooks insisted, cutting into whatever protest Robbins was about to make.

Robbins sighed. "Easy for you to say."

But, clearly under duress, the medical examiner unsealed the plastic bag and careful spread out its contents onto the slab right beside the miscellaneous body parts.

Both Robbins and Brooks observed Gwen as she looked at what turned out to be a pendant and a cheap, tarnished charm bracelet.

"Recognize anything?" Brooks asked her, carefully watching her face.

"I don't know," she confessed, then raised her eyes to look at Brooks. "I think I do, but I'm not sure."

"That's the way it goes sometimes," Robbins said dismissively. He went to pick up the pieces of jewelry that had been taken out. "Okay, let's just put these back in the bag and—"

"Would it be all right if I took a picture of these, please?" Gwen asked the medical examiner, stopping him just as he went to reach for the plastic bag.

Robbins glared at her. "What did you just ask me?"

"I asked if I could take a picture. I want to show these two pieces to my grandmother," she explained, then turned toward Brooks to make the rest of her appeal. "I think I recognize them from a photograph of my mother that my grandmother has framed on the mantel in the living room, but I'm not a hundred percent sure. My grandmother would be, though. She had a very keen mind and a great eye for details."

"Your grandmother," Robbins repeated incredulously.

It was easy to see that he was highly skeptical about any of this. But glancing toward Brooks had the medical examiner refraining from gathering up the two articles of jewelry and putting them into the drawer until after Gwen had finished taking the photographs.

"Is there anything else?" Robbins asked, looking at Gwen and then at Brooks. He definitely didn't sound pleased.

"Not right now. Thank you," Gwen added politely. "My grandmother has been trying to find out what happened to my mother for more than a quarter of a century," she told the ME. "You might have finally given her the answers she's been looking for."

"Glad to help," Robbins mumbled, flustered in the face of her genuine gratitude.

"YOU KNOW, YOU didn't need to flatter Robbins *that* much," Brooks told her as they left the morgue.

"I know. I did it for you," she said.

"For me?" That didn't make any sense, he thought.

"Uh-huh." She looked at him earnestly. "It never hurts to be polite—and you never know when you might need that man's cooperation again."

He sighed, putting his arm around her shoulders as they walked. "Right as usual."

Chapter Twenty

"Why don't we go out to dinner tonight?" Brooks suggested. "There's no denying that you've had a pretty rough day and a little diversion might help you relax and unwind."

Gwen thought it over for a minute. "Maybe you're right."

But deep down inside, she honestly didn't think anything could help her relax, or get that image of dismembered bones out of her mind. Still, it was worth a try.

She buckled up once she got in the car. However, she couldn't resist looking at the photographs of the jewelry she had taken with her cell phone.

Brooks glanced over toward Gwen when he came to a stop at a red light. He saw that she was looking at the jewelry she'd photographed. It was all too fresh in her mind. Was that good or bad? he couldn't help wondering.

"So do you recognize those pieces?" he asked her, nodding at the jewelry.

She raised her eyes to his face and gave Brooks an honest answer. "Depends on what minute you ask me.

I keep going back and forth on that. That pendant and that bracelet *look* like the pieces that are in that photograph on the mantel, but then, those pieces weren't exactly rare."

"Tell you what, why don't we drive over to Kansas City in the morning, go see your grandmother and show the photographs to her?" he proposed.

She bit her lower lip, vacillating. "I really hate putting her through that, but you're right. Grandma would be a much better judge in determining if those pieces belonged to my mother. Grandma was the one who gave her that pendant." She'd heard the story countless times. "It was a graduation gift."

"How about the bracelet?" Brooks asked. "Do you know who gave her that?"

Gwen frowned a little. "According to my grandmother, she thought the bracelet came from my father. When she asked my mother about it, my mother became very vague and secretive. She wouldn't really say one way or another. My grandmother came to her own conclusion about the bracelet. She just assumed the bracelet was a way for him to string my mother along."

Brooks had another thought. "Tomorrow, before we go to see your grandmother, I'm going to call Yvette and have her request those dental records from that dentist you told me about. Dr. McClellan's son," he recalled, then changed his tone, sounding a little more upbeat. "But right now, I want you to put everything else out of your mind and just focus on enjoying the best Italian cuisine outside of New York City."

He was trying so hard to make her feel better, Gwen

thought. She did her best to smile as she told him, "Sounds good."

"Tastes even better," he promised as he pulled up in front of a warm, inviting restaurant.

GWEN TRIED VERY hard to at least *look* as if she was enjoying herself. She felt that she owed it to Brooks because he was going out of his way to make her come around, to stop dwelling on those bones she had insisted on viewing.

But no matter how hard Gwen tried to make Brooks think that she was having a good time, she just couldn't seem to come out from beneath the oppressive blanket of sadness that had descended over her. It had come over her from the moment she'd first viewed the remains that had literally fallen out of the wall.

"Would you like to order some dessert?" Brooks asked her when they had finished the main course— or at least he had. It was not lost on him that Gwen had barely eaten half her dinner. This was definitely not going the way he'd hoped. "Or would you just rather skip dessert and just go home?"

Home.

He was talking about his place, she thought. Funny how quickly that had become more of a home to her than the apartment she had rented.

"Would you mind terribly if we just skip ordering dessert and go back to your place instead?" Gwen asked.

"If I minded, I wouldn't have suggested it," Brooks pointed out.

Looking around, he saw their server walking toward

another table. He raised his hand to catch her attention. When he did, he asked the woman to bring the check.

Rather than use a credit card, Brooks paid for the dinner putting a hundred on the tray. He assumed the server would keep the change.

"Let's go," he said to Gwen, escorting her out of the restaurant.

"I'm sorry I'm such a wet blanket," Gwen apologized as they walked to his vehicle.

"You're not a wet blanket," he told her. "You're dealing with a lot of emotions right now, not the least of which involved you seeing what you believe to be your mother's remains. All things considered, I'd say you were bearing up really well. Give yourself a little credit, Gwen. I certainly do."

They had reached his car. Gwen turned to say something to Brooks, to thank him for being so understanding. But when she looked in his direction, she suddenly froze. Her eyes widened as she stared at something in the distance.

"Gwen?" Brooks said her name. When she didn't respond, he raised his voice to get her to snap out of it. "Gwen, what's wrong?"

She grabbed his arm, her fingers digging harder than she had intended. Her entire body had gone rigid.

Stunned, Brooks looked around, but he didn't see anything that would cause her to react this way.

"What is it?" he asked. Pulling his arm away, he took of her shoulders, shaking her a little to make her around. "What is it that you see?"

e exhaled, releasing the breath she hadn't even realized she had drawn in and was holding. She blinked, stared harder and realized that she was staring off into the shadows.

"He's gone."

"Who's gone?" Brooks asked, scanning the parking lot. There were a few people there, either getting out of their cars or going into them. But he saw nothing that would have made Gwen grow so pale that he saw the difference even in the moonlight.

Gwen shook her head, feeling foolish. "You're going to think I'm crazy."

She had genuinely looked spooked. Something had scared her. All he wanted to do was help her. "I'd never think you were crazy."

"Well, I'll think it for the both of us," she told him. Then, because she could see he was still waiting for an answer, she said, "I thought I just saw Daniel."

Brooks scanned the area again, more slowly this time. He didn't see anyone who resembled Shelton.

"Where?"

"Here. Across the parking lot," she said, pointing at an area that was now empty. "He was staring at us."

"Those are just your nerves, overreacting," Brooks assured her. After what she'd been through, he could understand her seeing the man behind every building and tree. He'd seen it before. "Besides, I know what the man looks like and he's not out there, Gwen." He was keenly alert for any signs of the man. "Your mind is playing tricks on you."

"Or maybe I'm just losing it," she countered, referring to her mind.

For a moment, she looked so stricken, his heart went out to her. All he wanted to do was comfort her. He did the only thing he could. He took her into his arms and held her.

"I promise I'm not going to let anything happen to you, Gwen." Her head was lowered but he could tell that she was crying. Very gently, Brooks turned her head up toward him, making her look at him. "I care about you, Gwen. I care a great deal and should that stalker actually turn up anywhere around here, I'm going to make him regret he ever intruded into your life."

But Gwen only heard him say one thing. "You care about me?"

Why did she look so surprised? "Of course I care about you," he said. "What did you think the last few nights were all about?"

She shrugged helplessly. "You being a male?" It was more of a question than a statement.

His brow furrowed. "Is that what you really think?"

A long, heavy sigh escaped her lips, followed by another shrug. "I really don't know what to think," she confessed.

"Then I will *tell* you what to think," he said. He saw the confused, hesitant expression on her face. He pulled out all the stops. "You mentioned 'crazy' earlier," he reminded her.

Had he changed his mind about her mental state, after all? "I did," she admitted tentatively, waiting to hat he would say next.

ell, I am crazy about you. Understand? To the tent of what that word implies. Crazy about you," he repeated, his eyes on hers. "So my advice is deal with it."

As she looked up into his eyes, she realized that he actually meant those words. Suddenly, the world was back in balance.

"Oh, I will. I will." Moved, relieved, happy, Gwen threw her arms around his neck and sealed her lips to his, managing to steal his very breath away, as well.

After several beats had gone by, Brooks carefully removed her arms from around his neck. Surprised, Gwen looked at him quizzically.

"I think this is better continued behind closed doors," he explained. He found himself wanting her and it was really hard not going with his instincts, so he knew he had to get her home before his resolve completely disappeared.

"Are you propositioning me?" she asked, a provocative smile playing on her lips.

"Propositioning, begging, whatever gets us out of this parking lot and into my house," he told her, the look in his eyes already transporting her from here to there.

Suddenly Gwen didn't feel nearly so lost and alone anymore.

"Works for me," she whispered to Brooks. "How fast can you drive without breaking any laws?"

"Fast enough," he replied.

Her eyes were smiling at him as she said, "Then let's go."

The next moment, she slid into the passenger seat and buckled up.

Gwen assumed that he would just take off, driving to

his house at what would be considered the legal limit. But the route Brooks took wasn't one that she recognized. Finally, she just had to ask. "Um, Brooks, where are we going?"

"My house," Brooks answered, checking his rearview mirror.

"I don't really recognize the route," she told him honestly.

"That's because I'm not taking the usual route," he explained.

"We're taking the scenic route?" she asked him. "You do realize that it's kind of dark for that to be enjoyable, right?"

"I'm not doing it for that reason," he said.

"All right, I'll bite. Why are you doing it?" she asked.

"Let's just call it evasive driving," he answered, keeping one eye on the rearview mirror.

"Which you're doing because?" she asked, her voice going up at the end of her sentence. He had managed to stir her curiosity.

"Because in case you *did* see Shelton out there in the parking lot before, I'm not about to lead him to my front door."

Gwen sank down farther in her seat, doing her best to deal with what he was suggesting. "If he wants to know where you live, Daniel's resourceful enough to hire someone to find that out for him. You're a Colton, ⸻aven's sake. Your address would be easy enough ⸻e."

⸻ sure you're right, but I am not about to help him

do that," Brooks pointed out. "If you're worried, I can stash you at Jordana's house."

"Thanks, but if it's all the same to you, I feel safer with you," she told him.

She was putting an awful lot of faith in him, Brooks thought, although he had to admit that having her trust him this way did make him feel even more protective toward her than he already did.

Still he felt it only right to point out to her that "Jordana has a state-of-the-art security system, if you're interested."

"So do you. Besides," Gwen said as they pulled up into his driveway, "you can distract me in a way that your sister can't."

Brooks laughed softly under his breath. "Guess I can't argue with that."

Her eyes all but caressed him as she looked up at him. "No, you can't," she agreed.

Brooks unlocked the front door, disarming his alarm system. Holding the door open, he gestured for her to come inside.

"Shouldn't you be saying something like "'Will you walk into my parlor?" said the spider to the fly'?" she asked him, grinning.

"That all depends," he said as he took her purse and put it on the table.

"On what?" Gwen asked.

Lord, but this man could make her feel breathless faster than anyone had ever been able to do prior to Brooks.

Right now, her heart was fluttering so fast she was certain it could easily just take off.

"On whether or not you'll let me devour you," he told her, pressing a wreath of kisses gently all along her face.

Brooks was doing it again, she thought, making her feel dizzy. Every single thought floated out of her head without leaving a single trace in its wake.

"Devour away," she gasped, breathing hard but unable to catch her breath sufficiently.

"Yes, ma'am," he replied solemnly.

Gwen couldn't contain herself any longer. It felt as if emotions had suddenly exploded in her veins. She began tugging at his shirt, pulling it up over his head and tossing it aside.

She splayed her hands along his hard, rippled chest muscles, her pulse quickening as she initiated the contact.

It was all he needed.

The next second he was pulling off the clothes from her body, sending the garments down to the floor in a heap, right on top of his.

His mouth hungrily devouring her lips, he knew that they weren't going to be able to make it up to his bedroom. They weren't even going to make it to the base of the staircase.

Picking up her now nude body, he pressed her against him, filling his senses with her scent, her taste, her hunger and doing his very best to match it. It was almost a competition.

Every time they made love, it was a completely new revelation to her. She discovered things about this man she hadn't known before, took comfort in and reveled in the way he made her feel, the way he made her body sing in response to the lightest of his touches.

Rather than be rough, he was incredibly gentle yet so very arousing and she was seriously afraid she might just lose her mind.

She was so caught up in what was happening between them, she didn't think about Daniel right now, wasn't concerned that he might have been the man she had seen lurking in the background earlier. For this small isolated space of time, Brooks was all that existed for her. Being with him defined both the beginning and the end of her world.

And just for now, that was enough for her.

Something whispered within her soul that that very well could be enough for forever.

If only he wanted her forever.

Chapter Twenty-One

"Do you want to call your grandmother to let her know that we're coming?" Brooks asked Gwen the following morning after they had gotten dressed and ready to leave. "That way we can make sure she'll be home and we won't be making the long trip for no reason."

"There's no need for that," Gwen told him. "My grandmother's almost always home, especially in the morning."

The inflection in her voice caught his attention. "You don't want to tell her about that second body turning up, do you?" he guessed.

She debated denying it, but then didn't even try. "Not over the phone. I'd rather tell her about that face-to-face. That way I can be there for her when she has to deal with the realization that my mother is never going to be coming back. That she died a long time ago."

He fought the urge to just take her into his arms and hold her. Instead, he pointed out, "That jewelry might not be your mother's. I know that this might be clutching at straws, but..."

A smile quirked her lips. "Until I can show my

grandmother the picture with those pieces of jewelry, straws are good," she commented.

He gave up fighting his urge. Brooks took her into his arms and held her close. "I hate that you're going through this."

She appreciated his saying that. She also appreciated having him hold her like this. There was something very comforting about having those strong arms around her.

"At least I'm not going through it alone." She took a deep breath, as if that would help her face the ordeal ahead of her. "Ready?"

He nodded, giving her hand one quick, final squeeze before heading toward the front door.

"Ready."

"You're very quiet," he observed. They had been on the road for almost fifteen minutes and she hadn't said a single word.

"It's kind of hard to talk when your heart's in your mouth." A sad smile curved her lips. "For most of my life, part of me was waiting for my mother to walk through the front door and back into my life and now... and now that's not going to happen," she said, forcing the words out.

He drew the logical conclusion from that. "Then you're really sure that's her jewelry, aren't you?"

Gwen grimly nodded her head, holding her emotions in check. "Pretty much, yes."

"Look, we don't have to go see your grandmother with this right now. We can wait until after Yvette gets those dental records and confirms that the second body in the wall belonged to your mother. For that matter, it could be that making a conclusive identification even *with* the dental records will be impossible," he pointed out.

But Gwen shook her head. She'd come this far, she was going to see this through all the way. "My grandmother deserves closure."

"And you?" he asked, glancing at her. "What do you deserve?"

He saw her jaw clenching. "I deserve to find the SOB who did this, who killed my mother, and make him pay. I also deserve to find out who my father was."

A thought occurred to him. "And if they turn out to be one and the same person?"

He had seen cases when a philandering husband took extreme measures to protect his secret and keep his wife from finding out that he was cheating. Brooks really hoped that Gwen's grief wouldn't wind up being compounded by having her father turn out to be the person who killed her mother.

Gwen squared her shoulders, as if bracing herself against a physical blow. "I'll deal with that when and if it turns out to be true. Right now I just want to get through showing these photographs to my grandmother," she said.

THEY MADE GOOD TIME.

Pulling up in front of the small house where Gwen had lived for most of her life, Brooks got out of the vehicle and rounded the hood to the passenger's side.

When he took Gwen's hand to help her out of the car, he thought that it felt almost icy.

His heart went out to her.

"You know there's still time to go home," Brooks told her.

"No, there isn't," she answered.

She flashed him a grateful smile, knowing he was just trying to comfort her. With that, she turned and walked up to her grandmother's front door. She still had the key but she didn't want to walk in and frighten her grandmother. If she'd called ahead to tell the older woman that she and Brooks were coming, that would have been a different matter.

But even that would have presented problems. Her grandmother would immediately be suspicious about a second visit coming so close on the heels of the last one.

It was best to keep all the questions down to a minimum. But now it was finally time to face the music, she thought.

So she rang the bell and waited for her grandmother to come to the door and open it. That took time. Gwen felt anxious and she would have wanted to ring the bell for a second time, but she forced herself to just be patient and wait.

Finally, the door opened and her grandmother was standing there in the doorway. The older woman's face lit up when she saw her.

"Gwennie, Brooks, you're back," she declared in surprise. But as her own words sank in, the woman's smile faded. "What's wrong?"

"Why does anything have to be wrong?" Gwen asked, her nerve faltering. "Maybe I just missed you."

Rather than say anything to her granddaughter, she turned toward Brooks. "I always knew when she was fibbing," she told him. "Her right eye would close just the tiniest bit, like she was really concentrating hard to get that fib out without giving herself away." The woman's attention shifted back to her granddaughter as she led the way into her house. "Now out with it, Gwen," she instructed. "What are you and this handsome young man of yours doing back here so soon?"

As she began to explain, the words seemed to stick in Gwen's mouth, refusing to emerge.

Brooks decided to step in and take the pressure off Gwen. "A second body turned up at the demolition site, Mrs. Harrison," he explained to the woman.

Rita's legs suddenly wouldn't support her and she sank down on the sofa.

"Was it—" The woman took a deep breath and tried again. "Was it my daughter's body?" she asked Brooks.

"We don't know yet. Unlike the first body, this one wasn't as well-preserved."

He saw the older woman's hands go up to her mouth, as if to keep the horrified sound that was building up in her throat from coming out.

Moved by what she saw, Gwen was finally able to find her voice.

"They found a couple of pieces of jewelry, Grandma. They let me take photographs of the jewelry," she said. "I brought them to show you."

But Rita continued to look at her granddaughter, a

host of emotions evident on her face. Her sharp eyes pinned Gwen where she sat.

"You recognized the jewelry, didn't you, Gwen?" she asked.

Gwen struggled to answer and finally just nodded her head. "I think I did," she told her grandmother. "One of the pieces they found was a pendant. It looked just like the one you said you gave Mom when she graduated high school."

"And you brought the photographs?" Rita asked, her voice almost stoic as she looked into her granddaughter's eyes.

"I did." Gwen slipped the two photographs she had taken and printed out of her purse. She placed them on the coffee table in front of her grandmother.

Rita continued to look at her granddaughter, but gradually, she lowered her eyes and examined the two photographs. The moment she did, she sucked in her breath. The next moment, there were tears shimmering in her eyes, threatening to spill out.

"You recognize those pieces, don't you, Mrs. Harrison?" Brooks asked the older woman kindly.

"Yes." Her voice was hardly above a whisper and broke as she answered him.

"Do they belong to your daughter?" he asked her gently.

"They do," Rita answered, her body almost trembling as her voice cracked again.

"Are you sure, Mrs. Harrison?" Brooks pressed.

It sounded almost callous to question the woman like this, but he wanted to make certain that the woman did recognize the pendant and bracelet as the ones that had belonged to her daughter.

"Yes," Rita answered hoarsely. "Very sure." The tears slid down her cheeks.

"Oh, Grandma," Gwen cried, putting her arms around the older woman and hugging her tightly. "I'm so very sorry about this."

"Don't be, dear," Rita said, stroking her granddaughter's hair. "In my heart, I knew this day would come. And now that it has, I am relieved. We can finally hold that memorial service for your mother." She looked at the photographs again. "My poor baby's been waiting a long time for that." Her voice broke again as she struggled not to cry. "Now you two go and do what you have to do," she told them, looking from her granddaughter to Brooks.

But Gwen made no move to get up. She looked at her grandmother with sincere concern. "Are you sure you're going to be all right, Grandma?"

"I'm fine, Gwen," Rita assured her, patting her granddaughter's hand. "I just have one request," she said, turning toward Brooks.

"Name it," he told her.

"I want you to find the bastard who did this to my girl. I want you to find out who killed her," Rita implored. "I don't have much, but whatever I have is yours if you can find out who did this to my Olivia, who buried her in that wall for all these years." She shivered as she thought about what that had to have been like, even if her daughter had been dead at the time.

"Keep your money, Mrs. Harrison," he said. "My

sister is already working the case for the police department." That wasn't strictly accurate, he thought and endeavored to set the record straight. "Technically, she's trying to find out who killed Crane and buried his body in the wall," he told her.

"Same thing," Rita said.

"So you think that the two murders are connected?" he asked Rita.

"I do," she replied. She scrutinized the look on his face. "Don't you?"

Brooks laughed quietly. "You know, Mrs. Harrison, if you ever decided you want to leave retirement behind, you would make a pretty good detective."

Rita eyed him, amused despite the dark subject they were discussing. "Are you flirting with me, young man?"

"I don't think I'd stand a chance if I was," he replied with a very straight face. And then he changed the subject and became serious. "But I did want to say that Gwen told me about you getting your daughter's dentist to maintain her dental records. I am very impressed by your farsighted thinking."

She shrugged slightly. "I don't know about farsighted thinking, but I was always taught that desperate times deserve desperate measures and those dental records were the only thing I could think of."

"Well, it's a very lucky thing that you did. This could finally put at least this part of your long ordeal to rest."

He saw the tears beginning to shimmer in the woman's eyes again. "Oh, I'm sorry, Mrs. Harrison. I didn't mean to make you cry again," Brooks said, feeling contrite about the matter.

Rita shook her head. "No, no, you misunderstand. These are tears of joy, young man."

Gwen and Brooks exchanged looks. "Joy?" Gwen questioned her grandmother.

"Please don't misunderstand, dear. I would have much rather that they had found your mother alive and well, but I am really glad that I—we," she amended, "finally know what happened to your mother and that we are, at long last, able to honor her life.

"I was afraid that I would go to my own grave never knowing what happened to my daughter. Now, at last, I do," she concluded.

Brooks smiled at Gwen's grandmother. "I'm glad I could be part of that, Mrs. Harrison," he told her honestly. "Now, if you could please give me this Dr. McClellan's address, I'll pass that along to the lab technician in the crime scene investigative lab and see if we can pin down an ID."

"Your sister," Rita said.

"Yes, my sister." His eyes crinkled as he smiled at her. "You remembered." He had only mentioned Yvette in passing the one time he had been here to meet Gwen's grandmother. "Again, I must say I'm impressed. You are a very impressive lady," he told her. "You remind me of my mother."

"Thank you, dear. And your sister, she'll handle the identification?" Rita asked Brooks, getting back to the subject that was uppermost in her mind.

Brooks nodded. "That's what she does."

"You do have quite an interesting family, young man," Rita said, then smiled nostalgically. "You don't know how lucky you are."

"At times," Brooks allowed.

"No, all the time," Rita stressed. "Family is family, Brooks. That isn't something to be taken for granted. Trust me, I know. Gwen and I have been alone for most of our lives and being alone is not something I would have chosen on my own. But my husband died shortly after Olivia was born and after a while, you get used to shouldering your way through life, especially when you have a child depending on you. And I've been lucky to have that twice in my life. Once with Olivia and then with Gwen here," she said, nodding at Gwen. "I couldn't have asked for more—except maybe for a young man who knows how to cherish my granddaughter," Rita said, pointedly looking up at the private investigator.

"Grandma!" Gwen cried, embarrassed. After all this time, was her grandmother suddenly deciding to play matchmaker?

"What, I should keep that to myself?" Rita asked, surprised. "At my age, Gwen, I don't know how much longer I have. That means I should tell people what I'm thinking, because I might never get another chance to share something that I really feel is important." The older woman looked back at Brooks. "You understand, don't you, Brooks?"

Gwen could feel herself turning very red. "Grandma, please. You're putting him on the spot."

Rita smile as she looked at Brooks. "You don't mind, do you?"

His eyes met Gwen's. He had been thinking more and more about what life would be like if they spent it together. There was a great deal he liked about that, Brooks thought.

"Not in the slightest."

Chapter Twenty-Two

Gwen waited until they were back in Brooks's car and on their way back to Braxville before she said, "I'm sorry about my grandmother."

He glanced in her direction, not quite sure what had brought this on. "What's there to be sorry about?" he asked. "I think your grandmother's a really nice lady."

Gwen paused, digesting what he had just said. She liked the fact that Brooks appreciated the most important person in her life.

"Well, she is," she agreed, "but she shouldn't have put you on the spot like that."

"Like what?" he asked innocently.

Gwen sighed. "Are you really going to make me say it?"

He suppressed the smile that rose to his lips and said, "I guess you'll have to because I'm not sure what you're talking about."

"Okay." Gwen forced the words out of her mouth. "My grandmother was blatantly hinting that the two of us should get together and be a couple. There," she declared. "Satisfied?"

"Getting there," he answered, grinning at her. "Personally, I think that's a great idea."

Now he was just having fun with her, Gwen thought. "You don't have to continue this act. We're in your car. It's not as if she can hear us. I used to think she was all knowing, but super-hearing is a little out of her league."

"I don't care who hears us," he said seriously. "And it's not an act. I wasn't kidding when I said I really care about you. Because I do." He looked in her direction for a second, his mouth curving just the slightest bit. "Is that going to be a problem for you?"

He was really serious, she thought. This was no longer something he said just before they made love together. He had real feelings for her. Gwen felt as if there was a parade going on inside of her.

She grinned at him. "Not at all."

His smile widened. "Good."

It took several minutes for her pulse to settle down. When it finally did, Gwen took in her surroundings. This didn't quite look like the road back to the police station.

"Where are we going?" she asked. "I thought you said we were going to go to the precinct to see Yvette and give her the name of the dental office." Had he changed his mind about that? she wondered.

"I already took care of that. I texted Yvette the information. Right now I decided that maybe I should swing by the demolition site. I know that there's a work stoppage order in place," he told her, thinking Gwen might protest and bring that up, "but I just wanted to see if Jordana or any of her team found anything else at the

site. You know, something that might be useful in helping us find out who killed Crane and the second victim."

He had her complete attention. "Like what?"

"I don't really know, but then I never expected this
turn of events to happen either," he confessed. It occurred to him that she might not be up to this, given
that it involved her mother. "If you'd rather, I could drop
you off at home first."

"No, I wouldn't *rather*," she informed Brooks, re-
minding him that, "We're in this thing together, you
know."

He smiled at Gwen, silently approving her choice to
come along. She was fearless despite the emotional toll
that joining him in this investigation might take on her.
He liked that about her. He liked, he realized, everything about this woman.

"Glad you see it that way," Brooks told her with approval.

It took them another few minutes to get to the initial
demolition site of what had once been Ruby Row, a
popular shopping center in its time. All that had been
marked for clearance in order to build the new center
and thereby usher in a new phase of progress.

Because of his father, Brooks knew all about the current mayor pushing his campaign to put a stop to what
that man referred to as *urban sprawl*. The term highly
incensed his father. Other than angering him, the label
wasn't exactly conducive to helping Colton Construction to continue to grow.

If that label persisted to hinder the company's newest project, not only would the company not grow, it would be in serious financial trouble. A great deal of money had been put into making this new center a thriving reality.

Piecing together miscellaneous conversations he had overheard, Brooks had also picked up on the fact that there were additional problems plaguing the company. Problems that, when questioned, his father didn't want to talk about.

But nothing really stayed secret in Braxville and word had gotten out that some of his father's longtime employees were beginning to get sick on the job. Really sick. Whether this was just a coincidence or there was something more serious at play here remained to be seen. But Brooks secretly felt that this work stoppage might have a positive side effect. If there was something behind the rumors, being away from the construction site might help those men heal.

Rousing himself from the grim thoughts, he realized that Gwen was leaning forward in the passenger seat, taking in what she saw.

"This looks like a scene out of an old war movie," she commented.

Brooks parked his vehicle as close as possible to the demolished building and they both got out of the car.

Gwen looked in awe at the debris that had once been a warehouse. "How soon do you think your father's company can get back to building the center?" she asked. Anything had to look better than this, she couldn't help thinking.

"For my money, it can't be soon enough," a deep voice behind them said, answering her question.

Surprised, Gwen and Brooks both turned around to look at the man who had just spoken.

Brooks had recognized who the voice belonged to immediately. Markus Dexter.

There were many other people whom Brooks would have rather introduced to Gwen than his father's business partner, a man who had been in his life far longer than he and his siblings cared for. For reasons known only to the man himself, Dexter liked to refer to himself as their "Uncle Markus" although none of his siblings or he thought of him that way.

"Well, hello," Dexter said, his green eyes all but lighting up when he looked at Gwen.

Brooks imagined that jackals had the same look in their eyes when they saw their next potential dinner.

Dexter's eyes were all but devouring Gwen. His question was for Brooks, but his father's partner never looked in his direction. "And who is this lovely young creature?" he asked.

Not wanting to come across like a boor, Brooks had no other choice but to make the introductions. "Gwen, this is—"

Taking Gwen's hand, Dexter brought it up to his lips, kissing it in what had once been an accepted courtly gesture but had now, in Brooks's opinion, become hopelessly antiquated.

"Uncle Markus Dexter," Dexter said, completing the introduction. "Charmed," he pronounced, his eyes continuing to slide along her face, taking slow measure of the young woman.

"He's not really my uncle," Brooks said, disavowing the familial connection.

What Brooks said didn't seem to bother his father's business partner. "I've watched all those little Coltons grow up so it just *feels* as if I'm their uncle," he told Gwen. "Brooks, why would you bring this ravishing young creature *here*? She'll just get her clothes, not to mention her shoes, dusty. Surely there are much nicer places you could bring her to, Brooks." Dexter pretended to chastise his partner's son.

Dex's eyes slid back to their primary target. Gwen. "If I had someone as exquisite as you to escort, I'd certainly take you to somewhere much finer than this dreary, dusty demolition site."

"We're not here to take in the scenery, Dex," Brooks informed the older man. "We're here looking for some answers."

Dexter's brow furrowed just a tad as he pretended to think about what Brooks had just said. "He always liked to talk in riddles," Dex *confided* to Gwen. "He liked to do that even when he was a young boy. Do you like riddles—?" He went to say her name and found that he'd forgotten it. "I'm sorry, what did you say your name was?" he asked, eager to begin the game with this new player who had just walked into his life.

"Gwen," she answered, feeling just a shade uncomfortable.

"Gwen what?" Dexter asked, his smile growing larger and more encouraging. Brooks had always thought that when Dexter smiled like that, he almost seemed smarmy.

Maybe it was the situation, or because this was Gwen, but for some reason, Brooks found Dexter to be behaving in a particularly disgusting manner. Just being in the man's company seemed to contaminate everything around him.

Brooks just wanted to get Gwen away from this man who liked to prey on an ever younger class of women. "Look, Mr. Dexter, this was a bad idea—" he began.

"Harrison," Gwen answered Dexter's question at the same time. "My name is Gwen Harrison."

For just a moment, the expression on Dexter's already pale face froze. If Brooks hadn't known better, he would have said that the man had seen a ghost. But there was just the three of them here.

The next moment, Dexter recovered, his voice becoming more like its normal self. "I just remembered that I'm supposed to be attending a meeting clear across town in twenty minutes. I regret I have to cut this short." His smile was almost forced as he said, "Really nice meeting you, Gwen. Brooks, tell your dad I'll be by to see him later on this week."

"You'd be better off telling him yourself," Brooks advised, "because I really don't get to see him that often."

Fitz Colton's dedication to his company, and the fact that he was rarely home was well-known. Certainly, his business partner was aware of this.

But then, Brooks thought, when the man was focused on the conquest of a new woman, everything else seemed to fly right out of Dexter's head.

The man was a womanizer, pure and simple. It was one of the things he particularly disliked about Dexter, along with a dozen or more other things.

To say the least, Dexter's sudden exit surprised him. Brooks found it nothing short of odd, but given the circumstances, gratifying.

"So, what do you think of him?" Brooks asked once Dexter had dashed off.

Gwen didn't want to insult someone who had obviously been part of the Colton Construction Company for many years, especially since she wasn't sure just how Brooks felt about the man. So she couched her words carefully.

"This is probably unfair for me to say, but I feel like after talking to the man, even this little amount of time, I need a shower."

When Brooks laughed at her answer, she was relieved. "Nice to know we're in agreement. I have to admit there's just something about that gentleman-of-the-world act of Dexter's that makes my skin crawl. I don't think my father likes it—or him—very much either."

"Then why are they partners?" she questioned. It didn't make any sense to her.

"Not really sure," Brooks admitted. "As near as I can figure it, Dex came along when Dad ran into a cash flow problem or something like that. Dad's very close-mouthed when it comes to the business," he explained. "I think his favorite phrase is, 'Let me worry about that.' I must have heard it a dozen times. Eventually I just stopped trying to ask questions."

"You know, Mr. Dexter doesn't seem like your father's type of friend," Gwen commented.

"He's not," Brooks told her. "My father might not be the warmest, most outgoing individual, but he's an honest, hardworking man who has worked for everything he has ever gotten.

"As for Dexter—" he looked off in the direction the man had taken even though Dexter was now long gone "—he never worked a day in his life." There was no missing the animosity in Brooks's voice. "His family had some money and then he married Mary. His wife came from old money. I honestly believe that was the *only* reason he married her. I've seen him operate. The man is not above using flattery, manipulation or even resorting to small crime to get what he wanted."

"Small crime?" Gwen questioned. "You know that for a fact?"

"I've heard rumors to that effect, but none that I've ever witnessed," he admitted. "What I do know for a fact is that Dexter has had his share of mistresses on the side—young, attractive women who enjoy getting pretty things and having attention lavished on them."

Gwen ran her hands along her arms, warding off a sudden chill that had nothing to do with the weather. She tried to imagine being like one of these women— and just couldn't. "I don't think there are enough trinkets in the world to make me consider selling myself like that."

Gwen debated leaving it at that, but in all honesty, she couldn't. She needed to tell Brooks what she'd felt, even if it didn't make any sense to her.

"But there was this, oh, I don't know, strange connection between Dexter and me just the briefest of seconds. But then it turned into—"

"Revulsion?" he asked.

She reflected on the word for a brief moment.

"No, I think it's more like— You know in those horror movies when you know the actress is about to be killed by the mass murderer, or eaten by an anaconda, but you just can't look away? You have to watch. Well, it's like that," she admitted. "Your father's partner strikes me like that."

Brooks heard her out, and then he began to laugh. Really laugh. "You know, if there were more women like you around, Dexter wouldn't ever have been such a legend in his own mind. He'd realize that he was the pathetic, stomach-churning low-life subhuman that a lot of us take him for."

She felt her own stomach twisting, making her want to get away from here as well as from the topic. "I don't want to talk about your father's partner anymore," she told him. "Let's just go talk to the people we came here to talk to."

"Good idea," he agreed softly. He regretted the run-in with Dexter, regretted having put Gwen through it.

BROOKS APPROACHED SEVERAL people who were working to clear the portions of the site that were far from where the second body parts had been found.

One of the older workers, Kyle Jackson, a hulking giant of a man, recognized Brooks.

"You here to shut down another part of the site?"

Jackson asked. "Your sister already came yesterday to limit our work space." He appealed to Brooks. "You know, if we don't work, we don't get paid."

"I'm not here to close anything down," Brooks assured the man. "I'm just here to find out if anyone found anything else interesting while combing through the debris."

Jackson stared at him, ignoring the young woman with the boss's son. "You think anyone would admit that now, given that the last time anything 'unusual' turned up, we had to stop all work until told otherwise?" The big man laughed, but there was no mirth in the sound. "I don't think so."

Jackson looked around at the three other workers who were there with him and they merely nodded their heads in agreement.

"I understand, but I want you to know that I'm not working with the police, we just happen to be interested in the same set of events." Reaching into his pocket, Brooks took out one of his business cards. "So if you *do* happen to come across something unusual, *anything* at all, I'd appreciate it if you called us first."

Jackson took the business card and looked at it. "I've got a question for you, Young Colton."

"Go ahead, ask," Brooks encouraged, mentally bracing himself for whatever was coming.

"Why is one of the boss's kids out there, working as a detective—"

"Private investigator," Brooks corrected.

"Yeah, that. Why are you working as a private investigator instead of—you know—being out there, partying every night?" Jackson asked. "I know that's what my own son would be doing, given half a chance."

"That's easy," Brooks said, not commenting on Jackson's son. "I like earning my own way. So do my sisters and brothers."

Jackson nodded. It was obvious that he was rolling over Brooks's statement. "Well, I can tell you that having all you kids choosing your own paths in life is a mixed bag for your old man."

"A mixed bag?" Gwen questioned. She'd kept silent up until now, not wanting to interfere, but at this point, she needed to have things clarified. "I don't understand. What is that supposed to mean in this context?"

"Well," Jackson answered with surprising authority in his voice. "Mr. Colton's both annoyed that none of his kids followed him into the construction business, and proud of the fact that none of them are leeching off him but making their own way."

"He told you that?" Brooks asked, amazed.

Jackson looked surprised by the question. Fitz Colton didn't share his feelings with his employees.

"Your father? Hell no. That man doesn't stand around and chew the fat with his employees. But I can tell, the look on his face says it all." Jackson nodded at the card he was holding before he put it into his pocket. "I'll let you know if anyone finds anything," he promised, patting his pants pocket.

Brooks smiled his thanks. It was the best that he could hope for.

Chapter Twenty-Three

At a temporary impasse in the investigation, Brooks and Gwen went back to his house.

His cell phone rang just as they crossed the threshold. He saw the hope that instantly sprang into Gwen's eyes. Seeing her this way was painful for him. She was hoping someone was calling him with news about her mother, but that wasn't the case. The ringtone identified the caller as Bridgette.

Bridgette was the one member of his family that Gwen hadn't met when he'd brought her over to his parents' estate. That was because his triplet sister lived in Kansas City.

Not wanting Gwen to harbor any undue hope, before answering his cell phone he told her, "It's just my sister calling."

The information didn't immediately dampen Gwen's spirits—or answer any questions. "Which sister?" she asked. "Jordana or Yvette?"

He could tell that Gwen thought getting a call from either one might mean hopeful news. Brooks really hated disappointing her.

"Neither," he told her. "It's Bridgette." The call was about to go to voice mail, so he answered it. "Hi, Bridgette. What's up?" he asked while Gwen eyed him curiously.

"I could ask you the same thing," he heard Bridgette say. From his sister's tone, he could tell that there was a smile on her face.

Much as he loved his sister, he wasn't about to get drawn in to a long word exchange. "Bridgette, I'm a little busy right now. This isn't the time for riddles and frankly, I'm really not in the mood for games."

He heard Bridgette chuckle. "At least not with your sister, right?"

Out of the corner of his eye, he saw Gwen slipping out of the room. Was she disappointed by this exchange, or bored by it? Time to wind this up.

"Okay, I'll bite," Brooks said. "What are you talking about?"

Bridgette backtracked. "I was put on an assignment that will have me coming back to Braxville for several months. I was going to ask if you could put me up for the duration, but I happened to mention that to Mom when I called her with the news and she thinks that I might be intruding."

Brooks braced himself for a barrage of questions, but just in case he was wrong, he played dumb for a second. "Why would she think that?"

"Really, Brooks? You want to play it that way? Okay," Bridgette said gamely, "according to Mom, you have a new girlfriend and she's staying with you at your place." Pleased, his sister laughed softly. "You're coming up in the world, Brooks. I can't remember the last time you had a girl living with you—present company excepted, of course," she said. "So tell me, dear brother, just how serious is this?"

Brooks might have been slightly annoyed by his sister's prying question if he hadn't been as pleased about the existing situation as he was.

"I guess there's no such thing as privacy in this family," he concluded.

"Nope," Bridgette replied with an extremely smug laugh. "So it is serious, huh?"

"Tell you what, Bridgette, we'll talk when you get here," Brooks told her.

Just in case he misunderstood, she informed him, "Oh no, I'm going to be staying at Mom and Dad's for the duration of my assignment. I'm not going to be the third wheel getting in the way of whatever you have going on here," Bridgette told him. "Just make sure she's worthy of you or I'm going to be forced to gut her like a fish."

"Very colorful," he commented dryly. "And for your information—" he glanced toward the doorway to see if Gwen was close by, but she wasn't "—Gwen's the best thing that ever happened to me," he told his triplet.

Bridgette whistled softly. "Wow, you do have it bad, don't you?"

Brooks was about to protest, then decided, what was the point? All in all, that was a pretty accurate assessment of the situation.

"Yeah, I guess I do," he admitted.

"I can't wait to meet her. And I'll have plenty of opportunity to do that because I'm going to be hanging around Braxville for a while. Possibly indefinitely."

"Please don't take this the wrong way, Bridgette, but why?" His curiosity aroused, he told her, "You said something about being here on assignment. What kind of an assignment?"

He heard his sister sigh and caught himself thinking that this couldn't be good.

And he was right.

Bridgette had never lied to him and she wasn't about to start now. "There's a rumor circulating at the health department that there's been a spike in the number of people coming down with cancer in the last couple of years."

Brooks remained silent, waiting for the other shoe to drop. When it didn't, he decided his sister needed prodding. "And?" he asked.

"And most of the people who have come down with it either work or did work for Colton Construction."

Although he thought he'd braced himself, when the news finally came, it felt as if he had been sucker punched in his gut. One glaring question formed in his mind, begging to be put to rest.

"You don't think that Dad's somehow involved in all this, do you?" he asked.

"Honestly, Brooks," he heard her say wearily, "I don't know what to think. I'd like to believe he isn't, but you and I both know that Dad's always been secretive to a fault.

"Anyway," she maintained, "I'm just here to investigate the situation and try to get to the bottom of it."

That meant that some time or other, she was going to have to corner their father and ask questions that the man was *not* going to take kindly to. "Good luck with that," he told her.

"Yeah, thanks," Bridgette responded. There were several moments of hesitation and then she said, "Look, if you happen to hear anything, anything at all about people getting sick on the site, or something along those lines, no matter how trivial it might sound, I'd appreciate you letting me know."

He didn't like being put in the middle of something like this. Choosing sides when it came to family matters left a bitter taste in his mouth. "Bridgette, I don't think—"

Bridgette played her ace card. "You're a private investigator, Brooks. Investigate. You know, I could hire you on the q.t. Nobody has to know. You'd be working for just me, not the health department if that makes you feel any better."

"You want me to investigate Dad?" he asked incredulously.

"No, not Dad," Bridgette immediately corrected his misinterpretation. "Dad's *company*."

"In case a small fact managed to escape you, that's one and the same thing," Brooks pointed out.

"Not really," his sister protested quickly. "Not entirely."

Brooks sighed. "You're clutching at straws, Bridgette."

"I'd clutch at a giant tarantula if it meant getting an answer that didn't implicate our father," she informed her brother. "But I do need an answer."

He couldn't see this going any other way than as an indictment of their father's business transactions. The threat had always been there, lurking in the shadows, behind the scenes.

"You know that a lot of people would like to see Dad taken down," he said. "If for no other reason than the fact that he's a Colton and he managed to make something of himself through a lot of hard work that in turn amassed him a lot of money."

"You don't have to tell me that," Bridgette said. "Jealousy is a poisonous, blinding emotion that manages to contaminate everything it touches. I run into it myself," she admitted. "I can't tell you how many people think I got my position because of my last name."

He could hear the resentment in his ordinarily easygoing sister's voice. It made him wonder what she'd had to deal with.

"They don't realize that my job isn't exactly an enviable one," Bridgette told him. "But then I suppose that haters have to hate, right?"

That was true almost by definition, he couldn't help thinking. "Unfortunately."

"So, can I hire your services?" she asked her brother, thinking she had won him over.

"No," he replied, completely surprising her. And then he negated that by adding, "But I will look into the matter for you when I can. However, right now I'm working on another case. And that comes first."

She knew he was talking about Gwen's case. Their mother had said the woman had been a client first before things began to develop between her and Brooks.

"Tell Gwen she's a lucky lady," Bridgette said by way of ending the conversation.

"It goes both ways," Brooks answered. "I'll let you know if I find out anything."

"I'm counting on it," she said. "In the meantime, we need to get together real soon. I want to make sure that this 'Gwen' person is actually worthy of my brother."

He laughed. This was an unusual side to Bridgette. "She is."

"You're not exactly an unbiased judge here," Bridgette reminded him. "I'd rather check the lady out for myself. I'll see you at the homestead, Brooks."

After they ended the call, Brooks went looking for Gwen, who had gone into the next room to give him some privacy.

She looked up when Brooks walked in. "Anything?" she asked, eternally hopeful.

"Nothing that would enlighten either of us about what might have happened to your mother," he told her. "That was just my sister Bridgette letting me know she'll be in town for a while."

"Is she here for business or pleasure?" Gwen asked.

"Oh, definitely business," he answered. "Although she wants to get in a little personal time, as well." He only thought it fair to warn Gwen ahead of time. "There's another family dinner in the offing."

"That sounds nice," Gwen said.

He had a skeptical look as he said, "I'm not quite sure about that."

"You know," she said, rising from her chair, "I hadn't

realized this before, but you do have this habit of talking in riddles."

Her assessment made him laugh. "That's what makes me more interesting," Brooks told her.

Her eyes washed over this man who had become so dear to her in such a very short amount of time. "You don't need riddles to make you more interesting, Brooks."

His mouth curved in a smile that seemed to encompass everything it came in contact with. "Is that a compliment?"

"If you have to ask," she responded, "then I didn't say it with the right inflection in my voice."

"Sorry," he said, sliding his thumb along her bottom lip, "I'm a little preoccupied."

"With the case?" The question came out sounding breathless.

Brooks slipped his arms around her, drawing her so close to him, it was almost hard to say where he ended and she began.

"With you," he told her. The smile on his lips grew deeper. "Are you hungry?" he asked her.

When he looked at her that way, she felt as if he had trapped her soul in his eyes. "Absolutely."

"What are you in the mood for?" he asked Gwen, serious for once. He knew there was nothing in the refrigerator, but he was more than willing to make a run to one of the local restaurants to pick up something and bring it back.

She tilted her head back just a touch and there was a wicked glint in her eyes as she answered, "Guess."

When she looked at him like that, everything within him melted quickly, like butter that had accidentally been left out in the sun.

His pulse quickened, hitting a tempo that had it been attached to a monitor, would have set off all sorts of alarms.

"What do I get if I guess right?" Brooks asked.

"Me," she breathed.

That same breath feathering along his face became his undoing.

He completely lost himself in her, sweeping her into his arms and kissing Gwen over and over again. Each time his lips came in contact with hers, there was even more passion being unleashed than the last time.

His mother had called it, correctly assessing the situation before even he had. This was definitely the woman for him.

All he had to do now was convince Gwen of that fact.

The thought of dinner was put on hold as other appetites quickly took over. Each time he made love to her, Brooks just couldn't get enough of her.

Might *never* get enough of her.

And that was all right because he intended to keep on doing it until there was nothing left inside him to give.

There definitely was no sin in that.

And even if there were, he didn't care. Just as long as he could go on sampling her lips and filling his soul with the essence of her, he knew he was going to be all right.

THEY FINALLY MADE it upstairs and into his room, although it was during the second time they made love to one another tonight, not the first. And it was because she had made the request, saying something about doing it in his bed made her feel a little more secure about it.

Brooks didn't even think to question her about what she'd said until they had finished this time around and were lying, all but spent, in each other's arms.

"What did you mean by that?" he asked her out of the blue when he could think clearly again.

"Mean by what?" she asked, her own mind all but a total blank.

"That making love in my bed made you feel a little more secure. Secure?" he questioned, looking at her. "What do you mean by 'secure'?"

"Maybe I should have said 'protected,'" she said, re-thinking the matter.

That still didn't answer his question. "Now I'm really lost. Why would you need to feel protected?"

Gwen stared at the ceiling. "You're going to think I'm being paranoid again."

"No, I'm not," he promised. He propped himself up on his elbow, looking at her. "Talk to me, Gwen. What's going on?"

She might as well level with him. The man seemed to be able to look right into her head. "I can't seem to shake the feeling that someone was watching us when we were downstairs."

"And they're not watching us when we're upstairs?" he questioned.

She shrugged, knowing that she wasn't making any sense, but she couldn't help what she was feeling. "Maybe by the time I'm up here, I'm just so eager to make love with you, I don't notice," she guessed. And then she reddened slightly. "I don't know, it sounds crazy, right?"

"I wouldn't go that far," he said kindly, "but I do have a great security system and it's programmed to go off if it detects motion or someone breeching the system. Does that make you feel any better?" he asked her.

"Yes," she said before she threaded her arms around his neck again and kissed him. She said it because she felt that it made *him* feel better about the situation.

But not her.

Chapter Twenty-Four

Gwen found the lovemaking to be glorious and at the same time, extremely comforting.

Once again, Brooks had managed to block out the rest of the world for her. She reveled in that feeling of warm solitude that he always managed to create for her.

And when it was over, she absorbed the peaceful shelter of his arms.

Gwen was just about to fall asleep when a distant noise registered somewhere in the back of her mind. Before she was even fully conscious, Gwen bolted upright in Brooks's bed.

Her sudden movement managed to wake Brooks up, as well.

"What's the matter?" he asked her, reaching for Gwen with the intention of drawing her back into his arms and sleep.

"I think that I heard something," she told him, scanning the darkness and trying to make out an actual form.

Finding nothing, she leaned over toward the nightstand beside the bed and turned on the lamp.

"Are you sure it wasn't something that you actually *heard* in a dream?" he asked her. Physically exhausted, he had quickly fallen asleep himself and he hadn't heard anything.

"No," Gwen insisted. "This was real. It sounded as if something had been knocked over downstairs." She looked at him. She was disappointed by what she saw. "You didn't hear anything, did you?"

"No, but you did and that's enough for me. You stay here," he said, throwing off the sheet. "I'm going to check it out."

That made her sound helpless, like some damsel in distress. She rebelled against the image. "We can check it out together."

"No reason for both of us to go prowling around," he protested. "You just stay here."

Pulling on his jeans, he took a flashlight with him and went to check out the source of Gwen's "noise"— if there actually was a source.

Gwen decided that arguing about this would just take up precious time. So instead, she waited long enough for Brooks to leave the bedroom.

Less than a minute later, she was out of the bed and had put on the nightshirt she'd discarded when they began to make love again for the second time.

Padding barefoot across the carpeted floor, she silently made her way out of the bedroom. But not before grabbing some Hall of Famer's baseball bat that Brooks had hung up on his wall. It was a gift from his father's brother back in the day when baseball still had some sort of significance to Brooks.

Gwen was aware that taking the bat for protection was probably just silly, but in lieu of any other weapon, the bat made her feel as if she had some sort of control over the situation and could protect herself—and Brooks—if she needed to.

She had just gotten to the top of the stairs, ready to go down, when she heard a loud crash.

Not *my imagination*, Gwen thought as a cold chill descended up and down her spine despite the warm August night.

Squinting, she could barely make out the outline of two men fighting downstairs.

But despite the poor lighting, she could see that one outline belonged to Brooks. The other—she struggled to focus on the other man as she tiptoed and made her way down the stairs—the other she could have sworn belonged to Daniel!

The next moment, her heart hammering hard, she was sprinting down the stairs, determined to get the drop on the man who was still obsessed with stalking her. All she could think of was that she fervently wanted to make him back away from Brooks.

Shelton had somehow managed to get the drop on Brooks. From the looks of it, Shelton had gotten in several very heavy blows on the other man's face and upper torso before Brooks had even started to defend himself.

It was obvious that the element of surprise had gone a long way in Shelton's favor.

Reaching the bottom of the stairs directly behind Shelton, Gwen dug in and took one big swing at the back of her target. Hearing her, Shelton shifted just enough so that her blow didn't land where she had intended. She had been aiming for his kidneys, but what she managed to make contact with was the side of one of his hips.

Stunned by the blow, Shelton screamed out in pain as he spun around to see his attacker, his face a mask of fury.

"You're going to get yours, Gwen!" Shelton shouted just as a pummeled Brooks fell to the floor, all but unconscious.

Meanwhile Shelton tried to grab Gwen's hair, wanting to pull her over to him. At the last moment, she ducked her head, managing to elude his grasp.

"Whatever you were thinking of doing, *don't*," Gwen warned her stalker, her eyes blazing. She was fighting the urge to rush over to Brooks, knowing Shelton would use the opportunity to grab her. "I've already called the police. They'll be here any minute."

There was hatred etched into Shelton's face. "You're bluffing," he sneered just as he made another lunge at her. Again, she managed to stay out of his grasp, knowing that if he caught her, he would undoubtedly squeeze the very life out of her body.

Moving quickly, her eyes on him, Gwen continued to keep Shelton at bay. Glancing at Brooks, she could see that he was trying to pull himself together and get up. With renewed determination, Gwen did all she could to distract the stalker, giving Brooks more time to come around even if it was just a little more.

Seeing she was momentarily looking toward the private investigator, Shelton dived for possession of the gun he'd lost when he first overpowered Brooks. At the same time, Gwen realized what was happening and managed, just by a hairbreadth, to get to the gun first.

But before she could pick up the weapon herself, the gun was sent flying again. The very next second, Shelton dived down, a different target in mind this time. The stalker caught hold of her leg, his hand closing around her ankle.

"I've got you now," he gloated, a nasty laugh escaping his lips.

The stalker was pulling her in toward him when he suddenly cried out in anguished fury. Brooks had rallied enough to turn the tables. He had planted his foot in the small of Shelton's back, sending shooting pains up and down the stalker's spine. At the same time, where he had planted his foot managed to paralyze Shelton, as well.

Shelton let loose with a barrage of curses.

"Gwen, call 911," Brooks ordered, knowing that she hadn't done as she'd boasted earlier to the stalker. Meanwhile, Brooks pinned and twisted Shelton's arms behind his back in such a way as to send the man into very vocal screams of anguish.

"Gladly," she answered, hurrying to pick up the phone receiver on the landline in the living room. Within seconds, she was talking to the 911 dispatcher.

"There's been a break-in," Gwen told the woman in response when she asked the eternal question: What is your emergency?

"Is the intruder there now?" the dispatcher asked.

"Yes," Gwen answered. "Please hurry." And then,

anticipating the woman's next question, she rattled off the address of the house.

With no further questions coming, Gwen hung up the receiver. Turning, she looked again in Brooks's direction. Incensed, Shelton was screaming and cursing at both of them.

Brooks's eyes met hers and he shook his head. "Look at him." There was contempt in his voice. "He's not even bright enough to be afraid."

"Afraid?" Shelton cried, the expression on his face mocking Brooks. He twisted so that Brooks was forced to momentarily loosen his grip. "You're the one who should be afraid because after the police finish with their stupid games and let me go, I'm going to be coming back for you and your cheap, two-bit whor—"

He didn't get to finish the insult because Brooks sent a right cross straight to his chin. Gwen's stalker wound up biting down on his lip. Blood came oozing out.

"Maybe that'll teach you to stop talking," Brooks said.

Instead of falling silent, Shelton let loose with another string of curses, just as the doorbell rang. Gwen hurried to answer it, although at the last minute, she cautiously opened the door. To her relief, there were two tall, imposing police officers standing in the doorway.

"You called about a home invader?" the taller of the two officers asked.

"He's right here, Officers," Brooks called out, still holding Shelton.

"We'll take it from here, Mr. Colton," the other officers told him.

"Looks like they sent two more lackeys to bow and scrape and do the almighty Colton's bidding," Shelton sneered. "You disgust me!" he shouted at Gwen and Brooks.

Suddenly, he screamed bloody murder and tucked in his head. He went charging into the two unsuspecting police officers who had just entered the Colton house.

Gwen stared, openmouthed and stunned at what she thought to be Shelton's incredibly stupid move. Startled, the officers issued two verbal warnings in quick succession.

Shelton didn't seem to hear them so the tall, thin officer farthest away from Shelton fired a shot at him, wounding the stalker, and more important, stopping him in his tracks.

"You just sealed your own fate, buddy." Officer Ed Marrow told Colton, "He's going to be going away for a long, long time." Officer Marrow ushered a far from silent Shelton out the door and into the squad car while his partner tied up the loose ends.

"We're going to need to have the two of you come down to the station and give your statements," Officer Hathaway said.

"No problem," Brooks told the officer. "Just give us a few minutes to get dressed."

"I can give you more than a few minutes," Hathaway said. "There's no hurry. Tomorrow morning is soon enough. That guy's not going anywhere. I'd say that you and the lady here have been through enough for one night. Why don't you just try to relax and get some sleep?"

"Thanks for coming so quickly." Brooks escorted the second officer to the front door. "We'll try to do that. I've got one question, though."

Turning around to face him, Hathaway said, "Okay, shoot."

"I've got a state-of-the-art security system, but Shelton managed to get into my house without setting it off. How did he?"

"Wire cutters," Hathaway told Brooks. "Simple wire cutters. He cut your system. Saw the wires when he came in."

"You're kidding."

"I'm afraid not," Hathaway said, clearly sympathizing with Brooks. "You really need to update your system. You know that old saw about the shoemaker's kids going barefoot. Think about it. Anything else?" he asked.

Brooks shook his head. "No, that answers my question."

Hathaway offered them an encouraging smile. "You two have a nice night now—what's left of it," the officer said, taking his leave.

Brooks locked the door. "Tomorrow morning I'm having Ty come out and go over my whole system from top to bottom. And then put in a brand-new one, the best he can recommend."

"Well, with that maniac under lock and key, there's no immediate hurry for that," she told Brooks philosophically.

"Maybe not," Brooks allowed, "but I'm not going to

stop being vigilant about your safety until I've taken every precaution that I can think of—plus a few more."

She smiled at him. "I appreciate you looking out for me like that, but I think we can finally relax on the stalker front."

As if to negate her words, the phone rang just then. This time, it was his cell phone rather than the landline. She watched Brooks take out his phone and saw the odd expression on his face when he looked at his screen. She felt her stomach sinking.

"What now?" she asked.

"Beats me. That's Yvette calling," he told her, swiping to answer his phone. "Yvette, isn't this kind of late for you to be calling? Is there anything wrong?"

"I'm pulling an all-nighter," his sister explained. "And I thought you'd want to know this as soon as I found out."

"Found out what?" he asked.

"You know that dentist you directed me to? The one who had Olivia Harrison's dental records," she prompted when he didn't say anything in response.

"What about him?" Brooks asked cautiously. He could feel Gwen's eyes on him. He tried to keep his expression blank.

"The dental records he sent me were a match," she told him.

Brooks could feel his heart sinking. It occurred to him that he'd been clinging to a shred of hope that the records didn't match, that Gwen's mother was still alive somehow.

"You mean—?"

"Yes," Yvette answered, her voice almost hollow as it seemed to echo in his phone. "The body that was found at the demolition site belongs to Olivia Harrison."

Brooks looked at Gwen the moment his sister said Gwen's mother's name. "Thanks, Yvette," he said quietly, ending his call.

Gwen immediately caught the look on his face and although it was plausible that there could have been a lot of reasons for that expression, her mind zeroed in on just one reason.

The main reason.

Suddenly the room felt as if it was closing in on her. She had been braced for this for a long while, but now that she was on the cusp of having her supposition become reality, she could feel her pulse beginning to race and the very room spinning, making her dizzy.

"It's her, isn't it?" Gwen asked him in a hushed whisper.

He didn't want to just walk right into the confirmation, he wanted to ease his way into this cautiously.

"Gwen—"

"Isn't it?" she asked again, her voice more forceful this time.

There was no dodging her question. Cornered, he had no recourse but to tell her the truth.

"Gwen, I'm so sorry," he began. He got no further. He was halted by the tears that he saw springing into her eyes. All he could do was take her into his arms, hold her and repeat what he had already said to her. "I am so very sorry."

She began to cry then, cry until there were no more tears left to shed.

He held her tightly, stroking her hair and saying nothing until she finally stopped.

Taking a deep, shaky breath, she slowly raised her head and looked at him. "I guess now the healing can finally begin."

He tightened his arms around her, kissing the top of her head.

"I guess it can," he agreed. "For both you and your grandmother."

Epilogue

Brooks and Gwen went to deliver the news to her grandmother in person.

The moment that Rita Harrison opened her front door and saw her granddaughter and Brooks standing there, she knew.

She clutched the door for support.

"That second body they found, it was Olivia's, wasn't it?" Rita asked, her voice echoing with sadness.

"Yes, ma'am," Brooks answered.

Rita nodded, bearing up to the news with a mixture of both relief and sorrow.

"I guess in my heart, I've known for a long time that she was gone," she said to the two people on her doorstep. She opened the door wider, admitting them into her house as she went to sit down. Her legs were threatening to give way again. "Now at least we can hold Olivia's memorial service."

"I still intend to find out who killed your daughter, Mrs. Harrison," Brooks told Rita. "I give you my word."

Rita smiled at him, temporarily making the years

fade from her face. "You're a good boy, Brooks," she murmured, touching his face with affection.

In the end, despite their offer to help with the arrangements, Rita told her granddaughter and Brooks that she had it all under control. She had planned this memorial service in her mind a dozen times over the years.

Gwen knew that finally being able to do so would be cathartic for her grandmother.

She and Brooks let Rita get started as they left to go back to Braxville.

GWEN HAD REMAINED rather quiet on the trip home. Brooks knew she had a lot on her mind and he gave her space until he pulled up in his driveway and got out. Then, unable to remain silent any longer, he had to ask her what she was thinking.

"I guess with Shelton going away for what looks like a long time, thanks to the testimony of the police officers, not to mention that he tried to barrel right through them—" Gwen began.

"Don't forget the testimony of all those other women that he stalked before he went after you," Brooks reminded her.

She nodded, still looking rather grim in his opinion. "That was all your doing," she said. "They wouldn't have come out of hiding if you hadn't managed to locate all of them, telling those women that he would be out of their lives permanently if they just spoke up and testified against him."

He wasn't about to take credit for that. "Nobody

should be able to do that to another human being and get away with it," he told her simply.

"Still, you did it. You said you'd keep me safe and you have." Sighing, she looked away, not wanting him to be able to look into her eyes. "I guess you'll be able to go back to your own life now."

Brooks cocked his head, looking a little confused by her words. What was that supposed to mean?

"Where's this going?" he asked her. "What are you trying to say?"

She took in a deep breath. "I'm saying that I'm going to be going back to my apartment."

"I still haven't located your mother's killer, or found out who your father is," he pointed out. "Those are some of the reasons that you hired me, remember?" There was something about her expression that was beginning to worry him. "And I was serious about what I told you the other day. I've come to care about you a great deal. Hell, I love you," he said, finally getting up his nerve to tell her. "I don't want you moving out of my house, I want you moving into my life—unless you don't want to," he said suddenly, thinking that was the reason she'd been so quiet.

"Don't want to?" she echoed, stunned. "How can you possibly even think that?"

He didn't understand. "Then why did you just say you were going to move out?"

"Because I didn't want to crowd you, you big dummy!" she said.

"Crowd me!" he said, making it sound like an order. "And while you're at it, marry me."

That came out of nowhere. Gwen stared at him, wondering if she'd misheard him. "Marry you?"

"Yes. You'd make my mother very happy," he told her, his mouth curving.

"Your mother?" she asked, confused.

"Yes. You're just the type of woman she would have picked out for me."

A voice whispered in her head that it was going to be all right. She could *feel* it. "Well, I wouldn't want to disappoint your mother," she replied.

"And there's an added bonus to marrying me," he said.

"And that is?" she asked, not bothering to stifle her grin.

"You won't have to pay me to find out who your father is. Think of it as a wedding present," he said, then coaxed, "Say yes."

"Stop trying to sweeten the pot. I would have said yes without the added bonus." Laughter entered her eyes. "After all, I really do like your mother."

"And me?" Brooks asked. "How do you feel about me?"

"I'd rather just show you." She wrapped her arms around his neck as she started to kiss him.

He drew his head back just a little. "So that's a yes to the marriage proposal?" he asked.

"It's always been a yes," she cried, this time sealing her mouth to his.

Again he drew his head back. When she looked at him quizzically, he told her, "Let's go inside so we can really settle this."

Gwen didn't waste any words, she just pulled him across the threshold and into the house.

This time, when she kissed him, he didn't move his head away. He just kissed her back.

For a very long, long time.

* * * * *

COMING SOON!

We really hope you enjoyed reading this book.
If you're looking for more romance, be sure to
head to the shops when new books are
available on

Thursday 9th
July

To see which titles are coming soon, please visit
millsandboon.co.uk/nextmonth

LET'S TALK
Romance

For exclusive extracts, competitions
and special offers, find us online:

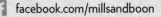 facebook.com/millsandboon

@MillsandBoon

@MillsandBoonUK

Get in touch on 01413 063232

For all the latest titles coming soon, visit
millsandboon.co.uk/nextmonth

MILLS & BOON

THE HEART OF ROMANCE

A ROMANCE FOR EVERY KIND OF READER

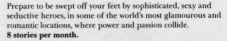

MODERN

Prepare to be swept off your feet by sophisticated, sexy and seductive heroes, in some of the world's most glamourous and romantic locations, where power and passion collide.
8 stories per month.

HISTORICAL

Escape with historical heroes from time gone by. Whether your passion is for wicked Regency Rakes, muscled Vikings or rugged Highlanders, awaken the romance of the past.
6 stories per month.

MEDICAL

Set your pulse racing with dedicated, delectable doctors in the high-pressure world of medicine, where emotions run high and passion, comfort and love are the best medicine.
6 stories per month.

True Love

Celebrate true love with tender stories of heartfelt romance, from the rush of falling in love to the joy a new baby can bring, and a focus on the emotional heart of a relationship.
8 stories per month.

Desire

Indulge in secrets and scandal, intense drama and plenty of sizzling hot action with powerful and passionate heroes who have it all: wealth, status, good looks…everything but the right woman.
6 stories per month.

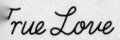

HEROES

Experience all the excitement of a gripping thriller, with an intense romance at its heart. Resourceful, true-to-life women and strong, fearless men face danger and desire - a killer combination!
8 stories per month.

DARE

Sensual love stories featuring smart, sassy heroines you'd want as a best friend, and compelling intense heroes who are worthy of them.
4 stories per month.

To see which titles are coming soon, please visit

millsandboon.co.uk/nextmonth

MILLS & BOON
MEDICAL
Pulse-Racing Passion

Set your pulse racing with dedicated, delectable doctors in the high-pressure world of medicine, where emotions run high and passion, comfort and love are the best medicine.

MILLS & BOON

Desire

Indulge in secrets and scandal, intense drama and plenty of sizzling hot action with powerful and passionate heroes who have it all: wealth, status, good looks… everything but the right woman.